KT-425-980

Sue Fortin

I am a member of the Romantic Novelists' Association, having come through their New Writers' Scheme, and a part of the online writing group The Romaniacs who all met through the NWS. I am also a member of the Crime Writers' Association.

Lover of cake, Dragonflies and France. Hater of calories, maths and snakes. I was born in Hertfordshire but had a nomadic childhood, moving often with my family, before eventually settling in West Sussex.

I am married with four children, all of whom patiently give me time to write but, when not behind the keyboard, I like to spend time with them, enjoying both the coast and the South Downs between which we are nestled.

www.suefortin.com
@suefortin1

WITHDRAWN

ABERDEEN LIBRARIES

The Girl Who Lied

SUE FORTIN

A division of HarperCollins*Publishers*
www.harpercollins.co.uk

Harper*Impulse* an imprint of
HarperCollins*Publishers*
1 London Bridge Street
London SE1 9GF

www.harpercollins.co.uk

A Paperback Original 2016

First published in Great Britain in ebook format by Harper*Impulse* 2016

Copyright © Sue Fortin 2016

Sue Fortin asserts the moral right to
be identified as the author of this work

A catalogue record for this book
is available from the British Library

ISBN: 9780008194857

This novel is entirely a work of fiction.
The names, characters and incidents portrayed in it are
the work of the author's imagination. Any resemblance to
actual persons, living or dead, events or localities is
entirely coincidental.

Set in Minion by Palimpsest Book Production Ltd, Falkirk, Stirlingshire

Printed and bound in Great Britain

All rights reserved. No part of this publication may be
reproduced, stored in a retrieval system, or transmitted,
in any form or by any means, electronic, mechanical,
photocopying, recording or otherwise, without the prior
permission of the publishers.

MIX
Paper from
responsible sources
FSC˙ C007454

FSC™ is a non-profit international organisation established to promote
the responsible management of the world's forests. Products carrying the
FSC label are independently certified to assure consumers that they come
from forests that are managed to meet the social, economic and
ecological needs of present and future generations,
and other controlled sources.

Find out more about HarperCollins and the environment at
www.harpercollins.co.uk/green

For my mum and my daughters, with my eternal love.

PART 1

'I can't go back to yesterday – I was a different person then.'
Lewis Carroll

Chapter 1

London, England

This is the moment I've been dreading. It's time for me to go back. I play with the Triskelion pendant around my neck, my finger rubbing each of the three edges in turn. *Father. Mother. Child.* I read the email once again.

From: Roisin Marshall
To: Erin Hurley
Subject: Meeting Up

Hello Erin

You can't keep ignoring me. I'm sure you never really thought you could walk away from everyone and everything.

I have something that might interest you.

Call me.

Roisin

My finger hovers over the reply key. For a fleeting moment I consider deleting the message. If I ignore it, she may go away. She may give up. I sit back in my chair and let out a long, slow breath. The anxiety that has lain dormant for all this time, having now been stirred, stretches its hand, grips tightly and twists my stomach. No matter how many times I have anticipated this moment, prepared myself to confront my past, right now, it's insufficient.

'Aha! Caught you.' A voice from behind startles me. Somehow I manage to click on the inbox icon, clearing the screen of the email. I plaster on a smile and spin round in my chair to face Ed.

'You made me jump,' I say, noting that I sound overly cheerful. 'How long have you been there?' My mind replays the last few minutes. How long had I been staring at the email? How long was it visible on the screen? Could Ed have read it from where he was standing?

Ed gives a small laugh. 'What are you trying to hide?'

I know he's only joking but he has no idea how true his words are.

'Now, it wouldn't do for a girl to tell her boss and her boyfriend all her secrets, would it?' My turn to laugh. It sounds forced. Ed cocks his head to one side, weighing me up.

The phone on my desk rings and I offer a silent prayer of thanks that I am saved from having to continue the conversation.

'Good afternoon, Hamilton's Health and Beauty Spa.' I glance back up at Ed, who winks before returning to his office.

The immediate danger has passed, but the ever-present fear remains, which only serves to convince me I must do something about it. I cannot afford to let chance or luck, bad luck even, take control. I can afford even less to let my old school friend be in charge.

I turn my attention to the call and quickly deal with booking an appointment for a back massage. Replacing the phone in its cradle, I peek back through to Ed's office.

He's busy looking at his computer screen. I return to mine, calling up Roisin's email again. Instead of replying, I forward it onto my own private email address. One I will have to sacrifice giving to her. I don't want her trying to contact me at work again.

4

I check my phone and see the email has been received. Next job is to delete the email coming in and going out of the work computer. I know there will be some sort of cyber-footprint, but no one will be looking for that.

It takes less than a minute to carry out, just in time as my next client arrives for her full leg wax. 'I won't be a moment,' I tell her as I double-check that all traces of the email have been eradicated.

For the rest of the day, try as I might, I can't put the email and Roisin out of my mind. Up until now, I've been pretty good at ignoring her. Naively, knowing Roisin, I had hoped she would go away if I didn't reply. That she would give up. Her first email had been unthreatening. The sort you'd send to someone you hadn't been in contact with for a long time. The second, thinking back, had a more insistent tone. And now the third, well, she's certainly not going away and the bait she's dangling, the something that might interest me, how can I ignore that? Not after what I've done.

The day slowly comes to a close and as I'm tidying up and checking the diary for tomorrow's clients, the telephone rings. I let out a sigh, hoping it's a straightforward query.

'Good afternoon, Hamilton's Health and Beauty Spa,' I reel off automatically. 'How can I help you?' There's silence, but I know someone is there. I can hear their breath. 'Hello,' I repeat. 'Can I help you?' A bead of sweat pricks the skin at the back of my neck and my mouth dries. I know who it is before they speak.

'Hello, Erin,' she says. 'It's me. Roisin.' The soft roll of her country accent seeps out of the receiver, winding itself into my ear.

I haven't much of my Irish accent left any more. Ten years has seen it dwindle and I've never had any particular desire to hang onto it. In the early days of our relationship, Ed used to mock it, which just served as another reason to leave it behind. Another connection with my past that I don't want. I adopt my best English accent as I reply.

'No. Sorry. You have the wrong number.' I can't speak to her. Not now. Not at work.

'Oh, I don't think I have,' she replies. I can hear amusement in her voice. It's the same patronising voice I remember from when we were at school. 'And before you hang up, you might want to listen to what I have to say.'

I look up towards Ed's door. It's closed. The frosted glass blurs his outline, but I can see him there, sitting at his desk.

'What do you want?' My voice is low, almost a whisper. I hope she can't detect the undercurrent of fear.

'We need to talk,' says Roisin. 'Oh, and you can drop the accent.'

'What do you want?' I repeat, ignoring the snipe.

'If you hadn't ignored my emails, you would know.' She's enjoying this, I can just tell. It reminds me of when we were kids. She loved being in control then, whether it was as five-year-olds in the playground, twelve-year-olds listening to music or teenagers deciding what to wear for a party. It always had to be on Roisin's terms. And I'd let her. She was pretty, she was popular, she was rich, she was all the things I wasn't. She used to tease me then and she's doing it now. Except, I'm not the same person as I was then. A little flicker of defiance ignites within me.

'Look, Roisin,' I say. Perhaps if I stand up to her now, like I should have done all those times before, I can call her bluff. 'Whatever it is you want to talk about, spit it out. I haven't got all day. I'm about to go home.'

'Don't go getting yourself all worked up now, Erin,' says Roisin. 'I've found something of yours.'

'What's that, then?' I can't for one minute think what it is and for that reason the unease shifts up a gear.

'A photograph.' She pauses for effect. It works. Then she continues. 'A photograph of you and Niall.'

'Roisin, can you get to the point,' I say, noticing through the glass that Ed is standing up, getting ready to leave.

'I tell you what, I'll scan it and email it over to you.'

I hold in the sigh of exasperation. I don't want her to know I'm riled. I can see Ed putting on his jacket. Any minute now he'll be out of the office and waiting to take me for a drink. Neither of us has work tomorrow, so we had planned an evening out, which usually meant my staying over at his place.

I need to get Roisin off the phone. 'Don't email my work. Send it to my private email.' I quickly rattle off the address.

'Make sure you get back to me,' says Roisin. 'We need that talk.'

I put the phone down without answering just as Ed walks out of his office, his sports holdall in one hand and car keys jangling in the other.

'All set, then?' he says.

'Erm, I'm not feeling too well,' I say, not quite able to meet his eyes. 'I feel a bit sick.' That's not actually a lie. I feel queasy at the thought of what Roisin is sending me.

'That's not like you,' says Ed. 'We can go straight to mine, if you like. Skip dinner.'

I smile at him. 'To be honest, I think I'd better go home.' Again that's no lie. 'I don't think I'd be much company tonight.' I pick up my bag and take my coat from the peg. 'Sorry.'

'Hey, that's okay,' says Ed. 'Are you going to be okay to drive or do you want me to drop you home?'

'I'll drive. I'll be fine.'

'Text me when you're home,' he says. He gives me a hug and drops a kiss on top of my head. 'I'll give Ralph a call and see if he fancies a pint. Now, drive carefully and don't forget to text.' He's scrolling through his contacts list and calling up Ralph before he's even out the door. 'Ralph, mate! What you up to tonight?' And then he's disappearing out of the door.

When I get back to the house, where I rent two rooms on the top floor, I call out a quick hello in the hallway and then head straight up. I hear Stacey, one of the house-sharers, call out a greeting. She rents the room at the front of the house. We're friendly, but not friends. Same for the guy who rents the middle floor. I'm not even sure what he does, but he keeps himself to himself. We each do our own thing. I like it that way. Everyone at arm's length.

I unlock the door at the top of the second staircase and step into my own bastion of safety. I make myself a cup of green tea and sit down in front of the laptop. I notice my hand shakes slightly as I move the mouse around on the pad and access my emails.

Roisin didn't waste any time. Her email is sitting there in the inbox. The paperclip icon indicating an attachment.

I take a deep breath and open the email.

Call me by six o'clock this evening or you'll be sorry. Last chance.

Her mobile number is typed below. I move the cursor to the attachment. It's a jpeg. I double-click and wait for the image to download.

It takes only a matter of seconds.

My stomach lurches and for a second I think I'm going to be sick.

'Oh God, no.' I drag at my face with my hands, rubbing my eyes as if I can rub away what I've just seen. But I can't.

There in front of me, filling the screen, is a picture of myself and Niall Marshall. Any other picture and I wouldn't have batted an eyelid, but this one…Where the hell did she find it? I had totally forgotten about it.

Somewhere in the distance I hear the doorbell ring, followed by footsteps taking the stairs two at a time. I don't fully register this or my name being called until there is a rapping of knuckles on the door.

I jump in my seat, knocking the cup of green tea flying. The earthy-coloured liquid performs a jump only physics could explain and cascades across the keyboard of my laptop.

'Erin? Erin? You there?' Ed is knocking on the door.

For a moment I'm paralysed as I stare at the door and then

back at the laptop. 'Erin!' He's more insistent and there's a note of agitation in his voice. 'Are you okay?' He bangs harder on the door.

Adrenalin kicks in and I grab the laptop, turning it upside down, hoping the tea hasn't reached the vital components. 'Won't be a minute!' I call out. I rush through to the bedroom and into the small en suite. Grabbing a towel, I wipe at the keyboard.

'Erin!' He's definitely gone past the agitated stage now.

I stand the laptop upside down, like a tent and hope it's enough to save it from permanent damage. 'I'm coming!' As I bustle past the table, I upright the offending cup and throw a tea towel on the table to soak up the remains of the tea. Unfortunately, most of it seems to have gone on the laptop.

When I open the door, Ed is standing there, his face taking on a pink tinge. His mouth is set in a firm line and there's the familiar crease between his eyebrows he gets when he's annoyed.

'I was just about the break the door down,' he says.

'Sorry, I was in the bathroom.' I step back so he can come in. 'I wasn't expecting you. I thought you were going out with Ralph.'

'Yeah, well, Ralph is busy,' he says. 'I wanted to check on you anyway. Come back to mine if you're not well. It's much nicer than here.' He waves his hand around with disdain. Ed has never made any secret of what he thinks of my living accommodation. It couldn't be more different from his plush bachelor pad on the fourteenth floor with views of the Thames.

'I'm okay here,' I reply. I think of the laptop in the bathroom and check my watch. Thirty minutes until Roisin's deadline.

'Don't be daft,' says Ed. 'I insist. Come back to mine.'

'I just want to go to bed.'

'Perfect. You can go to bed in much more comfortable surroundings than this.'

'No, I mean here. I just want to go to bed here.'

'Really, Erin, you're so stubborn at times.' The note of irritation is back. He picks up my jacket and handbag. 'And silly. Now come on.'

I feel like a child as he ushers me out of the door. 'My stuff,' I say in a final act of protest.

'Your overnight bag is still in my car. You put it in there this morning. Remember?'

He's right. I did put it in the boot of his car earlier. I could kick myself. I glance at the clock. Twenty-five minutes to the deadline. Even if we get through the rush-hour traffic and to Ed's apartment by six, there's no way I can make a phone call to Roisin. Not with Ed there. I'll have to nip to the loo and text her that I'll call tomorrow. Hopefully that will hold her off from whatever it is she has planned.

County Cork, Ireland

Kerry wiped the petrol tank of the Yamaha with the polishing cloth. It looked good. His latest commission was to spray-paint an image of the human rib cage down the centre of the black tank and pop in a few mini skulls sitting on the rib bones. Unusual, but effective. He liked the less-than-ordinary private jobs he got in. Bike mechanics might be his trade but spray-paint artwork was his passion. A bike tattooist, if you like.

Draping a soft cloth over the tank to protect it, Kerry checked his watch. It was after six. He should call it a day soon. His cousin, Joe, had already finished and Max, Joe's dad and owner of the workshop, wasn't in today. That had given Kerry time to get the paint job finished.

Locking up behind him, Kerry left by the rear of the workshop. He only lived in the flat above but he wanted a quick smoke before he went up. Despite it being the middle of May, the day had been a particularly wet and dreary one. Kerry gave a little shiver, the sea breeze drifting in from the Irish Sea chilling his arms. He rolled a cigarette and, standing on the path, he looked across the High Street and to the service road opposite, which ran behind the parade of shops.

He saw something. At first he thought it was a pile of black bin bags that hadn't been put in the commercial wheelie bins, but as he took a draw on his roll-up and looked closer, he realised it was someone kneeling down, bent over something. Or rather someone.

The person kneeling raised their head and flicked their hand towards the end of the service road. Then, as if sensing they were being watched, turned to look over their shoulder at Kerry.

'What the…?' said Kerry, instantly recognising Marie Hurley, not least because of her distinctive bobbed auburn hair.

She jumped to her feet and began running towards him. 'Kerry! Kerry!' she shouted. 'Help me. Please.'

Kerry chucked his half-smoked cigarette to the ground and dived across the road. He caught Marie as she bundled into him in a blind panic.

'It's okay, Mrs Hurley,' said Kerry, holding onto the tops of her arms. 'Mrs Hurley. What's wrong?'

She looked up at him. Her face was paler than normal, if that was possible. Her eyes were wide with fear. 'It's Jim,' she said. 'He's had a fall or something.' She pulled away from Kerry and then, taking hold of his forearm, started dragging him back down the service road. 'He's bleeding. Come quickly.'

Jim Hurley was indeed bleeding, badly. A dark crimson pool of blood was leaking out from under the back of his head. One of his arms was twisted underneath his body, which was sprawled flat out on the tarmac.

Kerry snatched his mobile from his pocket and dialled the emergency services.

'Get a blanket and some towels,' he instructed Marie, while he waited for his call to connect. He reached over and tried to locate a pulse in the man's neck. It was there. Weak, but there.

The operator answered the call and after a few minutes' exchanging information and advising on basic first aid, she assured Kerry the ambulance was on its way. Marie reappeared with a blanket.

'Is he going to be okay?' she asked as Kerry draped the pink candlewick bedspread over Jim's body.

'The ambulance will be here soon,' said Kerry. He had no idea if Jim was going to be all right. He bundled the towel up and placed it at the side of Jim's head.

'If you can't see where the wound is, then don't move him,' the operator instructed. 'He might have spinal-cord injuries. Wait for the medics. Keep the towels either side of his head to stabilise him.'

'I think I can see part of the wound,' said Kerry. 'It's right at the back of his head. It looks pretty deep.'

'Just leave the towel there. Don't apply pressure. You could end up causing more damage.'

Kerry was no doctor but the trickle of blood from Jim's ear that appeared didn't look good to him. Marie was standing over her husband, looking down on him in a trance-like state. She was probably in shock.

'It's okay, Mrs Hurley. Come and kneel down. Hold his hand,' said Kerry. Marie glanced around. 'The ambulance will be here very soon. Come on, now.' Marie nodded and, kneeling down, she took Jim's hand, making soothing noises and offering reassuring words. Kerry suspected this was as much for her own benefit as for her husband's.

Jim's breathing was becoming shallower with each beat of his heart. Kerry willed the ambulance to get a move on. Rossway village was a bit out of the way, ten miles south from Cork itself on the Irish coast and the roads were twisty and narrow. Not exactly the easiest of routes to be throwing an ambulance around.

The sound of an empty bottle being knocked and rolling across the road made Kerry look up. He thought he saw something move in the shadows of the evening sun. A cat jumped out from behind one of the wheelie bins, trotted across the road and then sprang up onto the fence before disappearing into the grounds of the doctor's surgery.

A thought broke into Kerry's consciousness. The doctor's surgery. Why didn't he think of that before? He looked at the building. It was in darkness. He dismissed the small beacon of hope with his next thought. Half an hour earlier and one of the doctors might still have been there. Now, though, they would all have gone home. As far as he was aware, neither of the GPs lived in Rossway. It wasn't as if he could get one of them here to help. There was, of course, Diana Marshall. She used to be the local GP, but he dismissed the idea pretty much straight away as well. She lived on the edge of the village. It would take over ten minutes to get there and back. The ambulance would be here by then. Besides, he couldn't be sure she wouldn't have been drinking tonight. From what Roisin had told him in the past, her mother more than liked her sherry.

Eventually, there came the reassuring sound of an engine turning at speed and blue lights bouncing off the walls of the High Street. Kerry ran out to the main road and flagged the ambulance down, pointing to the service road.

With an assured confidence and professionalism, the paramedics examined Jim, wrapped his head with a temporary dressing and manoeuvred him from the ground to the back of the emergency vehicle. It took less than five minutes.

Kerry stood with his arm around Marie's shoulder as they watched.

'Is he going to be all right?' Marie asked.

The paramedic pushed the stretcher into the back of the ambulance. 'We need to get him to hospital straight away,' he said. 'Are you coming with us?'

'Oh, but I haven't locked up,' said Marie, looking anxiously back up the steps to her flat.

'Don't be worrying about that now, Mrs Hurley,' said Kerry. 'Give me the keys. I'll do it for you.' He was aware of the undercurrent of urgency and had registered that the paramedic had offered no comment to Marie's question of Jim's prognosis.

Marie grappled in her coat pocket and pulled out a set of keys. 'The flat and café keys are all on there.'

Kerry took the bunch. 'Off you go, now,' he said. 'Do you want me to contact Fiona?'

'Yes please. Tell her to phone Erin too.'

Chapter 2

London, England

When the call comes, it strikes me numb with fear. I don't know what to think or what to feel. Thoughts and emotions are crashing around in my head like bumper cars, bouncing and rebounding, stopping and starting. Confusion reigns.

'How bad is he?' A thread of compassion laces Ed's voice. 'What exactly did your sister say?'

'Fiona said it's serious. He's in intensive care. Apparently, Dad fell down the steps to the flat and hit his head,' I reply with a hint of impatience. I was uptight enough that I hadn't been able to phone Roisin earlier. This is only adding to my agitation. 'Fiona was in a bit of a fluster when she rang.' I hit the print button on Ed's laptop and the image of the document on the screen is sent to the printer.

'Have you booked a return flight?' Ed moves behind me as I loom over the printer. He squeezes my shoulders in a reassuring gesture.

'No, I'll see how things are first. I need to go and make sure Mum's all right, really.' Then more because I feel I ought to, I add, 'And see how Dad is, of course.' I silence the voice that also wants to add the need to face Roisin.

'Okay, I'll sort out some cover at work.'

'I'm sure Amber will do my shifts, she's always saying she needs more hours.' I take the sheet of paper as it glides out of the printer.

'Keep me in the loop, though, won't you? You know what it's like organising the staff rota.'

Whilst it's nice being the boss's girlfriend, it sometimes irritates me that Hamilton's Health and Beauty Spa always comes first with Ed.

'I'll do my best,' I say. 'I'll have a better idea once I'm there and can speak to the doctors myself.'

There's a small silence before Ed speaks again.

'Will you be okay on your own? Do you want me to come with you?' I can detect an apprehension in his voice. 'It will be a bit tricky with work, but I could manage a couple of days away, I should think.'

I withhold the sigh that threatens to escape. I know Ed better than he realises. His priority is work and the offer to accompany me is more out of duty than concern. I take care to respond in a conciliatory manner, not wishing to get into an argument.

'No, it's okay. Probably best if I go alone.'

'Are you sure you're up to it? You were feeling sick earlier.'

'It was nothing. I'm fine now and I'll be all right on my own. Thank you, anyway.'

'Sure? Okay. Look, I'll organise you a cab home so you can pack and I'll book another to take you to the airport.' This time the relief in his voice is very much apparent. 'I would take you myself but you know what it's like at work…really busy…I've got meetings…' His voice trails off.

'Thank you. And don't worry. I know what it's like.' I ignore the fact that Ed actually has the day off tomorrow.

As I climb into the cab, this time I release the sigh unrestricted. Ireland definitely isn't a place I want to be going. Since moving to England, my visits home have been few and far between. Far too many unhappy memories linger around the coastal village where I grew up. And now I'm being forced to face them. The unease begins to transform into fear.

Once the cab turns the corner, leaving Ed and his apartment behind, I take my phone from my pocket and find the email Roisin sent me. Her number is highlighted blue and I double-tap. After a few seconds the call is connected and I hear the sound of the phone ringing.

The phone goes to voicemail.

'It's me...' I hesitate. I need to be careful what I say. I'm not paranoid, merely cautious. Maybe overly, but it has stood me in good stead all this time and I'm not about to get caught out now. 'I'm coming over. I'll ring you again when I'm in Rossway.'

County Cork, Ireland

Looking at my father lying in his hospital bed, crisp white linen and a cellular blanket surrounding him, his face seems to have taken on a grey tinge. He looks older, frailer and smaller, somehow, as if he has suddenly aged without me noticing. His chest rises and falls as he lies motionless in a medically induced coma. He's hooked up to a ventilator, which wheezes up and down, helping him to breathe as the heart monitor bleeps a steady beat.

'How is he?' I ask Mum who, having embraced me, is now settling herself back into the plastic bedside chair.

She puts her forefinger to her lips and whispers, 'They're going to give him a brain scan in the morning. They want to see if the swelling will go down first.' She gives me half a smile, which I suspect is supposed to be reassuring. 'It's all right. Your dad's a fighter. Don't go getting yourself upset now.'

I turn my gaze away from the ashen look on her face. The guilt weighs me down. Guilt I feel because I cannot summon as much sympathy for my father as I know I should.

Our relationship has always been a strained one, with any feelings of compassion finally quashed ten years ago. I swallow

17

down the anger that always accompanies the memory. This time I am able to meet Mum's eyes.

'What exactly happened?' I fiddle with my necklace. I need to keep my hands busy. Nerves are making them shake.

'I came out of the café and found your father at the bottom of the steps,' says Mum. 'That's it, really.' She sniffs and when I look up, she's fumbling with her sleeve and finally produces a tissue. She dabs her eyes and wipes her nose.

'Do you want anything, Mum? Have you eaten?' I change the subject, not wanting to upset her.

'No, I'm grand,' she replies quietly, a fleeting smile of gratitude dashes across her face. She stuffs the tissue back up her sleeve. 'The nurses have been looking after me, so they have.'

I'm not convinced Mum looks grand at all. She looks tired and strained. 'I'll make you a fresh cup of tea,' I say. 'I could do with one myself. Back in a minute.'

One of the nurses kindly shows me to the community kitchen, where all the tea and coffee making paraphernalia is housed. While I wait for the kettle to boil I can't help feeling more concern for Mum than for Dad. I don't like the dark circles under her eyes or the depth of the hollows below her cheekbones. She looks exhausted. No doubt she has been working herself hard at the café. Now, with Dad incapacitated and set for a long recovery, I wonder how on earth she will manage to look after him and run the business on her own.

The next thought snakes its way from the back of my mind, where it has been lurking, waiting to strike. What if he doesn't pull through? How do I feel about that? I don't trust myself to examine the notion too closely. I'm not quite sure I'll like what I might find. Instead, I focus on producing an acceptable-looking cup of tea for Mum and venture back to collect her. We're not allowed to take food or drink into ICU so we sit in the small family room at the end of the corridor.

'You just missed your sister,' says Mum, resting her cup on her knees. 'She had to get back for the kids. Sean's on duty this evening. You know he's a sergeant now?'

'Yes, Fiona said. He deserves it. He's a good police officer.' It seems a bit surreal talking about normal, everyday things when this situation is anything but normal.

After drinking the tea, we venture back to my father's bedside. It's very quiet, apart from the rhythmic bleep of the monitor and the sighing of the breathing apparatus as it wheezes air down the tube. *Inhale. Exhale. Inhale. Exhale.*

'Time's getting on. There's no point in you hanging around with me,' says Mum, breaking the silence that has settled. 'You go on back and stay with Fiona tonight, she's expecting you.'

'What about you? I don't want to leave you,' I reply frowning. 'You can't stay all night, surely.'

'I'm not going anywhere.' My mother pats my knee. 'Please, go to Fiona's. Get some rest and then come back in the morning. I'll ring if there's any change. Besides, they won't let you stay here on the ward.'

I'm not entirely convinced, but deciphering her subtly placed eyebrows, I determine she isn't going to take no for an answer.

'Okay, only if you're sure,' I relent.

'I'm positive. In the morning go over to Wright's motorcycle shop and get the keys for the flat and the café. You can nip up to the flat and bring my wash bag and some clean clothes.'

Mum stands up. I take this as a signal it's time for me to leave. I walk round and give her a kiss.

'It will be okay, Mum. I'll see you in the morning,' I say, hoping to sound positive before I beat the retreat. 'Do I need to ask for anyone in particular at the bike shop?'

'Er, yes...Kerry,' replies Mum distractedly as a nurse approaches us.

'I'm just doing some routine observations,' the nurse explains.

'I'll get out the way,' I say, giving Mum a reassuring smile. 'Bye, Mum.'

19

'What about your Dad?' says Mum. 'You should say goodbye to him too.'

'We like to encourage family to still communicate with the patient,' explains the nurse. 'Sometimes, it can help with their recovery.'

I hesitate. 'What should I say?'

'Just speak to your father as if he's awake,' says the nurse. 'It seems a little odd at first but once you've done it a few times, it becomes much easier.'

I go over to the bed and reach out to touch his hand. 'Bye, Dad,' I say, feeling terribly self-conscious. The nurse smiles encouragingly and I feel I need to say something else. 'I'll see you tomorrow.'

It's awkward and it's not without relief that I escape the hospital and head over to Fiona's.

*

Mini lights and precision-planted marigolds line the brick path to Fiona's front door. The outside light bathes the garden, high-lighting the alternating dark-and-light-green stripes running up and down the lawn. Tidy to the point of being manicured. The black gloss of the door with shiny chrome furniture is smart and exact. Fiona, my older sister by eight years, opens the door before I reach the end of the path.

Meeting me on the doorstep, she draws me into an embrace. The familiar smell of Fiona's perfume clings to me in the same way I cling to her. A feeling of relief seeps out. Fiona has always been able to do that. To take away my troubles. To fix whatever needs fixing.

'Hi-ya, hun,' she says, giving me a squeeze. 'How are you? How's everything at the hospital? No change, I expect.'

'I'm fine. It's lovely to see you. Dad's still sedated and Mum is happy to be there by herself.' I give a little shiver in the night air. 'I didn't want to leave her, but she insisted.'

'I know, but there's nothing we can do. Anyway, come on in out of the cold. The kids are fast asleep, so we'll go quietly.'

Sitting in Fiona's immaculate kitchen, I hold my hands around the fine-bone-china cup. The heat from the cup warms my fingers. On the fridge door there is a family snapshot of the Keanes: Fiona, Sean, Sophie and Molly. It looks like it was taken last year on their holiday to Spain. Sean is giving Sophie a piggy-back. Fiona and Molly are looking up at them and everyone is beaming with happiness. Sean is a tall man and none too skinny either. He must look very imposing in his Guard's uniform. In this picture, though, he reminds me of Roald Dahl's *BFG* and I think how aptly named their daughter, Sophie, is.

'How's Sean?' I ask, as Fiona sits down beside me.

'He's fine. Well, that's not entirely true. He's exhausted, if I'm honest. We both are. His mum needs a lot of looking after. We're thinking about moving her in with us.'

'Is she getting to that stage where she needs a lot of care?' I ask.

'She can't cook properly, she's a danger to herself.' Fiona gives a weary sigh. 'Not so long ago, she left the frying pan on the stove and burnt right through it, setting off the fire alarms. There was smoke everywhere. The fire brigade turned up, it was chaos. Since then, I've been cooking for her. She's lovely, though, so I wouldn't mind her moving in. After all, she is the reason we came home.'

I nod, remembering the day well when Fiona and Sean packed up their little family in London and headed back home to care for his recently widowed mother. I had managed to hold back my tears until the car and removal lorry disappeared around the corner.

Funny how Fiona regards it as coming home, whereas I look on her return as leaving home. To me, home means a place of love and fond memories, a feeling of being safe and cared for. Coming to Ireland is not coming home for me.

My thoughts turn to Roisin's email again and my stomach lurches as the fear that has pitched up and taken residency gives another kick. I had thought I'd tell Fiona about it but now I've changed my mind. Maybe I can get this sorted without her knowing. She has a lot on her plate at the moment, what with Dad and Sean's mother. I'll tell her only if I have to. I'm sure I can handle this. At least, I hope I can.

Fiona's mobile phone cuts through my thoughts. From this side of the conversation, I guess it's Sean. I busy myself with making another cup of tea while she wanders off into the living room for more privacy.

She returns a few minutes later.

'Sean's going to call by the hospital at some point in the night to check on Mum and Dad.'

'What exactly happened? How did Dad end up falling down the steps?' I ask.

'I'm still not entirely sure. Apparently, Mum was in the café tidying up at the end of the day and Dad went upstairs with the day's takings to put them in the safe for the night. When he didn't come back down, Mum went out to look for him and found him at the foot of the stairs.'

'Was there anyone else there? Did they see anything?'

'No, just Kerry from the bike shop across the way.'

'What time did all this happen?'

'Soon after six,' says Fiona after a moment's thought. 'That's what time he always puts the takings in the safe. Of course, we've no way of knowing if that's what he did.'

'What do you mean?'

'Mum can't find the key for the safe, so we can't check to see if Dad fell before or after he went upstairs. There was no bag beside him.'

'You don't think he was robbed, do you?'

'We just don't know,' says Fiona. 'It's all a bit worrying.'

'Doesn't Mum know where the key is so we can check?'

'No. She can't remember,' says Fiona. 'I tried to ask but she was so distracted with Dad, I didn't like to push it.'

'I don't suppose you know where the key would be or even if there's a spare one?' I ask half-heartedly.

Fiona gives a wry smile. 'You know what Dad's like. Top-secret information that is.'

'I'll have a look round when I'm at the flat,' I say. Much as my feelings towards my father are stifled, the thought that someone mugged him is not nice.

'To be honest, that's the least of our worries at the moment,' says Fiona.

'Yes, you're right.' I force myself to conjure up the compassion I know should be there. I change the subject to divert this uncomfortable acknowledgement. 'How are Molly and Sophie?'

'The kids are grand,' says Fiona. A smile spreads across her face at their mention. 'Molly is coming up to the last term of nursery. She goes off to school in September. She'll be in junior infants, and Sophie will be going into fifth year of senior infants.'

'So, two more years and then secondary school.'

'I know, I can't believe how the time has flown,' says Fiona. 'Remember when Sophie was born, she was such a scrap of a thing. All that red hair against her lily-white skin.'

'She looked like an alien,' I say, thinking back. A lump makes a bid to establish itself in my throat. I feel Fiona's hand cover my own and hear her soft words.

'It's okay,' she says. 'It's been a long day. Don't go upsetting yourself, now. You can't change anything. It will all be fine. I promise.'

When I go up to bed shortly afterwards, I stop and peep in the open door of Molly's bedroom. The five-year-old is fast asleep, her fair curls fan the pillow like a golden starburst. Molly has been lucky to inherit her mother's colouring, but not so lucky with the curse of the Hurley curls.

I can't resist looking in on Sophie, who is snuggled down

under the duvet. Admittedly she doesn't have the Hurley curls, but she most definitely has the ginger colouring, or auburn, as Mum likes to call it.

I touch my own hair, the colour I have grown to love, a dark-orangey brown, the curls haven't quite won the same affection and, every day, I'm grateful to whoever brought hair-straighteners to the mass market. I can remember the absolute relief I felt on my fourteenth birthday when Fiona gave me a set as a present so I would no longer have to use the household iron in an attempt to banish the unruly curls. The ironing effect didn't quite have the staying power and by lunchtime my hair had usually sprung back up into its familiar coils, much to the amusement of my classmates.

Fiona has always made things better. Right from making cakes when I felt fed up, taking me to the cinema to see the latest film, walking me to and from school when no one would walk with me because I'd fallen out with Roisin, to helping me fill in an application form for college and helping me find student digs.

Muffled footsteps on the carpeted landing bring me from my thoughts. Fiona appears at my side.

'I was just looking at them. Fast asleep. Oblivious,' I whisper.

'Oblivious to everything,' she says, putting her arm around my shoulder. 'Is everything all right? Apart from the obvious…Dad.'

I feel my resolve weaken. I want to tell her about Roisin. Fiona will know what to do. She always has and before I can check myself the words are out.

'Fiona, there's something I need to tell you.'

'Aha, and what's that?' says Fiona, unhooking her arm and pulling the bedroom door closed. She stifles a yawn.

Fiona looks tired. Even her hug had the air of exhaustion around it. Now isn't the time to burden her with news of the email.

'I'm glad I came back,' I say quickly.

She gives a smile. 'I'm glad as well. So is Mum. And Dad will be too.'

I don't challenge this. It's my turn to give out the hugs now.

Chapter 3

I walk round on to Beach Road and the familiar parade of shops greets me on one side and the Irish Sea on the other. The fishing boats are tied up on the shore and the tidal waters of the estuary slop back and forth.

Seahorse Café is on the end of the parade of shops. The buildings that make up the parade are stone-built to echo the traditional style of the area, as are the small-paned windows and wooden doors. Above the shops is the living accommodation. My parents' flat, my childhood home, stretches over four shop premises. Along the parade is a paper shop, hairdresser's, a charity shop and Seahorse Café, my father's pride and joy. The village road runs adjacent to the shops and on the other side is 'Wright's Motorbike Servicing & Repairs'.

My dad's car is parked in the bays outside the café. I have the keys, so I can use it while I'm here. Sean is sorting out the insurance for me. I'm not sure what my dad would say if he knew. He'd probably be horrified. The car is old, but you wouldn't think so. My dad has cared for that car like it was his own flesh and blood. I give a small laugh at the expression and correct myself. He cares for the car *more* than his own flesh and blood.

Crossing the road to the bike garage, I take a deep breath

before entering. I have no desire whatsoever to come here, but Fiona is taking the children to nursery and school so it's down to me to collect the keys to Mum's flat. I've yet to call Roisin, but I'll do that once I have the keys, then I can let myself into the flat and phone her in private.

I hope it will be only Kerry there and I won't have to see Jody Wright, his cousin. With any luck Kerry won't even remember me, our paths had only crossed a couple of times in our teenage years. However, I'm sure Jody won't have forgotten me, after all, we had been at school together.

Another feeling of disquiet settles over me. School days bring no comfort or feeling of nostalgia to me. I breathe deeply and exhale slowly, blowing away the dark memories from my mind.

A bell tinkles above the doorway as I open and close the door. It's a small reception area with a coffee machine in one corner that has seen better days. Either side are two chairs and a small table with a selection of bike and motoring magazines, all looking well-thumbed and dog-eared. The sound of a radio filters through into the reception area from the open doorway behind the counter, accompanied by the sporadic sound of some sort of power tool and the clanking of metal against metal. Obviously, the workshop. I stand at the counter patiently, hoping Kerry will appear.

After a minute or two I call out a 'Hello!' trying to time it with a lull in the noise. It appears an unsuccessful tactic, so I decide to go round the rear of the building to the workshop entrance.

Picking my way through a couple of oily patches in the court-yard, to avoid any stains on my white trainers, I head towards the open double garage doors.

'Hello,' I call out as I enter the building. The smell of oil and petrol, mixed with a dirty, greasy sort of smell, hits me, catching in the back of my throat. There are a number of bikes in the workshop, all in various states of repair. One looks like it has been stripped right down to the frame; there are bits of motorbike lying alongside. I assume they are bits of motorbike. To me it's a mass of metal and plastic.

To my right a curtain of thick industrial plastic strips separates one side of the workshop. A blond head pokes through, the face obscured by a white mask and a pair of thick protective goggles. Pulling the mask from his face, he speaks.

'All right?' he says looking over at me. 'Can I help you?'

I swallow hard. I recognise the voice instantly. It's Jody Wright. He doesn't appear to recognise me. Perhaps I can get away with this.

'Hi. I'm after Kerry.' I turn my face from view, looking around the workshop as if trying to locate Kerry.

'He's upstairs in the stock room. I'll get him.' I can hear Jody's footsteps come further into the workshop. 'Oi! Kerry! You've got a visitor!' His voice bellows out, followed by a shrill whistle.

A moment later, I hear the door at the top of the stairs open.

'All right?' comes another voice.

'Someone to see you,' says Jody.

I have no choice but to turn around this time. I look up at the figure standing at the top of the steps.

'Hi…I've come to get the keys for Marie Hurley.'

Before Kerry can answer, Jody interrupts. 'Hey, wait a minute! I know you.' I turn and watch him take a few strides across the workshop, coming to a halt in front of me, whereupon he whisks his goggles from his face. 'Well, well, well, if it isn't Curly Hurley!' I stand there in silence as I come face to face with my nemesis of those wretched childhood days. 'It's me…Joe. Jody Wright!' He grins at me, raking his fingers through his mop of longish blond hair. 'We were in the same class at Rossway School. Mr Capper's class, or Mr Crapper, as we used to call him. I sat behind you and Roisin Marshall. Come on, you must remember me.'

Despite feeling myself flinch, I remain composed. I'm older now. I'm in control. I can handle this.

Straightening up, giving him the benefit of my five-feet-eight-inches' height, I look at him unsmiling. 'How could I forget?'

'Nearly didn't recognise you without your curls,' Joe says, nodding towards my poker-straight hair, which hangs loose over my shoulders. 'Do you remember my cousin, Kerry? He used to come and stay sometimes during the summer.'

I give a shrug. 'A bit.'

Kerry is watching me. He has blond hair, not dissimilar to Jody's, actually, casually parting in the middle with longish layers giving a sort of dishevelled look. He wears a pair of blue overalls, which hang from his waist and bear the scars of many a battle with a paintbrush. The black t-shirt has suffered a similar fate, together with a rip at the left sleeve, revealing some sort of tribal-pattern tattoo around his bicep. He smiles at me and descends the steps.

'I thought you looked familiar, I was just trying to place you,' he says. 'You were at Shane's eighteenth birthday party, weren't you?'

I nod, impressed with his recall. Shane is one of Joe's older brothers. 'That's right. There was a big group of us.' I shift on my feet. The desire to take a trip down memory lane is furthest from my mind.

Joe gives a laugh and carries on energetically. 'There are quite a few of us Wrights. Kerry probably just blended in. One summer he came to stay and never went home, I don't suppose me mam even noticed an extra person at the dinner table.' I nod this time. He carries on enthusiastically. 'What you up to these days? It must be about ten years. You disappeared without a trace.'

'Working in London,' I reply, really having no wish to get into this conversation. 'Look, I don't mean to be rude but what with my dad and everything…' I wave my hand airily, hoping I don't need to explain. I'm relieved when Kerry speaks, ending Joe's desire to revisit our childhood days.

'Yes, of course, you've got more important things to do than reminisce about the good old days. You'll have to excuse my cousin's enthusiasm,' says Kerry, giving Joe a playful whack on the arm with back of his hand. Kerry ferrets around in the large side pocket of his trousers and after a moment produces a set of keys. He holds them out to me. 'How is your dad?'

'Not good. He's stable, but they're waiting for the swelling to go down before they can assess him further. He's taken a nasty bang to his head. Thanks for asking.' I take the keys from Kerry, his rough hands with grubby fingernails briefly brush my own well-moisturised and manicured fingers. 'Mum said you helped her yesterday evening?'

'It was nothing,' replies Kerry shrugging. 'I just happened to be out the back there. I called the ambulance and then locked up the flat. As I said, nothing really.'

'Thank you, anyway. Mum really appreciates it. We all do.'

'You should come down the pub one night and meet up with some of the old gang,' says Joe.

Looking at him for a moment before I speak, I can't think of anything less I want to do. 'I'm only here for a few days, so probably won't have time. And besides, if I wanted to catch up with everyone, I could have done that by now on Facebook.' I give a little laugh, which I so don't mean and then, turning my back on Joe, direct a slight nod at Kerry before heading out of the dirty workshop. I'm just congratulating myself on getting one over my old enemy when I hear him call after me.

'See ya, Bunny!'

For a split second I'm transported back to my school days. Bunny is the nickname Joe used for me. A loose connection between the colour of my hair and carrots, which still appears to amuse him. I force myself to walk on and not acknowledge his parting shot.

*

29

Roisin's heart pumped an extra beat. There was Erin Hurley walking across the green, heading straight to where Roisin and her mam had parked their car. Roisin had got Erin's voicemail but it had come too late. She hadn't been sure Erin would come but fate had intervened and made it impossible for her not to. The incident with Jim Hurley, unfortunate as it was for Erin, was fortunate for Roisin.

Suddenly, Roisin thought of her mam and how she would react. She looked across the roof of the car as they got out. Her mam, Diana, was having a good day today. She was calm. She was talking clearly. Thinking rationally. She had even been smiling a lot. Roisin was under no illusion that it was all about to end in a matter of seconds.

'Mam,' she called across to her. Diana looked up and smiled. Roisin didn't return it. She flicked her eyes towards Erin. Her mother followed suit. Roisin watched the recognition spread across Diana's face like a snow flurry. Her mother's hand grappled for the car, resting on the front wing for support.

The athletic figure of Erin Hurley walked purposefully towards them. The curls might have gone, but the distinctive red hair was unmistakable as it reflected back the sun, almost challenging it to be brighter.

This was not how Roisin had wanted the meeting with Erin to happen. It was supposed to be just the two of them. Alone. On Roisin's terms. Somewhere private. Not here in the middle of the village when she was caught by surprise.

Erin was only a few metres away and as she looked up, the recognition in her eyes was instant. The defiant look came a second later. She slowed her pace and came to a stop in front of their car. She fiddled with the bunch of keys she was holding.

'Hello, Erin,' said Roisin. She wanted to glance over at her mam to see if she was okay, but she didn't want to break eye contact with Erin. Roisin had nothing to be ashamed about. She wasn't the one who had done something so wrong. Roisin hadn't caused her family this never-ending pain.

'Hello, Roisin.' Erin held Roisin's gaze for a moment and then looked over at Diana. 'Mrs Marshall.'

'How is your father?' Diana spoke with a removed tone to her voice. Roisin wasn't sure her mam was really that concerned about Jim Hurley, but she asked as that was the polite thing to do.

'Not too good at all,' replied Erin.

'I hope he makes a good recovery,' said Diana. Her own recovery now in full swing. 'Please pass on our best wishes to your mother.'

'Thank you. I will.'

'I take it you'll be around for a few days?' said Roisin, sensing this reunion was coming to a close.

'That's right, yes. Until I know he's better and Mum is okay.' The reply was stiff and cold.

'We must catch up,' said Roisin. 'We have lots to talk about.'

'If there's anything I can do to help, please let me know,' said Diana, straightening her navy tailored jacket and dropping the car keys into her handbag.

'We're fine. Thank you.' A terse response from Erin, which irritated Roisin more than it probably should. A flutter of anger made itself known in her stomach at Erin's lack of gratitude. Old feelings of hostility broke free. *Shame on you, Erin Hurley, for what you did.*

'Is something wrong?' asked Erin, making her way round to the driver's door of the car parked next to Diana's. Roisin recognised it as Jim and Marie Hurley's car. An old estate car they used for their weekly trip to the trade discount supplier.

Roisin was perfectly aware of the lack of concern in Erin's voice. If anything, there was almost a mocking, challenging tone as she continued. 'Don't worry, I know we have things to catch up on.' She made quotation marks in the air. Roisin got the subtext.

'Good. I'll look forward to it,' said Roisin.

Without so much as looking their way, Erin reversed out of the parking bay and drove off up Beach Road. It was only once the silver estate car had turned the corner Roisin allowed herself to succumb to the tremors that rippled from the inside to the outside. She looked down at her hand. It was shaking. Adrenalin-fueled.

She took a deep breath. Slowly she exhaled. The feeling of control came back. She had to admit, she hadn't expected Erin to have that effect on her.

She looked over to her mam. Roisin could tell Diana was fighting with her emotions.

'You okay, Mam?'

Her mam turned to her. 'I need to get a few bits from the shop. Why don't you get what you need from the chemist and I'll meet you back here in, say, fifteen minutes?' She totally ignored Roisin's question. Roisin knew the subject of Erin Hurley was off-limits.

She also knew her mam wanted her out of the way so she could stock up with sherry. Then the subject would have no limits.

Once again, Roisin cursed Erin Hurley for what she'd done to the Marshall family.

*

Diana turned the car into the drive, the gravel scrunching under the tyres. The Manor House looked down on them, casting its shadow across the drive. Roisin looked up at the home she had lived in all her life. It used to be filled with happiness, now it was empty and devoid of any warmth. She ignored the sound of the bottles clanking together as her mam came to an abrupt halt. The wheels ground into the stones. Diana cut the engine and, holding on to the top of the steering wheel, rested her head on her hands.

'I suppose I should have expected her to turn up,' said Diana, sitting back in the seat. Her fingers unfurled from the steering wheel. 'It's just she's so brazen. Full of attitude. No shame.'

'Come on, let's go inside,' said Roisin, opening the door. She wanted to distract her mam, to stop her going into a full rant. Roisin knew the routine. Anger followed by despair as the pain was numbed by alcohol. 'I'll make us a cup of tea and some lunch.'

As Roisin took the shopping into the kitchen, she noted Diana peel off into the drawing room, the bag with the bottles chinking in time with her step.

Roisin made a pot of tea and hurriedly put together two ham sandwiches. It was probably futile. Diana would be well into the sherry by now, but she had to try. She couldn't give up on her mam. All Roisin ever wanted to do was to save Diana from herself. For her to be the mam she used to be. And since Roisin had found that photograph, she thought she knew how. She could make things right. Roisin could make her mam happy again.

Diana was standing at the fireplace, in one hand a sherry glass, in the other a photograph of Niall. It was taken when he was sixteen. They were on a family skiing holiday.

Roisin placed the tray on the coffee table and, going over to her mam, she took the photograph and replaced it on the mantel-piece. Niall's deep-blue eyes looked back at her, his ski goggles were strapped around the top of his ski helmet. Mam always insisted they wear helmets. She never took any chances. From when they were a very young age she had instilled in both of them the need to be safe. As a doctor who spent several years working in A and E, she had seen the result of many an accident where the injuries sustained could so easily have been avoided had the victim being wearing or using the correct safety equipment.

Roisin absently ran her finger across Niall's face. It was as if touching his photo would bring a small crumb of comfort. She wished, like she had every day since the accident, that he had held the same regard for his safety as their mam had.

Roisin guided her mam to the wing-backed armchair beside the fireplace.

'Here, sit down.'

The lid of the walnut art-deco drinks cabinet was down. The freshly opened bottle of sherry stood on the glass shelf, the lid beside it. Roisin replaced the lid.

'I've not finished,' Diana said, without turning to look at her daughter.

'At least have a sandwich,' said Roisin, putting the lid down and offering the plate to her. Diana took it, but her attention was caught by something else and she rested the plate on the arm of the chair.

'What's that sticking out of the sideboard?' she asked, nodding to the other side of the room.

Roisin swore silently to herself. That was her fault. She had been rummaging through the box of photos the other day. She thought she had put them all back neat and tidy, just as her mam liked it. Roisin was certain Diana had developed OCD over the years. She never used to be this particular about things; it had only been since the accident.

Roisin jumped up quickly and went to put the errant photograph away.

'Pass it here.' Diana held out her hand.

Obediently Roisin delivered it to her mam. It was a photograph of Roisin and Niall when they were about five and seven. A school photo. They were both smiling brightly at the camera. Diana drank in the image before her.

She placed the photograph on her lap. As she did, her elbow caught the plate balanced on the arm of the chair. It fell to the floor, the sandwich hitting the parquet tiles, quickly followed by the plate, which broke into two pieces.

Diana didn't give the plate a glance. Roisin knelt down and picked up the two halves. It reminded her of their hearts. Broken.

'I'll make you a fresh sandwich,' said Roisin, standing up.

'Don't bother. I'm not hungry.'

As Roisin left the drawing room and closed the door gently

behind her she could hear her mam sob. A guttural noise from deep within. A sound Roisin was all too familiar with.

Roisin took the crockery and sandwich out to the kitchen, choosing not to return to the drawing room. She was not sure she could deal with this today. After the sobs would come the blame. Her mam would say how she held Roisin partly responsible for what had happened. How Roisin should have said something sooner. How Roisin had let her down.

She slipped off her shoes at the bottom of the stairs and trod softly as she ascended the oak staircase, seeking solace in her room.

Her mam went through phases. Sometimes she barely drank at all and, during those dry times, she was easier to live with. However, when she befriended the sherry bottle, she became an emotional wreck. The sadness that emitted from her was so heavy Roisin felt she was drowning in it simply by being in the same room.

Roisin reached the top of the stairs and headed to the back of the house, where her bedroom was situated. Her mam's sobs were now, thankfully, out of ear shot. She closed the bedroom door behind her and slumped onto her bed.

She needed a few minutes' peace and quiet to work out what to do next. She needed to up her game. If she was to give her mam something to cling to so she could climb out of the pit of depression she had fallen into, then Roisin needed to make things happen.

Chapter 4

Teenage Kicks
Eight months before leaving

I hate my curly hair. I hate my red hair. I hate my curly, red hair. I hate that Jody Wright and his mates call me Curly Hurley at every opportunity. I walk out of the village-hall youth club away from them, my head held high. I should be used to it by now, but it still hurts.

'Hey, it's Erin, isn't it?'

I stop dead in my tracks as in front of me Niall Marshall is sitting in his car, smoking a cigarette, the driver's window is wound down and a plume of smoke floats out. He looks pretty cool. I throw a glance over to the passenger seat. His mate, Shane Wright, is sitting with him. They are listening to some drum-and-base music. Shane flicks his cigarette out of the window and nods in acknowledgement of me.

I realise Niall is waiting for an answer. I must try to play it cool. Niall Marshall is a bit of a catch in the quiet backwaters of Rossway. Nearly all the girls in my year have a crush on him. I swallow hard and, resting my hand on my hip, I stick it out to one side and place one foot slightly in front of the other.

'Yeah, that's right,' I say.

'You not staying at the youth club, then?' he asks.

I shake my head. 'It's boring.'

'Full of kids, right?' Niall looks over at Shane and they both laugh.

'There's nothing else to do in this village,' I say, as justification for being there.

'Is that right?' muses Niall. He leans over and mumbles something to Shane that I can't make out. I'm not sure whether I should stay where I am or carry on home. Back to where life is even duller. I can't wait to leave school and get out of this place.

I feel a bit of an idiot standing there and the pose is making my leg hurt.

Shane gets out of the car, saying his goodbyes to Niall. He holds the door open and gestures for me to come over.

'Aren't you going to get in, then?' asks Niall.

'Am I?'

'Come on, I'll take you for a ride. It won't be boring, I promise.'

I look back at the youth club door, the sounds of some club mix blares out. I look beyond Niall's car at the road leading to the flat, where I live with my mum and dad. There's no contest.

I'm sitting beside Niall. I want to squeal with delight and excitement, but I keep it in. He's two years older than me and the coolest thing since I don't know what. He flicks the control on his iPod, which is plugged into his stereo and 'Teenage Kicks' by The Undertones blasts out from the speakers. I grin to myself and, as I fasten my seat belt, Niall blips the throttle and does whatever you do with the pedals to make the wheels spin for a few seconds, before we lurch forward and Niall floors it. We speed down the High Street. I'm with Niall Marshall! Woohoo!

We drive around the village for a while. As usual, it's pretty quiet. There's not much going on in Rossway. There never is.

'So, where do you want to go?' he asks.

'I thought you were going to take me somewhere exciting,' I say. To be truthful, I don't mind where we go. If I'm with Niall,

I really don't care. I wonder briefly what Roisin would say if she knew I was out with her older brother. I don't know if she would be happy. Anyway, she's with Jody and his crowd. I don't know why I feel any loyalty towards her, it's not as if she ever sticks up for me when they start taking the mickey.

'I know, let's go out to The Spit,' says Niall. 'We can get burger and chips from the takeaway and eat it there.' The Spit looks out onto the Irish Sea, jutting out from the coastline for about half a mile.

I smile at him. 'That sounds great,' I say, even though I'm not really hungry. Mum always makes sure I have some tea at the café before they close at the end of the day. I had a burger tonight, but I'm sure a burger with Niall will taste better than one from the café.

It's peaceful out at The Spit. We come to a stop in the car park and look out across the dark water, the clouds cross the path of the moon, allowing snatches of light to peak out for only a minute or two.

I eat my burger and I was right. It does taste better.

'Why were you leaving the youth club early?' Niall asks.

'I was actually a bit bored,' I reply.

'I think everyone grows out of it after a while. You're what, sixteen now?' says Niall through a mouthful of burger.

'That's right.' I feel grown up that I'm sixteen, it sounds so much better than being the fifteen I was a month ago. I like being one of the oldest in the school year.

'I can't wait to get away from here,' says Niall as he screws up the burger wrapper and drops it into the brown-paper takeaway bag. 'Only one more year in the sixth form and then I'm off to university.'

'Where are you going?' I ask, ignoring the little flicker of disappointment that he will only be about for another year.

'Dublin. If I get my grades, that is,' he says. 'I'm going to study law.'

'Wow! You want to be a lawyer? You must be clever.'

Niall laughs. 'A little. My mam's got high hopes for me. She wants me to go into company law – where the money is.'

He imitates his mother's voice and I laugh.

'But what about you? Is that what you want to do?' I ask.

'I want to represent people who can't afford a proper solicitor. I want to make a stand for the underdog. Mam doesn't get that at all. She's all right, really,' he says with a smile. 'She says she just wants what's best for me. She's a bit of a control freak at times.'

'Sounds like my dad. It's his way or no way. My dad isn't ambitious for me, though. He'd be happy for me to work in the café when I leave school.'

'Do you want to?'

'No way. It's bad enough having to work in there at the weekends and during school holidays. When I leave school I want to go to college and do a beautician's course.'

'What like, make-up and leg wax, that sort of thing?'

'Yes. I want to have my own salon one day. Be my own boss.'

'And will your dad let you?'

'He doesn't think I'll stick at it. I'd like to live with my sister, Fiona.' I fold up the last bit of burger in the wrapper. 'She lives in London with her husband.'

'How old is she?'

'Twenty-four. We get on really well despite the big age gap. I'd be lost without her sometimes.'

'I've only got Roisin,' says Niall. He pulls a face, which makes me laugh again. 'I know she's your friend and all that, but as a sister she's a feckin' pain at times. She's another control freak. I think she must get it from Mam. My poor dad is going to be spending even more time hiding from them at work once I leave home. He says he going to get a huge man-shed in the garden and take up model train-making.'

A small silence settles between us as we contemplate our families.

39

'Let's make a pact,' he says suddenly. He turns in his seat to look at me. 'We promise each other we'll follow our dreams and not let our parents stand in the way. You promise you'll go to college and become a beautician and I promise I'll qualify as a solicitor and defend criminal cases. Is it a deal?'

He holds out his hand. I put mine in his. Just touching him makes me feel like a child at Christmas who has opened the best present ever. 'It's a deal,' I manage to say, trying to stay calm and cool.

Niall leans over and kisses me briefly on the mouth. Oh, my God! I've had my Christmas and birthday presents all in one go.

We sit for a little longer looking up at the stars, talking about what the future holds for us. What we're going to call our businesses. We fantasise about the sort of clients we will have. I will work on a cruise ship and travel to faraway places like the Caribbean and Mediterranean. Niall will defend high-profile celebrities and businessmen so he can make enough money to work for free, defending those who can't afford a solicitor. He sees it as a modern-day Robin Hood sort of figure.

We promise again we'll follow our dreams.

*

Seven months before leaving

'When exactly were you going to tell me?' demands Roisin.

'Tell you what?' I try to act all innocent.

We're sitting next to each other at registration. I know exactly what she means. She means me and Niall becoming a proper item. Proper boyfriend and girlfriend. I hadn't told her before as I didn't want her to tell the others. Jody Wright will no doubt find something funny about it.

'Come on, Erin. Don't pretend you don't know what I'm on about.'

Fortunately, Miss Martin, our form teacher, begins to call the register and I avoid answering Roisin. It gives me time to come up with a reasonable excuse.

As soon as registration is over and Miss Martin tells us to read in silence until the bell goes for first period, Roisin is hissing in my ear.

'So?' she demands. 'When were you going to tell me you were going out with my brother? Why did you keep it a secret? I thought I was your best friend. Best friends are supposed to tell each other everything.'

I resist the urge to say what else best friends are supposed to do, like stick up for each other. Instead I say, 'I was going to tell you eventually, but I was waiting until it was all official. We've only been out a few times.' I hope she doesn't press me to define 'a few times'. I've actually seen Niall eight times in the last three weeks. Last night, he said we were officially boyfriend and girlfriend. I think Shane, Jody Wright's brother, knows as he saw us together last night. He seems cool about it, though. He just said hello and carried on talking to Niall about what he was doing to his car. I suppose it is inevitable now that word will get around. After all, Rossway is only a small village.

I ask Roisin how she found out.

'You didn't come to the youth club again last night, so I went round to your house to see why.'

I gulp. 'Did you speak to my mum? What did you say?'

'Yes, I did, as a matter of fact. She said she thought you were at the youth club. That's where you told her you were going.' Roisin's eyes narrow. 'Your dad called out, wanting to know what you were up to.'

This time I can't gulp. There's a golf-ball-sized lump in my throat. I don't want my dad to know I've been lying about what I've been doing. Roisin continues, a small look of amusement on her face. She knows what my dad is like.

'Don't worry, I didn't give you away. I just said I remembered I was supposed to be meeting you there.'

'Thank you.' I look up over my book as I sense Miss Martin's eyes trained upon us. We wait a few minutes before we start up again, making sure Miss Martin is preoccupied with trying to get the new interactive whiteboard working for her next class.

'When I was walking back to the youth club, I saw Shane. He stopped to give me a lift. He said he'd seen you with Niall.'

'Ah, Shane,' I say. He would have just said it in conversation, I know. He's not like his brother, Jody. I like Shane.

'I had to act like I knew, of course,' says Roisin.

'I'm sorry. Like I said, I was going to tell you.'

The bell goes for first period and as I pack my book away in my bag, I feel a nudge on the shoulder. I turn round and Jody Wright is grinning, from his seat in the row behind.

'Hey, Roisin,' he says. 'I saw your brother in the shop this morning.' Roisin and Joe exchange a smirk. 'He was buying carrots.'

I groan inwardly. I know what this is all about. Hastily I zip my bag shut and stand up, my chair bashes into the table behind me. It doesn't distract Jody.

'Carrots?' questions Roisin.

'Yeah, a whole load of them. He said they were for his bunny.' He nudges me in the back again as I try to squeeze between Roisin and the tables. 'You like carrots, don't you, Bunny?'

'Get lost,' I say as I manage to execute my escape. I hear them laughing as I leave.

Niall tells me to take no notice of them. He's had a word with Roisin and Shane. He's sure the message will get through. He says he doesn't care what they say anyway, that Jody's a prick. I agree on that point. I say I agree on the not-caring point too, but really I do care. I wish Jody would let up. I don't know why he and his cronies find me so bloody amusing.

We drive out to The Spit that night. It's dark and cold. Niall has brought a blanket with him. We climb into the back seat and huddle together under the cover. We kiss each other. Up until now we haven't actually had sex. We haven't done anything yet. In fact, I haven't done anything with anyone. However, all that changes in the next hour. It's a bit of a fumble, not least because there's no room and we can't really see what we're doing. Had I known, I might have worn my skirt.

Niall told me he loved me tonight. I'm not stupid enough to fall for that: only having sex with him because he loves me, although that did help. No, I wanted to do it with him. I love him and he loves me, it seems right – the next stage of our relationship. Afterwards, he holds me and tells me he loves me. I know he means it. So do I.

I feel different when I go into school the next day. Grown up. I see Niall at school and when we pass each other in the corridor he pulls me out of the line. I see the other girls look, with a sense of envy. They wish Niall Marshall had eyes for them. He asks me if I'm okay after last night. Of course I'm okay. I'm in love. He kisses me and tells me he loves me before running down the corridor to catch up with his class. I float in the other direction. I feel grown up. I feel loved.

Chapter 5

I take the plate away from Mum, the pork chop barely touched and the vegetables only picked at.

'Would you prefer a light sandwich?' I ask.

Mum shakes her head. 'Maybe later. A cup of tea would be nice, though. I'll put the kettle on.'

'No, you sit there, I'll do it,' I say as I flip the lid to the bin and tilt the plate to let the food slide off. Mum hates wasting food and takes it personally if anyone leaves so much as a morsel on the plate, so for her to leave pretty much all her dinner isn't a good sign.

'Erin, did you remember to get the café keys?' says Mum.

'Yeah, they're in my bag.' I try to suppress a frown as I recall my encounter with Messrs Wright.

'I was so glad Kerry was there the other night,' says Mum. For a moment she looks lost in her thoughts, then giving herself a little shake, she's back with us. 'Nice lad, he is.'

'I remember him from when we were teenagers,' I say. 'He used to come down in the summer holidays.'

'He's been living here for quite a few years now. He works there with Max's son, Joe,' Mum explains, albeit needlessly, since I've established this myself.

'Didn't Max take him in because he was in some sort of trouble?' asks Fiona, as she takes on tea-making duty. 'I can't remember the details, but wasn't Kerry kicked out by his mum?'

'Yes, that's right.' Mum looks thoughtful again. 'Apparently, when Max's brother died, that was Kerry's father, the lad went off the rails a bit. Got into trouble with the Guards, I believe. The final straw was when his mum got a new husband. A clash of personalities, you could say. Lots of arguments. That type of thing. Anyway, Max felt he owed it to his brother to look after Kerry.'

We sit in silence for a few moments and I mull over the conversation. Kerry comes across as laid-back and I have a vague idea of him being pretty chilled out when we were teenagers. From what I saw today, I'd say he's not changed much. It sounds like he had a troubled home life. I can relate to that.

'So...,' begins Fiona bringing over a cup of tea for each of us. 'What's happening tomorrow with the café?'

'I've been thinking about that. I need to open up,' says Mum. 'It was closed all day yesterday and today; we can't afford to lose another day's takings or have our regulars find somewhere else. Your father won't be happy if we stay closed.'

'You should try and rest,' says Fiona. 'Anyway, aren't you going to be at the hospital tomorrow?'

'Of course I am, but I thought I'd go in the afternoon so I can open up the café first thing.'

'No you won't,' I say. 'I will.'

'You will?' The surprise in Fiona's voice is evident.

I take a sip of my tea to stall for time. I haven't actually thought it through properly, but I know Mum needs a break. She looks tired and drawn and I'm not entirely convinced that is just from the shock of Dad's accident. It looks a deep-rooted tiredness, one that has been weighing her down for a long time. I can feel Fiona's eyes on me, waiting for a response.

'I can open up and do the breakfast rush – I assume the menu

45

is the same: bacon, sausages, eggs, beans, that type of thing. I'm quite capable of cooking that and when you've dropped the children to nursery and school you can come and help me get ready for the lunchtime rush.' I smile at Fiona, pleased with myself for making it sound so easy.

'Ah sure, there's no need for that,' says Mum, looking at us both. 'I can manage, honestly.'

'No,' I say firmly. 'There's every need. Now, please don't argue. We want to help. Don't we, Fiona?'

'Yes, of course we do.' Fiona squeezes Mum's hand.

After we've finished our tea, Mum goes upstairs to the bathroom and I make a start on rinsing the plates and loading the dishwasher.

'That's good of you to offer to open up the café,' says Fiona. 'I seem to remember you saying something along the lines of never wanting to step foot in that greasy spoon again.' There is no malice in Fiona's words and we exchange a wry smile.

'I'm only doing it for Mum. One less thing for her to worry about.' I scrub at the saucepan to remove some of the mashed potato that has already hardened around the edges

'When do you have to go back to London?' asks Fiona.

'I'm not sure. Ed has shuffled the staff rota around, but I don't know how long he can do that for. I don't want to stay here longer than necessary.'

'It's not that bad here,' says Fiona, cleaning the work surfaces with anti-bacterial wipes. 'I came back and, if I'm totally honest, I'm glad I did.'

I pause from rinsing the saucepan. 'It was different for you, though,' I say eventually. 'You liked it here. You had lots of friends. You had Sean and Sophie. And since then, Molly. I have nothing and no one to come back for. You came back to happiness, I'll come back to misery.'

'That's not strictly true,' says Fiona. 'You have your family to come back to.'

'It's not that easy.'

'Things do change. People change.' Fiona drops the used wipe into the bin. She comes and stands beside me and brushes a strand of hair from my face, tucking it behind my ear. 'We miss you.'

'I know. I miss you and the kids too. And Mum.' I study the bottom of the pan as I tamp down the unchecked emotion churning in my stomach. Confident I have it under control, I look up at Fiona. 'Just meeting Jody Wright again and the mention of the Marshalls is bad enough. And then I bumped straight into them.'

'Oh no, did you?' Fiona's face creases into a wince. 'Did you speak to them?'

'Didn't have much choice. They were parked right next to me. I just explained about Dad.'

'Are you okay?' There's real concern in Fiona's voice.

'I'll be fine,' I say, as much to convince myself as my sister.

'There's something you're not telling me,' says Fiona.

I should have known it wouldn't be easy to hide anything from her. She has always had this uncanny knack of being able to read my moods, my body language, or whatever it was.

'Erin! Erin, your phone's ringing!' Mum's voice comes from the hallway.

'It's okay,' I call back, about to add that I'll leave it to go to voicemail, when Mum appears in the kitchen carrying my handbag. I dry my hands and take the bag, but by the time I've fished around for the phone, it has stopped ringing. I check the screen. 'It was only Ed. I'll phone him later.'

'Are you ready, Fiona?' asks Mum. 'I want to get back up to the hospital before it gets too late.'

'Sure,' says Fiona. 'Have you got your coat?' She turns to me. 'We'll chat tomorrow. It will be okay, whatever it is. Trust me, I'm your big sister.' She gives me a brief hug before ushering Mum out to the hall to find their coats.

47

Under normal circumstances, I wouldn't hesitate to believe her. She's never let me down in the past, but this...this thing with Roisin, well, it's bigger than anything either of us have had to face before. Certainly since I left Rossway as a teenager. For the first time in my life, I have doubts about Fiona's ability to make things right.

Chapter 6

Normally at six in the morning, I would be going for my morning run or sweating it out in the gym. Today, however, I'm standing inside the doorway of Seahorse Café wondering if I've stepped back in time. Nothing has changed since I walked away as a sixteen-year-old.

The easy-wipe Formica tables with their padded bench seats are lined up and down the café in three uniform rows of four. Each table is set the same as it has always been. I remember cleaning the tables every night and arranging the red and brown sauce bottles to stand behind the salt and pepper with the plastic menu slotted between to keep it upright.

The counter at the rear of the café looks the same too. A cold cabinet for cakes to one side and the cutlery and napkins to the other, next to a small selection of crisps and biscuits. Behind the counter is the tea and coffee making machine, together with a fridge for the milk and cold drinks. Through the serving hatch where the orders are pushed, I can see the stainless-steel kitchen equipment, all exactly as I remember.

Before I can do anything, I need to move the four silver bistro tables and their chairs from inside the café, where they have been stacked overnight, and take them outside. They aren't so much heavy as awkward and once accomplished I can tick that task off the list Mum gave to me last night.

Consulting the list, I continue to prepare the café for opening.

In the kitchen, I am just tying my apron when I hear the little bell above the door jangle to announce the arrival of the first customer.

'Right, here we go,' I say, as I tuck the order pad and pen into the front pocket of the apron. However, my breezy morning smile slips as I see who my first two customers are.

Kerry and Joe Wright.

'Morning, Bunny,' calls Joe as I make my way round the counter and walk down towards them. He grins broadly at me.

'Morning. How's your dad?' says Kerry. They sit down at a table.

'About the same,' I reply. I take the order pad and pen from my pocket, not wanting to get into small talk. Not with Joe, anyway. Kerry's okay. 'What can I get you?'

'Two house breakfasts, one tea and one coffee, please,' replies Kerry.

I head straight back to the kitchen and I'm just putting the bacon on to cook when I hear the bell jangle above the door. Peeking through the serving hatch, I see two more customers arrive. Painters, judging by their overalls, followed by another chap, who is probably some sort of tradesman too if his work clothes are anything to go by.

Three more breakfast orders later, I'm back in the kitchen hurriedly putting more sausages and bacon in the frying pan, whilst stirring the beans in one pot and cracking eggs in a pan for the first order.

Taking out the two breakfasts for Kerry and Joe, I'm greeted by yet another customer. I didn't realise the café was so busy this time in the morning.

I spend the next twenty minutes rushing round like a whirling dervish but, despite my best efforts, I manage to burn one of the orders. The scrambled eggs have stuck to the bottom of the pan.

'Sod it,' I say out loud as black bits begin churning up into the yellow egg. I try to pick out some of the bits and wonder whether I can get away with serving it. In all honesty, not: it looks like the scrambled eggs have freckles. Dumping the pan down into the sink, the clatter resonates around the kitchen. I grab some more eggs and break them into a clean pan. Glancing through the hatch again, I sigh inwardly as I see Joe standing there.

'Just want to pay,' he calls through to me. 'Run rabbit, run rabbit, run, run, run…'

'You should do them in the microwave. A lot quicker and less chance of burning.' A voice behind me makes me jump and I swing round. I watch, lost for words, as Kerry casually strolls over to the hob, turns the heat off completely then washes his hands in the small sink next to the fridge.

'Don't worry, all nice and clean,' he says as he dries them on a paper towel. 'I'll send Joe on his way. I'll settle up the bill.'

'Right, thanks.' I watch as he motions to Joe through the hatch then begins to rummage around in the cupboard. Surely he doesn't think he is going to help out in the kitchen. He takes out a plastic bowl and puts it on the counter.

'Yep, this will do,' he says. 'Pass the eggs and milk.'

'I'm not sure my dad would approve,' I say, as I open a fresh box of eggs.

'We won't tell him, then,' whispers Kerry conspiratorially in my ear. 'It will be our secret. Why don't you get on with the drinks? I'll keep an eye on this lot here.' He picks up the order slips, arranging them on the work surface and then, turning to me, the amused look still on his face, he waves the whisk in the direction of the doorway. 'Go on.' He has an air of authority yet calmness about him and I find myself obediently following his instructions.

Within ten minutes, all the customers are tucking into their food without complaint and Kerry is having a much-deserved cup of tea.

'Thanks for that,' I say gratefully. 'I'm a bit out of practice.'

'I gathered.' Kerry grins over the rim of his mug. Then, more seriously. 'Look, about Joe.' Immediately I feel myself tense. I don't say anything as I wait for him to continue. 'Don't take any notice of his teasing. He doesn't mean anything by it.'

'Oh, I'm not bothered about Jody, I mean, Joe,' I lie, forcing a laugh. 'Although it is a bit boring after all these years. You kind of think when you're in your mid-twenties you've grown out of all that stupid nickname business. Obviously, Joe has still got a bit of growing up to do.' I can hear the tone in my voice changing involuntarily as I speak, not quite able to suppress the irritation I feel. I turn my attention to rinsing out my cup.

'So, how come you and Joe have never crossed paths in all this time? You must have been back to visit your family and I certainly don't remember seeing you either,' Kerry asks.

I shift uncomfortably from one foot to the other as I concentrate on cleaning an imaginary mark from my cup. 'I usually pop over for a brief visit. It's very busy at work. I'm a beautician at a health-and-fitness spa so I don't always work regular hours. It's not easy.'

'Don't you keep in touch with any of your old school friends?'

'No, not really.' *Christ, wasn't it time he went to work rather than ask all these awkward questions?*

'What was the appeal of London?'

'You ask a lot of questions, don't you?' I'm not making a very good job of keeping my tone light-hearted. I put the cup on the draining board. 'Why have you ended up here in Rossway?'

Kerry shrugs. 'Needed a change, I suppose.'

I look at him, holding his gaze for a moment before speaking. 'So did I.' There, hopefully that would be the end of that conversation. I'm not the only one who has a past that needs to stay in the past.

52

Kerry doesn't blink as he looks back at me, the silvery flecks in his eyes for a moment don't seem so glittery. He nods his head slightly as if understanding something.

'Right, I suppose I'd better get over to the workshop and get on with my real job,' he says, breaking the mini deadlock.

'You won't get into trouble, will you? Being here when you're supposed to be working,' I say, trying to regain some equanimity.

'I can make the time up later – work through my break. It's no big deal.' Kerry puts his cup in the sink and heads for the door. 'Are you on your own for the rest of the day?'

'No, my sister's coming in later for a while to help with the lunchtime rush. I'll just have to close up on my own.'

'Okay, I'll see you later.'

I call after him through the serving hatch. 'If you're in for breakfast in the morning, it's on the house, by way of a thank you.'

Kerry turns and, with what I can only describe as a cheeky grin, followed by an even cheekier wink, calls back to me, 'I'm sure we can come to some arrangement!'

*

Kerry wiped the sweat from his brow with the sleeve of his overalls. It was a hot day for May and working inside the poorly insulated workshop wasn't pleasant. The air was still and the humidity high.

'Wouldn't be surprised if there's a storm coming,' said Kerry.

'You want a cuppa?' asked Joe, putting down the spanner he had been using.

'Got anything colder?'

Joe went over to the fridge in the corner of the workshop and opened the door.

'Beer, water or can of Coke?'

'A Coke will do,' said Kerry. He stepped forward and caught

the can that Joe chucked his way. 'I'm going to sit outside for five minutes. You coming?'

Joe followed him out. Kerry plonked himself down on the back seat from an old car, which had long since been separated from the vehicle and abandoned in the far corner of the yard. Joe grabbed a wooden crate to perch on. Skip, Kerry's little terrier dog, came trotting out of the workshop and jumped up onto the seat beside his owner.

As Kerry leaned back, grateful for the shade of the workshop, he glanced over at the service road, which ran along the back of Seahorse Café. His attention was caught by the sight of the willowy figure of Erin bringing out a bag of rubbish and lifting the big industrial lid of the wheelie bin to sling in the bag. Her chestnut hair, although tied back in a ponytail, seemed to shimmer down her back in the sunlight.

'Aha! Caught you!' At Joe's jibe, Kerry snapped his head back to look at his cousin. Joe nodded in the direction of the café. 'Admiring the scenery, were you?'

'What's that?' said Max, coming out of the workshop and wandering over to them.

'Kerry here, ogling the new waitress at the café. I think he's got the hots for her.'

Very rarely did Kerry ever feel like punching his cousin. Today, however, was one of those occasions. Annoyed that he had, indeed, been caught looking at Erin, Kerry didn't want to let on, otherwise he'd never hear the last of it. Instead, he made a great effort to keep his voice nonchalant as he replied. 'What? Oh, Jim Hurley's daughter.'

Joe laughed and mimicked Kerry. '*Oh, Jim Hurley's daughter.*' He turned to his dad. 'Like he doesn't know what her name is after hanging around the café for half an hour this morning, getting all hot and steamy in the kitchen.'

Max grinned at Kerry and raised his eyebrows. 'Is that so? You been rattling her pots and pans?' Father and son laughed.

Standing up and squashing his cigarette under his foot, Kerry gave Joe a shove on the shoulder, sending him sprawling backwards off the upturned wooden crate. 'That mouth of yours will get you in trouble one day.'

This seemed to fuel Joe's laughter even more. He picked himself up and, righting his makeshift seat, settled himself back on it. 'Touch a nerve, did I?'

Later Kerry was relieved to hear Joe down tools and announce he was finished for the day. Max had already gone and Kerry was left to lock up. He needed to get the bike he was working on ready for the customer to pick up in the morning.

Kerry wheeled the bike out into the rear yard and started the engine. Leaning over it, he revved the throttle several times, listening carefully to make sure the engine was firing properly. Then he left it to tick over for a few minutes, again listening for any stuttering in the rhythm of the rumble. At tick-over it chugged at a nice steady pace; no hesitation, no lumpiness.

After a few minutes he was satisfied everything was okay and, cutting the engine, took the bike back inside.

As he locked up the workshop doors, he glanced over to the café and suddenly fancied a coffee. Of course, he could simply go up to his flat and make a cup of instant, but that wasn't the same as a freshly made Americano. *What the heck? It was only a coffee.*

Kerry gave his hands a quick look and determined them presentable enough, having managed to get most of the grease off and dirt out from under his nails.

'Come on, Skip,' he called to the little terrier. 'Let's get a coffee.' He headed round to the front of the café. He had just taken hold of the handle when the door swung open and out bustled a very tired-looking Erin. She gave a little yelp of surprise.

'Sorry, didn't mean to frighten you,' said Kerry, feeling a broad smile spread across his face. A few tendrils of hair had escaped from Erin's ponytail and had curled slightly.

'That's all right,' she replied, touching her hair, as if checking it was in place. 'I was just about to close up. Did you want something? Please say no.' She clasped her hands together as if in prayer.

'In that case then, no?' replied Kerry.

'Is the right answer,' Erin laughed, then added, 'For God's sake don't tell my dad I'm turning away customers. He'll have a fit.' She moved round him and began stacking the outside seating.

'Here, I'll do that,' said Kerry, taking hold of the chair Erin now had in her hands.

'Tell you what, I'll do the chairs and you do the tables.' Erin gave the chair a little tug and then a much stronger one as Kerry realised he was still holding onto it. She raised her eyebrows slightly, a small smile turning the corners of her mouth upwards.

Kerry shook himself mentally and, letting go of the chair, turned to focus on the bistro table instead.

'So, how was your first day?' he asked, carrying a table in behind Erin.

'Not so bad in the end. It's been really quiet this afternoon. Not sure if it's always like this, but it was hardly worth being open.' They put the furniture to one side.

'It will probably pick up more in the summer, though,' said Kerry, holding the door open so they could go back out and collect some more tables and chairs.

'I suppose so. If it's like this tomorrow, I might close early.'

'When do you think you'll go back to London?' Kerry hoped he sounded only mildly interested.

'I need to see how things go with my dad first,' she said. 'There's still no change in his condition. The doctors were having a consultation amongst themselves today to decide the best way forward.'

'Is that good or bad?' asked Kerry, although he acknowledged it didn't sound good.

She shrugged and looked as if she was struggling to find the right words for a moment. He watched her swallow hard and then look up at him. 'I really couldn't say.'

Kerry placed another table inside the café. He felt he should comfort her with a hug or soothing words, but he got the distinct impression Erin didn't want a fuss made. He decided best to leave it. As he turned to get the last of the tables, he saw a familiar figure heading towards the café, their eyes fixed firmly on the back of Erin as she stacked the last few chairs

She wasn't hard to track down. She was going to be one of three places. At the hospital. At her sister's or here, at the café. It wasn't like she had loads of friends to catch up with.

Roisin neared the café, her thoughts solely on Erin. It wouldn't be so bad, but after what happened, Erin had no right to disappear and start a new life, washing her hands of her old one, just because it didn't work out the way she wanted it. Got herself a rich boyfriend in London and thought she was the bee's knees. Sure, she had barely been back here. What sort of daughter was she?

But, hey, look at her now, waiting on tables. Serves her right. Roisin was so looking forward to wiping that smug look off her face and making Erin admit to what she really did.

'How the mighty fall.'

Kerry looked from her to Erin and back again. His eyes were wary. He clearly wasn't sure how things stood between the two of them.

Erin put the chair down and turned to face Roisin. 'Hello, Roisin. I'm sorry but the café's closed now.'

Sure, she wasn't sorry at all. Erin knew Roisin wasn't here for a cosy catch-up over a one-shot-skinny-latte, or whatever it was she drank. Probably some detox green-leaf crap, knowing her.

'I'm not here for a coffee,' said Roisin. 'I didn't get a chance to speak to you before, not with me mam there.'

'I'm a bit busy right now,' said Erin, glancing back at Kerry.

'You got yourself a new job?' Roisin asked, looking at Kerry.

'Just being neighbourly,' said Kerry.

'Clearly. So, in the spirit of being neighbourly, has Erin been telling you all our secrets?'

'That sounds dangerous,' said Kerry.

The trouble with Kerry, Roisin could never read him. He could be so deadpan at times. She didn't care; it gave her another opportunity for a dig at Erin. Roisin quite liked the way Erin had that look of uncertainty in her eyes. She had no clue as to what Roisin might say next.

'Secrets are always dangerous,' said Roisin. 'Aren't they, Erin?'

'I need to get on,' said Erin, ignoring the comment.

'Yes, I'm sure you do,' said Roisin. 'Oh, meant to say, I got your text message…in the end.'

Erin looked up at her. 'Good.'

'It was too late, though,' said Roisin, enjoying the doubt on Erin's face. 'Maybe we can catch up another time? There's so much we need to talk about. Not least, why you did a disappearing act.'

'It wasn't a disappearing act.' There was a snap in Erin's voice and Roisin was rather pleased with herself. She had got the conversation to a place where she wanted it. A place Erin wasn't happy to be: talking about her past. Erin turned her back on Roisin and picked up the last of the bistro tables. 'I need to get finished here and go up to the hospital to see my dad.'

Before Roisin could reply, Kerry spoke. 'Sorry, we must be holding you up. We'll let you get on. Come on, Roisin, let's go for a drink at The Smugglers.' He whistled for Skip to follow.

Roisin went to protest, but Kerry took her elbow and whisked her away.

'Sometimes, Kerry, you're a proper gentleman,' said Roisin, as she fell into step with him. 'A drink is nice, although I'm not sure for whose benefit the offer is.' She looked back over her shoulder and called out before Erin disappeared inside. 'Don't worry, Erin, there will be plenty of time for us to catch up. I'll be in touch. Very soon.'

Chapter 7

Kerry always enjoyed spending time at Apple Tree Cottage. Joe
and Bex always made him feel at home. No one stood on
ceremony. Their home definitely had a lived-in feel, but one
that was warm and welcoming; just as Kerry thought a home
should be.

Kerry was in the garden with Joe, watching him fiddle around
with the lawn mower. Skip was laid flat out on the grass, basking
in the warm May sunshine.

'Aren't you fed up that you keep having to fix that old thing?'
said Kerry as Joe made yet another attempt to start the petrol
mower. 'Why don't you admit defeat and buy a new one?'

'No, there's plenty of life left in it yet,' said Joe. He knelt down
and took the cover off the engine.

Kerry leaned against the shed and surveyed the garden at Apple
Tree Cottage. Laid to lawn mostly, there were deep flowerbeds
either side in which Bex, Joe's wife, had randomly planted traditional cottage-garden plants. There was a semi wildness about it,
much like Joe and Bex themselves, thought Kerry. The rear of
the garden was fenced off, a small gate leading to the vegetable
plot. Bex embraced the whole home-grown, organic ethos and
could often be found tending to the many varieties of vegetables

and fruits. Even with the recent birth of their second child, Bex was still a dedicated gardener.

The other side of their garden was home to free-range hens, which Bex had rescued from a battery farm. Only last week, Kerry had helped Joe make another hen house to accommodate the recent additions to Bex's poultry sanctuary.

'You're wasting your breath trying to persuade him to buy a new one,' said Bex, coming out into the garden. 'I've been telling him for the past two years, but he likes a challenge.' She smiled as she spoke.

'I was thinking maybe we should go for the meadow look,' said Joe, as he picked up a spanner from the ground and began tightening a nut. 'Is Breeze asleep?'

'Yes, I've just fed her,' said Bex. 'She's gone straight off. It's hard to believe she's only a month old, she's such a dream.'

At that moment, their three-year-old son came tearing out into the garden, dressed in a Superman outfit.

'Watch out,' said Kerry, sidestepping the youngster. 'Superman Storm's arrived. Hey, buddy, who are you saving the world from today?'

'Marshmallow Man!' called back Storm as he raced around the garden, stopping by the path to have an imaginary fight with his adversary. Skip raised his head to see what all the fuss was about, but the warmth of the sun was a more tempting option and he rested his head back down.

Bex turned back to Joe. 'Why don't you borrow your dad's mower?' she said. 'We can't go for the meadow look, we've got the barbecue soon and then a couple of weeks after that it's Breeze's naming ceremony.'

'I'm...not...giving up,' muttered Joe and then cursed as the spanner slipped from the bolt and clattered to the floor.

'Want me to take a look?' said Kerry. He pushed himself away from the side of the shed.

'Nope. It's not going to win,' said Joe. Picking up his spanner again and issuing a series of threats to the machine, he set back to work.

'I'll take that as my cue to leave,' said Kerry. He turned to Bex. 'Shall I take Superman out for an hour for you? I'll get him an ice-cream or something.'

'Oh, would you?' said Bex. 'That would be great. I've got a load of nappies to wash out.'

'Definitely my cue to leave,' said Kerry.

'You can leave Skip here,' said Bex. 'He's no trouble. Won't be much fun for him sat outside the café.'

'Okay, thanks,' said Kerry. 'Hey! Superman! Do you want to recharge your powers with a bowl of ice-cream?'

'Ice-cream! Ice-cream! Yes. Ice-cream!' Storm ran over to Kerry and danced around his feet.

'That's a yes, then.' Kerry gave Bex a peck on the cheek and Joe a pat on the shoulder. 'Catch you later, cuz.' As he headed out of the garden, holding Storm's hand, he called back over his shoulder. 'You may want to turn the fuel supply on!'

He laughed out loud as he heard Joe curse at him. By the time Kerry stepped out onto Corkscrew Lane, he heard the mower's engine rumble into life.

Erin placed the bowl of ice-cream, vanilla with strawberry sauce, on the table in front of Storm. 'So, Storm and Breeze,' she said. 'They're unusual names. A bit like yours and Joe's.'

'Blame our mums for that. They collaborated,' said Kerry with a smile. 'As for this generation of Wrights, Bex says she named them after her pregnancies. A difficult first pregnancy and an easy second one. Plus the fact Bex is into all that being-at-one-with-nature business.'

'I remember she was a bit hippy looking when we were younger.'

'She's very environmentally friendly, loves nature, makes her own bread and keeps chickens. Very bohemian. You get the picture.'

'Hugs trees? Protests against urban development and smokes roll-ups?' suggested Erin.

'Something like that,' replied Kerry, smiling.

'She was a year below me at school,' said Erin. 'She's married to Joe? Neither of them left the village, then.'

'There's nothing wrong with that. I like living here, actually. There's a real sense of community. Everyone's really friendly.'

'Hmm, nosey, you mean.'

'You're really not a fan of Rossway, are you?' said Kerry, aiming a spoon of ice-cream in the direction of Storm's open mouth. It reminded him of the wildlife programmes where the birds came back with little grubs to give to the eager, open-mouthed chicks. 'Why don't you like it?'

Erin shrugged. 'Just don't. Anyway, I'd better get on. Do you want anything else?'

'No, I'm good for now. I'll have something later.' He held her gaze for a moment, the little smile now a broad grin. He didn't miss the small flush of colour to her cheeks before she turned away.

'What you doing two weeks Sunday?' The question brought Erin to a halt.

She turned to face him. 'Why?'

'Bex and Joe are having a barbecue. Didn't know if you fancied coming. You could catch up with Bex, maybe. It's all very casual and low key.'

'I'll be busy. I've got something on.'

Kerry raised his eyebrows. 'Really? You've got something to do in Rossway.' He could tell she was being evasive. It intrigued him. 'Come on, you never know, you might enjoy yourself. Or is it that you don't want to associate with the locals?' He gave a wink to show he wasn't being totally serious.

'It's not that.'

'So…' prompted Kerry. 'You going to enlighten me?'

'I hardly know you, for a start.'

Kerry let out a small burst of laughter. She dipped her head but he could see the smile on her face.

'Okay. I'm twenty-six. My star sign is Aries. My favourite food is Indian. I like rock music and ride a motorbike. I love the sea and hate the gym.' He rattled the facts off like a machine gun in rapid-fire mode. 'Oh, and I was kicked out of the Scouts for setting fire to a tent…by accident, of course. What more do you need to know? Come on, say yes.'

'Normally, I would say yes,' said Erin.

'Just say it, then,' said Kerry. 'It's not hard. Y. E. S. Yes. Go on, give it a try.'

'I have a visitor coming. From England,' said Erin. The smile slipped from her face. 'My boyfriend.'

Kerry hadn't been expecting that, but then he wasn't entirely surprised. Why wouldn't she have a boyfriend? 'Bring him too,' he said. Not because he especially revelled in the idea, but a certain morbid curiosity had swept over him. He'd like to see what sort of fella had won Erin's affections.

'I'm not sure,' said Erin. 'I haven't seen Bex since I left Rossway all those years ago. She might not even want me gate-crashing.'

'Bex won't mind. She's the most laid-back person I know.' Kerry lifted the bowl to scrape the last of the ice-cream for Storm.

'I'll have a think about it.'

The bell tinkled above the door as two customers arrived. Erin smiled at Kerry, before going off to greet them. Kerry turned his attention to his coffee.

'All done?' said Erin coming over to them some ten minutes later. She took the bowl and coffee cup from the table.

'If you do decide to come to the barbecue,' said Kerry ensuring a casual tone to his voice, 'it's Apple Tree Cottage, Corkscrew Lane, but I'll see you before then anyway.' He wiped Storm's mouth with a napkin and lifted him down from the chair. He pulled out a note from his wallet and gave it to Storm. 'Here you go, Superman, give the money to the lady and say bye.'

As Storm went to pass the note to Erin, he let go of it too soon and it fluttered to the floor. Erin stooped down and picked up the money, handing it back to Storm. 'My treat.'

'Say thank you to the lovely lady,' prompted Kerry, giving Storm a gentle nudge forwards.

Without warning Storm planted a rather sloppy kiss on Erin's cheek. 'Thank you, lovely lady,' he said.

'Thank you, Storm. You're welcome.' Erin stood up.

Kerry grinned and then, on impulse, he too gave Erin a surprise kiss on the other cheek. 'Thank you, lovely lady,' he said.

'What was that for?'

'Just being friendly,' said Kerry, feigning innocence.

Kerry left the café without so much as a backward glance, feeling very pleased with himself. He ignored the small voice of warning in his head. Erin Hurley was complicated, secretive and she had a boyfriend. He should be staying well clear, but never one to walk on the safe side, the intrigue was drawing him in.

Joe's parents, Max and Louise, were at Apple Tree Cottage when Kerry arrived back with Storm. While Louise cooed over the baby and made a fuss of her grandson, Max took Kerry to one side.

'You got a minute, Kerry?'

Kerry followed his uncle into the garden and lighting a cigarette each, they wandered towards the far end of the lawn, where the hedge and picket gate segregated the vegetable patch.

Kerry had no idea what Max wanted to talk about, although the troubled look on his face gave him a good indication he wouldn't like what was coming next. Max pushed his hand into the back pocket of his trousers and pulled out an envelope. He proffered it to Kerry. 'It's a letter from your mother. Go on, take it.' He waved the letter in his hand. Kerry could see his name written in his mother's hand-writing, no address, no stamp. 'It came in another envelope with a card for your aunt's birthday,' explained Max, as if reading Kerry's thoughts.

Reluctantly, Kerry took the letter, but made no attempt to open it. 'Thanks,' he said, folding it in half and slipping into the back pocket of his jeans.

'You ought to speak to your mother,' said Max, not unkindly. 'It's been a long time, Kerry. Time's a great healer and mellower of people.'

'I haven't got anything to say to her, and besides, if he's still about I'm certainly not having anything to do with either of them.'

'It's not Tom's fault your dad died.' Max absentmindedly stroked his goatee beard, a habit Kerry recognised whenever his uncle was concerned about something. It obviously still pained Max to think about his own brother's death, even though it was twelve years ago now. 'You can't blame him or your mother for it.'

'I'm not blaming him. I just don't like him. He's a tosser, that's all.'

Not wishing to hang around any longer than necessary, not least in case his aunt should start trying to convince him to contact his mother, Kerry made his excuses and left.

Once he was back in his flat, Kerry placed the envelope on the coffee table in front of him. For a long time he sat there looking at it. Should he open it, if only to see what she had to say? Would she be apologising or would she be berating him?

Kerry knew his uncle meant well, trying to encourage him to patch things up, but after all this time, Kerry still didn't feel ready to speak to her. He wondered whether he ever would. He exhaled deeply before getting up and going along the hallway to his bedroom. He knelt down at the side of his bed and slid out a shoebox. In it were nine other white envelopes. Each with his name and the same handwriting. His mother's.

He slipped the envelope into the box, alongside the others, and pushed the box back under the bed. The pain of her last words to him was branded on his heart.

Chapter 8

Seahorse Café has been steady all week and after being here for over two weeks, I feel I'm getting into my stride. I can definitely manage the early-morning breakfast rush now. Kerry and Joe don't come in every morning, but when they do, I can't deny it makes the morning much more pleasant. The only fly in the ointment is Roisin.

I debate whether I should, in fact, just leave matters. Should I start poking the hornets' nest? Or should I leave it? Maybe she'll grow bored and go away? However, my next thought is that I know Roisin too well. She won't let matters drop, especially as she has that photograph. She must be biding her time for a particular reason.

I decide I need to take the initiative rather than wait to dance to Roisin's tune.

With the mid-afternoon lull now upon me, I idly wipe down the counter and rearrange the contents of the chiller cabinet, moving the colder bottles to the front of the refrigerator and the more recent additions to the rear. I wonder what she's planning. She can't possibly know the significance of that photograph. It may give her a clue, but it's only half the story. And even if she did suspect the truth, she has absolutely no way of proving it. I hold onto this last thought.

The door to the café opens, breaking my thoughts.

'Hello, Erin! Remember me?'

I smile hesitantly as another ghost from my past resurrects itself. This ghost, however, is probably a more pleasant apparition. Perhaps because Bex is a year younger, she had never got involved with the teasing and tormenting I endured. As teenagers we had been friendly rather than friends, the crossover of groups unavoidable in a small place like Rossway.

'Hi, Rebecca, how are you?' I say, trying to assimilate the old memory of Rebecca the teenager with the up-to-date version: Bex the adult, wife and mum.

Bex certainly is rather boho, as Kerry had said. I take in the long, sinuous dark hair with streaks of indigo running through, matched by an equally flowing skirt that nearly reaches the ground. Bex's purple Dr Martens boots kick out from under the fabric as she walks and she appears to be carrying some sort of multi-coloured cloth bundle in front of her. I realise this bundle is, in fact, tied round Bex and snugly tucked inside is the baby.

'Kerry said you were here, so I thought I'd come and see you.' She smiles warmly at me. 'And no one calls me Rebecca these days, not even my mum. It's Bex.'

'Sorry, I'm a bit out of touch with everything. Although, I do know about your little one. Congratulations. How's everything?'

'Really good, thanks. Come on, Storm, you sit here.' She pulls out a chair for her son and then, adjusting the baby bundle slightly, seats herself on the opposite side of the table. 'There, she's fast asleep now. The fresh air obviously did the trick.'

I nod and give a courteous look at baby Breeze nestled peacefully in her fabric cocoon. Immediately, the familiar feeling, something akin to fear and regret, flits through me as I admire the tiny features of the baby and see the tender look Bex gives her daughter.

'She's lovely,' I say, then standing back, take out my order pad and pen. 'Now, what can I get you?'

'Black coffee for me, please, and a vanilla milkshake for Storm.' Bex looks at the menu. 'Think I'll treat myself to a toasted teacake and Storm can have a cookie.'

I jot the order down on my pad. 'Okay, I'll get that sorted.'

'How's your dad?' asks Bex. 'I heard what happened.'

'No change,' I say, touched that she has asked. 'He's being kept in a medically induced coma. They're waiting for the swelling on his brain to go down. They've given him a scan, but can't tell from the results. They said he needs to rest and this is the best way. Also, his breathing is affected. They're using a ventilator to give him a hand. They don't think he can manage on his own.'

'I'm sorry to hear that,' says Bex. 'It is nice to see you, though, despite the circumstances.'

I smile. I'm taking to Bex already. 'Thanks.'

'What did you do when you left here? I heard you went to London?' asks Bex.

I'm grateful for the change in subject.

'Yes. I went to live my sister, Fiona. Went to college and did a beautician's course, worked in a couple of places before ending up where I am now, at a health and fitness spa.'

'This is a bit of a change for you.' Bex grins as she indicates the café with a slight nod of the head.

'You could say that. I'm only helping out while my dad's not well. I've been given some time off from work, but I'm not sure how long they'll be so understanding.'

'You don't fancy moving back for good?'

There's something about Bex's easy manner that doesn't seem to challenge my departure from the village. It's a nice change from the usual reaction I've been getting from customers once they realise who I am. It's almost like an accusation when they refer to my leaving.

'Moving back? Not really.' That's an understatement. 'I don't think village life, well Rossway life, is for me.'

Bex nods, as if understanding. 'No, it can be a bit claustro-phobic at times, I must admit.'

'Not enough that it ever drove you away, then?'

'For a bit, but only as far as Cork. You can't really call that a life-changing move.' Bex chuckles as she takes the salt and pepper pots away from Storm, who looks like he's about to attempt to lick them. 'Once myself and Joe became serious there really wasn't any debate about where we would live. He's very close to his family and, of course, working for his dad.'

'Have you been with Joe a long time?' I ask. I don't know why this idea surprises me. I hadn't pictured Joe as the childhood-sweetheart type.

'Oh yeah, since I was eighteen and he was nineteen.'

'Good for you,' I say.

'It's not always been easy, don't go thinking that,' says Bex. 'We've had our ups and downs. We called off the wedding once and I went away with my sister. Thought it was all over. But it was all sorted out in the end and that was a long time ago. We don't count it. Not when you look at the big picture. We're love's young dream.' Bex grins and although she's laughing at herself, I can tell she is obviously very happy, courtesy of Joe. Maybe he does have some redeeming features after all.

'Look, I'd better get your order before the baby wakes up,' I say, although I actually think Storm needs distracting by way of his milkshake as he now seems intent on squeezing tomato sauce out of the plastic bottle and onto the table.

When I come back, Bex is in the middle of what looks like a game of chess. As she moves one item away from Storm he reaches over to grab another.

'There you go, Storm,' I say cheerily. 'Lovely vanilla milkshake and a biscuit.'

'What do you say?' prompts Bex.

'Thank you, lovely lady,' pipes up Storm.

Bex laughs out loud. 'Oooh, cheeky! Where did that come from?'

'Don't worry. Kerry taught him that.'

Bex raises her eyebrows. 'Did he now? Actually, he did tell me he had invited you to the barbecue we're having at the weekend.'

I nod. 'That's right. I'm sorry, though, but my boyfriend is coming over from the UK.'

'Bring your man along too,' says Bex. 'We'd love to see you there. I'll make sure Joe behaves himself, if that's what you're worried about.'

I try to smile confidently. I'm not quite sure how Bex is so perceptive. In a strange way, I find it reassuring. Maybe it would be a nice thing to do. 'Okay, I'll see how it goes,' I say.

After Bex leaves, I find myself clock-watching. I've decided to confront Roisin and sort this business out once and for all. I don't want it hanging over me any longer. I close up the café at four-thirty and spend the next half hour clearing things away and setting up for the next day.

Locking the door, I hurry round to the doctors' surgery. The car park is virtually empty, except for a handful of cars, which I presume are staff vehicles. I spot a black Mini and something tells me it's Roisin's car. I wander over to it.

I don't have to wait long before I see her emerge from around the corner. She has her head down, looking in her handbag. She pulls out a bunch of keys and looks up towards the Mini. I was right, it is her car.

Her step slows as she sees me. I remain leaning back against the car.

'I hope you haven't damaged the paintwork,' she says, tossing her hair over her shoulder and picking up her stride again. 'Wouldn't want to have to get Kerry to send you the bill for a respray.'

I wait until she reaches the car before I move off. 'I thought I'd have heard from you by now,' I say, ensuring there is no concern attached to the words.

'Getting jittery, are you?'

'Jittery? No. Not at all. More like bored.'

Roisin gives laugh. 'Well, you should be,' she says. 'Getting jittery, that is.'

'Over a photograph. I don't think so.' I'm holding my nerve so far in this game of brinkmanship.

'Yes, but this isn't any old photograph, is it? No, this is a very special photograph. One that my brother hid away because if anyone saw it and read what was on the back, then your sordid little secret would be out.'

The word 'sordid' is the trigger.

'There was nothing sordid about me and Niall.' I'm crowding her space, but she doesn't flinch. 'We loved each other.'

'Oh, please. Do me a favour…and yourself.' She takes a step closer. We are inches apart. 'You were a couple of young teenagers. It was puppy love. Do you really think my brother was going to stay with you once he had gone off to university?' Her smile, full of derision, turns to a sneer. 'Did you really think getting pregnant on purpose was going to keep him?'

'You've no idea what you're talking about. What do you want, Roisin?'

The smile returns and her shoulders relax. She side-steps round to her car, blipping the remote to unlock the car. 'Ah, now we're getting to the point.' Opening the door, she drops her bag onto the passenger seat, closes the door and turns to face me. 'I want to know the truth about what happened to that baby.'

I wonder how much she knows and how much she is fishing for. I study her while I decide how to answer this.

'There was no baby,' I say, after a few seconds.

'Well, you see, Erin, I don't believe that. And I'm going to make it my business to prove it.' She opens the door and slips into her seat, pausing with her hand on the handle. 'By the way, I hope your dad recovers soon from his *accident*.' She slams the door shut and starts the engine before I can react.

71

I bang on the glass. 'What do you mean by that?' She smiles, but says nothing, before driving off.

I'm left standing there, watching the car disappear out of the car park, leaving behind a foreboding, which settles around me like a shroud.

The next morning I'm up early and out for a run. I need to burn off the nervous energy that has been building inside me since I came back to Rossway. After the spat with Roisin last night, the reassurance that she can't do anything to cause trouble evades me.

I breathe deeply as I jog onto the estuary footpath, towards the village, the fresh sea air fills my lungs, the saltiness of it settles on my lips. This is perhaps one of my happier memories of living in Rossway: the freshness, together with the seagulls squawking in the sky and the sound of the tidal river churning in and out of the estuary.

As I near the bike shop, I find myself looking up towards Kerry's flat. I squint against the glare of the morning sun, realising someone is at the window. It's Kerry.

He has obviously seen me as he puts his hand up. I jog on the spot, not quite sure whether he is trying to get my attention or just waving. Kerry opens the window and leans out.

'Haven't you got anything better to do?' he calls. 'Like staying in bed?'

'You clearly haven't,' I call back, feeling myself smile broadly. 'Anyway, lie-ins are for wimps.'

'You saying I'm a wimp?'

'You're the one who looks like they've just got up. Me, on the other hand, I've been up for a couple of hours and now I'm out exercising.'

'Hmm, a bit of jogging around the village and you call that exercise?'

'It's more than a bit of jogging, I'll have you know.'

'Pah, anyone can jog!'

'Oh really? Get your backside down here and let's see what you're made of!' I can't help giggling. I'm enjoying the banter.

'I tell you what, you get your backside up here and then I'll show you what I'm made of.'

I laugh and look away for a moment while I try to think of a suitable reply. 'I asked first,' I call back, thinking what a crap response that was. I hope my face is red from running to disguise the blush that I feel race up my neck. Time to go. I look back up at him. 'Anyway, would love to stop and chat, but I'm a busy lady.' With that I sprint off, ignoring the cries of 'chicken' that follow me.

A pang of guilt shoots through me as I think of Ed. I increase my stride as if increasing the distance between myself and the bike shop will also push thoughts of Kerry away. I cross the road and run parallel with the estuary wall. The water looks calm today, the early-morning sun beginning to stretch its sparkly fingers across the sea with promises of a nice day ahead. A good day for friends, wine and lunches in pub gardens.

Unchecked, my thoughts return to Kerry and the invite to the barbecue tomorrow. Bex had been so easy to talk to the other day it really is a tempting offer. Bex is refreshingly unchallenging and we ended up having a long chat, catching up on the last ten years of both our lives and those of the Rossway folk. It's nice having a good old girly chat, I've been left thinking a few hours in the company of the Wright family might not be such a bad thing after all.

As I consider the prospect, I leave the footpath and head for the woods that cup the edge of Rossway. They aren't natural woods, but a man-made windbreak, about fifty metres deep, stretching the length of the village. Within ten minutes I've reached the end of the trees and, hopping over the stile, I realise I'm now in Corkscrew Lane.

I make my way up the lane past a variety of bungalows and

houses scattered along the way. About halfway along, I notice the crystals and lanterns hanging from an apple tree in one of the front gardens. 'That has got to be Apple Tree Cottage,' I puff to myself. What had Kerry said? Bohemian? Was this boho chic? That, together with the two motorbikes, an orange-and-white VW Campervan and a battered old blue Fiesta parked in the driveway, means I don't need to read the sign hanging from the gate to confirm it's where Joe and Bex live.

Pushing myself harder, I manage to negotiate the uneven gravel track and am thankful to reach the end of Corkscrew Lane, a winding road that curls round the back of the village and into the High Street. I check my watch. I have enough time to have a quick shower before opening the café up at nine.

I have spoken to both Mum and Fiona about the opening times, suggesting that opening later and closing earlier at weekends wouldn't do the business any harm. The early-morning rush is a weekday occurrence, usually tradesmen on their way to work. None of them came in over the weekend. Neither had protested at my suggestion.

'Ah, sure, close the café early,' Mum had said. 'You need a rest, Erin, and especially if Ed's coming over to see you.'

I sigh as my thoughts come full circle back to Ed. I really should be excited he's coming over, but I'm having a hard time convincing myself so. Truth be told, the prospect of seeing Kerry and spending time with the Wrights is rather more appealing.

Chapter 9

Teenage Kicks
Four months before leaving

I sit in front of the mirror in my bedroom and tease the straighteners through the waves of my hair. It takes forever and I am grateful, once again, for my sister buying these. I used the conditioner she got for me from a hair salon in London. Rita's hairdressers, along from the café, doesn't sell anything as nice as this, plus Rita charges a fortune for cheap stuff.

Finally, I'm happy with my hair and can begin to do my make-up. I glance at my watch. Niall is coming to pick me up in half an hour. We are going to a party. It's Shane Wright's eighteenth and his parents have hired the function room at the back of The Smugglers. To be honest, I'm not keen on going as, of course, Jody Wright and all the crowd will be there. Obviously that includes Roisin. We're not so close any more since I've been seeing Niall. I don't know what it is. I get the feeling she's disappointed. Disappointed that Niall hasn't got an uber-cool girlfriend that she can show off, rather than just me: plain old Erin Hurley from the café. I'm not exactly exotic. Anyway, Niall said not to worry about Jody, he will be on his best behaviour, after all, it is his brother's party and even Jody wouldn't do anything to ruin that. I hope Niall is right.

I apply my foundation, mascara and blusher. I stop short of using the red lipstick I have as I know Dad won't approve. For some reason he hates me wearing lipstick. I heard him mutter something to Mum about me looking like a tramp. Mum told him off and said it was a sign I was growing up and he should simply accept it. He did a bit more muttering after that. Still, I won't wear it in front of him if it upsets him. I don't want to cause problems between him and Mum.

I wriggle into the black stretchy dress, with really pretty lace sleeves, I bought. I'm sure Dad won't be keen on that either, so to keep the peace I put on my long maxi skirt over the top. I'll slip it off when I get into Niall's car. Just have to remember to put it back on when I come home later.

Mum taps on the door and comes in as I'm stepping into my Amish get-up. She raises her eyebrows but says nothing. I continue with my disguise.

Mum stands next to me and we look at ourselves in the full-length mirror. Our hair colouring is identical. She hasn't got the curls, though; I have Dad to thank for those. Mum and I both have the same lily-white skin, although mine is a shade darker due to the foundation I'm wearing.

'You look pretty,' says Mum. She gives me a hug and we smile at each other's reflection.

'Thank you.' I want to say she looks tired and is working too hard but I don't. Instead, I tell her she's pretty herself and I must take after her. Her green eyes crinkle as she smiles at me and lets out a little laugh.

'Now, you will be back by midnight, won't you?' she says, a more serious look settling on her face.

'Do I have to? Can't I stay out a bit longer? One?'

She looks at me for a long moment before finally speaking. 'Okay, one o'clock, but no later.'

I give her a big hug and plant a kiss on her cheek. 'Thanks, Mum.'

'Don't mention it to your dad. I'll sort it out once you've gone.'

I keep a look out from my window for Niall. I've told him to park over near the road leading to The Spit. It's easier that way. I don't want Dad questioning him about what time I'm coming home.

'I wish Dad wasn't so strict and uptight about everything,' I say.

Mum sits on the bed and smoothes out imaginary creases in my duvet cover. 'Your dad is not that bad,' she says. 'He's just a bit over-protective, that's all.'

'Controlling,' I respond.

'It's out of concern for your well-being. He's got your best interests at heart and he does love you.'

'He has a funny way of showing it. I wish he wasn't so stressy all the time. If he could relax and not be so uptight about everything, it would be so much better, but he wants to control everything I do.' I drop myself down on the bed next to her. 'It's his way or no way. That's why Fiona left.' I register the look of pain on Mum's face. 'I'm sorry. I shouldn't have said that.'

'I know what you mean about Fiona,' says Mum. 'And I don't want the same thing to happen with you. That's why I'm trying to help. So things are different this time. He does know he needs to give you more freedom and choice in matters. It's hard for him to change, that's all.'

With silent mutual consent we leave the conversation there. I take another glance out of the window. I can see Niall's car under the streetlight.

Mum follows me out of the bedroom and down the hallway. I pass the living room and casually call out a goodbye to Dad.

'Okay, have a nice time and don't be late,' he calls back.

I don't respond, but hastily close the door, leaving Mum to break the news to him.

Like most parties, Shane's birthday bash takes a while to get going. As Niall is one of Shane's closest friends, we arrive early, when it's mostly just the family there. Shane comes from a big family and they are all very close.

Niall's parents have been invited: Diana and Pat. Out of politeness, explains Niall.

'My parents and Shane's parents are very different,' he says. 'You know what my mam's like at times.'

'I didn't realise they were friends,' I say.

'They're not really. They know each other from living in the village so long and because Shane and I have been friends since we were kids.'

My dad says Diana and Pat Marshall like to think they are very middle class, with their money, fancy cars and expensive holidays. Diana is a GP at the local surgery in the village and Jeff works from home. Niall says he does something in IT. He doesn't really know what, but it means his dad has to go up to the Dublin office regularly.

Shane and Joe's parents are very down to earth. They go to the pub a lot and are into their motorbikes. Shane's dad, Max, has the bike shop he's just opened across the road from the café. Dad keeps moaning about the motorbikes and the noise they make.

Diana and Shane's mum, Louise, are chatting when we arrive. Diana has that funny look on her face, like she has something really nasty stuck underneath her nose. Louise has an empty wine glass in her hand and is doing most of the talking, by the look of it.

Diana spots us first, then says something to Louise and the two women come over to greet us.

'Hello, darling,' says Diana to Niall. 'I thought you were going to wear a jacket and tie?'

'No, Mam, I told you, it's not a formal do. I'm not going to a wedding or something. It's just smart-casual.'

'I think you look lovely,' I say.

Diana turns to me. I hate the look she gives. 'Hello, Erin.' I watch her eyes take in the black mini dress I'm wearing. She has that same disapproving look I've seen in Dad's eyes. Before she can say anything else, Louise is hugging us and thanking us for coming.

As more guests arrive and the adults return to their conversation, we make our way over to rescue Shane, who has been cornered by an elderly relative.

'Thanks, man,' he says as we bundle him away. 'I hope the others get here soon. Much as I love the olds, I can't do any more small talk.'

Within an hour The Smugglers' function room is filling up and the party gets going. The DJ starts off with some rather more party-like songs that get some of the older guests up dancing. I have to say, Louise and Max Wright are pretty cool on the dance floor. They are having an absolute whale of a time. Everyone is watching them.

Someone nudges my shoulder. I turn and inwardly groan. It's Jody Wright.

'All right, Bunny?' he shouts in my ear above the noise of the music. He peers around me and nods at Niall. 'Want to come outside, for a bit of, you know, fresh air?'

'Okay,' says Niall and takes my hand. 'Come on. Don't want to leave you alone. You might get dragged onto the dance floor with Max.' He grins as Max and Louise are now literally in the throes of a very energetic jive. At least, that's want I think it is.

The night air cuts through the lace sleeves of my dress, sending little goosebumps along my arms. Shane, Roisin and Rebecca, a girl in the year below us at school, are already there. We huddle round the corner, away from prying eyes. There's also a blond boy there who I don't recognise. He's laughing with Shane about something as they share a cigarette. I wonder for a minute if it's one of Jody's brothers, but I think they're older than Shane and this one looks about the same sort of age. He looks over and nods at us but doesn't break his conversation.

As we stand there, I'm very aware everyone is smoking except for me. This is Jody's idea of fresh air.

'Do you want some?' Roisin holds out her half-smoked cigarette in my direction.

'No, I'm good, thanks,' I reply. I really don't want to smoke. I don't care if others do; it's something that has never appealed to me.

'Goody Two Shoes,' Roisin says. She masks the remark with a smile. 'What about a drink?' she adds, as she rummages in her bag. She pulls out a large plastic bottle.

'Cola?' I ask and then immediately regret it as Roisin and Jody snigger.

'Yeah, cola,' says Roisin, 'and vodka. Jesus, Erin, I wonder at you sometimes.'

'I thought it was just cola too,' says Rebecca. She tosses her long black hair with pink-tinted ends behind her shoulder. 'Easy mistake to make.'

She looks over and smiles at me. I return the smile.

The bottle is passed around and this time I do participate.

The boy talking to Shane pulls a tobacco pouch from his pocket. 'Anyone want a proper smoke now?'

To the encouraging agreement from the others, he unfolds the pouch and, crouching down, begins to roll a cigarette. It's at this point I realise it's not a normal cigarette, not with those large papers and the extra sprinkling of green he mixes with the tobacco.

He stands up, lights the joint and takes a draw, long and slow. He puts his head back and closes his eyes. After a moment he lets the smoke drift out of his mouth. He blinks a couple of times, refocuses and looks appreciatively at the roll-up between his fingers. 'That's good,' he says. He offers the joint around.

'Cheers, Kerry,' says Jody, before taking an equally long draw. 'Now that's why I love my cousin. He gets seriously good gear.' He gives Kerry a friendly punch on the upper arm.

So the boy is Jody and Shane's cousin. That would explain the blond hair and ease with each other. Looking at the three of them, I can see the family likeness now.

The joint finds its way to me. I debate whether to take a drag, just to pacify them, as I'm sure there will be some comment if I don't.

'No big deal if you don't want to,' says Kerry. 'It's cool.' He sends a look in Jody and Roisin's direction and then the decision is taken away from me as Kerry reaches over and, taking the joint from my fingers, passes it on to Niall.

Kerry smiles at me briefly and I am thankful the moment has passed.

Niall, on the other hand, has clearly done this before. I don't know whether I'm shocked or not. I suppose I am a little bit. I know he smokes, but he's never mentioned weed before. I'm not sure how I feel about this as his eyes glaze over.

The vodka and coke is following the joint round our little group. I take a larger gulp than before, conscious the others are getting merrily stoned and drunk while I'm not feeling the effects of anything. I don't want to be the only one sober; it makes the night less fun. Nothing is quite so funny when you've not had a drink but everyone else has.

Suddenly the sound of door to the function room can be heard as it clatters open. The dull beat of the music is now sharper as the sound escapes into the night air but not so loud that we don't hear footsteps crunch purposefully across the gritted car park. Roisin pops her head around the corner and almost chokes on the vodka and coke she has just swigged. She dives back.

'Feck! It's Mam,' she hisses and thrusts the bottle into my hands. There's a flurry of activity as Niall drops his cigarette and crunches it underneath his foot.

I'm left holding the bottle of alcohol. I turn, looking for somewhere to hide it, but there's nowhere.

'Oh God, what shall I do with the bottle? Niall?'

He shakes his head. The bottle is then snatched from my hands just as Diana appears. I look over at Kerry, who now has it. Diana isn't stupid. She scans our faces. Her eyes rest on the bottle and then flick to me. I'm sure she saw Kerry take it.

'I hope that's just coke in there,' she says, her eyes still trained on me. 'And I can smell cigarettes.' This time Roisin is under scrutiny.

'That will be me,' says Kerry, holding up his cigarette, which fortunately is a normal one. I have no idea where the joint has gone.

I don't think Diana believes him but she can't prove otherwise. 'Shane, your mother was wondering where you were. She wants you back in. Now.'

'Right you are,' says Shane. He turns to us. 'Come on, we'd better go in. Don't want to upset me mam.'

'I'll say,' says Kerry.

We make a move and head back into the hall. Diana is at the helm. I link my arm through Niall's, but behind me I can hear a barrage of whispered swear words and scuffling. I glance back over my shoulder as Kerry extracts the joint from his pocket and is frantically flapping at his jacket with the palm of his hand.

Jody is smothering a laugh. 'He hid it in his pocket,' he whispers with a grin. 'It didn't go out, though.'

We are quite a gaggle staggering our way back into the party, all with varying degrees of success. Diana holds the door open and practically counts us in. I let go of Niall's arm so we can single-file in through the door. As I pass Diana she puts her hand on my shoulder.

'I'm watching you,' she says. 'I know that bottle was yours and there's more than just coke in it.'

I go to protest but decide against it. Grassing up Roisin is not on my agenda and, besides, I don't think Diana would believe me anyway.

Chapter 10

Kerry couldn't help glancing up the garden of Apple Tree Cottage every few minutes. The barbecue was in full swing and still no sign of Erin. He really thought she would turn up, especially after Bex's chat with her.

'Another beer?' said Joe, coming over with a cold bottle he had hooked out of a barrel of ice.

Kerry accepted the beer and, using the bottle opener Joe passed his way, flicked off the top and took a long slug.

'You been stood up?' said Joe.

'She's bringing her boyfriend,' said Kerry. 'Hardly call it stood up.'

'Maybe she got a better offer.' Joe gave his cousin a gentle punch on the arm.

Kerry resisted the urge to tell Joe where to go. He refused to rise to the bait. Besides, he was pissed off at himself for even thinking Erin would want to come to the barbecue, least of all because he was there.

He watched Storm and the other children race around the garden, squirting each other with water pistols. Skip was scampering after them, clearly enjoying all the excitement. As Storm tore past Kerry and Joe, screaming with laughter, one of the older kids grabbed the hosepipe and turning it on, pressed his thumb over the opening. The resultant jet of water sprayed both Kerry and Joe.

'Hey!' shouted Kerry, jumping back out of the way.

'Little shit,' muttered Joe, but he was laughing all the same.

'Right, that does it,' said Kerry good-humouredly. He thrust his beer bottle at Joe and strode across the grass. The lad screamed and, dropping the hosepipe, fled round the corner of the house.

Kerry picked up the hose and waited for the boy to come back into the garden. A movement caught Kerry's eye and he squirted the hosepipe at the lad.

There was a scream and a curse.

A cheer went up from the guests in the garden.

'Shit.' Kerry dropped the hosepipe.

Standing in front of him wasn't the lad, but Erin. Her clothes clung to her like she had entered a wet t-shirt competition. Water dripped from her hair. 'Jesus, Erin. I'm so sorry,' he said. He could hear Joe chortling in the background.

'What the hell was that for?' The man with Erin said.

Kerry noticed him for the first time. From the man's accent, Kerry assumed that it was Erin's English boyfriend. He wasn't quite so wet, unfortunately. It seemed Erin had caught the full brunt of it.

'Just messing around with the kids,' said Kerry. 'I didn't realise you were there.'

Erin squeezed at her hair and pulled the t-shirt away from her body. It slapped back against her stomach.

'So glad I came,' she said, her face deadpan.

Bex appeared at her side. 'Come on in, Erin,' she said. 'I'll find you some dry clothes. Hi, you must be Ed. Erin said she was bringing you. I'm Bex. You'd better come in as well. I'll get you a towel.'

The trio disappeared inside and Kerry returned to his beer. Joe was creasing up with laughter.

'What a classic,' he said. 'Way to go, cuz!'

Some ten minutes later, Bex returned with Erin and Ed. Kerry couldn't help doing a double-take. Erin had undergone some sort of transformation. Gone was the city slicker, with subtly expensive clothes and perfectly styled hair. Instead, was a country girl in a pair of Bex's cropped denim shorts, a white gypsy top floated gracefully over her body and copper curls bounced off her shoulders.

Joe let out a low whistle. He gave his cousin a nudge.

'I know,' said Kerry. 'What a difference a hosepipe can make.'

'Now, that's how I remember you,' quipped Joe, as Erin approached them. 'Curls galore. Curly Hurley.'

This remark earned him a thump on the arm from Bex, a glare from Erin and a muttering from Kerry to behave himself. Joe feigned innocence. 'I was only saying.'

'Well don't,' added Kerry, just to be sure Joe got the message.

'Your hair is looking a bit wild and mad, thanks to someone,' said Ed, throwing a cold glance towards Kerry. 'Can't you tie it back or something?'

'Oh, I think it looks nice,' said Bex, she flicked at her own long black-and-blue locks, a silent reminder that Erin wasn't the only one with untamed hair.

'Thanks, Bex,' replied Erin. 'Ed's not a fan of the natural look, are you Ed?'

'It's not that. I prefer it straightened, that's all.'

Kerry couldn't resist joining in. 'I'm all for the natural look myself.' He offered a beer to Ed. 'Don't like anything contrived.' Kerry was sure he heard Ed mutter something like 'clearly' under his breath, but he let it go. It was worth the smile Erin sent his way. 'I'm Kerry, by the way, and this is my cousin, Joe. And you've met the lovely Bex already.'

Ed offered a tight smile. 'I'm Ed Hamilton. Erin's boyfriend,' he said putting an arm around Erin's shoulders and pulling her into him. Just then, Skip came trotting over and, with perfect timing, jumped up at Ed, his front paws resting on the cream-coloured chinos. Ed stepped back, brushing the little dog away with his hand. 'Get off!'

'Skip, come here, boy' said Kerry, with less authority than he normally would.

'Did you train him to do that?' said Joe in his cousin's ear.

'No, but I think he gets an extra sausage off the barbecue for that,' said Kerry. He called Skip again, this time with more conviction, and grabbing a sausage from the table, dropped it into the eagerly waiting dog's mouth. 'Sorry about that, Ed.'

Ed was brushing at two muddy paw prints on his trouser legs, muttering something derogatory about bloody dogs.

'Now we've all met officially, let's get down to business. Who's hungry?' said Bex, shifting the attention away from the incident. 'Although I'm not sure what we've got left. I think there may be a couple of burgers going.'

'Not for me, thanks,' replied Ed as he regarded the barbecue. 'I'm not really a burger sort of man.'

'Why don't you get the hamper from the car?' suggested Erin.

'Hamper?' said Kerry.

'Ed brought a hamper for a picnic. I forgot to tell him we were coming here,' said Erin. 'We might as well share it out now.'

Kerry suspected that Erin's forgetfulness might have been engineered. He couldn't for one minute think Ed would have agreed to come here of his own free will. Kerry watched, amused as Ed shifted slightly on his feet and gave Erin a disapproving look at the mention of the hamper.

'I don't know if it's really the thing for a barbecue,' said Ed.

'Why ever not?' said Erin.

'You know, vol-au-vents, quiche, prawns – I'm not sure it goes with burgers and hot dogs.'

'Oh, prawns and quiche, now that does sounds posh,' said Joe. Kerry exchanged a look with him, only this time it wasn't one of disapproval, quite the opposite. Sometimes it was handy having a cousin whose main hobby was winding everyone up. Joe carried on. 'Perhaps you could educate us on the finer points of al-fresco dining.'

'Just go and get it,' said Erin, her tone of voice betraying the smile she tacked on. A slight pause and another look passed between the two of them, but Ed conceded and ever so slightly stomped off to the car.

'He's a bit precious, isn't he? Aptly named, though, don't you think?' commented Joe under his breath. Kerry looked at his cousin questioningly. Joe nodded in the direction of Ed. 'You know. Ed. As in Dick-Ed.'

For a couple of hours the barbecue passed without incident. Kerry took it upon himself to chat to Ed and find out as much about him as possible. Apart from working out and running, Ed liked to play squash, frequent high-class restaurants in the Covent Garden area and holiday abroad at all-inclusive resorts. Kerry also learned Ed was the manager of a health and fitness centre and Erin's boss.

'I was her saviour,' said Ed, looking very proud of himself. 'She was working in a beautician's concession at a local department store when I came in to buy a present for my mother. Erin helped me select some beauty products. I was very impressed with her service and knew she was wasting her time there. When a position came up at my place, I offered her the job. And the rest, as they say, is history.' Ed leaned over and patted Erin's knee. 'Once she started working for me, she simply couldn't resist me. Could you, darling?'

'Modest as always,' said Erin with a laugh. The smile looked a little false and Kerry was sure, as she dropped her gaze, there was a trace of embarrassment there.

Kerry's questioning was brought to a halt as some of the guests came over to say goodbye and he wandered out with his cousin Shane and Shane's family, who were also leaving. Joe appeared by his side as they waved to his nephew and nieces drawing away in the people carrier with Shane at the wheel.

'You and Dick-Ed seem to be getting on like a house on fire,' said Joe, poking his tongue out to his nephew, who was pulling a face through the back window of the departing vehicle.

'Just being friendly,' responded Kerry, turning to head back towards the garden.

'Yeah, right. Just checking out the competition, more like.'

They sat back down in the gazebo and as Kerry was about to start his second round of interrogation, Joe gave him a nudge in the ribs. 'Stand by your beds. Here comes trouble.'

'Hello everyone,' Roisin smiled, as she reached the gazebo. 'Hi, Bex, I just came to say congratulations.' She bent down to give Bex a hug and handed over a small gift-wrapped present, then proceeded to give Joe a hug too. She looked round for somewhere to sit.

'Here, have my seat,' said a man she didn't recognise but guessed, from his English accent, he was something to do with Erin. Her boyfriend, probably. He rose and held the chair back.

'Thank you. I can tell you're not a local, you've actually got some manners,' said Roisin as she sat down next to Erin. 'Hello, Erin, didn't expect to see you here.'

'Likewise,' said Erin.

Roisin was pleased to see an uneasy look cross Erin's face. She was going to enjoy this.

'So is anyone going to introduce me?' said Roisin, looking up at the Englishman as he brought over a plastic patio chair.

Erin made the introductions as he sat down.

'Ed Hamilton,' said Erin. 'Roisin Marshall.'

'So are you one of Erin's old school friends?' said Ed.

'That's right, we go back a long way, don't we, Erin?'

'Pleased to meet you,' said Ed, leaning over and shaking Roisin's hand. 'I would say Erin's never mentioned you before, but it wouldn't make any difference. She's never mentioned any of her old friends before.'

'Wonder why that is?' Roisin raised her eyebrows. 'Erin's got her reasons, no doubt.'

Roisin allowed a moment's uncomfortable silence to settle. Erin was playing right into her hands and making this very easy for her. Roisin turned back to Ed. 'So where's she been hiding you away all this time? Do you live in London too?'

'Yes. Fulham.'

'Live together, do you?'

'No, not yet. Although…' Ed looked encouragingly at Erin.

Erin looked like a startled doe, as her eyes shot open, seemingly surprised by Ed's inference.

'Oh dear, Erin, don't look so scared,' said Roisin. She gave a little laugh. 'Ed can't be that bad, well, at least he doesn't seem so from where I'm sitting.'

'Would you like a glass of wine?' said Bex. 'Something to eat?'

'Oh, that's kind of you,' said Roisin, aware Bex was trying to change the subject. 'I really don't want to intrude, but if you're sure, a glass of wine would be perfect.'

Joe got up and poured Roisin a drink.

'Thank you, Joe,' said Roisin, ignoring the warning look he sent her way. She settled back in her seat. 'This is nice. A real family get-together.'

Storm came running up to his mother, hopping from one leg to the other. 'Need a wee wee.'

'Daddy will take you,' said Bex.

'No, don't want Daddy. Mummy take me.'

'Okay, then,' Bex got up, cradling the baby in her arms. 'Who wants a cuddle?'

'Oh, can I?' Roisin placed her glass on the ground and, standing up, took the tiny baby from Bex. 'She's so beautiful. Aren't you Breeze? You're beautiful. Don't you think so, Erin?'

Erin nodded. 'Yes, she's lovely.'

Ed let out a laugh. 'She must be lovely for Erin to say so.'

'Why's that?' said Roisin, not missing an opportunity to undermine Erin. She took a sneak look round at the rest of the group. Kerry was immediately distracted from his conversation with Joe and was watching for Erin's reply.

'Erin's not really the maternal type, are you darling?'

'You've changed, then,' said Roisin, delighted with the way the conversation was going. 'I thought when we were teenagers a baby was what you wanted.'

Ed laughed again. 'I can't imagine that, never in a million years. Show Erin a baby and she runs a mile.'

'All right, Ed.' Erin's voice had a menace to it. If words were actions, those three would have walked right up to Ed and clamped themselves over his mouth.

'Sorry, didn't mean to upset you.' Roisin carried Breeze over to Erin. 'Here, have a cuddle. You can prove us all wrong, then.' Roisin smiled as she locked eyes with Erin. She could tell Erin wasn't happy about this at all. Erin hesitated slightly, glancing around the group before putting her glass down and taking hold of the baby.

She certainly looked awkward as she crooked her arm to support Breeze's head and placed her other hand under the baby's little legs. Shoulders hunched up, her whole body totally tense, Erin looked ill at ease with her precious cargo. To make matters worse, Breeze decided now was the time to begin to wriggle and, when finding no comfort from the staccato rocking offered by Erin, began to protest vigorously. More faltering swaying, the uneasiness radiated from Erin. Roisin couldn't be more pleased with how it was going.

Kerry jumped to his feet.

'My turn,' he said, going over to Erin and confidently taking charge of his cousin's baby. With ease, he rested Breeze at his shoulder and, gently patting her back, he returned to his seat. Almost immediately the baby's crying abated.

'You've got the touch,' said Roisin, disappointed, and then

turned to Erin. 'He'll make a fantastic dad one day. Some people were just meant to be parents.'

The reappearance of Bex and Storm gives me the chance to excuse myself and make for the bathroom. Once safely behind the locked door, only then do I let my composure fall and, leaning back against the wall, I close my eyes. Every nerve in my body is tingling and my heart throbs against my breastbone. It's been a long time since I held a small baby. In fact, it was when Sophie was born. The effect today was the same as it was then: overwhelming.

A gentle tap at the door brings me from my thoughts.

'Erin? You okay?' It's Kerry.

'I won't be a moment,' I call, attempting to sound cheery. I check myself in the mirror, flush the toilet for good measure and wait a minute before letting myself out of the bathroom. I smile at Kerry, who is standing across the landing, leaning against the slope of the dormer window, his hands in his pockets.

'I didn't ask you to hurry up,' he says gently. 'I asked if you were okay.'

The concern in his voice is apparent and for a second I'm uncertain if I can answer. I broaden my smile. 'Me? I'm fine. Whatever made you think I wasn't?'

'Roisin and Ed.' Kerry fixes me with his grey eyes, his voice is soft.

It's almost too much for me. A thread of sympathy and I can feel my composure unravelling. It only takes one stride and he is in front of me, his strong arms around me as he pulls me into him. I take in the smell of his aftershave, a spicy mixture, tinged slightly with cigarette smoke, which oddly enough I don't find offensive. He drops a kiss on the top of my head and I can feel his fingers entwining with my hair.

I pull away. 'We'd better get back to the party. People will wonder where we are.'

*

'That was interesting,' says Ed, exhaling loudly, as he slowly steers the hire car along Corkscrew Lane, avoiding the potholes where possible.

'What do you mean?'

'I didn't expect to be hanging out with a load of hippy bikers this afternoon.'

'They're not hippy bikers. Well, maybe a bit, but it doesn't matter, they're all very nice.' Even Joe had been quite pleasant, I reflect, if you didn't count the Curly Hurley jibe. After that, much as it pains me to admit, I couldn't really fault him.

'Yeah, nice but a bit, well, you know…' says Ed.

I feel myself bristle. 'Actually, I don't know.'

'You know…not very sophisticated. Country bumpkins. Bex with her mad hair and nose piercing, I half expected her to get out a guitar and start singing 'Kumbaya'. Then Joe and Kerry with their scruffy hair, frayed and faded jeans, t-shirts and tattoos. Can't quite see them at Jones' Wine Bar. Can you?'

I have to admit, I can't see any of the Wrights in the wine bar that Ed and I frequent but, then again, I can't actually imagine they would want to. 'They're just different,' I say. 'Anyway, you'll have to get used to them, Bex has invited us to the naming ceremony in a few weeks.'

'What? A naming ceremony? What's wrong with a traditional Christening?' Ed shakes his head as he steers the car out of the lane and onto the High Street. 'Please don't say you've accepted.'

I haven't actually said yes for definite, but Ed is annoying me now. He's been nothing short of pompous this afternoon. Showing off at every opportunity and being patronising towards me. He gets like that when we're in a crowd. It will serve him right if I make him go to the naming ceremony. You never know, he might stop being so dismissive of my friends if he got to know them properly. My friends, I note the reference and acknowledge subconsciously I am already thinking of them in this way. Ed is waiting for me to reply. 'Unlucky,' I say. 'I've accepted on behalf of us both.'

'For fuck's sake, Erin.' His eyebrows dart together in irritation. 'Why did you go and do that?'

'Because I would like to go. It will be nice.'

'The sooner you come back to London and civilisation, the better. Next they'll be brainwashing you, and before you know it, you'll be dressing in a floral smock, running around bare-foot with daisies in your hair. Speaking of which...' he flicks at my curls, 'you really need to get the straighteners out.'

Chapter 11

Teenage Kicks
Two months before leaving
I don't go to school the next day. I wake up feeling very sick. I clearly drank too much last night. Niall got some cider from the locally offy and we went and sat down on the beach. We went to the far end, where there are sand dunes and made ourselves a small fire to keep warm. We huddled under the blanket, drank the cider and ate leftover sandwiches from the café Dad let me take. We made love on the sand under the stars. It was very romantic. We stayed until the fire burnt out and we had no more driftwood to put on. It was very late. but I didn't care. I was with Niall and that was all that mattered.

Now, the morning after, I'm beginning to think it wasn't quite so romantic after all. The nausea notches up a gear and I rush to the bathroom. I retch but only some sickly sort of bile comes up. It tastes disgusting. All metallic. Yuk.

'You not well?' asks Mum, coming out of her bedroom. 'You look very pale. You'd better go back to bed.'

I'm grateful, Dad looks on from beyond and nods his approval. I clearly must look ill for him not to say something along the lines of, you'll feel better once you've had something to eat. Or, a bit of fresh air and you'll be as right as rain.

I fall into bed, pulling the duvet up around me, and drift back to sleep. I can't face going anywhere or eating a single thing. Cider is definitely my enemy. I swear I'm never going to drink again. Ever.

'Feck! Feck! Feck!'

Niall's response to our news. It's very similar to my own reaction when I found out, except I cried as well. I don't think Niall is going to cry, but he's holding both hands behind his head, pacing round in circles, scuffing the sand and leaving a track, which marks his anguish.

I can feel the tears welling up again. I was dreading telling him. I can hardly believe it myself.

'Are you sure?' he demands, momentarily halting.

I nod. 'Of course, I am.' It comes out rather more angrily than I intend, but I'm not an idiot. I wouldn't be saying this unless I was sure. 'I've done three tests and they are all positive. My period is now three weeks late. I'm definitely pregnant.'

I'm not sure what sort of reaction I expected from Niall. He's eighteen, about to go off to university, and I'm sixteen, hopefully with a place at college in London waiting for me. A baby was definitely not on the agenda. A baby? It doesn't sound real. I can't quite believe I have a baby growing inside me. It just doesn't seem possible. Yet at the same time, it very clearly is possible. What a mess. If this was ten years down the line it wouldn't matter but we are only kids ourselves.

Niall recommences his pacing and swearing. Then he goes quiet and stops walking, looking out at the monotone waters of the sea before us. Finally, he turns round and comes and sits beside me.

He puts his arm around me. 'Don't cry,' he says. This just makes me cry even more. He holds me tight. 'It will be all right, I promise.'

I have no idea how it will be all right. I stifle the tears and sobs. 'How?'

'Do you want to keep the baby?' he asks.

'Yes. No. I don't know,' I admit. I am so confused. 'I can't bear the thought of having an abortion, but at the same time I don't know how we will manage. I don't want to be a teenage mum.'

'I don't really want to be a teenage dad,' says Niall. 'How the hell did it happen?'

This makes me want to laugh. I'm pretty sure Niall attended sex-education classes, but I appreciate my humour will not be well received at this precise moment. 'I don't know,' I say instead. I seem not to know a lot of things. 'The only time I can think would have been after Shane's party. You know we were both a bit drunk then and we fooled around in the car.'

'Yeah, but I didn't think…you know…I thought we stopped in time.'

'So did I.'

'Let's think about this rationally,' says Niall. 'If you keep it, I will need to get a job to support you and the baby. We could get a place together. We'll probably have to get some financial help but I'm sure we will manage. Lots of people do. There are all sorts of benefits and then there are our parents. They could help. Maybe?'

'But what about university? You want to qualify as a lawyer. You won't be able to do it if you're working.'

'It's okay. I can go to evening classes, study part time. If I get a job at a solicitor's, as a clerk, they may even pay for my training.'

'You really think so?'

'Yeah, I'm sure. You can study to be a beautician in the same way too. There's loads of evening courses for that.' He smiles at me and seems excited and relieved all at the same time. 'It may be hard for a few years but once we are both qualified, we will be able to support ourselves and the baby.'

I'm buying into the idea. I imagine us both sitting at the

kitchen table; Niall surrounded by law books, me surrounded by beauty products. I imagine tucking the baby up in his or her cot and, dressed in my beautician's uniform, picking up my bag of products, kissing Niall bye and heading off for college. When I come home, he will finish his studying for the night and we will sit and have a cup of tea and talk about our day and the course-work we have to do. We will go up to bed, look in on the baby, who will be fast asleep. We will smile at each other because we are happy and proud parents and we will go to bed, still very much in love, knowing that despite the odds and what everyone said, we have made it. Our very own family. We will probably have another child once we are both qualified and I will work part-time from home and Niall will get a partnership in a law firm.

I smile at him. 'We could really make it work, if we try. I know it's not ideal, but we can do this. Together we're strong.'

'I love you,' says Niall.

'I love you too.'

Fiona has come over to visit. Her timing couldn't be better. Mum and Dad are in the café and Sean has gone off to meet with some of his friends. It's just me and Fiona at the flat. She is the first person, other than Niall, who I'm going to tell about the baby.

Fiona sits down beside me. 'So, what's up? You've been on edge ever since I got here yesterday.'

She knows me so well.

'I don't know how to say this…' I stumble over the words. I can't bring myself to say them out loud. I feel I've let her down. I look bleakly at her whilst my mind rushes to think of something else. I feel the tears begin to sting my eyes and I rapidly blink them away. A lump forces its way up my throat, sticking right at the back, where I can't seem to swallow it down.

Fiona's eyes penetrate mine. She's searching for the answer.

'Erin?' Her voice is soft and I can hear a tentativeness I'm not used to. Usually, Fiona is strong and able to deal with anything and everything. She reaches over and holds my hand in hers. 'Are you pregnant?'

How does she know without me having to say a word? I still can't get rid of that lump in my throat. It swells some more and the tears flood my eyes, spilling over and racing down my cheeks. I nod and manage to croak out a yes.

'Oh, Erin,' says Fiona. There's compassion in her voice. She draws me to her and holds me tightly. I don't know what she's thinking. She doesn't say anything, just holds me while I sob.

'It will be all right, though,' I say, when the tears subside. 'Niall is going to get a job and study at evening classes. I'm going to do the same. Once we're both qualified it will be great. We'll be able to support ourselves properly.' I'm rambling, the words are tumbling over each other in a bid to free themselves. They gather pace. 'I know it will be hard at first and everything, but we are going to make it work…'

Fiona listens patiently. Every now and then she gives a little smile and nods. She waits for me to come to an end.

'You seem to have it all worked out,' she says. 'You know, Erin, it's great you and Niall are being positive about it all and I do admire that, I really do, but you do also know it won't be that straightforward. You're both giving up great opportunities ahead of you and you may never fulfil your dreams. Life has a habit of putting obstacles in the way and sometimes there are just too many to get round.'

'Are you saying I should have an abortion?' Although it is something I've thought about and talked over with Niall, I never expected this suggestion from my sister. Not Fiona. She's never made any secret of the fact that her and Sean want to start a family soon. Why would she suggest it to me?

'Absolutely not. You must know how I feel about it,' she says, without a moment's hesitation. 'All I'm trying to say is, whatever decision you make, you must do it with the full knowledge, realistic knowledge, of what lies ahead. I would never dream of telling you what you should and shouldn't do. I'm here for you. Always have been and always will be. I'll support you, but I won't tell you what to do.'

With an understanding of where we stand, we talk our way through the rest of the morning. Fiona starts making a list of things I will need to do. The list is endless. Go to the doctors. Start taking folic acid. Avoid eating soft cheese and pâté. No alcohol. Find out about financial support. Find out about my rights to education. Research evening classes. I feel overwhelmed with the enormity of what I have to do. Practical things. Grown-up stuff that before I never had to even consider.

'And then, of course, there's Mum and Dad to tell and Niall's parents,' says Fiona.

'Dad is going to kill me,' I say. I've been avoiding this issue. Telling him is going to be the worst thing ever. 'And then he's going to kill Niall.'

'If I was you, I'd tell Mum first. On her own. Give her a couple of days to get used to the idea. That way you'll only have to deal with one of them at a time.'

I look up from the tissue I've been tearing apart, bit by bit, for the last few minutes, and I see so many things on my sister's face. So many emotions. There's compassion, love, protectiveness, strength and there's pain. I wish the last one away. I'm sure the pain is not just for me, but for her too. How did God muddle up our wishes? It seems so cruel.

Chapter 12

Teenage Kicks
Six weeks before leaving

Niall is waiting for me at the school gates this morning. He doesn't usually wait. I'm pleased to see him. However, as I approach him, I can see by the look on his face something is wrong.

'Hi. What's up?' I ask. I put my arms around him for a hug, as if this action itself will take away the trouble. His reaction quashes any such thought as his hands remain stuffed in his pockets.

'Get in the car. We need to talk.'

I take a moment to stand back and read the expression on his face. It's not anger. It's fear. He's upset. I do as he says, even though I know this is going to make me late for school.

'What's up?' I ask again.

'Mam knows.' The two words are like a physical blow and I reel back from the verbal punch. His voice cracks. 'She knows you're pregnant.' He really doesn't need to qualify his mother's knowledge. I'm already there.

'How?'

'How do you think? She's a GP. She must have seen your notes.'

'But, I went to see the nurse. Your mum wouldn't have been

100

able to see them, not without going to look for them. It's all done on computer.'

'I don't know how and it's irrelevant now. She knows.'

I open the door and lean my head out as the bile in my stomach makes for a quick exit. Niall barely seems to notice. When I'm done retching, I take the bottle of water from my school bag and rinse my mouth, spitting into the road. In the depths of my bag I have a packet of ginger biscuits. Fiona gave them to me. She said they were supposed to be good for morning sickness.

The biscuits are hard and the sound of the crunch fills the space in the car. It sounds like a whole army is marching towards us. An army of fear. Niall's mum knows. Soon my mum and dad will know. Soon everyone will know. It's time for us to face up to what's happening. Suddenly the baby growing inside my stomach seems real. It's no longer a word. I'm no longer simply pregnant. I actually have a baby inside me.

'Do you have to eat so loudly? You sound like a horse.'

I put the remaining part of the biscuit back into my bag.

'What did your mum say?'

'She went ballistic. Had a screaming fit at me. Dad joined in too.'

'And Roisin?'

'She was out and doesn't know. Thank, God.'

'Ditto.'

'Mam wants to speak to your folks.'

Suddenly the sickness is back. 'She can't. I mean, I need to tell them first. What does she need to speak to them for?'

Niall shrugs. He looks away from me and I get the feeling he's being evasive. There's something he's not telling me.

'Did you tell her about our plan?' I ask. My voice is quiet. The confidence in our ideas for the future suddenly feeling fragile.

Niall takes a long time before he answers. 'She wants you to have an abortion.'

The breath I draw is sharp and grazes the back of throat. 'It's none of her business,' I almost shout.

'That's what I said, but she said it was her business as she will potentially be a grandmother and it's not on her agenda yet. She said we would regret it and there's plenty of time for babies in the future.'

'You sound like you agree with her.'

'It's not that, well, maybe I do a bit…'

I sit bolt upright in my seat.

'You've been brainwashed.' I feel crushed. 'I thought we had it all planned. We were going to go to college in the evenings. You said it would be okay.'

I want to shake him. Make him see sense. He puts his head in his hands.

'Feck. What a mess.' We sit in silence for a long moment. Finally, Niall lets out a sigh. He rubs his face with his hands and then, turning in his seat, he puts his arm around me and lays one hand on my stomach. 'We'll be okay. I'm sorry. It's just Mam making me twitchy. Of course I want all this. I want us to be a family. You'll be a fantastic mam. It's just, in an ideal world, I want all this in ten years' time.'

'So do I, but it's not an ideal world. We have to deal with what's real. I'm as scared as you. Every time I think about it, I dart from being terrified to brave, from sad to happy.'

'We'll be okay as long as we have each other. I'll look after you.'

'I'll have to tell my mum first,' I say, feeling better now Niall seems to be back on track and has reassured me he is serious about the baby. 'Just ask your mum to wait before she says anything.'

Mum takes the news as I imagined she would. Shock. Disbelief. Silent. Then with love. She cries, only for a moment, as she cuddles me. It makes me cry. I'm doing that a lot now. Fiona says it's my hormones. Mum holds me for a long time as she lets it all sink in.

She listens patiently as I tell her my and Niall's plans. I get the feeling if it wasn't for the seriousness of the situation she would probably find it amusing, or rather my ideas amusing.

'Sure, it's such a big commitment,' she says. 'I don't know how a sixteen-year-old and an eighteen-year-old can truly manage.'

My tentative hopes of her embracing grandmotherhood begin to slide away. I wanted Mum to be my ally in this.

'We need to tell your dad,' she says. 'Jesus, he is not going to be happy.'

That surely has to count as the understatement of a lifetime.

I'm sitting on my bed, pretending I'm reading the book on my lap. Pretending I don't really know Mum is telling Dad about the baby. I'm trying hard to focus my eyes on the words, but my brain is connecting with my ears only. All other senses diminish as my hearing heightens.

The tones of their voices start off low, but now Mum has broken the news the pitches are rising, becoming louder and finally I hear Dad as clear as if he were right next to me.

'Erin! Get yourself in here. NOW!'

Mum is silent. She knows it's not worth trying to appease him now. He's in a temper, for sure. Before I even reach the door, I hear him shout for me again. I feel sick. My hands are trembling. I hold them together over my stomach, close my eyes and take a moment to compose myself. I have to be strong. I need to prove to Dad that although I'm only sixteen, I'm grown up enough to take on the responsibility of a child.

He rants and raves. He calls me stupid, irresponsible, naive and a tramp. The last hurts the most. Whoever said sticks and stones were the only things that could hurt you was lying. Even Mum draws in a sharp breath at this attack.

'Jim, please...'

He dismisses her protests with a wave of his hand. 'I didn't bring my daughter up to go sleeping around and getting herself pregnant at sixteen.'

'She's not been sleeping around. She's been in a relationship with Niall for a long time now.'

I appreciate Mum's defence. She may not like what's happened, but she is taking her usual pragmatic approach.

'But she's only sixteen and he's only, what, eighteen?'

Dad hasn't yet taken his eyes from me. He shakes his head. I force myself to hold his gaze and not look down. I won't let him shame me. Instead, I stand myself taller, swallow hard and tell him about the plans Niall and I have made.

Amazingly, he listens without interruption and as I finish with, 'We love each other,' the corners of his mouth turn up and, for a fleeting second I feel a surge of joy, as I believe he has been convinced by my argument. But the smile doesn't come – it turns out to be a derisory smirk.

'That's just great, Erin,' he says, sarcasm coating his every word. 'You've got it all sorted out, haven't you? You're going to have the baby, get a house, go to college, get a job and live happily ever after. I'm worrying about nothing, aren't I?' He taps Mum's arm. 'Hey, did you hear that, Marie? Erin has it all sorted. We've nothing to worry about.'

Mum looks uncomfortable and throws me a look I can interpret immediately. I prepare myself for the second onslaught.

'And where do you think you're going to get all the money for this? We're not rolling in it. Do you really think Mrs High and Mighty Diana Marshall is going to fall over you with handouts? Get real, Erin.' He clicks his fingers inches from my face. 'This is not some fairytale out of one of those romance books you read. This is real life.'

My bravado is waning. 'What are you trying to say?' I can't quell the tremble in my throat that makes my words wobble.

Dad looks at me for a long moment. I see his shoulders sag and he exhales a deep sigh. Is that compassion in his eyes? He places a hand on the top of my arm and when he speaks his voice is soft but firm. 'You can't keep the baby.'

'I can. And I'm going to.' The wobble has become a tremor and the words are catching in my throat.

'Erin…' Mum takes a step towards me.

I take a step back. And another. 'It's not up to you.' My eyes flick from one face to the other.

'Think about it,' says Dad. 'It won't work. You're both too young and don't know what you want in life. You can't tie yourselves down at this age. Not to each other and not to a baby.'

'Listen to your dad,' says Mum. 'He's only thinking of you and your future.'

I shake my head in disbelief. Mum is siding with Dad. He curses under his breath and when he speaks again the softness has gone and the dominating father I'm accustomed to returns.

'You're not keeping the baby and that's that. I'll hear no more about it.' He adjusts his cardigan around his shoulders. 'Now, I suggest, young lady, you go to your room and have a proper think about things. Tomorrow we'll contact the Marshalls and get this mess sorted out.'

We're sitting in the Marshalls' living room. Me, Mum and Dad. Mum and I are perched on the sofa and Dad is standing by the fireplace. Niall is sitting opposite me in a chair. His father is standing too. Diana is making tea and coffee. The silence that fills the room is oppressive and heavy. I feel as if the ceiling has an invisible force field that is slowly pushing down on top of us.

I wanted Niall to sit by me. When he came into the room, I went to get up, to greet him. I wanted to show some sort of unity to our parents. But his body language told another story. He didn't meet my eyes. We haven't seen each other since Dad found out three days ago. Niall hasn't been at school and I was so sick this morning, I couldn't face going in. I'm not sure if it's nerves or morning sickness. Mum seems to think a bit of both.

Last night I wanted to ask her why she was siding with Dad. I went to say something but she just put her hand on my cheek and shook her head. She didn't need to say she was sorry. I knew she was. She thought she was letting me down. She's tried to talk to Dad – I've heard them for the past three nights arguing about it, but Dad won't be moved.

Today is my last chance to convince them they're wrong and that Niall and I are right. That we can do this. We can have this baby and be happy. We will get our happy ever after.

Diana comes in with a tray of cups. We're all having tea except for Dad. He's gone for a black coffee.

I'm not sure what happens next. One minute we're sitting stilled, awkwardly accepting our drinks and thanking Diana, and the next there is a full-blown conversation going on between both sets of parents about how they're going to sort this mess out as quickly as possible, without any fuss: no one need ever know.

'I can make the arrangements. I have professional contacts in London who deal with this sort of thing,' Diana is saying.

'And they're discreet?' asks Dad.

'Absolutely,' says Diana.

'And safe?' Mum asks.

'Very. As much as you can be with these sorts of things,' says Diana. 'Erin's not very far gone, there shouldn't be any complications at all.'

They carry on talking. I look over to Niall, who is still staring at his shoes. I want to cry. Why isn't he defending us? I've tried to speak, but it seems only I can hear my voice. I am silent to the adults in the room. He looks up and I can tell he's hurting too. I send a pleading message with my eyes. He nods. He mouths 'It's okay.' He moves his hand slightly, as if very gently patting down the air. He's telling me not to say anything. To go along with it. I send a questioning look this time. Again, the mimed words, 'It's okay,' come back to me. I don't understand. What's okay?

Is it okay what the parents have decided? Or is it okay, as in we're going to be okay? I just don't know.

The next thirty minutes go by in a haze. It seems my fate and the fate of my unborn baby, their grandchild, has been decided. I am to go to London to have a termination. The sooner the better. And then we can all go back to our normal lives, Niall can go off to university and everyone will carry on as if nothing has happened.

Niall texts me that night. He wants to meet in secret. I tell him he has to meet me at midnight, when I know Mum and Dad will be asleep and I can creep out. He's to wait at the top of the road to The Spit. I will keep a watch out from my window.

It seems forever before Mum and Dad go to bed. I lie still in mine, listening for the tell-tale sign of the light switch in the living room and the plug behind the TV being flicked to off. Dad doesn't believe in leaving things on standby.

By eleven-thirty they will both be in a deep sleep, so by the time it's midnight, they won't hear me at all. I put my dressing gown on over my clothes, in case I get caught in the hallway.

At midnight I peer through my curtains. Niall's car is parked under the streetlight.

I make a stealthy exit and pad in my stocking feet down the metal staircase. I don't put my shoes on until I'm at the end of the service road and then, keeping to the shadows, I run along the parade of shops, across the road and hurl myself into Niall's car.

We drive off out of the village, along to a deserted part of the tidal river. The light of the moon fans across the water as it laps its way down towards the sea, the pull of the outgoing tide leading the way.

'You okay?' asks Niall.

I shrug. 'Sort of.'

'Look, I know what it must have looked like earlier at my mam's, but I couldn't say anything in front of them.'

'Why?'

'It would have caused a big argument again. Whatever we've decided, they've decided the complete opposite. Don't think I didn't try and get my parents to see it my way, because I did. I argued and argued, but they won't budge. You know what my mam's like.'

'So, we're letting them decide our future?'

'No. No, we're not.' He pulls out a little blue book from his jacket pocket. I read the gold writing stamped across the cover. It's a savings book. Niall opens it and shows me the figure.

I look and look again.

'Is that how much you have in your account?'

Niall nods. 'Yes. It was left to me by my grandparents for when I was eighteen, to pay for university. Seven thousand euros.'

I don't know what to say. My mind is racing ahead, but I may have this all wrong. 'Why are you showing me this?'

'Oh, Erin, you are such a daft thing at times,' says Niall. He leans over and kisses me on the head. 'This is for us. We can use it for rent and food. I've looked into it all. We have enough for a deposit and a month's rent up front. I'll have to get it in my name and you will need a guarantor. I was thinking maybe Fiona would do it.'

I nod, still not quite daring to believe what he is saying.

'And...'

'I'll still go to uni, but I'll go to one nearby. You can do your college course. We'll get part-time jobs, like we said. We'll get by. I promise.'

'But, what about the termination?'

'Just go along with it all. The night before you're due to fly out to London, we'll leave. We might need to stay in bed and breakfast to start with until we get somewhere, but if we can wait as long as possible before we leave, we won't be using so much money.'

'Oh, Niall, I don't know what to say.' I put my arms around him and we cling to each other. 'I'm so happy. I thought you had changed your mind about everything. I'm sorry I doubted you.'

'Here, I almost forgot. I have something for you,' says Niall. He takes a small box from his pocket and presents it to me.

I take the lid from the box and inside is a silver Triskelion pendant. The three points are curled around into a scroll at each end. 'It's beautiful,' I say.

Niall takes it from me and fastens it around my neck. 'There are lots of variations on what the three scrolls represent,' says Niall. 'I like to think it's the symbol of family. Father. Mother. Child.' He touches each edge in turn. 'Me. You. And our child.'

'Thank you,' I say. 'I will treasure it forever.'

Chapter 13

The days seem to be rolling into one. I ponder my new, but temporary, routine as I open up the café one morning. I'm surprised at how quickly I've adapted to living in Rossway, I hadn't expected the transition to be so simple. I certainly hadn't been expecting to actually enjoy it.

And then the black cloud of reality descends. Of course, I shouldn't get used to living here. Once Dad is out of danger, I'll have to return to England and pick up my old life. Once I had been so certain London life was for me, but now the doubts are kicking in.

Since the barbecue, Bex has called in several times for a coffee and a chat, which I've really enjoyed. We even went out for a drink one evening, complete with Breeze snuggled safely in the baby sling so Bex could still breastfeed when necessary. Apparently Bex breastfed Storm up until he was two years old and fully intends to do the same with Breeze. When I relay this to Ed during a phone call, he annoys me up by uttering the words 'gross' and making a retching noise.

'God, I hope she's not going to start all that at the naming ceremony,' he complains.

'For goodness sake, Ed, you make it sound disgusting and

110

unnatural,' I say. 'Anyway, speaking of the naming ceremony, have you booked your flight?'

'Yes, all done. I won't be coming over in the interim, though.'

I'm aware my immediate reaction is one of relief. It surprises me. The disappointment is mild by comparison. 'Oh, that's a shame,' I say. 'Why's that?'

'I have a lot of work on and Ralph and Melissa have invited me over for dinner.'

'You'd sooner be with Ralph and Melissa than with me?' It irks me slightly, but I know I have no right to be put out, not least because of my initial response to Ed cancelling on me. I speak again before Ed can. 'It's fine. I'm sure you'll have a great time, anyway.'

'Mmm, thanks,' says Ed. 'It's a bit stressful at work at the moment, not helped by your absence. Look, Erin, how long do you think it will be before you're back?'

'Honest answer? I don't know,' I say. 'There's still no change with Dad. They've carried out a neurological evaluation but they said it's difficult to get an accurate understanding of what's happening in his brain. Sometimes his brain is quite responsive but other times not so much because he's sedated. They're talking about bringing him out of the induced coma. I can't come back to England yet. Mum still needs me.'

'Can't come back to England,' repeats Ed.

'That's right. Not until the doctors can give a more definite prognosis.'

'Yes, I heard that bit,' snaps Ed. 'That's not what I was referring to. You used the words *can't come back to England*. Don't you mean you *can't come home*? England is your home, Erin, not Ireland. God, how many times have you told me that?'

'Don't be so pedantic,' I say. I totally hadn't noticed my turn of phrase. 'Does it really matter?'

'It matters to me. Besides, I'm not sure how long I can keep this imposed amendment to the staff rota. Amber can't cover all your clients forever.'

'Seriously, Ed, I really could do without that sort of pressure at the moment,' I say. 'Look, I've got to go, I'm at the café and I've got customers waiting to be served. I'll speak to you later.'

'And you've got clients waiting here,' says Ed. 'To put it bluntly, I may have to start looking for a replacement for you. A permanent replacement.'

That had been yesterday and I have no more desire now than I did then to pick up the phone and call Ed. What's the point? We would only end up rowing. No, I'll wait until next weekend when he is over for the naming ceremony. We can talk face to face. It's always much better that way.

I'm not entirely sure whether Ed was serious or whether he was just having a frustrated temper tantrum. Would he really find a replacement for me? And when he said replacement, what exactly was he referring to? My job or me?

I mull this over as I take some rubbish out to the wheelie bin later that afternoon. As I close the lid to the bin, something makes me turn and look up at the rear of the two-storey doctor's surgery. I scan the windows, but the one-way glass prevents me from seeing anything other than the reflection of the shops.

I have the sensation of being watched. It makes me feel uneasy and I hurry back inside.

Roisin was standing at the upstairs window of the surgery. She often stood there in her coffee break looking out at the rear of the shops. Her eyes were automatically drawn to Seahorse Café.

Sometimes, she would get a glimpse of Erin. Today, Erin actually turned around and gazed up at the building. The one-way glass meant Roisin couldn't be seen. It gave her an amazing sense of power. She stared straight at Erin. It brought a small smile of satisfaction to Roisin's face.

It had been several weeks since Erin arrived in Rossway and Roisin had been playing the waiting game. Erin seemed to be fitting rather too well into the village again. The Wright family had certainly taken to her. If only they knew the truth, especially Kerry. Roisin was sure he wouldn't be so fascinated with her then. But first, Roisin needed to get some sort of confirmation as to what she suspected the truth about the pregnancy was. The Hurley family had a secret.

She thought of Marie at the hospital. It must be tiring to have to sit there every day watching her husband. Surely it was taking its toll on the woman. Maybe now her defences would be weak…

Roisin continued to stare at the café, long after Erin had disappeared back inside. Her fingers drummed a steady beat on the side of the coffee cup she clasped in her hands. Roisin needed to up her game.

It was mid-afternoon and Roisin had timed her visit to the hospital just right. Erin would be busy in the café and Fiona would be picking up the children from school. Marie would be alone.

Roisin came to a halt at the end of the corridor and took a moment to steel herself. She found the small four-bed ward on her right. Looking through the glass in the door, she could see Marie sitting beside Jim. She was slightly slumped forwards and her head hung down, like she had nodded off.

Roisin pushed open the door. There was a soft release of suction as it swung inwards. Her trainers squeaked on the flooring and the nurse looked up from the patient she was attending to.

Roisin gestured towards Marie and smiled. The nurse didn't challenge her and nodded before returning to her patient.

Marie must have sensed Roisin's presence as she looked up with a start. Her eyes widened and her whole body tensed.

'What are you doing here?'

'Don't look so alarmed, Marie,' said Roisin, taking the seat alongside the older woman.

'I don't know what you want, Roisin, but you're not welcome.'

'Now now, Marie. There's no need to be nasty. I've merely

come to see how Jim is.' Roisin rose slightly to take a closer look at Jim's face. The machine bleeped steadily in the background. 'He seems peaceful enough. Which is probably a good thing, for now. I don't suppose you want him to wake up just yet.'

'I've no idea what you're talking about,' said Marie.

'If he wakes up, then he might remember what happened to him. You know, he might tell someone.'

'How did you get to be so wicked?' said Marie. 'What is it you want?'

'You know exactly what I want.' Roisin sat back down on her seat. 'I want that picture and I want to know the truth about the baby.'

'I don't have the picture any more.' Marie looked straight ahead. 'I destroyed it.'

Roisin tightened her grip on her bag. She was not entirely surprised. Cross, yes, but not surprised. She had prepared for this. Marie was so predictable, really.

'That's okay, I don't need the original,' said Roisin. 'I made a copy of it.' She still had the scan she'd sent to Erin – that was only the front of the photo, it didn't show what was written on the back, but Marie didn't need to know that.

'So what are you here for? If you think you know what happened to that baby, then you will need to prove it. There's no way you can prove Erin had it.' Marie spat the words out.

It took a moment for Roisin to realise what Marie had said. It must have dawned on Marie at the exact same time. If Marie could look paler than she already did, then Roisin had just witnessed a miracle. Marie's jaw dropped open and her eyes burned with horror. Her hand flew to her mouth. She went to speak, but Roisin beat her to it.

'Thank you, Marie, you've just confirmed what I've been wondering since I found that photo.' Roisin gave a laugh. 'Erin was pregnant and had the baby.'

'Don't be so ridiculous,' said Marie quickly. She was making a valiant attempt at recovering from the horrendous faux pas she had made. 'Of course, she didn't.'

'You said there was no way I could prove Erin had the baby,' said Roisin. Her words galloped to keep pace with her thoughts. She moved to the edge of her seat. 'So, you're admitting Erin was pregnant. Not only that, you're telling me she had the baby.'

'You're fantasying now, Roisin,' said Marie, her voice rose a level. She glanced over at the nurse and then back to Roisin. 'You don't know what you're talking about.'

'Oh, I think I do,' said Roisin. 'Now, do you know what I'm going to do? I'm going to give you a few days to think about this. You and your scheming daughter. And then I want you to tell me exactly what happened to that baby. I have a right to know. My mother does. My father does. Do you understand?'

She could see Marie's hand shaking. God, she was right about this. She just didn't realise how right she had been and now she had Marie exactly where she wanted. Roisin had the power to save her mother, to give her mam something to live for. Diana could live for the future, instead of living for the past.

'And if I don't go along with you?' said Marie, breaking Roisin's thoughts.

'I might have to tell the Guards the truth about Jim's fall.'

With that, Roisin marched out of the ward.

Victory.

Chapter 14

I'm surprised to see Mum step out of a taxi that afternoon. She has taken to staying at the hospital until the evening, when she either comes back home with Fiona or decides to stay overnight with Dad.

'Hello, Mum,' I say as she walks into the café. 'Is everything okay?'

'Sure, it's grand,' says Mum. 'I was feeling a bit tired, so I thought I'd come back and have a rest. The nurse will call if there's any change.'

I study Mum. She does indeed look tired. She has a washed-out appearance and there are dark circles under her eyes.

'Go up and lie on the bed,' I say. 'Do you want me to make you a cup of tea to take up?'

'No. It's fine. I'll make myself one upstairs.'

'Okay. I'll be closing soon and I'll come up to check on you,' I say. Mum is agitated and it bothers me. Mum's not usually flustered by anything. I watch her hurry through the kitchen and out the rear of the café, towards the steps. It's then I remember there's no milk in the flat. I had used it up that morning.

Looking round the empty café, I quickly go over to the door and flick the lock. I will only be gone a minute, it won't matter.

I doubt whether I'll have any more customers now, it's nearly four o'clock.

Taking a carton of milk from the fridge, I nip out of the café and up the staircase. The door to the flat is open and Mum is standing at the kitchen sink. A small plume of smoke curls up into the air.

'Mum, what are you doing?'

Mum jumps. She steps in the doorway, preventing me from coming in.

'Nothing,' she says. 'What's that you have there? Milk? Oh, thanks.' She reaches out and takes the carton from my hand.

'What are you burning?' I peer over her shoulder. The blackened remains of some sort of card or paper lies in the sink. The flame gives one last puff and extinguishes.

Mum turns and runs the tap. 'Oh, that. Nothing,' she says. 'I couldn't get the gas to light, so I used an old piece of card.' She swishes the water around with her hand and then drags the charred remains up the stainless-steel side with the palm of her hand. Taking a piece of kitchen roll she wipes them off into the bin.

I look over at the hob. One of the burners is alight. 'Are you sure that's all it was?'

'Erin! Please,' says Mum with an unusual impatience. 'I'm tired and need a lie down and you should be in the café.'

'Okay, I'm sorry,' I say, slightly bruised from her reaction. 'I'll get back. Make sure you get some rest, won't you?'

An hour later, having closed the café up for the day, with a certain amount of trepidation I go back up to the flat. I'm still a bit confused about Mum's reaction earlier, but I've decided to put it down to the stress of Dad being in hospital. It's only natural, now I come to think about it. Mum is, in fact, doing a great job keeping it all together.

I needn't have worried. Mum is in a much better mood than

when I left her earlier. The rest has obviously done her some good. I make a light tea for us both and while Mum takes a shower, I settle down in front of the TV.

I flick through the channels, but nothing really holds my attention. The weight of trying to juggle my new-found responsibilities here in Ireland with those of work back in England, and not to mention Ed, are bearing down on me. Will he really sack me? If he does, how will that impact on our relationship? That's if you can call it a proper relationship at the moment. We've hardly seen each other and I have to admit, the physical side of things is pretty non-existent. Last time he was over, I turned him down for sex, citing it was my time of the month. It had been a lie, but I hadn't been able to bring myself to have sex with him. I'm not quite sure what made me do that. I like to think it's stress, although I suspect it might have something to do with a certain Irish mechanic.

Speaking of which, what is going on there? I know I like him. Like him a lot. But is this impairing my usual rational judgement? Is there even a point in liking him as more than just a friend if I'm skipping off back to London soon? The latter thought doesn't fill me with any cheer.

'Oh, this is so confusing,' I groan to myself, pushing a cushion to my face. 'I can't think straight any more!'

'You all right?' Mum is standing in the doorway, refreshed and relaxed from her shower. She tightens the belt on her dressing gown. 'Anything you want to talk about?'

I smile fondly up at her, not wishing to share my dilemma. 'I'm fine, thanks. A bit tired, that's all.'

Mum looks sceptical. 'You sure? You can talk to me. Don't want you bottling things up and then, you know…' She waves her hand airily.

'Scoot off?' I offer. 'Don't worry, I'm not about to hot-foot it off to London in the still of the night. It's all under control.'

Mum nods her head. 'It's nice having you back, if only for a while. I've missed you, Erin.' She turns away and heads for the kitchen.

I jump to my feet.

'Mum.' I follow her into the kitchen and put my arms around her. I hug her tightly. 'I've missed you too.'

As Mum returns the embrace, I'm aware of the shift in dynamics between us. Now, as a grown woman myself, I feel responsible for Mum, it's almost as if our roles have been reversed. I know people speak of this as their parents age and the child becomes the carer, but this isn't so much a physical need, but more of an emotional need. I won't let her down, not this time.

'Look at us daft pair,' says Mum, as she pulls away from the embrace to wipe a few stray tears from her face.

'What are we like?' I sniff through a smile. 'Look, it's still light out, I think I'll go for a quick run. Clear my head a bit. Will you be all right on your own?'

'Of course I will be. I don't think I'll go back to the hospital tonight. I could do with a decent night's sleep,' says Mum. 'Off you go now.'

I take my usual route out onto the High Street, past The Smugglers and turn left to take the outermost road of the village which leads to the church and then, looping back onto the High Street, I head for Beach Road.

It feels good to be out in the fresh air, stretching my legs and breathing in the sea air. I try not to think of anything other than my feet rhythmically pounding the tarmac and keeping my breathing steady as I listen to my iPod and shut away my troubles. I'll think about them later.

I sense him a nanosecond before he appears at my shoulder, but it still makes me jump. I stop running and pull out my earphones.

'Sorry, didn't mean to frighten you,' says Kerry smiling. Skip follows closely behind, excited at the unexpected chase.

'Where did you spring from?' I say to Kerry. I bend down to give Skip a stroke. 'Hello, boy. Your owner making you run, is he?' I stand up and begin to jog on the spot to keep my muscles warm.

'Saw you running past The Smugglers. Guessed you'd probably loop back round, so I thought I'd see if you wanted to come in for a drink.'

'What, dressed like this? All hot and sweaty?'

'Nothing wrong with that.' His grey eyes glitter with mischief.

I shake my head. He's a terrible flirt at times. 'Right, don't let me keep you from your pint,' I say. 'I need to get on. It will be dark soon. I'll see you tomorrow.'

I begin to jog away, fiddling to get my earphone in, and am surprised to see Kerry appear at my shoulder once more. I carry on jogging, slightly amused by the thought of seeing how long he can keep up for.

'I actually wanted to speak to you,' he says, falling into step beside me.

I give up with the earphones and tuck it into my bra strap 'Uh-ha. Go on, then.'

'I've been meaning to call in for the last couple of days, but I've been tied up with a private paint spraying job. Whenever I've called in to the café, you've been really busy.'

'Or you've had Joe in tow.'

'Exactly,' Kerry says as we jog side by side. 'So, what are you up to at the weekend? Got anything planned?'

I fight to stop myself smiling. Kerry is trying to sound casual, but doing a very poor job of it. 'Nothing. Why?' I say.

'Ed not coming over?'

'No. That's why I'm doing nothing.'

'Great. I mean, that's a shame.' Kerry takes a few deep breaths, his pace slows slightly. 'Shit. I'm such liar. I don't mean that's a shame at all.'

I raise my eyebrows. 'You don't?'

'Fancy spending the day with me on Sunday? We could have a ride out on the bike.'

'Your motorbike?' I say. Kerry doesn't answer me immediately. His breathing becomes deeper. 'Do you want me to stop?' I ask.

'No. Not at all,' he says. He gives a whistle to attract Skip's attention as the little dog dives into some bushes, hot on the scent of a rabbit, no doubt. 'And in answer to your question, I don't have a pushbike, if that's what you're thinking. This running lark is enough exercise for me. I've…no intention…of extending it to include a pushbike. Skip! Come on. Good boy.'

'I've never been on the back of a bike before,' I say.

'What, never?'

'Never.'

'We will have to remedy that, won't we?' he says. 'Unless you tell me Ed is a black belt in martial arts, or something like that? SAS-trained and can kill me with his little finger.'

I laugh at the thought. 'No. I think you're safe there.'

I can hear Kerry's breathing getting heavier as we continue the run. 'Are you sure you don't want me to stop?' I ask. 'I'm not saying you're a wimp or anything…'

'I told you before,' he puffs. 'I'm no wimp…but there are other ways to…prove it.'

I laugh again. He has a habit of making me laugh. I remember back to the other week when I had jogged by and he had called out of the window to me. I lengthen my stride and begin to pull away from him.

'Hey…that's not…fair.' Kerry catches up with me, again matching his step to mine. 'You're dressed…for running…I'm not.'

'Admit it, then,' I tease. 'You're no match for me.'

Kerry stops running and bending over, rests his hands on his knees, breathing hard. 'Not in these boots.'

I turn around and once again jog on the spot. 'Excuses, excuses! You've got no stamina.'

'No one's ever complained about my stamina before.'

And there, he is doing it again, making his eyes glitter mischievously. 'First time for everything.' I turn and sprint off down the road.

'Be ready first thing Sunday morning,' Kerry calls after me.

I wave my hand in acknowledgment but don't turn round. I don't want him to see the ridiculous grin that has involuntarily plastered itself over my face. Going on the back of a motorbike is something I would never normally dream of doing. Ed wouldn't approve, for a start. However, I'm beginning to suspect Kerry Wright is having a bad influence on me. And I don't mind in the slightest.

Chapter 15

My eyes fix on the black crash helmet Kerry is holding out to me. Should I do it? Do I have the nerve? Ed would disapprove. It's this thought that makes me take the crash helmet.

Shaking my hair over my shoulders, I pull the helmet down over my head. The padding, although soft and spongy, holds my face firmly in place, squeezing the sides of my cheeks against my teeth. There's a funny smell to the inside of it; musty like a charity shop, with a dash of petrol. I struggle with the woven chinstrap, not being able to see the D rings makes it difficult to fasten. I feel Kerry's hand on my wrist as he pulls me towards him and takes over, securing the strap in a matter of seconds. Then, turning the key in the ignition and thumping down on the kickstart with his foot, the vintage Triumph Bonneville erupts into life, the noise rumbles through the exhaust pipes like a purring lion awakening from its slumber. A few flicks of the wrist on the accelerator and the beast roars into life, louder, deeper, faster, now snarling. I flinch and screw my nose up at the fumes emitting from the exhaust. A hot, burning oily smell, once again mixed with a hint of petrol that I can taste as it drifts in the air.

Kerry pats the pillion seat and holds out his hand. For the briefest of moments, I hesitate. My stomach is jiggling around so much I imagine my insides must look like a snow dome that had been vigorously shaken by an over-enthusiastic child. I'm unsure if this is fear or excitement. I glance at Kerry.

'Trust me,' he calls, his voice muffled by the visor and the growl of the engine. 'You'll be okay. I promise.' His grey eyes ooze sincerity and, in that second, from just that one look, I really do believe I can trust him with my life.

Swinging my leg over the seat, I rest my feet on the pegs and shuffle closer to Kerry. Excitement zings through me as the insides of my thighs come to rest against the outsides of his and, slipping my arms around his waist, our bodies mould together.

'Do what I do,' instructs Kerry. 'If I lean, you lean with me. Any problem and you want me to stop, just tap my shoulder. Okay?'

I give the thumbs-up sign and raise my voice above the engine noise. 'Yep. That's fine.'

I'm surprised by how excited I feel and although I know Kerry is pulling away slowly, I can't help but tighten my grip on him.

Steadily, we cruise out onto Beach Road and follow the estuary up-river, then turning at the end away from the water down the High Street, we head out of the village. Hitting the open road, I hear the change in the engine noise as Kerry moves down a gear and accelerates away.

It's a totally new feeling being on the back of a motorbike. It's a beautifully warm morning and I feel cocooned in the leather jacket and gloves Kerry insisted I borrow from Bex.

The feeling of the wind rushing over me, being so close to the road as it zips underneath the bike, together with the noise of the engine rumbling and growling, roaring occasionally, gives me a real sense of freedom.

We ride up the hill towards a semi-derelict croft we used to frequent as teenagers. We often held late-night parties up there away from the adults of the village. Okay, parties might be stretching it a bit, but we took alcohol up there, sat around a camp fire, a few of them smoking, while one of the lads boomed out the music from his car stereo.

Kerry reaches back with his hand, patting my thigh.

'You want to go faster?' he shouts above the noise.

I can just about make out what he's saying and looking in the mirror on the handlebar, I nod my head. He winks back at me and then moves his hand to cover mine, pulling me tighter to him.

The speed at which we accelerate takes me by surprise and for a second, as I jerk backwards, I think I might tumble off the rear of the bike, but the momentum flicks me forwards again and my crash helmet taps the back of Kerry's. I cling on and snuggle up against his back as close as I can, dipping my head to stop the wind buffeting it backwards. It's scary but exhilarating all at the same time as I feel the adrenalin rush through me.

We reach the foot of the hill and Kerry slows the Triumph down, coming to a gentle stop. I hop off the back and nearly fall over, my legs have a jelly-like feel to them. Kerry laughs and puts out a hand to steady me.

'Here, let me do that for you.' Pulling me towards him, he fiddles with the chinstrap. I'm suddenly aware of how very close we are. His face only inches from mine. His hand brushes the underside of my jaw as he works the strap free. He pauses. When he speaks, his voice is soft. 'How was the ride?'

Aware my heart is racing and my throat dry, I somehow manage to force a response. 'Amazing.'

'That's what they all say,' he replies.

For a second I think he's going to kiss me. If I'm honest, I hope he does. However, he lets go of the straps and slides the helmet from my head. Jumping off his bike he tugs my arm. 'Come on, let's walk to the top.'

We walk up the steep grass bank that leads to the very top of the hill. The old croft has taken a beating from the coastal elements over the years. One half of the roof is completely caved in. The door and windows are boarded up now.

'What have you done with Skip today?' I ask.

'He's with Joe,' says Kerry. 'I can't exactly bring him on the bike and I don't like leaving him on his own. Storm loves him and he's got the garden to run around in.' After a few more minutes' walking, we reach the very top of the hill. 'You get a great view of the Irish Sea from here,' says Kerry, shielding his eyes from the sun.

Standing behind me, his hands rest on my shoulders. He lowers his head so his line of sight is level with mine, our faces touch. Once again I'm very aware of our closeness. It's difficult to concentrate.

Kerry is now pointing across the hill. If I lean back I will be in the crook of his shoulder. He carries on pointing out landmarks, oblivious to the intimacy of our bodies.

'Now, if you turn slightly, over that way is Cork.' Like the wind blowing a weather vane, he leans into me and turns my body. 'Over there, you can see where the estuary comes in and Half Penny Bridge. And if we turn all the way round, we have the beautiful rolling countryside.'

We stand together, silently admiring the scenery and I secretly enjoy being in such close proximity with him. We've barely been out of physical contact since I got on the bike.

'You can see for miles up here,' I say. 'It's a beautiful view. Funny how I never really appreciated it all the times I came up here as a teenager.'

'We had far more important things on our mind in those days,' says Kerry. 'Like getting drunk. Having a smoke. Making out. But you're right. It is beautiful up here. I really appreciate the view today.'

I can feel his warm breath on the side of my cheek. I have no doubt what will happen if I look at him. Even before I am fully facing him, his lips are on mine. More forceful than I expect. More demanding. And definitely more exciting.

Kerry pulls me even closer, our bodies fusing together from

126

top to bottom as his hand slips under my t-shirt, his fingers spreading wide across the bare skin of my back. Oh God, help me. I'm sure if he wants to, I'll have sex with him right here on top of the hill.

Fortunately, the need to breathe imposes a brief embargo on the kissing, breaking the tension. With that, I feel a pang of guilt surge through me. I close my eyes, willing it away.

'I think it's at this point I should be saying I'm sorry and what just happened was a mistake,' I say, looking intently at his jacket zip.

'But you're not.'

'No, I'm not, but let's pretend that never happened.' As if it was going to be that easy, I think.

Kerry seems to be weighing up the suggestion. After a moment he speaks. 'I'm not very good at pretending, but I'll give it a go if that's what you want.' His trails his fingers through a lock of my hair and exhales deeply.

I peel myself away. Despite my change in feelings about Ed, I am officially still in relationship with him. I have no intention of overlapping with Kerry, no matter how appealing the idea is.

We sit on the grass looking down the hillside. I'm pleased to be able to take off the leather jacket, even though I only have a t-shirt on underneath. Kerry lies down on the grass, propping himself up on one elbow while I sit with my knees up, resting back on my hands. I tip my head back to soak up the warm rays of sunshine.

'It's so peaceful and quiet up here.'

'I'll make a country girl out of you yet.' Kerry gives a small chuckle. He plucks a blade of grass and begins twirling it around his finger. 'This is actually one of my favourite spots. It's a great place to come if you have something on your mind and need some thinking space. You get a clarity you can't get when everyone and everything is buzzing around.'

I sit forward and wrap my arms around my knees. 'You really like the quiet life, don't you?'

'Suppose I do these days. Life hasn't always been this calm.'

I assume he's referring to life with his mum and step-dad. I want to ask but am frightened in case it opens up the way for him to ask about my past. I rest my head on my knees and exchange a smile with him.

'I imagine it must be nice to work with your cousin, seeing as you get along so well,' I say, going for the positive angle.

'Most of the time.' Kerry sits up himself now so we are side by side. He throws the blade of grass away and, resting his arms on his knees, picks at the cuticles of his fingers.

'Ew, don't do that.' I screw up my face. 'Stop picking.' I tap his hands away, but when he doesn't respond I grow concerned. 'Everything all right?'

Kerry takes out his tobacco pouch and rolls a cigarette. He draws deeply on the lighted roll-up before puffing out perfect smoke circles. At last he speaks. 'I've had my hours cut at the bike shop, well, not hours more like days. I'm on a three-day week as of tomorrow.'

'Oh no. Were you expecting that?'

Kerry nods and flicks the ash from his cigarette. 'Things have been pretty quiet for a while now and although Max is my uncle, his loyalties are to Joe, besides the fact Joe has Bex and the kids to look after.'

'Will you manage or will you have to look for another job?'

'Think I'll manage. I get the odd paint job in now and again. It pays well and I can live pretty cheaply for now.' Kerry stubs his cigarette out on the grass and flicks the end away. He gets to his feet and, picking up his jacket, he holds his hand out to me. 'Come on, let's go for a spin. You don't want to hear all my troubles.'

I'm becoming more relaxed and comfortable on the bike, feeling braver about leaning into the bends and ducking down behind Kerry's shoulder to make myself more aerodynamic. We cruise through the countryside and after an hour wind our way back towards Rossway.

As we reach the High Street, a car shoots out from a shop car park right in front of us. Kerry's reactions are fast and I instantly feel the bike lock up, the back wheel snatching and biting into the tarmac before sliding out to the left. The squeal of the tyre and blast of the horn are simultaneous.

I hear a shriek and realise it's come from me. I shut my eyes, certain we are going to collide with the car. I feel the bike swerve to the right, flip back to the left and then come to an abrupt halt and the engine cut out.

When I open my eyes, I'm relieved to see we have stopped safely at the side of the road, the silver car having sped off down the High Street, apparently ignorant of the incident.

Kerry's gloved hand pats my leg. 'You okay?'

Even though I can feel myself shaking, I don't want to make a fuss. 'I'm fine. That was close.'

Kerry mutters some expletives directed at the car driver and shakes his head. 'Right, let's get back. Hold on.'

Within a couple of minutes we are parked up on the forecourt of the bike shop. 'Fancy a coffee?' asks Kerry. Before I can answer, a toot of a car horn interrupts us and we both look up to see a silver BMW M3 pulling up into a parking bay outside the café.

'I don't feckin' believe it,' says Kerry. 'It's that prick who pulled out in front of us.'

As the driver emerges and heads our way, I groan out loud. 'Oh shit, it's Ed.'

'Don't look so worried,' says Kerry, as he hangs his crash helmet on the handle bar and begins to undo my chinstrap. 'You haven't done anything wrong.'

'In theory,' I reply.

'And in practice. *You* did nothing wrong.'

I give him a small smile of gratitude. Kerry leans back on his bike and begins to roll a cigarette.

Ed is striding over to us. The scowl on his face isn't a very promising prospect. 'Hi, Ed. This is a surprise.'

'So it would seem.' He stops in front of me, dropping a kiss on my cheek. 'What's going on?'

'Nothing. Kerry gave me a ride on his bike, that's all.'

'Humph. You never said.' Ed continues to frown.

'All right, Ed. How's it going?' Kerry draws on his cigarette. He thinks he looks disinterested, but I can tell he's pissed off, it radiates from him.

'Kerry,' acknowledges Ed, before turning his attention back to me. 'What are you doing going on the back of a motorbike anyway? Bloody dangerous things.'

'Oh, Ed, you sound so pompous, that's the sort of thing my Dad would say.' I smother a laugh. 'Anyway, look, I'm in one piece, no harm done and, besides, Kerry was very careful.'

'Those things are a one-way ticket to an early grave, if you ask me,' replies Ed, seemingly unconvinced.

Standing up, Kerry drops his cigarette and squashes it under his boot. He has a bad-tempered look on his face. 'Careless drivers are just as dangerous.' Hooking his thumbs into the belt loops of his jeans, he looks steadily at Ed. 'Especially when pulling out on a main road from a shop car park.'

I throw Kerry a look that pleads with him not to cause trouble, before turning back to Ed. 'Anyway, what are you doing here?' I ask in an overly cheerful voice.

'Thought I would surprise you.'

'Oh, well, it's a lovely surprise. I was just about to go home. Come on, let's get a coffee.' I slip the jacket from my shoulders and hand it back to Kerry. 'Thanks for taking me out today. I really enjoyed it. I'd better...you know...go now.'

'Sure. Have fun.' He takes the jacket, his fingers brushing mine. Our eyes lock. I can feel the intensity between us as I'm sure he can. Kerry folds the jacket over his arm. 'Hey, Ed, if you're about this evening and fancy a pint, we're down at The Smugglers.'

'What? Oh, right. Maybe, if we have time, this is just a flying visit,' says Ed. He pauses. 'Although, maybe I should be keeping a closer eye on Miss Hurley here, keep her out of mischief.'

I nudge Ed towards the car. I need to get away from Kerry. The guilt is swirling around me like a storm cloud. Any longer with Kerry and I'm not sure I'll keep it together.

'If I don't catch up with you later, I'll see you at the naming ceremony next week,' calls Kerry.

'Yeah, sure,' Ed responds, before muttering so only I can hear, 'We don't still have to go to that do we?'

Without even looking, I know Kerry is still standing there, his eyes following us as Ed takes my hand and heads for the café. He strides round to the service road at the back and I have to run a little to keep pace. He ascends the staircase, still holding onto me. We reach the top and he holds out his free hand.

'Key.'

'What's going on, Ed?'

'Key.' He wags his fingers impatiently. I find myself taking the key to the flat from my pocket and passing it to him.

Ed beckons me into the kitchen, closing the door behind me.

'This is what's going on,' he says. A smile plays at the corners of his mouth, then he slips his arms around my waist and draws me to him, kissing me. His kisses grow longer and his hands begin to roam over my body. I squirm free. 'Stop, Ed,' I whisper, looking furtively around in case Mum appears.

Ed smiles. 'Don't worry, your Mum's at the hospital. I phoned and spoke to her earlier when I couldn't get hold of you.' He begins kissing me again. 'I've missed you, Erin.' He cups my breast under my t-shirt and gives a small moan. 'Let's go to your bedroom.' His voice is deep and low.

For the second time, the thought of making love to Ed isn't appealing whatsoever. In fact, even referring to it as 'making love' is making me recoil, it doesn't seem right to think of it as that. It's more like just sex. Sex that I'm not the least bit interested in, especially not in Mum and Dad's home.

'Oh, Ed, I can't,' I say, pulling his hand out from under my top.

'Of course you can.' He looks surprised. 'Come on, Erin. You turned me down last time. Don't insult me again. It can't still be your period. We haven't done it for ages.'

'I didn't know we had to keep to a schedule,' I reply, trying to keep the irritation from my voice. His tactics are doing nothing but turning me off even more. If that's possible. 'What if my mum comes back?' I add lamely.

'She won't be back for ages. Come on, Erin, it will be fine.' Once again, he pulls me towards him and once again I push him away. 'Christ Almighty, Erin! What's wrong with you?' His eyes narrow and his lip curls as anger sweeps his face. 'What's going on? Is it that hillbilly?'

'Who?' I do, of course, know exactly who Ed means.

'Who?' scoffs Ed. 'Kerry, the hippy biker, of course.'

'Don't be so ridiculous, Ed. It's nothing to do with Kerry at all. Trust you to jump to conclusions.'

'What is it, then? You've got to admit, from where I'm standing it all looks a bit suspicious.'

'I'm not in the mood, that's all,' I say. 'I'm tired. I've been working long hours.'

'Didn't stop you going out on the bike with him, though, did it?'

'I am allowed some time off,' I say, disentangling myself completely from his grip. 'You've been to Ralph and Melissa's, and I don't suppose that's the only thing you've done in your free time.' I know full well Ed has a wide circle of friends and as long as I've known him he's never been short of an invite to go somewhere with someone.

'That's different,' says Ed.

'How is it?'

'I've been out with my friends.'

'Likewise.' I sigh at our argument. 'Look, why don't I make us a coffee?'

'If you like.'

I make the coffee in silence as Ed sulks and then carry the two cups through to the living room. Ed sits down on the sofa and I feel obliged to sit next to him. 'So what do I owe the pleasure of this visit?' I ask, aware there is little gratitude in my voice.

'Spur-of-the-moment decision,' says Ed. He leans forward, his arms resting on his legs. 'Actually, that's not quite true. There is a reason.'

'Which is?'

'I need to know when you're coming back to work.'

'In all honestly, I don't know,' I say. 'Dad's not recovering as quickly as they had hoped. They put off waking him but he is breathing on his own now, which is a good sign. They are having another meeting about it next week to decide on the way forward. I can't possibly come back until I know a more certain prognosis.' I sip my coffee. My life in London seems a million miles away, whereas my life here in Rossway, working in the café, seems more like the norm. 'And even then, I might have to stay to help Mum.'

'Anyone would think you like being here.'

'It's not as bad as I thought, to be honest.'

Ed gives me an old-fashioned look. 'Are you serious? You are, aren't you? For God's sake, Erin.' He picks up the teaspoon and taps the palm of his hand with it. 'I need to have a firm date for when you're coming back to work.'

'I wish I could give you it.'

'You can't expect me to treat you any differently to the other girls.' Ed has a slightly belligerent tone to his voice and then more softly. 'I've barely seen you for weeks, let alone had any real close contact.'

I roll my eyes. 'We're back to that again, are we?'

'It's only natural.' He puts the spoon down and turns on the sofa to face me. 'I don't want to argue and I don't want to put you under any more pressure, but I have no choice.' He takes my hand. 'If you're not back at work in two weeks, I'll have to let you go.'

'Let me go? What do you mean? Finish with me?'

'That's up to you,' says Ed. 'What's the point staying together if you're living on the opposite side of the Irish Sea to me?

'When do you need to know?' I ask, whilst acknowledging I'm not as heartbroken at the prospect as perhaps I should be.

'I'll be over next weekend for the naming ceremony, you know, the one I absolutely can't wait to attend,' he says, making his fingers into the barrel of a gun and pretending the shoot himself in the temple. Then, looking seriously at me, 'You can let me know what your decision is then.'

Chapter 16

'Say bye to everyone,' said Kerry, standing at the door of Apple Tree Cottage.

'Bye Mammy. Bye Daddy. Bye-bye baby Breeze,' said Storm, waving solemnly in turn at each of them.

'Now you be good for Kerry,' said Joe. 'And be nice to those Keane girls too, I don't want Sean Keane coming round here after me. He might put your daddy in jail.'

'And that will be a blessing to us all,' said Bex.

'Ah sure, you'd miss me, so you would,' said Joe.

'What, your smelly socks lying around, t-shirts covered in grease and oil, your snoring,' said Bex. 'Yeah, sure, I'd miss those, all right.'

'Well, you're the child's mother,' retorted Joe, winking at Kerry. 'If he does anything wrong, that's down to you, I'd say. You're the one at home with him all day.'

'Jody Wright, you're walking a fine line,' said Bex.

Kerry grinned at the easy banter between husband and wife. 'We promise to be on our best behaviour, don't we, Storm? You'll be nice to Sophie and Molly and I'll be nice to Erin.'

'Yeah and that's what I'm worried about,' said Joe. He gave Kerry a punch on the arm. 'You and Erin playing happy families.

135

Although, I like your thinking, the two of you. Taking out the little ones. It's a trial run, so it is. To see how you like it.'

'Leave them alone, Joe,' called Bex. 'Now come back in here, your daughter wants her nappy changing.'

Kerry left his cousin to it. He loved the relationship Joe and Bex had and he hoped that one day he'd find someone he was as comfortable with. Someone he'd like to have a family with. Despite his own fractured relationship with his mother, the thought of his own family one day warmed him. If he had learned anything from his mother, it was how not to mother. He would love his own children forever, unconditionally. He had absolutely no doubt about that. He would never treat his children the way he had been treated by his mother. He used the term loosely. Being pregnant and giving birth might give a woman the right to be called a mother, but there was far more to it than that.

He cursed to himself. He could feel his mood beginning to drop. Just thinking about his mother could do that to him. He made a conscious effort to put all thoughts of the woman out of his mind. He didn't want it to darken the day. He was looking forward to spending some time with Erin.

Kerry walked up Corkscrew Lane, heading towards the new estate where Fiona and Sean Keane lived and where he was meeting Erin. It had been a spontaneous idea to invite Erin and all the kids out for the afternoon, after he'd called into the café that morning and caught her looking through a small pocket photo album. She had shoved it in her pocket when she saw him approaching the counter.

'What you got there?' said Kerry.

'Nothing,' she said and then when Kerry had raised his eyebrows, she had taken it out again. 'It's just a small album with pictures of Sophie and Molly. Fiona sends me photos and regular updates.'

'Do you miss your family being so far away?'

At first Kerry thought she was going to tell him to mind his own business, but she must have changed her mind. 'Yes. Yes, I do miss them,' she said. 'Very much. When I see you with Storm and Breeze, it makes me wish I could take the girls out and do normal things with them.'

'And what's stopping you?'

'I'm not here very much, am I?'

'But you are now,' said Kerry. 'Why don't we have, what is it they call it these days, a play date? You bring the girls out and I'll bring Storm. We can go down the beach or to the woods. Take a picnic. You know, the sort of thing you do with kids. What do you say?'

A smile spread across her face. 'I say I'd like that very much.'

And so they had arranged this play date. Although Kerry had to admit, he was probably looking forward to it far more than Storm was. He wondered what Erin felt about it. He had definitely sensed something between them the other day after the bike ride and back at the barbecue, when she had come out of the bathroom. Not only had she had to put up with Dick-Ed, but Roisin had been spoiling for a fight too. Kerry sensed there was history between Roisin and Erin, history that he was unaware of. He knew that Erin had dated Roisin's brother, but there was something else he was, as yet, unaware of.

They soon reached the new estate where Fiona lived. Any doubts that Erin wasn't looking forward to it were dispelled as soon as he turned into their road. Erin and the girls were waiting in the front garden for him. Erin was sitting on the doorstep but jumped up and waved at him. Her smile lifted his heart.

Erin gathered the girls up and met him halfway up the road.

'Hey, there,' she said. She was carrying a small rucksack. 'I've got us a few snacks. It's not a huge picnic but it will do us fine.'

'What? No hamper today with Champagne and vol-au-vents?' He put his hands on his hips and gave her his best old-fashioned look.

'Oh, don't,' said Erin, rolling her eyes. 'That's so embarrassing.

Look, let's make a deal. No talk about the barbecue or Ed.' She held out her hand.

Kerry shook it. 'Deal.'

'Okay, girls, hold my hand. One each side,' said Erin. 'Storm, you keep hold of Kerry's hand. Make sure he doesn't wander off into the road.'

They made their way to a sheltered part of the beach. It wasn't quite a cove, but the hollow in the coastline gave shelter from the sea breeze, which could be fierce at times.

Erin spread a blanket out on the sand and took out the snacks from the rucksack. The beach bag contained the buckets and spades.

'Has Storm got sun cream on?' said Erin, making sure Molly's sun hat was securely in place on the little girl's head.

'Yep. Bex said she'd already done it.' Kerry slipped off his trainers and stood up to undo his trousers. 'Who wants to go for a paddle?'

'I hope you've got something on under there,' said Erin as she kicked off her flip-flops.

'It's okay, you're safe,' said Kerry. 'I've my shorts on. What about yourself? You got your bikini on under that dress?'

'You must be joking, this is the Irish coast, not the Bahamas. I'll just be paddling, thanks.'

The party of five made their way down to the water's edge. The children rather more brave in their t-shirts and shorts, running on ahead and wading straight in.

'Don't go too deep,' said Erin. 'No further than your ankles.'

Kerry watched on as Erin held onto Molly and Storm's hands and jumped the incoming waves with them. The little ones were loving it. Sophie, although that bit older at ten, was having just as much fun splashing about alongside them.

'Come on, Kerry,' said Erin. 'You've not gone all chicken on us, have you?' She turned and kicked some water in his direction, only to get some sent back her way.

'You're lucky you have the little ones with you, or you'd be in trouble,' he said, coming to stand next to them. He held Storm's other hand and they jumped the waves together, laughing when Kerry mistimed it and sent a huge splash of water over them.

It was nice seeing Erin laughing and so relaxed after the last time they had been together.

Later, sitting on the blanket, eating their picnic, Kerry found himself watching Erin as she sorted the children out, making sure they all had something to eat, that their hands were clean from sand, reapplying sun cream and generally making sure they were all catered for.

She caught him watching her a couple of times and he looked away, making out he was admiring the beach. On the third time, he didn't look away.

She grinned at him, a small moment of self-consciousness settled on her face. 'What?' she said.

'What?' said Kerry innocently.

'You know what. You keep looking at me.' She sat back next to him. 'You're going to tell me I've got sand on my face or cake or something, aren't you?'

'No, I wasn't, actually,' said Kerry, rolling onto his front. 'I was thinking how relaxed you looked. You're a natural with the children.'

'Hmm, maybe,' she said, her smile dropping from her face. She looked out at the horizon and let out a small sigh.

'You okay?' said Kerry.

The smile returned. 'Of course I am,' she said, lying down next to him on her back. 'Anyway, you're pretty good with the kids yourself. And I have to admit, Joe is too.'

'You sound surprised.'

'I guess I saw him in a different light at the barbecue. More Joe the husband and dad, rather than Joe the boy who teased me relentlessly when we were kids.'

'He's all right, is Joe. Just likes a laugh, that's all. He's like his mum, Louise.'

'I remember Louise.' said Erin. 'She always seemed good fun. I remember at Shane's eighteenth birthday party, her and Max were giving it some on the dance floor.'

'That sounds about right.'

'Was your mum there that night?' said Erin. 'I mean, Shane's her nephew, so presumably she came.'

Kerry sat up. 'No. She didn't go.'

'Sorry, I didn't mean to pry. Ignore me.' Her voice was tender.

Kerry gave her a small smile. 'You're not being nosey. It's just, I didn't get on well with my mum when I was a teenager.'

'And now?'

'We haven't spoken for years. I can't see us ever patching things up.'

Erin slipped her hand into his. 'Is it really that bad?'

'You know you didn't want to talk about Ed and the barbecue…?' He left the rest of the sentence unsaid. He lifted her hand and kissed it. There were lots of things Erin didn't want to talk about. She'd understand.

She held his gaze. Her soft-green eyes looked intently into his, as if she could read not only his thoughts but his soul too.

Kerry moved his head closer to hers. For a moment he thought she was going to kiss him, but instead she rested her forehead against his. A feeling of mutual understanding passed between them.

Erin pulled away first. 'Sandcastle competition anyone?' She turned to the children. 'Boys against girls?'

This was met by a resounding and excitable yes from the children.

Kerry took a moment to watch her organise everyone. There was something special about Erin Hurley. There was just one fly in the ointment. Dick-Ed. Still, there was time to work on that.

The afternoon went far too quickly and, before he knew it, Erin was looking at her watch, saying it was time to get them all back.

'They should sleep well tonight after all this fresh air,' said Erin, as they gathered up their belongings. 'Storm looks like he's about to zonk out right now.'

They rounded the children up and tramped their way back up to the road, then ambled along, no one in any rush to get back.

'The kids have had a great afternoon,' said Kerry. 'And so have I.'

'Me too,' said Erin. They exchanged a smile.

A car pulled up alongside them. 'Ah, would you look at you two playing happy families!' came the unmistakable voice. Kerry knew who it was before he even looked round.

'Hello, Roisin,' he said, and then muttered to Erin. 'Keep walking.'

Roisin cruised alongside the kerb. 'Been out to the beach, have you?'

'Clearly,' said Erin, as she held up the bag with the bucket and spades poking out.

Roisin pulled a face. 'Only asking. You're a bit tetchy, aren't you, Erin. I noticed your man's not about. Gone off back to London, has he?'

'Did you want anything in particular?' said Erin.

'What do you think?' said Roisin. 'I'll give you a call.'

With that Roisin sped off down Beach Road and out of sight.

'What was all that about?' said Kerry.

'You don't want to know.'

'As it happens, I do.'

'Let's not spoil the afternoon,' said Erin.

By the time they reached Fiona's house, Erin seemed to have relaxed.

'There you go, lovely lady,' said Kerry. 'Delivered safely to your door.'

'Thank you for this afternoon,' said Erin. 'I really enjoyed it.'

'We'll have to do it again sometime.' Kerry couldn't deny the disappointment that was creeping up on him. The afternoon had come to an end far too quickly. 'Do you fancy a drink this evening at The Smugglers?'

'Oh, I...I...' She shifted uncomfortably on her feet, not meeting his eyes.

'It's okay. Sorry. I shouldn't have asked,' said Kerry quickly, wishing he could kick himself right there and then for pushing his luck.

'It's not that,' said Erin quickly. 'I'm going up to the hospital to see my dad. I promised Mum.'

'Okay. Well, give my regards to your mum,' said Kerry. 'I'll catch you later. Come on, Storm. Let's get you home.' He paused. 'So would you have said yes? To the drink, if you weren't busy?'

Erin walked over to him and, rather unexpectedly, rose on her tiptoes and gave him a quick kiss on the cheek. 'Well, that would be telling,' she said. 'You'll have to ask me again another time.'

This time it was her turn to wink and walk away without turning.

Kerry knew he was going to have a hard time getting rid of the grin that had spread across his face.

Chapter 17

Breeze's naming ceremony couldn't come around quick enough for Kerry. He had made a point of not going over to the café. He felt Erin needed some space and he wasn't quite sure what the situation was with Ed. As Joe had pointed out to him, he would find out soon enough. He didn't want to add to the pressure she was already under, what with her dad and having to work at the café. He wanted to be there for her when it got too much, as he was sure it would sooner or later. He wanted her to run to him, not from him.

Now everyone was standing in Joe and Bex's back garden next to the olive tree they had planted for Storm's naming ceremony three years earlier. The proud parents had just pledged themselves to bringing up Breeze in a safe and happy family, where the natural beauties and all living forms of the world would be respected. Where love would always be in their hearts, warmth in their souls and protection in their arms.

Joe stepped forward and, with the help of Kerry, they manoeuvred a new olive tree into place and shovelled in the earth around the roots. Once they had trampled the soil back down, Bex tied a pink ribbon around the trunk and hung a wooden heart with the name 'Breeze' painted on it. This matched the blue ribbon and now rather weather-beaten heart with the name 'Storm' tied around the other tree.

'For my beautiful Breeze,' smiled Bex, stroking the bark before kissing her daughter on the head.

'Beautiful Breeze,' echoed the Wright family, which was then repeated somewhat randomly by the other guests.

Kerry glanced around and caught Ed rolling his eyes towards another couple standing with Erin who Kerry didn't recognise. Erin looked lovely as the sun bounced off her red hair. She had it tied up in some sort of bun at the nape of her neck. A few strands of curls hung loosely around the side of her face. She was wearing a pale-pink floating dress, which reached just below her knees, with a cream-coloured wrap across her shoulders. Her casual look was at odds with the rather starchy look of Ed and his companions. They looked like they were attending a sailing regatta with their navy blazers and cream chinos, while the woman was done up like a dog's dinner. Skip whimpered beside him, as if agreeing with his master's thoughts. Kerry bent down and ruffled the dog's head.

'Yes, you look dashing too, so you do,' he said, adjusting the blue bandanna tied around Skip's neck.

He looked back at Erin and she met his gaze. He wondered if she would look away. Did she regret going out with him last week? She smiled at him. It warmed his heart. That was definitely a no-regrets smile.

Then, as casually as the naming ceremony had begun, it was over. The guests began milling about, chatting, while Joe went off to crack open some beers and tend the barbecue. Kerry wandered over to Erin and her group.

'Hi, Kerry,' smiled Erin, as he approached. 'That was a lovely ceremony.'

'If you like that sort of thing,' Ed muttered to the couple standing with them. Kerry ignored the snigger the other man tried to suppress, while the woman pressed her lips together to try to hide her smirk.

'Good job we're not all the same,' Kerry couldn't help responding.

He noticed the uncomfortable look on Erin's face. Jesus, for the life of him, Kerry didn't know what she saw in Ed. She was talking now, introducing the other couple. 'This is Ralph, he's an old friend of Ed's, and his girlfriend, Melissa.'

Kerry nodded briefly. 'Can I get anyone a drink?'

'We've got some champagne in the car, actually,' said Ed. He patted his trouser pocket and then pulled out the car keys.

'Champagne?' replied Kerry, irritated by Ed's aloof manner. 'We're quite happy with the beer and homemade wine.'

'I'll have a white wine, please, Kerry.' Erin smiled at him, although it was somewhat strained.

'No, Erin. Have some champagne. Ralph and I brought some especially.' Ed jangled the keys. 'I'll go and get it.'

'Really, Ed. I'm fine.' Erin turned to Kerry. 'I'll still have that glass of wine, if that's okay?'

'Sure.' Kerry looked at Ralph and Melissa. 'What about you two? Are you waiting for the champagne or can I get you something?'

Ralph spoke first. 'I'll wait, thanks. Shame for it to go to waste. In fact, I'll give Ed a hand.'

'I'll wait too,' replied Melissa. 'I'll nip to the loo. Back in a minute.'

Kerry watched Melissa tiptoe across the lawn to avoid her heels digging into the soft ground. He looked down at Erin's flat shoes. 'You're learning.'

She gave a small, wry smile. 'Just for the record, I didn't know Ralph and Melissa were coming.'

Kerry shrugged. 'Are they the cavalry? Back-up?' He rested his hand between her shoulder blades and guided her towards the gazebo, which was a permanent fixture in Joe's garden, whatever the weather. The drinks were stashed on a trestle table, which had been painted random colours and patterns by Bex and Storm.

Kerry poured Erin a glass of homemade elderflower wine. 'Here, tell me what you think of Joe's home brew?'

He watched as she took a sip and then blinked a couple of times, probably surprised by the strength of it, before she took another taste.

'It's strong but very nice,' she said.

'A bit like us Wrights,' he teased, moving to stand closer to her than was necessary.

'Something like that.'

The bottle in his hand was the only thing keeping their bodies apart. 'Do you want a proper taste now?'

Erin looked down at the bottle and then up at Kerry. She smiled. 'I think that might be dangerous.'

Kerry, not to be outdone, replied without hesitation, 'But it might also be fun.'

She let out a small sigh of resignation. 'I guess I'll have to take your word for that.'

It was Kerry's turn to sigh now. He glanced down at the bottle, his hand wrapped around the base, so close to her waist. He uncurled a finger and with the lightest of touches, traced the waistline of her dress. He thought he heard her take in a small breath as he ran his finger back again. 'Seems to me there's something coming between us.'

Erin looked over his shoulder towards the house. 'In more ways than one,' she said. 'Here comes Ed.'

The party drifted through the afternoon. A very relaxed affair, although Kerry found himself becoming increasingly distracted from conversations as his eyes, time and time again, sought out Erin.

Ed seemed to be keeping a tight rein on her today. A proprietorial arm over her shoulder or round her waist. Kerry was aware of the little feeling of irritation that crept through him at this sight.

'So, Erin, when are you coming back to civilisation?' Ralph asks as he gulps the last of the champagne from his glass. 'Or have you defected?'

I feel myself bristle slightly at the scornful tone in Ralph's voice. Before I can answer though, Ed speaks.

'Oh God, don't start on that for fuck's sake,' he groans. 'Bit of a moot point.'

If I was bristling before, I feel positively spiky now. 'It's not that.' I look to Ralph. 'My dad is still in a serious condition.'

'Yes, well, time is running out.' Ed's clipped voice has a note of danger in it. 'We need to have that discussion.'

'It's not as simple as that, but can we save the discussion until later?'

'Frightened your country-bumpkin friends will ostracise you if they think you're leaving them? Maybe they'll cast some ancient pagan spell over you.' Ed laughs at his own pathetic joke. Encouraged by Ralph and Melissa laughing along, he continues, 'They might even put you on a ducking stool in the local village pond.'

'Don't worry, Erin, we'll come and rescue you.' Ralph sniggers. 'Headline news. Beautician rescued in a daring night raid from sleepy Irish village cult.'

'You're not actually funny,' I snap. 'In fact, you're bloody insulting.'

'Oh, lighten up,' says Melissa. 'The boys are only joking. You've got to admit, this is like something from one of those Hollywood movies, you know, where they live in some backwater town and all marry their cousins.'

'Er…excuse me, I wasn't joking,' chips in Ed, the smile now nowhere to be seen. 'Bloody new-age pagan hippies. They've certainly got Erin brainwashed.'

'Just stop it now.' I try to keep my voice to a hiss. I look round the garden, conscious we can probably be heard. Shit. Kerry's watching, although hopefully he can't hear what we're saying.

*

147

'I don't know what's happened to you since you got here,' huffs Ed. 'I mean, a few weeks ago you hated this place. After all, you did leave it as soon as you could. What exactly drove you away? You know, you've never told me?'

The pain of the memory sticks like a thorn in my throat. I can't answer. I can feel the tears stinging the back of my eyes. I need to escape.

Blindly, I head towards the cottage, trying to keep a dignified and composed walk, but the need to escape Ed drives my feet faster than I want. As I approach the cottage, I realise it will be full of people and I will only have the bathroom in which to hide. I detour round the sandpit and pass the other side of the gazebo. Lifting the latch on the gate to the vegetable garden, I hurry through.

The laurel bush that shields this part from the main garden is high enough to hide behind if I sit on the ground. Finally, I let the tears fall, but only a few before the anger rises to the surface, quelling them. How dare they laugh at Kerry and my friends? Ed and Ralph know nothing about the Wrights. Melissa is just as bad. Then for Ed to bring up why I left Rossway is the final straw.

The click of the latch on the gate as it closes makes me look up. It's Kerry. Furtively I wipe my face clear of any tears. Without saying anything, he comes and sits down beside me, a bottle of homemade wine in one hand and two plastic beakers in the other. He pulls out the cork with his teeth and puffs it onto the grass before pouring the pale-gold liquid into the cups.

The silence remains as he hands me a cup, which I accept and take a large gulp. The first mouthful catches in the back of my throat but the second slides down a lot easier.

'So, what's up? Ed living up to his name?'

I give Kerry a sideways look. 'Which is?'

'Dick-Ed. I can't claim the credit for coming up with that one, but it kind of fits.'

'I don't suppose I need to ask whose idea it was.' I take another gulp of wine. No doubt it was Joe's idea. I ought to feel offended by the nickname, but somehow I can't quite summon up that emotion.

Kerry tops up my glass. 'What are you doing with Ed? You know you'd be much happier with me.' He grins and gives my shoulder a squeeze. I like the feel of his arm around me and am in no hurry to shrug it off.

I give a wry smile back. 'You are funny.'

'Hmm, that wasn't quite the impression I was going for.'

An easy silence falls between us as I close my eyes and lean my head on Kerry's shoulder, soaking up the warm summer rays. The music and chattering coming from the other side of the hedge, together with the effects of the alcohol and sunshine, make me feel decidedly relaxed again. I push thoughts of Ed, Ralph and Melissa from my mind.

For a moment I wonder if I'm dreaming and haven't managed to clear my mind after all. The low voices of Ralph and Melissa drift over the hedge.

'You're looking very sexy today.' It's Ralph.

I sit up and exchange a look with Kerry, who puts his finger to his mouth, giving a wink as he does so.

Melissa's giggle is followed by some murmurs, which I can only guess is the two of them kissing. I pull a face at Kerry.

'Stop it, Ralph,' comes Melissa's giggling voice.

'Can't wait to get you back to the hotel room,' replies Ralph. 'Thank God we're not staying at the flat with Erin. We'd end up sharing a room with old Ed.'

'Sharing a room with Ed?'

'Yes, didn't you know? Erin won't let him share a bed with her at her parents' place.' The sneer in Ralph's voice is obvious. 'How bloody old-fashioned is that?'

'Ooh, I bet Ed's not happy.'

'No-fucking-way is he.'

I can feel the anger bubbling inside me. Ralph taking the mickey. It's none of his business. Kerry's hand holds firm on my shoulder, preventing me from moving. He slowly shakes his head.

'I don't know what he sees in her, if I'm honest.' Melissa is talking again. 'I mean, she's nice enough on the surface, but there's something about her I can't quite put my finger on.'

'Yeah, I know what you mean. We've all known her for about two or three years and, yet, we don't know her at all.' Ralph's voice is clearer now, as if he's forgotten they're supposed to be whispering.

'They say the quiet ones are the ones to watch. There's definitely something she's keeping a secret. I wonder if Ed knows what it is.'

'If he does, he hasn't said anything to me,' says Ralph. 'If I'm honest, I don't think the two of them will last much longer. She was his little project.'

'Project?'

'You know the film *My Fair Lady*? Eliza Doolittle. That's what Erin's like.' Ralph sniggers. 'Ed's project was to see if he could re-educate her. Turn her into a more sophisticated, classy sort of woman.'

Melissa lets out a laugh. 'Oh, that sounds awful, but I can quite see what you mean. Trouble is, it's all obviously an act for Erin. She can't keep the sophisticated thing up. As soon as she's back home, she's gone all Mother Earth. Well, as far as you can without doing the mother bit.'

'Speaking of which, wonder where she went?'

'Come on, let's see if Ed wants to leave yet. This is sooo fucking boring. My heels keep sinking into the grass and if I have to hear another word about motorbikes or babies with ridiculous names, I swear I'll scream. Take me back to civilisation, Ralph, please, I'm begging you.'

Melissa's voice trails off, indicating she's already walking away.

'You don't need to ask me twice,' Ralph calls back.

Then there's silence.

I don't want to look at Kerry. Humiliated doesn't even begin to cover it.

'Why do you stay with him?' asks Kerry again.

'That's a bit of a direct question.'

'I like direct. Everyone knows where they stand.'

'Direct can be confrontational,' I say, trying to steer the conversation away from his original question.

'It depends if the other person doesn't like what they're hearing or are in denial,' he says. There's no challenge to his tone, just matter of fact. Still it prickles me.

'Is that a jibe at me?'

'No jibe, merely an observation.'

'I'd like you to keep your observations to yourself.' I try my best to keep my tone even. 'Pour more wine instead.'

Kerry obliges, without taking his arm from me. He puts the bottle back down before speaking again.

'I wish I knew what was going on in that head of yours.'

'Trust me, you don't.' I take a large sip of the wine.

'You really think I'll be shocked by something you've done? Any secrets are safe with me.'

'Really? Is that because you have secrets of your own?'

'Fighting talk, eh? Don't usually get to keep anything secret around here. Most locals know about me. I'm not news any more. I'm not ashamed or embarrassed.'

I sit up and study him for a moment. His grey eyes have a blue tint to them, reflecting the cloudless sky above.

'But you do have secrets. I can tell. You have that look about you,' I say with a soft voice. There are things about Kerry Wright I don't know, things nobody else in the village knows. Things he's most definitely keeping a secret – and they hurt. They are buried deep, but they are still painful. It's his understanding that convinces me. He seems to know what I'm feeling. He empathises with me because he's felt the pain too.

His gaze continues for what seems like ages. I don't look away. I can hear the distant chatter of the guests, the sound of *Guns N' Roses* playing out 'Sweet Child of Mine'. Despite the rock music, the backdrop of bird song and leaves rustling in the gentle summer breeze, everything seems to be at one with each other. That includes me and Kerry. I sense some sort of invisible bond pulling our souls together.

His fingertips rest on the side of my face. 'You know what, Erin, me and you, we've got a lot in common.' He dips in for a brief kiss, before standing up and taking my hands in his, hauling me to my feet. 'Go out there with your head held high. You're better than them.'

Chapter 18

Sitting at the dining table in my parents' flat, I know the conversation I'm about to have with Ed is going to be difficult. I barely slept at all last night. Thoughts were tossed around in my head continuously, until they had eventually merged into a kaleidoscope of ever-changing suggestions and solutions, where I could no longer distinguish one from the other.

Finally, I had drifted off into a sleep, plagued by images of Ed standing next to Jody Wright, laughing at the colour of my hair, and then for me to be whisked away in a little blue hatchback, like the one Niall used to drive, except this time it was Kerry at the wheel but with Diana and Roisin Marshall in the back. All very bizarre, I conclude, as I sip my tea.

'You're up early,' says Mum, standing in the doorway. 'Ed asleep, is he?'

'As far as I know. I haven't seen him this morning.' I change the subject. 'You haven't remembered where the keys for the safe are yet, have you, Mum?'

'I wish everyone would stop asking me about the keys. Sean was on about them the other day. Had I found them? The Guards wanted to know whether to rule out an accident or not. Honestly, I don't really care right now.'

'Sorry. I didn't mean to upset you.'

'No, I'm sorry. I shouldn't have got all cross like that. Now, are you coming to the hospital today?' Although Mum fields this as a question, I know it's a request, bordering on an instruction. I haven't been to see Dad for several days now and I'm aware it pains her.

'Yes, I'll come up this morning,' I say. 'I'll ask Fiona to mind the café. She did actually mention it herself yesterday.'

'I know it's difficult for you,' says Mum, 'but he is still your father and he is critically injured. You should be there.'

'I know.' I feel ashamed my own feelings are so transparent. It hurts her, which, by default, means it hurts me. 'Sorry. It's just...'

My voice tails off. Now isn't the time for this. I'm already facing a difficult talk with Ed; I really don't need to get into another with Mum. When things are a bit more stable and not in such a state of flux, maybe then I can have the conversation that we have both been putting off for the past ten years. It's waited this long, it can wait some more.

As if sensing my reluctance, Mum changes the subject. 'Is Ed heading back home this morning?'

'Yes, I'll wake him up in a moment. He needs to get back because of work.'

'How are things between the two of you?'

'Fine.' It's an automatic response, a bit like when someone asks how you are and really, you could be on your last legs but you still say you're fine.

'It's your mother you're speaking to now,' says Mum, clearly understanding that fine doesn't always mean fine.

Mum is quiet and unassuming, yet underneath that gentle exterior is a perceptive, intuitive and steely woman.

'Not great.'

'I didn't think so.' Mum takes a sip of her tea before speaking again. 'Is it salvageable?'

'Probably, but I don't know if I want to launch a rescue mission.'

'If you don't know, then I suspect you do know, deep down inside,' she says. 'Sometimes you have to take a deep breath and be brave. Now, I must get on. Sean is picking me up soon.'

Ed looks at me as if I've taken leave of my senses. I can see him visibly compute what I've said, only to then disbelieve it.

'You want to finish with me?' The incredulous tone serves to back up my appraisal. 'This really is your choice? When I said you had to make a choice, I didn't really think you would choose *here*.' He emphasises the last word.

I nod before I speak in an attempt to soften my words. 'I think we both know it's the right thing to do. Neither of us has to pretend we are "the one" for each other any more.'

'It's those bloody tree-huggers, isn't it? They've brainwashed you.' Ed stands and paces to the living-room window and back again. 'Many a true word said in jest and all that.'

I can see he's making a visible effort to compose himself. I want to make this as easy as possible for both of us. I suspect it's his pride that hurts more than his heart.

'It's for the best. I'm going to be here for a while, helping Mum, and when Dad recovers they are both going to need support. Mum can't do everything on her own.'

'So you're going to defect over to this backwater for good? Is this what you really want?'

'Mum needs me.'

'You didn't answer my question. I said, is this what you really want?'

'It's a temporary thing.'

'Bah! I can't believe you want to give everything up: London, your flat, your job, your lifestyle…me…for this.' He gestures around the room with his hand. 'Your old bedroom, working in a café and a load of hillbillies.'

'They are NOT hillbillies.'

'As good as,' says Ed. 'I always thought you hated this life, here. That you never wanted to come back to it.'

'Things change. People change.' I'm conscious that I'm echoing exactly what Fiona has said to me. It seems there is some truth in it after all.

'Don't say I haven't tried to talk you out of it,' says Ed. 'After all I've done for you and this is how you repay me. You're like some sort of leech. I hope you'll be happy now in this shit-hole because you won't get another chance like mine again to get you out of it.'

He slams the door and I can hear his footsteps stamp angrily down the hallway. The bedroom door reverberates throughout the flat as he throws it closed behind him.

I sit still, analysing my feelings. I'm not sad. It surprises me. In fact, I'm already beginning to feel like the weight on my shoulders – to always live up to his expectations – is lighter. It's the right decision.

Five minutes later I'm standing at the window watching Ed jump into his hired BMW and rev the engine excessively before tearing off down the road. His farewell had been terse and business-like. He would post my P45 out, check his flat for any of my belongings and take them round to the house I share. And just in case I thought about changing my mind – tough, because Ed didn't do second chances.

Chapter 19

Teenage Kicks
Leaving day

I jump in the car, the engine is running and Niall pulls away before I've even shut the door properly.

'We've done it,' I say, stuffing my bag deep into the foot well.

'Wahoo!' yells Niall. He punches the air, the car takes a little swerve, which makes me grab onto the side of the seat. Niall rights the car and we speed off through the main street of the village.

'Why are we going this way?' I ask, looking across at Niall. I'm not sure I like the look on his face. He is grinning wildly. 'We're supposed to be making a secret escape.'

Niall throws his head back and laughs. 'Just a little detour. Besides, I don't give a feck about this lot. Small-minded villagers. They can kiss my arse.'

He takes one hand off the wheel and reaches over to the stereo, cranking up the volume. Drum 'n' bass music blares out. Normally, I'd enjoy this but there is something about Niall that is making me nervous.

I turn the volume down and glance over at the speedo.

'What are you doing?' He attempts to reach over again and I

push his hand away. 'Stop it. It's too loud and you're driving too fast.'

We near the end of the road and at the last minute Niall applies the brakes, yanks the steering wheel to the right and the car throws itself around the corner. I'm flung into the side of the door.

'For God's sake! Slow down!' I'm shouting at him. He's scaring the life out of me. I've never seen him like this before. His pupils are dilated and he's throwing his head back, laughing. 'Niall,' I plead with him. 'Please slow down. What's wrong with you?' I hit his arm to make him listen to me. I can feel myself on the verge of tears. He's really scaring me now.

Suddenly he slams on the brakes. We are just outside the village boundary now.

Throwing open the driver's door he leans out and is sick all over the road. He releases his seat belt and stumbles out of the car across to the grass verge, where he vomits some more. I get out and rush around the car.

'Are you okay?' He looks a deathly white. He can't focus on me properly and as he stands up he sways. 'You're drunk,' I say. 'Or high.'

'Sorry,' he mumbles. 'Farewell drink with Roisin.'

'Idiot,' I say.

'We need to go to the old croft,' says Niall.

'Whatever for?'

He doesn't answer me and staggers back to the car.

We have only been going for a few more minutes when the first drops of rain begin to spit onto the windscreen. It's not long before the spits become drops, then morph into splats. Faster and faster, heavier and heavier.

Headlights sweep around the bend ahead of us. The trees are lit up and road is more visible. I can see the rods of rain now hammering out of the night sky. Then a car comes round the bend towards us. The two white headlights burn bright and I am transfixed by them. I can't see anything other than the burning globes. The car passes us quickly. Suddenly the road is darker, the only illumination coming from the headlights of Niall's car.

Neither of us sees the flood of water lying across our path as we come out of the bend. The car suddenly loses contact with the road; it slips to the left.

We are now sliding sideways. The tyres snatch at the tarmac as we veer out of the water. I hear myself scream as we skid and continue our unchecked slide into the grass verge. I feel like everything is happening so slowly when, in fact, it's only taking seconds. The car pitches into the ditch. We somersault over. I can hear the crunch of metal, the shattering of glass. I hear Niall give some sort of shout, it's impossible to make out what he's saying.

As the car turns over, Niall is flung to the side. His head hits mine with such force I feel a searing pain and then nothing. I see nothing. I hear nothing.

The first conscious moment I have is dominated by pain. A distorted human-like groan filters through. I realise it is me. The pain I can locate to my head mostly, but my left shoulder hurts too.

The next sense I become aware of is smell. The unmistakable aroma of petrol creeps up my nostrils and claws at the back of my throat.

My natural instinct to survive takes over and I no longer feel the pain in my head and shoulder. I am overcome with the need to escape.

The smell of petrol spurs me on.

'Niall!' I shout. I can't see him. The seat next to me is empty and the door has come off.

The smell of petrol is stronger. I realise I am chanting the first few lines of Hail Mary. Repeating the words that have been ingrained in me from early childhood. 'Hail Mary, full of grace, the Lord is with me. Hail Mary, full of grace, the Lord is with me.' I push frantically at the clip of my seat belt and am rewarded with the sound of a click and immediately the pressure of the strap is gone.

I grapple with the door handle but my head is throbbing and I can't see properly. 'Hail Mary, full of grace. Hail Mary, full of grace.' My vision blurs and blackness comes at me from all directions.

PART 2

You never know how strong you are until being strong is your only choice.

Chapter 20

I feel flat. It's been over a week since I called things off with Ed. I know I've made the right decision, but all the same, it isn't a nice feeling. There is no sense of freedom I thought I might experience, no standing on an empty beach and throwing my arms wide open, embracing my new lease of life. No, there is definitely none of that; more a deep feeling of sadness, mixed with embarrassment that I had let myself become his project. Looking back, the signs were there, I just hadn't seen them, or maybe I hadn't wanted to see them.

I find myself wandering along the road towards the seafront. The sea air, the sound of seagulls and the gentle lap of the incoming tide always have a calming effect. I often sought refuge at the beach when I was a teenager, hiding amongst the sand dunes, away from the teasing and name-calling. I could look out to sea and watch all my worries slip away on the outgoing tide.

The day is drawing to an end and the sun is dipping low in the sky. A lone figure and dog come into view. The sun shines brightly behind them, silhouetting their outlines. The dog bounds around the owner dropping a ball on the sand, waiting for it to be thrown once more into the sea. The dog obviously delights in the game and keeps coming back time and time again.

As they come closer, the figure stops and faces the sand dunes. Then changing direction, heads towards me. I groan. It's Kerry. The sun has conspired against me, making early identification impossible. I rest my elbows on my knees, cupping my chin in my hands. Maybe he'll get the hint I'm not in the mood for talking.

'You look deep in thought there,' says Kerry as he approaches. I continue to look out to sea. 'I was.'

'Ooh, tetchy. Someone got out the wrong side of the bed this morning, did they?'

'Something like that.'

'I'm surprised you're not running out your frustrations. Isn't that what you usually do?'

'You're being very nosey today, aren't you?' I look up, squinting as the sun blinds me. Kerry moves position so his shadow shields my face.

'Got out the wrong side and then some,' he says. 'I'll leave you to it.' He whistles to Skip, who comes bounding out of the sand dunes with a tennis ball in his mouth. 'Come on, boy.' As he goes to leave, he bends down and squeezes my hand. 'You know where I am.'

I reply with a squeeze of his fingertips as they slip from mine. No words needed. Unspoken communication. It's easy being around Kerry, despite my bad mood. He gets me, understands my need for space and time. A kindred spirit perhaps? I watch him plod through the deep sand of the dunes, encouraging Skip to follow.

'Kerry!' I call, getting to my feet. I call out again. He turns to look at me.

He smiles and holds out a hand. 'Coffee? Chez Wright?' he says as I reach him.

I slip my hand into his. 'How could I resist?'

He winks. 'My thoughts exactly.'

The coffee is rich and warming. I cup my hands around the mug as I sit back on the sofa. Kerry's flat is so different to what I'm used to with Ed. There are no highly polished surfaces, no clean lines, sharp edges and monochrome furnishings.

Kerry's flat is full of life and excitement. There is a multi-coloured striped throw draped over one side of the sofa, with a royal-blue throw over the other half. Several cushions, none of them matching, are bunched up at one end as a makeshift pillow. Grey carpet tiles are hidden by a large rug in the middle of the room. The reds, golds and browns long since faded and worn in patches. A coffee table, which looks suspiciously liked white-painted pallets with stripped scaffold boards as a top, sits in the middle. The curtains are a plain beige colour, as are the walls and above the sofa a wall hanging depicts some sort of Buddhist deity.

The lack of any other chair forces Kerry to sit beside me on the sofa. He looks around the room. 'I know it's not The Ritz, but it's home.'

'It lovely. I like it.'

Kerry gives a laugh. 'Lovely wasn't what I was going for, but I'm glad you like it.'

'It homely. Relaxing,' I say.

'I'm glad to hear it,' says Kerry. He places his cup on the coffee table. 'You should try it more often.'

'Not something I can turn on and off, but with the right company...' I take a sip of my coffee and speak again. 'I've broken up with Ed.'

Kerry raises his eyebrows and nods his approval. 'Good.'

'You don't seem surprised.'

'After what happened, what do you expect? He's a dick. Joe was spot on about him.'

'Yeah, well, Joe should know.' It's an unfair remark, as I have to admit, apart from one comment at the barbecue, Joe has been fine.

'Why have you got such an axe to grind with Joe?'

'A personality clash,' I say.

'It's more than that. What went on with you two in the past? You've obviously got some history with each other.'

'Not that sort of history,' I say.

'What, then?'

'Why don't you ask your cousin?' I let out a sigh. 'Look, I'm sorry. Ignore me. My bad mood seems to want to hang around.'

'Sometimes it helps to talk about stuff,' says Kerry.

'And sometimes it doesn't,' I say. I'm not sure what it is, but I feel compelled to expand. 'It's nothing, really. Joe and I, we didn't get on very well at school. He used to like to take the piss out of me. You know, the red hair, the curls...'

'And that's it?'

I tap my finger against the mug. 'He used to wind me up about going out with Niall, Roisin's brother. She hated me being her brother's girlfriend and it wasn't unusual for her to load the gun, as it were, and for Joe to fire it. Quite a team at times.'

'He's always been like that,' says Kerry. 'Roisin doesn't sound like she was much of a friend.'

I shrug. 'A bit limited for friends in Rossway. Sometimes she could actually be really nice, but there was always a price to pay.'

'Like what?'

I think back, choosing which of the many occasions to cite. 'Like the time she let me borrow one of her outfits for a disco because I couldn't afford anything new. Then she went around telling everyone that she had lent it to me, but it was an awful dress and looked even more awful of me.'

'Nasty.'

'That's a good word for her. I can remember the feeling of total humiliation. I went home. Said I didn't feel well. I remember looking at myself in the mirror in my bedroom and that gorgeous emerald-green dress that made me feel beautiful now made me feel worthless and ugly. Stupid, I know, but I was fourteen and that sort of thing was pretty crushing.'

Kerry takes the cup from me and places it on the coffee table alongside his own. He holds my hands. I look at him as he moves his head closer to mine. I feel transfixed, as if under a spell. 'I don't believe for one minute that you looked anything other than beautiful.' He kisses me on the lips and then moves away, but only millimetres. I can feel his breath on my skin.

'What was that for?' My voice a mere whisper.

'What do you want it to be for?'

'I don't like all these riddles,' I say, still unmoving. I want more of him. Another small, teasing taste is too much to bear. I've been suppressing all sorts of feelings for Kerry for some time now. I like the closeness of him, the intimacy. I don't want to break the moment.

'Let's do some straight talking, then,' says Kerry. He kisses me again, this time for longer, his lips encouraging mine to open and join in the rhythm. I relax, giving myself permission to respond, not just with my mind but with my body as well. The lure of the double bed through the open doorway isn't an option, the softness of the sofa envelops my body as I lie back, my arms around Kerry's neck, pulling him down into the nest of pillows and multi-coloured throws.

I let out a small moan as his lips travel down my neck and meet with his fingers, which are unbuttoning my blouse. His hand scoops around my side and underneath me. I lift my body enough to allow him to release the catch on my bra. His finger-tips are rough, hardworking manual hands, little rips of skin graze over my own soft flesh. The roughness is a contrast to those that usually grace my skin, but even so, there is more tenderness, more delicacy, more sensuality in those sandpaper fingers than there has ever been in the smooth, moisturised and manicured hands that have roamed my body in the past.

The past. Such a loaded word, which holds so many dark secrets. Ed is now in the past. I am living in the here and now. The future – a dot on the horizon. All I know is I want Kerry with every part of my body and right at this very moment, with all my mind. The past banished; Ed tips into the abyss of my memory.

Afterwards, Kerry pulls the throw around us, we squash alongside each other on the sagging cushions, holding onto each other with what I suspect is more than just physical reasons for both of us. There is an emotional dependency and unspoken understanding. We both have past demons, which are hot on our heels.

'Are you okay?' I ask, lifting my head from under his chin. He looks down at me.

'Is that a serious question?' The smile on his mouth and the look in his eyes tells me what I want to know.

'Just checking,' I say, snuggling back down.

The tugging of the throw and whining of Skip breaks the moment.

'Hello, boy,' says Kerry, draping his arm over me to give the dog a pat on the head. Skip hops up on his hind legs, resting his front paws on my back. He whines with a sense of urgency. 'I think he wants to go out,' says Kerry. 'Sorry.'

We manage to untangle our limbs and Kerry hops over onto the floor. He pulls on his trousers and tugs his black t-shirt over his head. 'I'll take him out for a minute. Are you okay there?'

I sit up, pulling my blouse front together and fastening the buttons. 'I'll make us a drink. I should give Fiona a call too at some point to see how my dad is today.'

'How are things generally?'

'Not great.' I flick my hair out from the collar of my blouse. 'I'll just use the bathroom quickly to freshen up.'

'Yeah, sure. It's through there,' says Kerry, pointing in the direction of the bedroom. 'I won't be long.'

Padding through to the bedroom, I can see that the eclectic mix of old and new is a theme throughout. A striped duvet cover sprawls across the unmade double bed and a pair of red faded velvet curtains are pulled across the window. I wonder when they were last opened. Maybe when he had called out to me from the window that time I was jogging by. There is one bedside table, a chest of drawers and a wardrobe, all from different bedroom sets and eras. I smile. There's something warming about it. Charming. Male shabby-chic. Totally the opposite to anything I have been used to in Ed's sterile apartment.

Coming out of the bathroom a few minutes later, I catch sight of a mirror propped up against the wall that I hadn't noticed before. There are two photographs stuck to the glass. I bend down for a closer look. One is of a young couple crouching down with a toddler in front of them. The little boy has a shock of blond hair and is wearing denim dungarees. The man has the same colour hair, a beard and is wearing a cut-off black-leather jacket with jeans torn at the knees. The woman is smiling, her fair hair hangs loose on her shoulders. Her steel-blue-grey eyes shine with happiness. I've seen those eyes before. I know who the little family is.

The other photo is of two boys. The older child is definitely Kerry. I can tell by the blond locks and sea-grey eyes, the same as those of the woman in the other photograph. Kerry looks to be about fourteen or fifteen, a few years before I first met him, I guess. The younger boy looks about five. His hair is darker, but he too has the same colour eyes as Kerry and the woman.

'My younger brother.' Kerry's voice breaks through my thoughts. He's leaning against the doorframe, hands in his pockets.

'I didn't know you had a younger brother,' I say. 'I've not heard you mention him before.'

'I don't get to see him much. He lives with his mum.'

I frown, not understanding where the connection lies. 'His mum?'

'My mum,' said Kerry. 'She got married again. Ronan is the only good thing to come out of that.'

'And this is your mum,' I say, my finger rests on the edge of the family snap. Kerry doesn't say anything. My voice is soft. 'That's you and your parents.' It's a statement not a question. 'You have your mother's eyes.'

'Is that supposed to be a compliment?' There's a chill to his voice.

'I think your eyes are beautiful,' I say. I stand up and put my arms around his neck, kissing his cheek. 'Do you think you'll ever speak to your mum again? It's a shame if it means you don't get to see your brother.'

Kerry pulls my arms away from his neck. 'There's no going back. Not after what happened. A real mother wouldn't treat their child the way she treated me.'

'Which was?'

'Badly.' He turns and walks back into the living room.

'Time heals,' I say. 'Things get said in the heat of the moment. At the end of the day, she's your mother and loves you.'

Kerry spins on his heel and marches over to me. He swallows hard. For a moment I think he's going to shout at me. I take a step back. He moves around to the side of the bed and, kneeling down, pulls out a shoe box. He upturns it, the lid falls off and the contents scatter across the bed cover. His voice is full of hurt when he speaks. 'She fucked up and she knows it. That's why she sends me a letter every year.' He picks up one of the envelopes. 'She may well be sorry now, but I don't want to hear it.' He tosses the envelope back onto the pile.

I sit down on the bed and sift through the white envelopes. None of them have been opened.

'Don't you think she deserves the chance to say sorry? A chance to explain herself?'

'Jesus, Erin, you're such a hypocrite. You haven't exactly got a great relationship with your own dad, have you?'

It's a cutting remark, despite the truth that laces it. 'But I do still see him and speak to him,' I say in my defence.

'It's not simply that,' says Kerry. 'She's a mother. Mothers are supposed to love their child, no matter what. Mother's aren't supposed to reject their own flesh and blood. A child they've carried inside them for nine months and given birth to. Looked after for sixteen years and then when someone else comes along, she washes her hands?' He shakes his head. 'She turned her back on me. She can't just pick up the pieces when it suits her.'

There is real pain in his voice. A deep-rooted pain.

'That was a long time ago,' I say.

'Why are you defending her? What would you know about any of this?'

I jump to my feet. The remark cuts deep. 'Don't you dare judge me. You know nothing about me.'

'Come on, Erin. You don't get on with your dad that well. So what? It's no big deal. Your dad hasn't rejected you. He hasn't turned his back on you. You weren't kicked out of home at sixteen.'

There's so much I could say to that. Kerry doesn't know the half of what I've been through. He has no right to judge me and make assumptions. I need to get away from him before I blurt anything out in temper. I choose to retreat rather than attack.

'As I said, you know nothing about me.' I march out of the room. I need to get out of here. I grab my shoes and shove my feet into them, treading the heels down as I do so. Once they're on, I leave, pausing only in the doorway for a final word. 'You really need to get over yourself. You think you're the only one who's had a tough childhood. Well, I've news for you. You need to lose that chip on your shoulder.'

'And you think you don't?' His voice races after me as I slam the door and hurry down the outside staircase.

Chapter 21

Before I have even reached my parents' flat across the road, I know I've overreacted. A feeling of shame and embarrassment begins gnawing at my insides. I shouldn't have snapped back at Kerry like that. I don't know exactly what went on between him and his mum. In the same way as I don't want him to judge me, I shouldn't judge him. We are as bad as each other. We are both damaged goods.

Reaching the flat, I let myself in and go into the living room. I've already decided that I'll apologise to Kerry later. I'll let the dust settle and when we are both calmer, I'll go over and say sorry.

I flop down on the sofa and switch on the TV. Nothing holds my attention. I feel restless. I make myself a cup of tea and bring it into the living room, placing it on the coffee table, next to the bunch of keys for the flat and shop. Idly I play with the keys, sliding them round the keyring itself, ticking them off in my mind like a school register. The key for the front door of the flat. The key for the back of the shop. The key for the front of the shop. The key for the till.

The bunch of keys is familiar. It's the same bunch my dad has used since I can remember. I know he always kept the safe key separate, for security reasons, but where in the flat he hid it, I don't know. It's odd that Mum can't remember, and even more odd that the spare key's whereabouts is just as much of a mystery.

I get up and go into my parents' bedroom. The safe is fixed in the bottom of Mum and Dad's wardrobe. Kneeling down, I look at the safe. There is no other way to open it than with a key.

I look around the room, trying to determine a suitable hiding place. It would make sense that it's in the same room as the safe. The dressing table seems the obvious place to start. I'm careful not to disturb anything too much and the things I move, I carefully replace. I feel a bit guilty looking through my parents' stuff, but I justify it with the need to know for definite whether my dad was mugged or not. The thought that someone would do that is not nice. I hope his fall was purely an accident and finding the takings in the safe will confirm this and put everyone's mind at rest. Not only that but Roisin's parting words in the car park still bother me. The way she emphasised the word 'accident'. As if she knew something about Dad's fall that I didn't.

After ten minutes going through all their drawers and both bedside tables, I find nothing. No sign of the key or even a clue as to where they might have put it.

'Well, Dad, you've certainly hidden that key well.' I huff in frustration and, giving up, I wander back through to the living room and gaze out at the grey waves and white horses crashing onto the shoreline. The wind has picked up and a flag attached to the radio mast of one of the fishing boats performs some sort of crazy hip-hop dance as it flaps wildly in the weather.

The earlier calm I gained from the rhythmic crashing of the waves eludes me now. The tide has turned not only out at sea, but here on land too. With Ed I had felt landlocked. Now I am bobbing like a piece of driftwood, the off-shore drift teasingly taking me into safe waters with Kerry and then pulling me back out again. I need to make a decision. To take control and not let the currents drag me along to unchartered waters.

The first step is to apologise to Kerry. He deserves it. I'm just about to turn from the window when a movement to the left catches my eye. In the dwindling clouded light of the day, I see Kerry as he emerges from the road between the bike shop and Beach Road. He stops by the shop front to light a cigarette. Whether he knows I'm watching or whether he looks up by chance, I'm unsure.

'Wait there,' I call through the glass, holding up my hand to him. Animatedly, I tap my chest with my finger and point at him. 'I'm coming down'

With that I grab my jacket and handbag from the back of the chair and race out of the flat. I go to run down the steps, but then, remembering Dad lying in hospital, slow myself to a more orderly descent.

Safely reaching the bottom, I jog round to the front of the shops. I expect to see Kerry standing there but the street is empty. I look around, completing a three-hundred-and-sixty-degree turn. Not a sign.

My shoulders droop, disappointment floods through me. He hasn't waited. Maybe he didn't see properly or misread my mad hand gestures. He's probably only gone to the pub, otherwise he would have been on his bike.

I take a deep breath. 'I'm no driftwood,' I mutter and, walking faster and more determined than necessary, head for The Smugglers.

As I turn the corner, the pub within a few hundred yards, I let out a spontaneous groan. Walking towards me is Roisin.

'Look who it is. I was just thinking about you,' says Roisin, standing square in the middle of the path.

'Not now,' I say. 'I'm busy.' I sidestep onto the road, intending the bypass her.

Roisin's step matches mine and once again blocks my way.

I sigh. 'Roisin, this is silly. We've nothing to say to each other.'

'We have unfinished business,' says Roisin, pulling herself up straight, ready to strike like a cobra.

'Not interested,' I reply. Again, I go to move round Roisin and again she anticipates the move.

'I know about the baby. Your mum told me what really happened.'

And there's the strike. Words of venom spit at me, piercing my skin, fangs spiking deep into my heart. I gasp. A physical reaction to the poison Roisin has administered. My mum knows? My mum knows about the baby and she told Roisin?

'I…I don't know what you're talking about.' A clichéd response, but I can't think of anything else as I succumb to the toxic shock.

'You had that baby,' Roisin's lip curls. 'You've lied all these years. You and your mum have kept that secret. My brother was the father. You denied my mother the right to a grandchild. If you hadn't convinced Niall to run away with you that night, then he would still be alive and my mother would be rejoicing at two lives instead of eternally mourning the loss of one.'

'You have absolutely no idea what you're talking about.' My voice sounds distant. I'm aware I'm not processing any kind of thought, let alone verbalising it. It's like watching a car crash in slow motion on the TV.

'I hold you wholly responsible for the death of my brother. Which also means, I hold you wholly responsible for the mental state of my mother. She is a broken woman because of you.'

'Me? You hold me responsible. Your mother is responsible, not me.' I snap out from the shock. I push the thought that my mum knows my secret from my mind. I think of the guilt I've had to live with all this time about what I did. How I was left with no choice. And yet, Roisin blames me when it was her mother who didn't want me to have the child. The injustice clouds my thoughts and I hear myself snarl back at my old school friend. 'Your mother wanted me to have an abortion. She wanted to kill her own grandchild.'

The words are out and in that moment I don't care. To see the look on Roisin's face is enough; a look of disbelief. For a moment the curled lip and angry eyes are gone. We stare at each other. I can hear nothing but my own breathing and blood pumping rapidly through my ears. Roisin breaks the stalemate.

'You're a liar, Erin Hurley, always have been and always will be.'

'I'm telling the truth.'

'My mother would never kill her own flesh and blood.'

'You really don't know her, do you? I've seen the real Diana Marshall and it's not that pleasant, I can tell you.'

Roisin grabs the collar of my jacket. 'Liar! Liar!' she screams into my face. I struggle, trying to free myself.

'Get off!' I shout back.

From nowhere, two pairs of hands push between us.

'Come on, girls. Break it up.' It's Kerry. Calm but strong, pulling me back whilst Joe steps between us and grapples with Roisin's hands.

'Much as it's every man's fantasy to see two women fighting, unless you can do it in bikinis and a mud bath, I'm not interested.'

Roisin continues to yell at me. 'You're a liar!' She jostles with Joe in an attempt to get at me. 'And I'm going to prove it.'

'Get her out of here,' says Kerry to his cousin. He turns to me, taking hold of my arm rather unceremoniously. 'You, come with me.'

I briefly consider protesting, but taking another look at Joe still keeping Roisin under control, I decide against it. Joe throws a 'What the fuck?' look in Kerry's direction.

'Don't ask me!' Kerry calls over his shoulder as he practically frog-marches me down Beach Road.

Kerry thought about taking Erin back to his flat but after their little set-to earlier, he decided against it. Getting Erin anywhere near his bed would be asking for trouble, he would only want get her into it again and, at the moment, he didn't think that was a good idea.

Instead he opted for the beach. It seemed the safest choice. Erin didn't appear to have any objection. In fact, she was the quietest he had heard her. He was holding onto her hand now, despite her being a step behind him. He glanced at her but she kept her eyes fixed on an invisible marker ahead. He thought for a moment he could see tears gathering but she blinked hard, denying their leave.

They reached the beach, the tide was at its peak, crashing noisily on the shoreline, throwing up seaweed and then dragging the dregs away, only to bring them back onto the beach with the next wave.

Kerry led Erin to the sand dunes, a familiar spot where the dunes dipped, forming a small valley and providing shelter from the threatening gale.

'Glad it's not just me you're spoiling for a fight with today,' he said, sitting down next to her, drawing his legs up and resting his elbows on his knees. 'Were you planning on having a row with everyone in the village or were me and Roisin singled out for special treatment?'

'I didn't pick the fight with Roisin,' she said, scooping up a handful of sand and letting it pour through her open fingers.

'But you did with me?'

She turned to look at him. 'I'm sorry about earlier. I didn't mean to come across all high and mighty. Whatever's gone on with you and your mum, it's not my place to criticise. You know, glass houses and stones and all that.'

Kerry studied her for a moment. She looked him straight in the eye, unflinching, her face open, she was genuinely sorry. 'There may have been a slight over-reaction on my part,' he conceded.

'Can we scrub all that?'

'Consider it scrubbed.' He was aware of the flutter of relief somewhere in the pit of his gut. Erin Hurley was definitely under his skin. Big time. To distract himself from this rather unnerving realisation, Kerry put his arm around her and pulled her close, dropping a kiss on top of her head. She responded by lifting her head, her lips seeking his.

'That's better,' she said as she drew away from him.

'I have a feeling making up with Roisin won't be quite as straightforward,' said Kerry. Immediately, he felt Erin's shoulders tense. It really was a tricky subject for her. What the hell had gone on between those two?

'I've no intention of making up with Roisin.' Erin ran the pendant back and forth on the silver chain around her neck.

'What is it with you two?'

'Please, Kerry, can we change the subject?'

'No. We can't.' said Kerry. 'Look, Erin, I think I've made it perfectly clear how I feel about you. I really like you, *really* like you. We get along well. We get each other. And, we've both got demons from the past.' He paused to gauge her reaction. She didn't pull away. He took this as a good sign and carried on. 'If we're to make anything of it, then I think we have to be honest with each other. We need to have complete trust in each other.'

'I know what you're saying and, yes, I agree, but you have to earn trust.'

'Of course you do and sometimes you have to follow your gut instinct about who you can trust.'

'Do you feel you can trust me?'

She was testing him. He was willing to play. 'I do. I know I can. You and me, we're from the same mould.'

'Tell me what it is that your mother said to make you hate her.'

He had been expecting this and he was willing to sacrifice this for her. It would also explain to Erin his reaction to earlier.

'As you know, my dad died when I was a teenager. Cancer. It wasn't diagnosed until it was very advanced. Three months from start to finish.' He looked out to sea, thinking back to his father. 'Me and mum, we were pretty cut up, as you can imagine. It was the worst time in my life.'

'I'm so sorry,' said Erin. She placed a hand on his arm and dropped a kiss on his shoulder.

'After a few years, Mum remarried. Me and my stepdad, we never hit it off. I was a rebellious teenager who didn't want anyone taking the place of my father. My mum had a baby with him and after that things really got bad at home. To cut a long story short, I wasn't exactly the model son and I rebelled a bit.'

'That's only natural,' said Erin. She sounded genuine and empathetic.

'I got into trouble a lot, both in and out of school. Basically, I had a big bust up with my mum and stepdad one night. They called the Guards and kicked me out. I spent the next two nights sleeping rough in a farmer's barn. Word got back to Max what had happened. He and Joe came and found me. Max gave me a job and roof over my head.'

'That was good of him. You're lucky you had someone who would do that for you,' said Erin.

A silence fell between them as Kerry thought back to when he was kicked out of home. It was so much more than just an argument, but even thinking about it now still cut through him. Sliced through his heart like a stake post being driven into the ground. 'I always thought a mother was supposed to love her child unconditionally. I always believed a mother would never turn her back on her child. I was wrong.'

He felt Erin shift her position next to him. Her body tensed. From out the corner of his eye he saw her swallow hard. Her first attempt to speak failed. Her second attempt brought with it a wobble to her voice.

'Sometimes,' she began. 'Sometimes, the motives aren't always clear, but I'm sure a mother always loves her child.'

Kerry let out a scoffing noise. 'Jesus, Erin, you've got some fairytale image of mothers. That may well be true of your mother or your sister, but it's certainly not true of mine.'

'So tell me what happened. Trust me,' she coaxed.

'She made it perfectly clear what she thought of me. The last words she said left me in no doubt.' He dug his hand in his jacket pocket, pulling out his baccy. Deftly he rolled a cigarette. Cupping his hands to shield the lighter from the breeze, he drew hard on his cigarette. He was aware Erin was waiting for him to continue. 'There was no place for me in her life. She had her new family. I didn't fit in.'

'What exactly did she say?'

Kerry drew on his cigarette again, buying time. He had never told anyone what his mother had said. The words gouged his heart too much. Fuck it. Hadn't he just preached to Erin about telling the truth and not having secrets? He dug his heel into the sand and drew a deep breath. 'She said she wished I had never been born.'

There. He'd said it.

'She said that?' Erin sounded shocked. In some perverse way, Kerry was pleased with her reaction. It meant all these years of pain, feeling rejected and unloved were justified.

'Yes. Those were her exact words.'

'Weren't they just said in the heat of the moment, though?'

'I don't think the heat of the moment lasts for nearly nine years, does it?' Kerry stubbed his cigarette end out in the sand. 'I don't want to speak to her. I've cut her out of my life completely.'

'But she sends you letters,' said Erin. 'Doesn't that tell you something? She might be apologising. Trying to make amends. I'm sure she still loves you. Maybe she…'

Kerry cut her off. 'Don't. You don't know her. You don't know what she's like.'

'Yes, but…' This time Erin stopped herself.

'But, what?'

'Nothing.'

'No, go on. What were you going to say?' He could feel himself getting angry. This was a stupid idea and more the fool him for thinking that by telling Erin that she would understand.

'That a mother loves her child no matter what.'

'That's easy for you to say. You've got a mum who loves you. You've come from a stable home. You weren't rejected by your own mother. A real mother wouldn't do that to their child.'

'It's not always that simple,' said Erin. She began drawing circles in the sand again.

'It is in my book.'

They sat in silence for a while. Kerry had no desire to continue the conversation about his mother's behaviour and he was glad Erin didn't seem interested either.

The wind blew across the dunes, making the long grasses bow in unison. Gradually, the thoughts of the confrontation with his mother and all he associated with it began to drift from his mind and, with it, the tension eased from his body.

'Sorry,' he said. 'This is why I can't deal with it. I get too mad.'

'It's because it hurts,' said Erin. 'And that hurt goes both ways.'

Kerry wasn't sure he agreed, but he didn't want to talk about it any more. 'I could do with a pint. You fancy a drink?'

'Now?'

'Yeah, now.' He stood up and held out his hand to help Erin to her feet. 'Don't think you've got out of telling me your secret.'

'Oh, I see,' said Erin with a smile. 'You're going to ply me with alcohol to loosen my tongue.'

'Something like that.'

The pub is quiet and I'm glad Kerry texted Joe to check Roisin wasn't about. Bumping into her again isn't something I would relish just yet.

Joe and Bex are sitting in the corner of The Smugglers and have already got a drink in for us.

'Where are the children?' I ask as we sit down.

'Max and Louise have taken them out for a while,' says Bex. 'It feels odd not having Breeze bundled up in front of me.'

'We can all relax and enjoy a drink together,' says Joe. He lifts up his pint. 'Cheers.'

'Let's hope it stays this way,' says Kerry, as we all make an approximation of clinking glasses.

'Don't be worrying about Roisin now,' says Joe. 'She's gone off home. She'll be fine tomorrow. Probably just having an off day.'

'When isn't she?' I can't help but mutter the remark, albeit quietly into my glass.

'Ah, come on, Erin. She's not that bad,' says Joe. 'She's had a lot to contend with since...' His voice trails off.

'Since the accident,' I say. 'Well, she's not the only one.'

'It was and has been difficult for all of us,' says Bex. 'Admittedly, more so for others.' She gives me a comforting look. Bex is kind, always the peace-maker. 'Don't mind Joe, now,' she says. 'He's always had a soft spot for Roisin.'

'That might be so, but Roisin and myself, we go back a long way,' says Joe. He leans over to Bex. 'But you, my love, know I have eyes for you and you alone.'

'Is that so?' says Bex, tapping his arm. 'I always remember when we were teenagers, how you and Roisin were glued to each other's sides. I used to think you were going out with each other.'

'God spare us,' says Kerry.

'We were friends,' says Joe. 'Sure, we were more like brother and sister back then. Wouldn't you agree, Erin?'

'A proper double act,' I say. I realise I haven't quite managed to inject the banter into my voice that everyone else has been enjoying. Three pairs of eyes look at me in an awkward moment of silence.

'Right, who's for another round?' says Kerry, putting us all back on an even keel. 'Come on, Joe, you can help me at the bar.' He gives his cousin an indiscreet kick under the table.

We spend the next couple of hours on safer subjects, the atmosphere being warm and enjoyable.

It's early evening when we part company with Joe and Bex at the top of the High Street. I lean into Kerry as we wave them off down the road.

'I think your plan to get me wrecked has worked,' I say.

'Not too wrecked, I hope,' says Kerry. 'I've got plans for you.' He gives me a tap on the backside.

'And I have plans for you.' I return the gesture.

I'm not sure what time it is when I wake up, but the evening is drawing in, the last flecks of daylight shimmer against the dipping sun. I pull the duvet up and snuggle against Kerry, who is sleeping soundly. I feel relaxed and happy despite the altercation with Roisin earlier.

I think about it rationally. Okay, Roisin found the photograph of me and Niall. I don't know how or where as I don't know what Niall did with it after I gave it to him. It's irrelevant, really. The fact of the matter is that Roisin has it. The words I'd written on the back, *one plus one equals three,* were obviously a giveaway and she must have guessed I was pregnant when I was with Niall. And the reason for her resurrecting it all now, well, that's simple. She wants revenge. She's always blamed me for the accident and hated that anyone should feel sorry for me or my family. I remember between the accident and the funeral, she was going around the village telling people it was all my fault. Apparently, she hated it if anyone sympathised with me. I'm not sure whether she's hedging her bets that she knows what happened to the baby or not.

Kerry stirs and rolls over, his arms slipping round me. 'Hello, there,' he says, his voice heavy with sleep. 'You okay?'

I wriggle even further into his embrace. 'Of course. You?'

'Silly question.' He squints and rubs at his eyes so he can see the face of his watch. 'Half-eight. We must've been asleep a good hour. Cup of tea?' He rolls over out of bed, pulling on his jeans and t-shirt.

I get myself dressed and follow him out to the living room, where I make myself comfortable on the sofa, curling my legs up underneath me.

'I'm not used to all that afternoon drinking,' I say, accepting the cup of tea Kerry offers me. 'I feel like I'm getting a hangover now. I'm such a lightweight.'

Kerry sits beside me and we drink our tea in silence for a while until he speaks. 'So...' he says.

'So?' I repeat, although I'm pretty sure I know what's coming next. I brace myself.

'Soooo, what's the story with Roisin?'

Chapter 22

I look at him. I know he's not going to like what I'm about to tell him. Not after the secret he shared with me about his mother. Briefly, I wonder whether I can make up something. Tell him a lie. But what would that achieve? Nothing. He's trusted me. I have to trust him with what I can.

'When I was sixteen and going out with Niall Marshall, I fell pregnant,' I say, measuring each word. 'It was in the spring, my last year at high school. Niall's last year in the sixth form. He was going off to university in the September.'

'That was before I came to live with Joe,' says Kerry. 'Was the pregnancy common knowledge?'

'No. Not at all,' I reply. 'And that was the way our parents made sure it stayed.'

'I'm not with you,' says Kerry. 'So your parents knew? What, did you tell them?'

'Niall's mum found out. She was a GP at the time. I went to see a nurse, but Diana must have got wind of my visit or seen me at the surgery and, I guess, started poking around, and it wasn't long before she found out.'

Kerry lets out a long, low whistle. 'I bet she was pleased.'

'You could say that.'

'So, what happened?'

Skip jumps up onto the sofa between us and I'm thankful for the momentary hiatus in the conversation before I continue. 'Our parents decided it was best if I had a termination. Diana went ahead and organised it.'

'Just like that?'

I snap my eyes up at him. There's a hint of distaste in his tone.

'Yes, as a matter of fact. Just like that.'

'What, you went along with it?'

'Don't judge me, Kerry,' I warn. 'You know nothing about what it was like. What my dad was like. What Diana was like. I was only a kid myself. So was Niall, to all intents and purposes.'

'Okay, okay.' Kerry raises his hands in defence. 'How did she manage to sort out an abortion?'

'She paid for me to go to a clinic in England.' I stroke Skip's ears as he wriggles further into the cushions and rests his head on my feet.

'And that's your secret? That's what Roisin has on you?' says Kerry.

'Mostly.'

'What does that mean?' Kerry puts his cup onto the table. 'There's more?'

'I never had a termination. Niall and I decided to run away. We had all these plans of setting up home. He'd get a job and go to college in the evening. All that sort of thing. Crazy, naive and wistful teenage dreams…' I know that now. I've known it for a long time. Our plan would never have worked, never in a million years. It was based on false hope and a romantic vision of life. 'The night we took off, we were in Niall's car. We had an accident.' It's so hard to say this out loud; I've never had to before. Never had to explain to someone else what happened. Everyone in the village knew. They had heard it from the Marshalls. No one had needed to ask me.

'Niall was killed,' says Kerry. His voice is soft in contrast to the

186

roughness of his fingertips that reach out and cover my hand. 'I know. Joe told me. He never said you were pregnant, though.'

'It was the best-kept secret of Rossway. Diana and my father made sure of it.' The tears blur my vision, filling my eyes and cascading over the brim. Kerry scoops the dog out of the way and shuffles closer and wraps his arm around my shoulder, pulling me towards him.

'I'm sorry,' he whispers. 'So sorry.'

For a moment, I let myself take comfort from his embrace. I allow the reassuring words to soothe my pain. If only this was the end of it. If only this was where my story ended, not where it began.

I sit up, wiping the tears from my face. I sniff, not caring as to how attractive it makes me seem. My next words will put paid to any notion of a relationship between us. Once I tell him what happened next, he won't want to know me.

'There's something else,' I say.

'There is?'

'I never had the termination. Not because I no longer needed one after the accident.' I close my eyes for a moment. 'I told everyone I had lost the baby, but really I kept it. I kept the pregnancy a secret. I went to live with Fiona and I told absolutely no one in Ireland I was having the baby.' I look at Kerry. Confusion pulls at every feature. 'I had the baby. A little girl. A beautiful red-headed little girl. Still I didn't tell anyone. Only Fiona and Sean knew. My beautiful little red-headed baby girl was our secret. Not even my mum knew.' I smile as I think back to those precious first days when I cradled my newborn in my arms. More tears come, collecting in the upturned corners of my mouth, running between my lips, their salty taste seeping into my mouth.

As I speak again, my voice begins to crack, little sobs escape. 'But I couldn't keep her.'

'Jesus Christ, Erin,' says Kerry, he pushes his hand through his hair. 'Don't tell me you did what I think you did?'

'I gave my three-day-old baby away.'

'You gave up your own child?' Kerry stands up, muttering more expletives to himself. He takes his cigarette pouch from his pocket and begins to roll up. 'How could you do that?'

'I had no choice.'

'Of course you had a choice.' He snaps, spinning round to look down at me. 'You could have kept the baby. You could have still been its mother. You were living with your sister, for God's sake. You could easily have worked something out.'

I jump to my feet. Skip sits up, his ears pricked, looking at us. 'We did sort something out,' I say.

'Something that didn't involve you giving away your child.'

'It was the best thing for the baby. I had nothing to give her.'

'Yes you did,' says Kerry. 'You had something special and unique to give that child. Love. You had a mother's love.'

'Fuck off, Kerry,' I shout. 'What would you know?'

'I know what it's like to be rejected. I know that feeling. How do you think your daughter is going to feel when she finds out?'

'She's not going to find out.'

'For an intelligent woman, you're fucking stupid at times. She has a right to know who her parents are. A legal right and one day she might come looking for you. What are you going to do then? And what about the Marshalls? Have you not thought of them?'

'They didn't want her.'

'But she might want them. She might come and find them. They might feel differently now. She has a right to be loved by her paternal grandparents.'

'They gave up that right when they told me I should have a termination. Diana Marshall didn't care then, she certainly won't care now.' I can hear the venom in my own words.

'This is wrong,' says Kerry. He shoves the half-rolled cigarette back into the pouch. 'I was wrong about you. How could you do that to your own child? Your own flesh and blood?'

I go to retort, but Kerry isn't waiting for an answer. As I open my mouth to speak he shakes his head, his eyes tell me what he thinks. He despises me. Never have I been surer about him. I close my mouth. There's no point trying to reason with him.

With as much dignity as I can muster, I rise from the sofa and, for the second time that day, I leave his flat under a cloud. One that I'm not sure I can come back from this time.

Chapter 23

I wake the next morning and for a moment am unsure where I am. The sun streams in through a slit in the curtains. Curtains I don't immediately recognise.

I can hear the sound of movement in another part of the house, the voices of children and adults.

Of course, I'm at Fiona's. I had felt so miserable last night that I couldn't bear going back to the flat and staying there on my own. I had rocked up at Fiona's, no doubt looking a complete mess, hair all over the place, make-up streaked down my face and struggling with the onset of an early hangover.

I roll over and groan at the effort.

The second groan I make is when I remember what happened last night.

As recollections of the previous evening's events make themselves known in a coherent order, my mouth dries and my stomach churns. I sit bolt upright. Oh, God. I told Kerry about the baby.

Panic is the next emotion to kick in. Frantically, I try to remember how much I had told him.

A knock at the door and the sound of Fiona calling my name interrupts my thoughts. The door opens and Fiona appears with a mug of tea in her hand.

'Morning,' she looks at me, the smile falls from her face. 'You okay? You look mortified. My cup of tea isn't that bad, is it?'

'Erin!' Molly bursts into the room and throws herself on the bed, bundling me back down into the pillows.

I laugh despite my sore head. 'Morning, my lovely. You okay? Where's that sister of yours?'

'Still in bed, not very well,' says Fiona, placing the cup on the bedside table and then drawing back the curtains. 'Come on, Molly. Leave Aunty Erin alone, she's just woken up.'

I blink at the sunlight and manage to sit up with Molly still in situ. I stroke her hair, planting a kiss on top of the golden waves. A great feeling of love fills my heart.

'Why don't you go downstairs and find Daddy?' says Fiona. With slow but firm actions, she extracts her daughter from my embrace and, jumping Molly down from the bed, escorts her to the stairs. 'Off you go! I'll be down in a minute. Sean! Molly's on her way down.' Fiona comes back into the bedroom.

I go to speak, but don't know what to say. Fiona comes and sits on the edge of the bed.

'What is it? I can tell something's wrong,' she says.

I've dreaded this moment, but I know I can't avoid it any longer.

'Roisin knows. I don't know how much, but she knows about the pregnancy and she says she knows I had the baby.' The tears well up in my eyes and my throat feels lumpy as I continue. 'Kerry knows as well. I told him.' The tears spill over and a sob escapes my throat. 'I'm sorry.'

Fiona holds me. 'It's okay. Don't cry, Erin. What happened? How do they know? And what exactly do they know?'

I tell Fiona the whole story from start to finish. How I had received a couple of emails from Roisin but ignored them to start with. Then the one I received the night of Dad's accident. The photograph Roisin had found. And about our arguments and everything else that has gone on since I have come back to Rossway.

'I'm sorry, I should have told you at the start,' I say. 'I thought I could handle it but it's all spiralling out of control. And now I've told Kerry. I'm scared Roisin is going to do something stupid. Something that will blow this whole thing wide open.'

Fiona hugs me and tells me not to worry. 'The photograph, what does it prove? That you were pregnant. It doesn't prove you had the baby.'

'But she said Mum told her.' I say, suddenly remembering what Roisin had said. I can feel the panic starting up again.

Fiona thinks for a moment and then speaks calmly. 'That's impossible about Mum knowing. If Mum knew, she'd say. I'm certain. Roisin must be making that up. You know what she's like – she says things out of spite sometimes.' She pauses again. 'Okay. So what if she thinks she knows you had the baby? What then? Nothing. That's where it ends.'

'I don't follow.'

'You had the baby and then the baby was adopted. That's what you've told Kerry and that's what Roisin thinks she knows.' I nod. 'So she can't do anything else about it. Under law, she can't trace the child. It ends there.'

'But she could cause a hell of a fuss,' I say. 'What if she…'

Fiona cuts me off. 'A bit of tittle tattle from something that happened ten years ago. I don't think even the residents of Rossway will find that too interesting. It might be a bit of gossip for a day or so but that's all.' She smiles at me with confidence.

'You don't seem at all worried,' I say, wishing I could buy into Fiona's confidence.

'Because I'm not. You should have told me at the start and then we could have nipped it all in the bud and you wouldn't have got yourself in this state.' She gives me another hug. 'Now, stop with your worrying. We're safe, Erin. Safe.'

The early-morning rush of emergency appointments and requests for same-day consultations had finally reached a lull.

'Why don't you go for your morning break now?' said Roisin, turning to speak to her colleague. She wanted to be alone at the reception desk. She needed to access the patient records without anyone looking over her shoulder or asking what she was doing.

Her colleague was only too pleased to escape to the staff room for fifteen minutes and, once gone, Roisin quickly logged onto the patient-record system.

She typed in the name 'Erin Hurley'.

Roisin had accessed them the day after she found the photograph of Erin and Niall. The same photo she'd sent to Erin.

The screen flicked up Erin's past medical records from when she was born, right up until when she had left to go to live in England. Roisin carefully read the notes again, hoping she had missed something the first time around.

Erin's words had haunted her for the past few days. Had Roisin's mam really told Erin to have an abortion? It was unbelievable. Her mam was a GP. She saved lives. She didn't terminate them. Not only that, but abortion was still illegal in Ireland. Roisin was certain her mother would not do anything to break the law. Diana was a well-known figure in the village, she held a position of responsibility. Breaking the law would only bring public humiliation to her and that was something Diana would avoid at all costs.

And it was this last train of thought that had, time and time again, brought Roisin back to the same place. Diana would want to avoid any sort of scandal and Erin being pregnant at sixteen by Niall would, in itself, bring shame on their family.

The uncomfortable and unanswerable question came trundling back to Roisin. Would her mam have done *anything* to avoid a scandal, even if it meant breaking the law? Which scandal was the lesser of the two evils? Which one would her mam consider the best option?

There was no mention of the pregnancy on Erin's records at all. Roisin wondered if Diana had something to do with that. It wouldn't be so difficult for her mam to change the notes. She could also have arranged for the termination in the UK without anyone knowing. That would tie in with Erin leaving almost immediately after the accident, either to have a termination, which Roisin doubted, or to have the baby and put it up for adoption in England.

The telephone ringing broke her thoughts. Closing the patient-record system Roisin answered the call.

'Good morning, Rossway Health Centre.'

'I'd like to make an appointment for my daughter, please? Sophie Keane.'

Roisin sat up a little straighter. 'Hello, Fiona, it's me, Roisin,' she said. 'You need an appointment for Sophie?'

'Ah, hello Roisin. Yes, that's right. She's running an awful temperature and has a sore throat, which is covered in little white spots.'

Roisin was sure she could detect an apprehension in Fiona's voice. No doubt, Erin had already told her about their confrontation in the street. Fiona would know about her sister's pregnancy. Erin told her sister everything. Roisin couldn't deny the sense of vitriol rolling around inside her. A small victory; making the Hurley girls squirm. Giving them cause to worry and stress. A small battle in the big war. Roisin took a moment to savour the sensation.

She checked through the appointment system. 'We're really busy today. Can I get the doctor to call you back for a telephone consultation first?'

'Yes, that's fine.'

'Okay, I just need to get Sophie's details up. Right, here we go. If you can confirm the address and date of birth.'

'Roisin, really, you know it's me,' said Fiona. 'You don't need to be doing all this, surely. Can you not just make the telephone appointment?'

'Sorry, rules are rules. I can't go any further in the system without ticking the boxes to say I've personally checked the details,' said Roisin, enjoying herself. The sense of control and power warmed her heart. 'I don't want to do anything illegal that will get me into trouble. I don't want to get found out for not doing things right.'

With more than a reluctant tone to her voice, Fiona relayed the information. Roisin checked off the details and took a telephone number for the call-back. 'Okay, thanks then, Fiona. Doctor Peters will call you as soon as he can.'

Roisin ended the call. Something was bothering her, but she couldn't put her finger on it. She tapped the desk with her pen. It was something to do with Sophie, but what? She read through the child's notes.

It was on the third time of reading, it struck her. There, in black and white, staring straight at her. Sophie's date of birth. Why hadn't Roisin noticed this before?

Her stomach gave a tumble and thoughts rushed through her mind, making connections so fast, it was hard to keep up. She closed her eyes and massaged her temples with her fingertips, letting the flow of thoughts wash over her like the gentle lapping tide on the shore. Slowly she began to make sense of it all. It wasn't concrete, but it was a start; it was the lead she needed.

'Okay, what have we got, then?' It was Doctor Peters' voice.

Roisin gave a start, relieved she had her back to the doctor so he hadn't caught her with her eyes closed. She fumbled with her pen. 'I've just put the list of call-backs through. There are three elderly and two children,' she managed to say, without the nerves sounding in her voice.

Doctor Peters looked over her shoulder at the list. 'Mrs Farrell, again, I see. What's up with her this time?' Roisin moved the cursor so he could read more details. 'Okay, usual complaint. Who else have we got? Oh, the Keane girl, Sophie. That doesn't sound too good. I'm sure we ran some blood tests recently. Can you have a look?'

Roisin tapped around on the keyboard, working her way to the correct screen. 'Here we are,' she said, turning the monitor to a better angle for the doctor. Roisin scanned the results at the same time as the doctor.

'They all came back normal,' said Doctor Peters, more to himself than to his receptionist. 'Okay, thanks, you can close that now. Roisin. Hey, you're miles away, girl.'

'What? Oh, sorry.' Roisin hadn't been listening. One box of the blood results caught her attention. Stopped her in her tracks. She had almost missed it. A tiny piece of information that made all the difference. She realised Dr Peters was looking at her. She apologised again and exited the results, aware that her hand was shaking ever so slightly and her heart was pumping faster than normal.

Once Dr Peters had returned to his consulting room, Roisin logged back on to Sophie Keane's results to check she hadn't misread anything. She then double-checked the child's date of birth before closing the records and bringing up Fiona's notes.

The excitement was building inside her. Roisin's hand shook wildly and her mouth was drying by the second. She could hear Sandra, the other receptionist, talking to one of the practice nurses. Roisin willed the patient-records system to work faster. Within a few seconds she was in Fiona's records. Luck was on her side. Fiona was pretty healthy and hadn't attended the surgery much, it meant fewer notes to wade through. Roisin scrolled back down through the data to her pregnancy with Molly. It had been Fiona's first pregnancy. This was all tying in so much better than Roisin could have imagined.

She searched for the information she was looking for and jotted it down in the notebook beside the phone. Next she needed to access Sean Keane's records. Her fingers tripped lightly across the keyboard, the dexterity and familiarity with the system aiding the need to work at speed. She made another note on the pad underneath Fiona's name.

Fiona 0+
Sean A+
Sophie B-

Finally, she went back to Erin's notes. This was where her luck ran out. There was no mention of Erin being pregnant and, therefore, no record of any blood tests or note of her blood group. Roisin tapped her pen on the desk. It didn't matter. What she had in front of her was enough. She might not be qualified in the medical profession, but several years of working at the surgery meant she had picked certain things up. She stared at the notepad. The implications were huge.

Chapter 24

Twice Kerry thought about going over to the café and twice he dismissed the idea. He had also had to put up with a cross-examination from Joe as to why he didn't want to go over for breakfast that morning.

'Lovers' tiff already?' said Joe, totally unaware that he was spot on.

Kerry was kneeling on the floor, fiddling around with the fuel pump on a Ducati, which was in for a service. He got up. 'Give it a rest. I'm not in the mood.'

'I take that as a yes, then.' Joe grinned and ducked out the way of the oil-cloth that Kerry chucked at him.

Kerry went into the small kitchen area and flicked the kettle on. He hated this indecisive feeling. On the one hand he wanted to go over to Erin and tell her he was sorry he had reacted the way he did. He was sorry for upsetting her. He was sorry she had walked out. And he was sorry he hadn't gone after her. However, on the other hand, he wanted to stay as far away from her as possible. He couldn't get his head around the fact that she had given up her own child. How could a mother do that? She was no better than his own mother. And what of the child now? How could Erin not put the child's feelings first? What would that little girl be thinking now, knowing her mother didn't want her?

All these conflicting questions and emotions had kept him awake for the most part of the night. His feelings for Erin and his feelings for what she had done were at odds with each other. It was doing his head in.

Joe walked in, his arms up in surrender. 'Don't shoot,' he said.

'Coffee?' said Kerry, accepting Joe's indirect apology.

'Cheers. So, want to talk about it?'

'Not especially. Anyway, since when did you become a relationship counsellor?'

'Ah, so it is Miss Hurley that's the cause of your bad mood.'

'That obvious, is it?' Kerry poured the boiling water into the two cups, adding a slosh of milk and two sugars to each.

'Matter of deduction. No football last weekend, so it's not that. Nothing wrong with your bike, so that's ruled out. The pub hasn't burnt down, so we're good there. Skip's still here.' Joe threw the dog a biscuit as he spoke. 'So that only leaves women. Well, one woman. Erin Hurley.'

Kerry slid the mug of coffee over to Joe and picked up his own. He took a sip while he considered whether to confide in Joe or not. Despite being disappointed by what Erin had told him, he still felt loyal to her and didn't want anyone else thinking badly of her. And it was disappointment. He thought she was pretty near-perfect but it had been naive and immature to think like that. No one was perfect.

'I found out something about Erin that I didn't like,' he said at last.

'Right, I take it you're not going to elaborate.'

'Nah.'

'Well, that's a good sign. She can't have pissed you off so much that you don't care about anyone knowing. You obviously feel some loyalty to her and that's good, right?'

Kerry shrugged. 'Suppose so.'

'Is it something she's done since she's been back? Something to do with whatever is going on with her and Roisin?'

'No. Something she did when she was a teenager.'

'What? Here? In Rossway?'

'No. After she left.'

'Right, I was going to say, if it was here in Rossway, I'm sure we'd know about it. You know what this place is like.' Joe placed his cup on the counter. 'Doing something at sixteen or seventeen isn't the same as doing something now, at twenty-six or twenty-seven. We're different people now to what we were then. Sure, you've no life experience at that age. You think you're grown up, but you're only a kid.' Joe leant on the counter. 'You can't judge what someone did as a teenager through the eyes of an adult. Jesus, I should know. I was a shit at times when I was a kid. Look at me now.'

Kerry gave a small laugh. 'You reckon you've changed? Grown up? Matured?'

Joe grinned back. 'To a certain extent. I don't seem to remember you being much of an angel when you were a kid either. Anyway, the point I'm making is, we do things as kids without the knowledge and experience of adults. That doesn't make us bad people as adults. Whatever she did then, she was a kid herself. It's what she does now, as an adult, you should think about.'

'Thanks for the counselling session,' said Kerry. 'Now, if it's all right with you, I'll get back to my work.' He wasn't entirely sure Joe was right. What made a person, the essence of who they were, that was embedded deep in their DNA. He wasn't convinced a person could change that.

Roisin spent the rest of the day at work barely able to concentrate. Once she called a patient Mr instead of Mrs and another time she took some urgent results back to the wrong doctor. She was glad she wasn't on a late shift that night. She wanted to get home and think clearly about what she was going to do next.

200

Finally, she made it back to the Manor House. She could hear the television on in the living room and poked her head around the door. Her father was there watching the evening news.

'Hello, darling,' he said. 'How are you? Good day at work?'

Roisin went over and gave her father a kiss on the cheek. 'Hi, Daddy. I'm fine. Glad to be home.'

'Your mother's in the kitchen getting tea ready.'

Although her father tried to say it in a nonchalant way, as if it was the most usual thing in the world for her mam to be cooking, they both knew that given Diana's current state of mind, this was something of an achievement.

They had never openly discussed Diana's depression and drinking habits. They were taboo subjects: ones Roisin and her father both pretended didn't exist. It was as if admitting to them, saying it out in the open, would mean they had to confront them and do something about them. Neither Roisin nor her father had the emotional energy to do so. It was simply referred to as Mam having a bad day. Her good days, when they happened, were to be savoured, although they were bittersweet reminders of the mother Roisin had lost. When Niall died the best part of her mother died too.

Roisin weighed up her options. Should she approach her mam whilst she was sober, knowing that it would probably kick-start the next cycle of drinking? Or, should she wait until Diana had had a drink, when alcohol was more likely to loosen her tongue?

Roisin stopped outside the kitchen door. She could hear the radio playing and her mam singing along. It reminded Roisin of happier childhood days. Sundays in the kitchen helping her mam prepare the roast dinner. They were precious times. Her mam had worked long days as a GP which often trailed into the early evening. Roisin hadn't always seen much of her during the week, but always felt at weekends her mam more than made up for it.

Roisin longed to have her old mother back and, for the first time in ten years, she thought she just might be able to make it happen. She now had the solution. The answer to all their problems. An answer that could also punish Erin Hurley and bring a sense of justice for what had happened.

Roisin decided to hold off speaking to her mam, she would wait until after dinner, when they were all relaxed after a nice evening meal together.

'Hello, Mam,' said Roisin, walking into the kitchen.

Diana looked up from chopping the vegetables. 'Hello, Roisin,' she said as a smile spread across her face. 'Dinner won't be long. I thought we would eat in here today. Less formal.'

Roisin took in the pine kitchen table set for three. Pale-blue table mats; matching napkins lay on top of white dinner plates. A white oilskin table-cloth with blue spots finished off the retro effect. Her eyes came to rest on the condiments and bottle of wine on the table. The wine was already open. She looked over to where Diana had returned to prepping the vegetables. To her right was a wine glass with the remnants of red wine sitting in the bottom.

Diana looked back over her shoulder and followed her daughter's gaze. She raised her eyebrows in question.

Roisin said nothing. What would be the point? It wouldn't stop what was surely to follow. Any hopes of a civilised evening and a heart-to-heart talk were slipping away.

And so it did.

Dinner was one of false cheer and fading hope. Each mouthful of food was matched by a slug of wine.

Roisin poured herself another glass that she didn't want but it was one less glass of wine for her mam to consume. However, it was a wasted attempt to limit her mam's intake. Diana simply opened another bottle and took it into the sitting room.

'I'll help you clear away,' said her father, rising from the table.

'No, it's fine. I'll do it. You go and sit down. I'll bring you in a cup of tea.'

He didn't argue. It was best that way. Pat would shut himself in the living room and watch the television. He wouldn't go into the sitting room to comfort Diana, to talk about his feelings, his wife's feelings or even what Roisin might be feeling. No, this was the Marshall way of dealing with their heartbreak. The remains of their family united in eternal grief, yet disjointed and alone in life.

I've just got back from a visit to the hospital. Mum had called both me and Fiona, asking us to come to up. The doctors wanted to speak to the family. I had closed the café early for the day and driven us in my father's car.

The doctor had explained that although Dad's condition remains the same: stable but critical, they are considering bringing him out of his induced coma. They want to monitor him for another twenty-four hours before they make a final decision. The doctor has warned us not to expect anything to happen fast or for there to be any great or sudden recovery. It's a long process that needs to be handled with care. No miracles are in the offing.

I left Fiona with Mum. Sean is going to call in on his way back from work and pick her up before they go home to relieve the babysitter. I got the impression Fiona wanted some time with Mum. She had encouraged me to go home to get some rest. I didn't argue. The hospital room makes me feel claustrophobic, saps my energy and stokes my guilt. The empathy for my father I thought might come still eludes me. And if that isn't bad enough, I know Mum is only too aware of this. More guilt.

I climb the steps to the flat, having declined Fiona's offer to stay over at hers. I feel down and, if I'm honest, a bit sorry for myself. I haven't heard from Kerry and it hurts. More than I care to admit. I hope he'll see things from my point of view. I can understand the way he's reacted in light of what he said about his mother, but it's not the same. Twice I had composed a text message to him asking him to get in touch, to meet up, but both times I deleted it without sending. He needs to come to me because he wants to, not because I'm asking.

As I reach the door to the flat, I look out across at the bike shop. A few hundred yards and a brick wall is the physical separation, but the emotional separation is far greater. Is it too great a divide for us to meet somewhere in the middle?

I let myself in to the flat. I really should try to stop thinking about Kerry so much. He has occupied pretty much my every other thought and it's an unhealthy state of mind to be in. I shouldn't let someone have so much hold over me. I've just got rid of Ed for the very same reason, so why I am allowing Kerry to take up so much headspace?

My phone rings, making me jump. I pull my mobile from my handbag and look at the screen.

It's Ed.

It's as if my thoughts have managed to conjure him up. I let it ring twice more while I debate whether to answer the call or not. I decide to speak to him. Knowing Ed, he'll only keep trying if I leave it go to voicemail. I might as well get whatever it is out of the way now.

'Hello, Ed,' I say, walking into my parents' living room and sitting in one of the armchairs. I sink into the sagging cushion. It's never been comfortable, even when I was a teenager, it's less so now, having had another ten years of use. I opt for perching on the edge of the seat.

'Hi, Erin. How are you?' His voice is warm and soft but it fails to have the same swooning effect as it once did.

'Not too bad. You?'

'You know…okay. What about your father, how is he?'

'No change.' I have the distinct feeling this call isn't really to discuss the welfare of me or Dad. I sense there's more to it. 'I wasn't expecting to hear from you.'

'I've wanted to call for a while, but I didn't want to crowd you,' says Ed. He seems hesitant, which isn't like him at all. I wait for him to continue. 'I wondered if we could talk. I've missed you.'

'Okay, now?' I'm taken aback by this. Ed's confession to wanting to talk surprises me. It also puts me on guard. Thinking back to the day of the barbecue at Bex and Joe's place prickles me more than I care to admit.

'Yes, now, but not on the phone.'

'What do you mean?'

'I'm parked up out the front of the café,' he says.

I nearly drop the phone in surprise as I jump to my feet and shoot over to the window. I pull the net curtain up and peer into the dusk of the evening. I scan the few cars lined intermittently along the parking bays. A set of headlights flash. A BMW, like the one he has hired before, is parked several bays down from where I left Dad's car. Three other cars separate them. I hadn't paid any attention when I had pulled up. Why would I? He must have been parked there all along, waiting for me to get back.

'You'd better come up,' I say, dropping the net curtain and cutting the call. He has totally caught me by surprise. I sift through the feelings that are charging their way through my mind, a riot of thoughts and emotions.

I don't have time to get them into any sort of order before I hear the rhythmic clang of footsteps on the wrought-iron staircase as Ed jogs up the steps. The rap of knuckles on the door announces his arrival.

Chapter 25

'Why don't you give it a rest now?' said Joe wiping the oil from his hands on a rag. He threw the stained cloth into his toolbox. 'It's late. Let's go for a pint.'

'You go. I'll finish off here,' said Kerry, not looking up from the spark plug he was cleaning. Despite his chat with Joe earlier in the day, he still wasn't in a great mood.

'Come on, cuz,' cajoled Joe. 'Let's go to the pub and then you can tell me exactly what's going on. Whatever it is, it's bigger than you can handle, judging by the mood you've been in all day.'

'Leave it, Joe,' said Kerry and then, because he knew he had been a bad-tempered bastard added, 'I'm knackered. I'll get this done and then go home. Going to get my head down early.'

Joe wandered over and crouched down beside him. 'Those spark plugs look pretty clean to me,' he said. 'You, my friend, are bullshitting me. Now, come for that pint and tell me what's really up.'

'Look, it's nothing,' said Kerry, placing the spark plug on the cloth spread out beside the motorbike. He wracked his brains for an alternative reason to the one thing, or rather person, who had been playing on his mind. 'Money worries. I'm on a three-day week now, so, you know…' He left the sentenced unfinished, confident Joe would fill in the gaps.

'Yeah, it's tough. If it's any consolation, I feel bad about it – guilty, like.'

'Hey, forget it,' said Kerry, glad the conversation had steered away in a different direction. 'You've got Bex and the kids to think about. I've just got me.'

'You've got a couple of paint jobs to do, though, haven't you?'

'Mmm, one's cancelled as he can't afford it. I'm thinking of getting back to him and giving a lower price, much as it pains me,' said Kerry, standing up. 'But I don't have a lot of choice at the moment.'

'What's that, the Honda?'

'Yeah, nice bike. Was a nice paint job too.' Kerry blew out a breath. Suddenly a pint seemed like a good idea. He could do with taking his mind off not only Erin but money worries too. 'Let's get that drink after all.'

Joe gave him a punch on the arm. 'That's the spirit.'

'You sure Bex won't mind?' He picked up the dog's lead and whistled for Skip.

'Not at all. You know, Bex.'

Kerry did know Bex. So easy-going and laid back. She and Joe were a good team together. They were lucky, they had found a kindred spirit in each other and now they had baby Breeze, their family unit was complete. Bex was a great mum and Joe, much to the surprise of a lot of people, although not to Kerry, had not just turned up but had totally owned being a dad. It kept a faint glow of hope burning in Kerry's heart that, in life, there were parents who loved each other and loved their kids without condition.

Locking up, they left via the back of the workshop and wandered round to Beach Road.

It was a clear evening, the longer daylight hours adding to the hint of summer that was promising to come their way. The sound of footsteps somewhere behind him made Kerry look round.

Two figures, one male and one female, were walking over to

the parking bays. They hadn't noticed Kerry or Joe. Kerry gave another look.

'What the…?' he muttered under his breath.

'What's up?' Joe looked back too.

Kerry pulled Joe by the sleeve of his jacket. 'Come on.'

'That's Erin and Dick-Ed.'

'I know. Now, come on.' He gave Joe a shove forwards.

'Thought we'd seen the last of him,' said Joe.

'So did I.'

As they rounded the bend, Kerry gave one final look back at the parking bays. The engine of a car sounded and it reversed out of its space. A rev of the throttle, followed by the tiniest of wheel spins, and the BMW accelerated along Beach Road, passing them both, heading out of the village.

'Dick-Ed,' said Joe.

'You can say that again.' Trouble was, Ed wasn't the only one that fell into that category, thought Kerry, as they walked on towards The Smugglers. He felt a complete dick-head himself. He had thought there was something between himself and Erin; that she had meant it when she finished with Ed. Now, it seemed, she had only been using him, rebound material, and Ed was back on the scene. Yep, Kerry had been a dick-head to fall for that one.

Two pints later and Kerry was still brooding. He had tried to make all the right responses to Joe's chatter, nod in the appropriate places, look happy, look sad, laugh as necessary, but he wasn't actually listening. All the time his thoughts were recalling the conversations he and Erin had shared, her upset at the barbecue, her confession about having a baby, the intimacy they had shared on his sofa and now his own reaction to seeing her with Ed.

On the one hand she came across as troubled and fragile and yet, on the other, she was cold-hearted and arrogant. She had played him, that was for sure. But he was also sure that sooner, rather than later, every lie she had built up around her was going to come crashing down.

'You've not listened to a word I've been saying, have you?' said Joe pushing his empty pint glass to the centre of the table.

'Sorry,' said Kerry, supping his pint.

'Seems to me you have two options, cuz. Either get over it, or more like get over Erin.' He raised an eyebrow at Kerry.

'And the other option?'

'Do something about it. Because you're one miserable fecker like this.' He stood up. 'I'd better get back. There is a limit to Bex's understanding. You coming?'

Kerry drummed his fingers on the table, pursing his lips then, coming to a decision, looked up at his cousin. 'You go on home, Joe. I'm going to take your advice and do something about it.' He took his phone from his pocket. 'Need to sort something out.'

'Okay, I'm all for you taking my advice, just nothing stupid, eh?'

Kerry gave a mock salute. 'Nothing stupid.'

The meal is probably good, after all it is a nice restaurant, a top restaurant. Ed wouldn't bring me to a run-of-the-mill one, that's not his style. And the food is, no doubt, of the highest standard, but I could be eating cardboard for all I notice. My palate is tasteless, each mouthful dries in my throat and I have to force myself to swallow the food down.

Ed is very attentive. Overly so. There's a distance between us, a tension as we play out niceties.

The talk we have both been avoiding finally comes as dessert is placed in front of us. I toy with the cheesecake, usually one of my favourites, but like the main course, this too is tasteless.

'I'm sure your dad will be okay,' says Ed, taking my disinterest in my food as a sign I'm worrying about my dad. 'The doctors know what they are doing. He's in the best-possible place.'

Platitudes, but I nod and thank him all the same. 'That's what we keep telling Mum,' I say, avoiding any reference to my own emotions. The truth is there's still a blank space, for the most part. Every time I visit Dad, tiny edges around that space erode and break away. At first I thought it was for Mum, but my visit today summoned up a thread of compassion, which I realised was for Dad. Perhaps only now am I really appreciating the seriousness of his condition and how thin the line between recovery, and not, is. Some deeply buried trace of feeling for him is beginning to surface. I'm not quite sure how to deal with it, so long has it been since it was out in the open, certainly before I was a teenager.

Ed's hand reaches across the table. 'You know I'm here if you need me,' he says.

I look up and meet his eyes. I can't read them. I've never been able to. I thought I knew him. I thought I knew he loved me, but did he just love the notion of rescuing me? He saved me then, did he want to save me now? Was he saving me or serving his ego?

I slip my hand away. 'Thank you.' I don't know what else to say.

'The other week, when we had our row,' says Ed. 'I know I stormed off, but I must admit, I was quite shocked by what you said. I realise now how much pressure you must have been under, are still under. Anyway, I thought I'd give you a bit of space.'

'I meant what I said.'

'I'm sure you did,' says Ed. He gives me a patronising smile. 'But now you've had time to think, how about we get things back on track? You should also think about work. I could still take you back.'

I can't believe his attitude. 'I'm not a child. I do know my own mind. I meant what I said,' I repeat the last sentence to make my point.

'Everything?' He has that supercilious look on his face. The one he uses when someone has told him something totally ridiculous.

I put my spoon down and push the cheesecake away. I rest

my arms on the table. My fingers pinch the stem of the wine glass. I think of Kerry and what he means to me. What he could mean. How can it ever compare to what I had, or can have, with Ed?

'Yes, everything,' I say. 'I'm sorry, Ed.'

'Oh, come on, Erin, you can't mean that.' Ed too pushes his plate away. He downs the last drop of wine in his glass. 'You think it's better being over here in the arse end of nowhere with simple country folk. Really?'

I feel myself prickle. 'Yes. Really,' I snap. I lean closer. 'As a matter of fact, despite everything, I do prefer it here. Here is real. Here is where my family is. People I love. Here is where my heart is.'

I sit back, my words surprising me as much as they appear to surprise Ed. In the heat of the moment, I've spoken without thinking. I realise my true feelings have come out. Defending my family, my heritage and my loved ones from the scorn of a London city snob, who can only measure happiness with a price tag.

Ed studies the bottom of his empty wine glass, which hangs between his finger and thumb. He lowers it back on to the table.

'How I misjudged you,' he says. He signals for the waiter and asks for two coffees. 'I take it you're still drinking coffee after a meal or would you prefer a cup of Barry's Irish tea?'

I don't dignify the cheap shot with an answer. I smile at the waiter. 'Coffee will be fine, thank you.' Once the waiter has left, I rise from the table. 'I'm just going to the toilet.' I need a bit of space to break the tension and row that is threatening to erupt. I also need time to let the thoughts that have bombarded me and taken me by surprise to settle.

Piped music filters through into the ladies' washroom. I inspect myself in the mirror. I've just discovered something about myself I didn't know existed, or rather something I thought had long been resigned to Room 101. The love for my family, in all its shapes and forms. Some loves might be greater than others and some loves might be on different levels for different reasons, but there is no doubt about it, the love is still there. The more I acknowledge this love and let it in, the stronger it becomes. I realise that love isn't painful. It's the not having love that hurts. The rejection. The betrayal. The loneliness. They hurt. Love doesn't.

The sobering thought of Roisin crashes to the front of my mind, shoulder-charging all other emotions to one side. Roisin has the power to destroy my family, to break it up and scatter it across the village. I can't let that happen. Despite what Fiona thinks about Roisin and her motives, I know Roisin better. I know what she's capable of. She wants to bring my family down. I have a bad feeling that she just might, somehow. My love for my family fuels the primal instinct to protect. I have to protect my family first. To protect them is to love them.

I rest my hands on the washbasin, my head bowed while I consider my options. There is no place for the faint-hearted here, only the brave.

I need to get home. Away from Ed. I have things to sort out.

I return to the table, where my coffee is waiting. Ed has already drunk his.

'It's probably cold now,' he says nodding towards my cup. 'Would you like me to order you a fresh one?'

'No, it's fine, thank you,' I say, noting the lack of confrontation in his voice.

'So, it's really all over?' he says. He looks sad, but I decide it's probably a sadness that he has been defeated rather than a sadness that he has lost me.

'I think so,' I reply. 'And, about my job…I won't be coming back for that either.'

Ed nods. 'Saves me trying to think of a legitimate excuse to sack you.' He gives a laugh, which I'm not entirely sure he means, but I let it go. I have other things on my mind.

'Would you mind dropping me back now?' I ask.

'Let's go, I've already paid the bill,' says Ed, rising from his seat.

We travel back in silence, each lost in our own thoughts. There's nothing more I want to say. We both know it's over between us. It was over a long time ago. I could argue it had never really started. Not in the way a true lifelong relationship does, on equal terms, an equal footing, equal motives and equal goals. I was his Eliza Doolittle and there's nothing equal about that.

Ed pulls up in the parking bay outside the café. 'I'll walk you round,' he says, his hand reaching for the door handle.

'No, it's okay,' I say quickly. I look over at Ed and we exchange a smile of acknowledgement. This is the end. 'I'm sorry things never worked out the way we wanted. I think this is for the best. For both of us.'

'You're probably right,' he says. 'You never really fitted in with the crowd.'

Another remark that I won't dignify with a response.

'Goodbye, Ed.'

I get out the car. It's raining, but I don't care. I stand on the path, watching him pull away until the tail lights disappear out of sight.

That part of my life is over. I now have a new part ahead of me.

I check my watch. It's still quite early. The meal had been a quick affair. I dart in the doorway of the café for cover and take my phone from my bag. I scroll through the contacts list, stopping at the name I'm searching for.

I take a deep breath and fire off a text. 'Only the brave,' I say out loud. 'Only the brave.'

Chapter 26

As the evening wore on, Roisin came to a decision. Asking her mam tonight about Erin would be a bad idea. Diana had shut herself in the sitting room and was now listening to the CDs Niall used to play all the time. It was a bizarre event. A middle-aged woman, ex-GP, listening to music from a decade ago, music that doesn't sit naturally with her. Music to which she knows the exact words and slurs them out in between sipping her wine whilst slumped in a wing-backed library chair. It was a sorrowful sight.

Roisin reassessed her plan. She would force the Hurley family's hand. She was going to make them admit to what she had found out. Roisin had the proof, so even if they didn't want to, she would be able to force them. She would do it publicly, if necessary. She didn't care. Not about them. She cared about her mam and what had happened to her family.

If her mam had something to live for again, if she knew part of her son lived on, then Roisin was sure Diana would pull herself together. It would give her the incentive to sort herself out. She could be the mother Roisin longed to have back. The Marshalls would be well on the way to being fixed. There would be another Marshall to love and welcome into their arms. Just how it should be.

Her phone bleeped in her handbag. Roisin took it out and read the text message.

'Would you look at that?' she said out loud. She read the message again. A small smile spread across her face. She licked her lips, tasting victory already.

Grabbing her coat from the hall stand, Roisin wriggled her feet into her shoes. She looked from the closed sitting-room door on the left to the closed living-room door on the right. Would either of them notice if she went out? Would they care? Probably not, to both those questions. Checking she had her car keys, Roisin slipped out the front door, closing it quietly behind her. She would be back before they locked up for the night. She would nip back in, go up to her room and neither her mam nor Daddy would be any wiser.

The village was quiet. Roisin didn't notice anyone as she drove along Beach Road, heading out to The Spit. The gravel road that led out to the headland was unlit and her headlights cut through the darkness. The weather had taken an unhealthy turn at some point in the evening. The wind was picking up and as the wheels scrunched along the unmade track that ran alongside the water's edge, the rain came down heavier.

Arriving at the end of the track, Roisin parked the car. There was no other vehicle there and certainly no sign of who she was meeting.

The knock on her window made her jump and Roisin screamed with fright.

'Jesus!' she said. She couldn't see that well in the dark, but she knew who it was. They beckoned her out of the car and impatiently opened the door. 'You could have warned me you were here, instead of lurking in the shadows. Frightening me half to death. Haven't you got a torch?' said Roisin, swinging her legs out. The fierce wind swirled her hair around her head. She caught it in her hand, taming it and tucking it into the collar of her coat. 'Do we have to stand out here? I'm getting soaked.' But the figure, huddled into their coat, was already walking away towards the end of The Spit. Roisin swore under her breath. She had little choice but to follow.

I take the steps the flat as quickly as I dare in this weather, but at the same time with an urgency to get out of my wet clothes and to dry my hair, which has turned into a mass of copper coils. As I open the door to the flat, something makes me glance to my right and I see the bathroom light is on. I don't remember leaving it on.

As I walk into the living room, I sense I'm not alone. The door to the hallway is open and I can see a shadow move across the bottom of the closed bathroom door.

The door opens and I jump, letting out a small squeal.

'Mum!' I hold my hand to my racing heart. 'I wasn't expecting you to be here. You scared me.'

'Sorry, I decided to come home for the night,' says Mum. She's wearing her dressing gown and her hair is wrapped in a towel. In her hands is a bundle of wet clothing. 'I got caught in the rain.'

'What were you doing out in the rain? I thought Fiona and Sean were bringing you home.'

'Sean had to work late. Some emergency or something, so Fiona and I got a taxi back from the hospital.' Mum takes her wet clothes through to the kitchen and puts them into the washing machine.

'So how come you're so wet?' I ask

'I went for a walk. I needed some time to think about what the doctor said.'

I look at my watch. 'It's half-past nine. It's a bit late to go wandering around, especially in this weather.'

'Ah, sure, it wasn't raining then. Like I said, I just got caught in it.'

'Where was Fiona? Didn't she offer to go with you?' I don't like the thought of Mum wandering around in the dark.

'I didn't tell her. It was a spur-of-the-moment thing,' says Mum.

I follow her back through to the bathroom, where she plucks a towel from the airing cupboard and passes it to me. 'You're a fine one to talk, you're soaking yourself.'

I take the towel and rub vigorously at my hair. 'So where's Fiona now?' I ask.

'She had to get back for the babysitter. She had a couple of things that needed sorting out.'

'Well, don't be going off again like that without telling someone,' I say.

Mum laughs. 'Yes, Mummy.'

'It's not funny,' I reply, although I can feel the corners of my mouth turning up. I give in and a broad grin spreads across my face.

'Now you know how I felt all those years ago when the two of you were out.' Mum comes over and kisses me. 'Am I grounded now?'

'No, but you can have an early night for your cheek.'

'I'll have a cup of tea first, though.'

'I'll ring Fiona. Check she got home okay,' I say, as I head to my room to get changed into some dry clothes.

Mum has taken to coming home the last few nights. Fiona and I have managed to persuade her she will have a better night's sleep in her own bed and reassure her that the hospital will ring if there is any change at all.

I call Fiona's mobile number, but can't get through, so I call the house phone instead. An unfamiliar voice, who I assume is the babysitter, picks up the call.

'I was trying to get hold of Fiona,' I say. 'It's her sister. Is she there?'

'Hi. It's Karen. I'm the babysitter,' comes the reply. 'Fiona's not back from the hospital yet.'

'Oh, right. I expected her to be back by now.' I wedge the phone between my shoulder and chin as I wriggle out of my jeans and into my pyjamas.

217

'She called me to say she had been held up, but she'd be back as soon as possible,' says Karen. 'Shall I get her to call you?'

'If you could. I'll try her mobile again. I might get hold of her that way.'

I end the call, puzzled as to where Fiona might be. She and Mum had come home by taxi, dropping Mum off first. I consider questioning Mum, but decide against it – she has enough to worry about without me inventing things. I'm not my sister's keeper. Maybe she's called in to see a friend. I give Fiona's mobile one more try. This time it rings.

My sister's out-of-breath voice comes on the line.

'Hi, Erin. Everything okay?'

'Yes. All good. Are you okay? I rang the house, but your babysitter was still there.'

'I've literally just walked in now. I had to pick up a bit of shopping on the way home and bumped into one of the mums from school. We got chatting – you know what it's like. Where are you?'

'I'm at the flat. Mum's here. I was just checking you got back.'

'Yep, all safe and sound,' says Fiona. 'I'll call by the café tomorrow after I've done the school and nursery run. One of us can take Mum to the hospital and the other can stay in the café. How does that sound?'

'That sounds fine. I'll take Mum up to the hospital, if you like.'

'Really? I mean, that's great,' says Fiona. 'I'll see you in the morning.'

I don't miss the note of surprise in Fiona's voice and I appreciate the quick recovery she makes. Both Fiona and Mum will be pleased with my change of heart about visiting Dad, but I'm not ready for a big discussion about it. Knowing my family as I do, I'm confident they will let it go, silently accepting and approving of my new attitude.

Mum looks comfortable in the armchair, her big blue dressing gown pulled tight around her, a cup of tea resting in her hands on her lap. She nods towards the other cup, which she has made for me, on the coffee table. Finishing my call with Fiona, I replace the receiver in its cradle.

It's dark outside now. I switch on the table lamp and go over to close the curtains. As I draw them together, the sound of a motorbike's engine rumbling along the road catches my attention. I look out and as the bike passes under the street lighting, turning from Beach Road on to the main road into the village, I recognise the rider as Kerry.

He draws to a halt and lifts the goggles from his eyes. He looks up at the flat. I look back at him. I'm too far away and it's too dark to see his face properly, but I know he can see me. After a moment, he blips the throttle and, flicking the bike into gear with his foot, pulls away from the kerb, disappearing out of sight. I can hear him as he turns into the bike yard. A rev of the engine before it's cut.

I snag the curtains closed.

Chapter 27

I'm up early the next morning and am surprised to see that Mum is already dressed and sitting in the living room.

'Morning. I thought you might have a bit of a lie-in.'

'Old habits die hard,' says Mum. 'I wondered if you would like a hand opening up the café.'

'I'll be fine,' I say. 'You stay here and have a rest. Unless you really want to, that is.' I wonder whether a bit of normality might help her. Perhaps seeing and chatting to the customers might be good.

'I'll come down with you,' says Mum. 'No point sitting up here on my own.'

The usual early-morning customers are in for their breakfast and I'm pleased to see they make a fuss of Mum. Asking how Dad is, offering their sympathies and any help she might need. It's nice to see and I suspect it's having a positive effect. She's actually smiling and there's a light behind her eyes: one I haven't seen since arriving back in Rossway.

With each tinkle of the bell above the door announcing the arrival of a customer, I look up, expecting to see Kerry or Joe walk in. I'm not quite sure how I'm going to react. I can feel the apprehension building in my stomach as every minute passes.

It's only a matter of time before they get here. Sure enough, at seven-thirty the two cousins bowl in.

'Mrs Hurley,' greets Joe. 'Now, there's a fine sight. Are you cooking breakfast today?'

'It's good to see you, Mrs Hurley,' says Kerry. 'How's Jim?'

'They're going to try to wake him from his coma soon,' says Mum and then turning to Joe. 'Have you missed my cooking, then?'

'Ah, we have, indeed,' says Joe. He leans on the counter, beckoning Mum to do the same. 'Much as I appreciate Erin's culinary delights, they're no match for yours.' He shields his mouth with his hand and in a mock whisper, 'But don't tell Erin I said that. She's a sensitive thing, that one.' He winks.

Mum gives a chuckle while I force a smile. Kerry is looking at me, his face expressionless. I feel my heart sag, but try to disguise it by turning my attention back to Joe.

'I'm not good enough now, is that it?' I say, trying to sound light-hearted but not entirely convinced I'm doing a good job of it.

'Ah, now, your mother here, she is the queen of the cooked breakfast,' says Joe straightening up. 'It would be more than my life's worth to dethrone her.'

Mum laughs, which makes me smile. It's nice to see her happy, if only for a while.

'Go and sit down, boys,' she says. 'I'll bring your food over in a while and Erin will be along with your coffees.'

I take the coffees over a few minutes later and, despite the hostilities from Kerry, decide there is nothing I can do for now but carry on.

'How are Bex and the children?' I ask as I place the drinks on the table, deliberately avoiding eye contact with Kerry.

'They're doing well,' says Joe, his face lighting up as he speaks. 'Breeze is living up to her name. She's just a breeze to look after, says Bex. So easy, it's like she's always been with us.'

'Bex is such a great mum,' says Kerry. 'A real natural. You've got a good one there, cuz.'

'That's good. Tell her I was asking after her,' I say.

'You might be able to tell her yourself,' says Joe, stirring sugar into his cup. 'She's calling in at lunchtime to see me. I'll get her to pop over.'

'I won't back from the hospital until around two,' I reply. 'If I don't see her then, I'll call by at some point.' I could do with a friendly face, that's for sure. I loiter for a moment. I want to ask Kerry if I can speak to him. We've unfinished business. We both know that. He didn't stop outside the flat and look up at me for no reason and, yet, going by this morning, it would seem it's the last thing on his mind. I feel confused, hurt and, above all, controlled. I don't like that feeling, it's far too familiar. A feeling I experienced for too long via Ed. I will just have to tell him now that I want to speak to him, but, as if he has anticipated the words, Kerry speaks to Joe.

'What's on agenda for today? Is that Ducati being collected? I noticed last night the exhaust could do with a polish before we let it go.'

The moment is lost. The conversation doesn't include me as the cousins discuss the day ahead. Fortunately, one of the other customers calls me over and I leave the Wrights to it.

Some twenty minutes later Joe and Kerry finish their breakfast. Kerry appears at the counter.

He pushes a five-euro note and some coins over towards me 'We'll talk later,' he says.

I slide the money off into my cupped hand. 'I'm going to the hospital with my mum today. I'm not sure when I'll be back.'

'You know where to find me,' he says. His face is unsmiling and his voice gives no clue as to his thoughts.

The hospital room doesn't feel as oppressive as it had when I first arrived back in Ireland. Before, I hated coming here to visit. I hated having to look at Dad and feel nothing for him. I hated only feeling for Mum and what it was doing to her.

Today, I don't feel any of that hate. Dad's eyes are closed and he breathes steadily of his own accord.

'He's been breathing very well on his own,' says the doctor, reading from the clipboard of notes. 'The scan we did yesterday reveals that the swelling has gone down on his brain, so it is all looking good to begin to wake him.'

'How exactly will you do that?' I ask.

'We use medication, an antidote to the anaesthetic we used to sedate him. I've attached an I/V line to drip through the medication,' says the doctor. 'Now, his legs and arms have been twitching a bit too, which is a good sign that he's ready to wake up, but please don't expect anything to happen quickly. It can take around six hours before the patient responds.'

Since arriving at the hospital, when the nurse gave us the heads-up that today is the day, Mum has lapsed into a silence.

'Thank you, Doctor,' I say, when I realise Mum isn't going to say anything.

'I'll come back in about ten minutes once we have the medication sorted out,' says the doctor as he leaves the room.

I turn to Mum. 'Are you okay?'

Mum closes her eyes and nods. 'Yes, sorry, I'm a little nervous, if I'm honest.'

'It will be okay,' I say, guiding her to the bedside chair. 'The doctors know what they're doing. They wouldn't be trying to wake Dad if they didn't think it was the right thing to do.'

'I know.'

'Let's try and be upbeat about this,' I say, feeling concern and frustration at the same time. 'It will help Dad if we're positive. It's all good.'

Mum looks at me.

'Is it?' she says. 'Is it all good?'

'Yes, it is.' I pull the other plastic chair round so I can sit next to her. 'I know things have been difficult between myself and Dad, and for good reason, but things have changed.' I reach over to the bed and place my hand on top of Dad's. I hesitate for only a moment before curling my fingers. 'Sometimes good things come out of bad things.'

'And sometimes, bad from good,' says Mum.

I look at her. 'What do you mean?'

'A mother's love knows no bounds,' she says. She looks out of the window. 'Everything I have ever done, or not done, has been for many reasons, but at the heart of it all, the underlying reason has always been because I love you and Fiona more than anything or anyone in the world. You do know that, don't you?'

'Yes, Mum, of course I do,' I say. I don't understand why she's telling me this, but it seems important to her and it seems equally important that I understand. A feeling of unease weaves its way around me. 'Mum…has something happened?'

Mum blinks hard and gives the faintest of smiles.

'Nothing for you to worry about.' She brushes a curl back from my eyes. 'That's my job.'

I go to protest, but the doctor comes back into the room, accompanied by a nurse. The moment to question Mum is lost and although I try to focus on what the doctor is saying and doing, my concentration keeps stalling. All I can think about is what Mum said. *And bad from good.* The unease grows tighter with every thought.

Chapter 28

'That's what I like to see, you two hard at work,' Bex's voice called out. Kerry looked up and smiled as she entered the workshop. As usual, she was carrying Breeze in a baby sling, one hand protectively around the bundle, her other hand holding Storm's. He was straining to free himself like a puppy on a lead.

'Hey,' called Kerry.

'There she is, the love of my life,' said Joe. He wiped his hands on a rag and greeted his family. Kisses all round. The greeting extended to Kerry as Bex came over and gave him a peck on the cheek. Skip trotted out from the office and wagged his tail madly as Bex and Storm made a fuss of him.

'How you doing, Bex?' said Kerry. He dipped a kiss onto Breeze's head. 'And how's our little princess?'

'And me. I'm a prince.' Storm pulled on Kerry's trouser leg.

Kerry picked up Storm. 'Hey there, buddy. I mean, Prince Buddy.'

'I've brought some lunch,' said Bex, lifting the bag she was carrying. 'Sandwiches, beer and cake. Thought we could sit on the beach.'

'Give us five minutes,' said Joe.

'What's this, then? A tea party?' Max came out onto the landing from the upstairs office. 'Hello, Bex, sweetheart. How are you?' Max came down and made a fuss of his grandchildren. 'So, I expect you're wanting a lunch break, Joe?'

'And Kerry,' said Bex.

'Oh, I see how it is,' said Max. He winked at his daughter-in-law. 'No invite for me.'

'You're more than welcome to come too,' said Bex.

Max shook his head and smiled at his family. 'Nah, I'm only teasing. I'll stay here and man the fort.' He looked at Joe and Kerry. 'Well, go on then, before I change my mind.'

The beach was quiet and the Wright family settled themselves on the blanket Kerry had grabbed from his flat, along with a golf umbrella from the corner of the workshop. He opened it out and stuck it in the sand, wedging some stones around the base. 'There, that should keep the sun off the little ones,' he said. He pulled out a tennis ball from his pocket and threw it for Skip to chase after.

'Cheers, cuz,' said Joe, cradling his daughter in the crook of his arm.

'Oh, look,' said Bex. She squinted against the sun, holding her hand up to shield her eyes. 'It's Sean Keane. He's coming this way.'

Kerry glanced up. Sure enough, Fiona's husband was yomping through the sand, heading directly towards them. Kerry felt himself bristle. An automatic response to the blue uniform of the Guards; a reaction left over from his wilder teenage years.

Kerry exchanged a look with Joe, who shrugged in response.

'No idea,' he said.

'Likewise,' muttered Kerry.

Sean Keane reached the Wrights.

'Kerry. Joe. Bex.' Sean nodded at each in turn and gave a smile towards Storm.

'Everything okay, Sean?' said Joe, his voice wary.

'Have any of you seen or heard from Roisin Marshall at all today?'

226

The three looked blankly at each other. Bex spoke first. 'No. I'm afraid not. To be honest, I don't see much of her these days anyway.'

'Me neither,' said Joe. 'Is something up?'

Sean looked at Kerry, waiting for a response.

'No, I haven't seen her either,' said Kerry. He looked away to where Skip, having lost interest in the tennis ball, was bounding in and out of the water.

'When did you last see her?' pressed Sean.

Kerry looked back. 'The other day, maybe. I think I saw her walking through the village. Couldn't swear to what day exactly.'

'What's happened?' said Bex, standing up.

'Don't be getting yourself all worked up, now,' said Sean. 'She didn't come home last night. Her mother phoned the station this morning to report her missing.'

'Oh, no!' said Bex.

'Her phone's off. No one can get hold of her,' said Sean.

'I hope she's all right,' said Joe, standing up next to Bex and putting an arm around his wife's shoulder. 'Who have you asked so far?'

'We're doing the rounds now,' said Sean. 'I called by the bike shop. Your dad said I'd find you here.'

'When was she last seen?' asked Bex.

'Around suppertime last night. Her mam and dad thought she had gone to bed, but when she didn't come down for breakfast, they realised something was wrong. Her bed hasn't been slept in. Diana has been phoning around. No one has seen Roisin at all. Anyway, I'd better get on. If you see or hear anything, let me know.'

'Yeah, sure.'

'Of course. Bye, Sean.'

'Sure, that's awful if anything has happened to Roisin,' said Bex sitting back down on the blanket. 'That family are blighted.'

'Nothing's happened to Roisin,' said Joe. He passed Storm a juice carton. 'Sit down there, Storm. That's a good lad.'

'What makes you say that?' said Bex.

Joe shrugged. 'Well, I mean, I'm sure nothing's happened to her. She's probably gone off in a mood somewhere,' he said. 'She's not been herself lately.'

'I know, but you'd think she'd let her mother know,' said Bex. 'Can you imagine what Diana must be going through? She's already lost one child, to lose another…'

'Aren't you jumping the gun a bit?' said Kerry. 'Joe's right. Roisin might just have gone off with a friend or something.'

'Like I said, I'm sure she'll turn up,' said Joe.

'Do you think it's anything to do with Erin being back?' said Bex. 'Joe, you said yourself, her and Erin had a massive row in the street. What was that all about?'

'You best ask Kerry that,' said Joe.

Kerry hesitated. He didn't want to break Erin's trust. He was aware that Joe and Bex were expecting a response, though.

'It's not for me to say,' he said at last. 'Sorry, but it's something between Erin and Roisin. I can't say. I'm not even sure I know the whole story anyway.' He felt bad not sharing what he knew with Joe and Bex. He would trust them with his life, but despite his disapproval of what Erin had done, it would feel like he was betraying her trust.

'I won't waste my time trying to get you to tell,' said Joe. 'I know what you're like. You're loyal, if nothing else.'

'Now, wait a minute,' said Bex. 'If this secret is anything to do with Roisin and her disappearance, then you have to tell.'

'No. No, I don't,' said Kerry. 'As I said, it's not for me to tell.'

'Kerry's right,' said Joe, much to Kerry's relief. 'Let's leave it for now. Roisin will rock up later. She's probably got herself a fella and spent the night sha…'

'Okay, that will do,' said Bex cutting in. She nodded towards Storm. 'Little ears.'

'Yes, Daddy, you can't say rude things in front of me,' said Storm.

'That's me told,' said Joe. He ruffled his son's hair.

The appeal of the leisurely lunch on the beach waned with every minute. The news of Roisin's disappearance weighed heavy on Kerry and he could tell it was the same for both Joe and Bex.

'I'll go and see Erin,' he said standing up. 'I'll let her know what's going on. Will you take Skip back to the workshop for me?'

'No worries,' said Joe.

The café was quiet now the lunchtime rush was finished. A couple of older women were talking over a pot of tea, but other than that, the place was empty. Erin and Fiona were deep in conversation at the counter when Kerry walked in. The concern and anxiety on their faces told him they already knew about Roisin. They both looked up as he neared the counter.

'Kerry,' said Erin. 'Have you heard about Roisin?'

'Yes, Sean just told us. I was coming over to see if you'd heard.'

'It's terrible,' said Fiona. 'What on earth could have happened?'

'No one seems to know,' said Kerry. 'Let's think positive, though. I'm sure she'll turn up later.'

'I hope so,' said Fiona. 'Her mum is distraught, Sean said. They had to call the doctor out to her to give her something to calm her down.'

'Poor woman,' said Kerry. He looked at Erin. Was that a look of disapproval she had tried to lift from her face without him seeing?

'Look, I best get on,' said Fiona, taking the car keys from Erin. 'My turn to sit with Mum while we wait for Dad to wake up.'

'No change yet, then?' said Kerry.

'No. I've just come back from there,' said Erin. 'It can take some time.'

'I'll see you later,' said Fiona, giving Erin a quick hug.

'Call me as soon as there's any news,' said Erin, as Fiona went out the door.

'I was going to come and speak to you before I heard about Rosin,' said Kerry.

'I sent you a text,' said Erin.

'I know.' Kerry dug his hands in his pockets to stop them from drawing Erin to him. He wanted her, he really did, but every time he thought about what she had done, it pulled him up short. 'I've tried to get my head round what you told me. About the baby. Really, I have.'

'Let's go in the kitchen,' said Erin, glancing up at the two customers still chatting. Kerry followed her through to the back. He waited while she appeared to choose her words.

'I did it out of love,' said Erin. Her voice was soft, yet Kerry was aware of the steel that laced her words. She continued. 'I did what I thought was the best thing to do at the time.'

'And now?'

'It doesn't matter what I think now. What's done is done.'

'You don't want to undo it?'

'No. No, I don't. And I can't. It will only cause everyone pain. There's been enough pain in our families. I don't want there to be any more. I can't let it happen. I won't let it.'

He could see tears in her eyes. She looked away, blinking hard to stop them falling. Despite his best intentions not to have physical contact, he found his hands on her shoulders. He turned her to face him.

'How far would you go to stop it from happening? To stop the truth from coming out,' he said. She didn't answer. She gave a sob and the tears raced down her face. 'Jesus, Erin, tell me you didn't have anything to do with Roisin going missing?'

She gave a laugh between the sobs and drew deep breaths, while wiping her face with her fingertips.

'And there's me thinking I needed to ask you the exact same question,' she said. 'God, what a bloody mess this is turning out to be.'

'You didn't answer the question.'

'Nor did you.' She gave a final wipe of her face. 'Of course I didn't.' She raised her eyebrows, tilting her head, waiting for his response.

'Of course I didn't.'

'Good, that's cleared that up,' said Erin.

'What about Ed?' He had to ask.

'As in…?'

'As in, what's the craic with you two? I saw you going off with him last night.'

'Nothing is going on with Ed,' said Erin. He felt her shoulders sag under this hands. 'It was his last-ditch attempt at patching things up. That's all.'

Kerry registered the relief he felt. He nodded. 'Good.'

'So, where does that leave us?'

'I know where I want it to,' said Kerry. 'I'm just having a hard job getting there.'

'I know you like to see things in black and white, that things are usually cut and dried for you,' said Erin, 'but life's not like that. Not for me. Not for you.'

The sound of the bell above the door broke through. 'Let's talk about this later,' said Erin. 'I've got a customer.'

She gave him the briefest of kisses on his mouth. He went to respond, even though part of his mind was screaming for him not to. He couldn't help himself. But it was only a fleeting brush of her lips. 'Meet me tonight?' he said.

'I'll call you. I've got to go back to the hospital later. I don't know what's happening with Dad yet.'

'Sure.'

'We'll sort this out,' she said. 'I promise.'

He watched Erin go out to the front of the café. In his heart, he wanted to believe her that they could sort it out, but his head was putting up a fight. He couldn't be sure what would win.

Chapter 29

I had hated my father for what he had forced me to do. Or rather, what he assumed I would do. But my hate was that of a teenager who already had a tenuous relationship with him, a relationship that was already fractured. The insistence of a termination breaking the last of the links. I had given my baby up and I had hated my father even more.

Over the years I had stoked the hate. Every time I felt the flame was waning and at times diminishing to an ember without my notice, I poured petrol on it. It was the anger that kept me going. Without it I was afraid I would crumble under the weight of grief. Not only had I lost Niall but I had lost my child; this was Diana and my father's fault. I blamed them entirely. It had helped me cope.

I wander into the hospital on autopilot as I continue to analyse my thoughts and feelings. Now that I'm on the verge of losing my dad, I realise it scares me. If he dies, then I will have to face that our relationship will forever in time be a scared memory. A deep wound in my history, where life has healed over and left a mark. I don't want to lose the opportunity to reconcile things. Life, love and families are precious. I want to make things up with my father, despite the choices I've been forced to make. All this time I was in the driving seat, I was in control. It was up to me how our relationship played out and now I'm on the verge of losing that control, I'm frightened. I realise that all this time, deep down, I actually do want to make things up with Dad, but I've always thought I had time on my side. Now, of course, I don't.

I want Dad to recover. I want him to forgive me for distancing myself, for not understanding he had my best interests at heart. Whether I agree or not, it was because he loves me. In his own way, yes, but he loves me. And I love him.

I quicken my pace. I'm anxious to get to Dad's ward. I don't want to waste any more time. Time is precious, there's never enough time.

Walking into the small ward, I glance across at the other beds. All three are empty. Only Dad is in the ICU. A nurse sits at the desk writing up notes. She looks up and gives a smile of acknowledgement.

Mum and Fiona are sitting either side of Dad's bed. They look tired. I guess by the inactivity that nothing has changed over the course of the afternoon.

'I closed a bit early. The café was quiet. How is he?' I ask approaching the bed. As I do, his leg jerks. I look at Mum and Fiona. 'Did you see that?'

'He's done that a few times now,' says Mum. 'It's a good sign. Involuntary movement. It means he's not in such a deep coma.'

I latch onto her words. Coma. He's still in a coma.

Fiona pats the chair next to her. 'Come and sit down,' she says. 'The next twenty-four hours are crucial. The sooner he comes round, the better.'

'What about any long-term…' I search for the right word. 'What's the long-term prognosis?'

'They won't be able to tell properly until Dad's conscious,' says Fiona.

The speed at which my feelings towards Dad align themselves

233

with him surprises me and I settle into the chair at his bedside as I get used to this new emotion.

I must have nodded off, which is quite a feat given the hardness of the plastic chair, when I'm woken by Fiona tugging on my arm.

There's a flurry of activity as Mum calls the nurse over.

Dad's arms are flailing around. His eyes flutter open and then close again. I can see lots of REM behind his eyelids and he lets out an indistinguishable sound from the back of his throat.

His eyes come open again, this time for a bit longer, but he struggles to focus.

'Jim. Hello, Jim,' says the nurse, leaning towards him. 'Can you hear me?'

Dad's eyes hold her gaze for a moment before they roll back and his lids droop. They are in a half-open, half-closed state.

The nurse assures us this is normal and he could have several episodes like this. He is, after all, coming round from a very deep sleep. Each time he'll be able to stay awake for longer.

'I'll be right here,' she says, going back to her desk. 'Just talk gently to him each time he comes round. I'll let the doctor know.'

Her smile reassures me. It's routine to her. Nothing she's not expecting.

While we sit watching Dad breathe in and breathe out, now and again accompanied by little jerks or movements of his body, I think of Roisin.

'Did Fiona tell you about Roisin?' I ask Mum.

'Yes, she did,' says Mum. 'Sure, she'll turn up safe and sound.'

'Diana's been sedated,' I say. The similarity of Diana and my father's situation is not wasted on me.

'Lucky her,' says Mum. It's an out-of-character comment. I shoot a look at Fiona, who shrugs, a look of surprise on her face.

'I thought Roisin would have turned up by now,' I say. 'I mean, it must be getting on for twenty-four hours now. Have you heard from Sean if they've found her yet?'

'No, nothing at all. He phoned me earlier to say that he would probably have to work late,' says Fiona. 'They're extending the search. I think she's officially missing now.'

'God, I hope she's okay,' I say. 'Despite everything, I wouldn't want anything to happen to her.'

'Oh, for God's sake,' says Mum. 'Will you listen to yourselves?' Both Fiona and I jump at the outburst from Mum. I look over at the nurse, who raises her head but returns to her paperwork.

'Mum…' says Fiona.

'No, don't *Mum* me. That girl is trouble and don't you two pretend she's not. Sitting there all concerned for her.' Mum leans forwards over the bed. 'I don't care if I never see that girl again. That Marshall family have brought nothing but trouble to us. What goes around, comes around, I say.' She sits back in her chair, folding her arms and maintaining a defiant look.

'You can't be saying things like that,' says Fiona. 'Would you like me to make you a cup of tea?'

'No. No, I don't want a cup of tea. Don't patronise me,' says Mum. The anger is still in her voice. 'You think I'm a silly old woman who doesn't know anything. Well, I tell you now. I know everything.'

Goosebumps prick the back of my neck. Fiona's face is pale, as I'm sure mine is too.

'What do you mean?' I have to ask. I have to know if she means what I think she does.

Her eyes soften. The muscles in her face and neck relax. Her shoulders sag and she lets out a sigh. I hold my breath as I wait for her to speak.

'I'm sorry,' she says at last. 'Take no notice of me. I'm a bit tired. Saying things I don't mean. What is it you say these days? Having a mini melt-down.' She takes Dad's hand in hers and strokes it. 'Don't you two be worrying now, do you hear me? I've got it all under control.'

The goosebumps extend across my shoulders and down my

arms. What exactly does she have under control? Herself? Is that what she means? It's certainly what I want her to mean, but somehow I don't think it is.

Dad hasn't woken again and seems to have settled down. The doctor has been to visit and concludes that he's now in a normal sleep, as indicated by the NREM and EEG readings.

'He looks very calm,' says Fiona. 'Why don't you come and have a cup of tea with me?'

'I don't want to leave him alone,' says Mum.

'Erin will stay with Dad.'

'Yes, you go, Mum,' I say.

Reluctantly, Mum agrees and leaves the room with Fiona. I take the opportunity to rearrange the chairs and plump up the cushion Mum has brought in from home. A welcome relief from the hard, plastic chair seats.

As I slide one of the chairs over to pick up a tissue from the floor, Mum's handbag, which is resting on the seat, topples over. Several items fall from the unzipped bag, scattering across the tiled floor.

I mutter a curse under my breath as I drop to my hands and knees to retrieve the items. A lipstick. A packet of tissues. Mobile phone. A key.

I scoop up the items and slip them into the bag. I stop as a gold key slides down my palm. My fingers curl and catch it before it can fall back into the depths of the black-leather handbag.

I open my fingers and study the key in the palm of my hand. It hasn't been attached to the small bunch of keys Mum usually carries around with her, but I know exactly which lock it fits.

It's the safe key.

The key that Mum has claimed not to have.

Why is she lying about it?

I make a snap decision. I zip up the bag and replace it on the chair. The gold key, I poke into the front pocket of my jeans.

'You okay?' Fiona's voice makes me jump. I spin round as my sister and mother come back onto the ward.

'Yes, fine,' I say, tagging a smile on the end. I glance at my watch. 'I suppose I had better get back. Early start and all that. What are you doing, Mum? Are you coming back with us?'

'No, I'll stay the night, just in case,' she says, settling herself into the chair.

I feel guilty as a small wave of relief washes over me. It's wrong to be pleased Mum is staying at the hospital tonight, sat hunched in an uncomfortable hospital chair. However, it gives me the ideal opportunity to look inside the safe.

Saying our goodbyes, Fiona and I leave the hospital.

'Sean's working overtime,' says Fiona, checking her phone as we drive out of the hospital grounds. 'He texted me to say they are having one last search for Roisin before it gets dark. They'll start again in the morning.'

'Did you tell Sean about Roisin stirring up all this trouble?' I ask. Fiona turns her head to the passing scenery. I ask again. 'Fiona, did you tell Sean?'

'No. I didn't. I was hoping to keep him out of it. I didn't want to worry him,' she says, continuing to gaze out of the window. She rests her head against the glass. 'If Roisin doesn't turn up, I'm going to have to mention it.'

'Why?'

'Because he needs to know all the facts before someone gossips in the village and tells him.'

'But no one knows, other than us.'

'And Kerry.'

'He's no gossip.'

'Let's hope he's not.'

'He is NOT.'

Fiona turns away from the window. 'I didn't mean to offend you, but you don't know him that well.'

'Let's agree to disagree. Innocent until proven guilty. I'm sure, married to Sean, you must know that.' I try to keep the edge out of my voice. I don't want to fall out with Fiona, but my instinct to defend Kerry is great, even though my sister does have a point about not knowing him that well.

'It's not just Kerry, anyway,' says Fiona. 'We don't know what Roisin has told anyone else. What if she's said something to Diana?'

'I'm sure if Diana knew anything, she wouldn't be quietly sat at home.'

'I have to think of Sean too,' says Fiona. 'I don't want him to have any surprises. Not while he's investigating Roisin's disappearance. He could get into trouble at work. Conflict of interest. Or accused of not doing his job properly because he doesn't want Roisin found.'

We continue the journey in silence until I pull up outside Fiona's house. 'I hadn't thought of it like that,' I say. 'I suppose you had better tell him everything.'

'He doesn't want any of this to come out any more than we do. But it could put him in a really difficult position,' says Fiona.

'What were we thinking of back then? Why did we ever think we could pull this off?'

'At the time it was very straightforward,' says Fiona. 'Never in a million years did we think anyone would find out, least of all Roisin. Don't start with the recriminations. It's too late for that. We have to deal with the here and now.'

When I get back to the flat I go straight to Mum and Dad's bedroom. Opening the wardrobe doors, I kneel down in front of the safe. I'm glad Dad didn't invest in one of those safes with a keypad and secret number, having a key makes life so much easier.

My hand is shaking with both excitement and fear. Never in my life have I ever been allowed anywhere near the safe. Dad is the keeper and doesn't even allow Mum to open it. I wonder what I'm about to find. It's as if I'm committing a crime merely by having the key, let alone opening the safe. Dad would be furious if he knew. In the past, defying his wishes would have given me a sense of satisfaction, but today it's not there. Today there's guilt and fear.

I've taken the key from my mum without her knowing because I am suspicious of her. Guilt. If I find what I think I will in the safe, then the implications are huge. Fear.

I wipe my sweaty palm on my trouser leg, buying myself a few seconds.

The key turns easily. I can feel the internal locks moving and hear a clank as the bolt is freed from its position. I open the door and peer inside.

The navy-blue coin bag is sitting folded neatly in half at the front of the safe. I lift it out. Inside the cloth bag, bundled up with an elastic band, is a collection of notes, twenties, tens and fives. A till receipt is on top. I examine the date and check on my phone. Fifteenth of May. Yep, that's the day Dad had his accident.

I sit back on my heels as the implications float around in my mind, settling in an uncomfortable order. Mum has been lying about the key. She's lied about the takings in the safe. Why? And what else has she lied about? For whatever reason, she wants us to think that my dad might have been mugged for the takings. There's something about that night that she's not telling us.

I sink back onto the carpet, bringing my knees up and resting my chin on them.

The only reason Mum would be lying would be to protect someone. Who would she go to such lengths to protect?

I know there is only one answer.

'Oh, Jesus, Mum,' I say out loud. 'What have you done?'

Chapter 30

Kerry rubbed his hair dry with the towel and pulled on his black t-shirt before going in search of his jeans. Ten minutes earlier he had seen Erin pull up outside the café. He had been thinking about what she'd told him. In fact, it had never been far from his mind, trying to reconcile her actions with his morals. It made him sound pompous when he said it like that, but the divide was there. However, ignoring it wasn't solving it.

He sat down on the sofa and slipped on his boots. He'd go over on the pretext he was checking she was okay after her visit to her dad. It was partly true, but it would also give him the opportunity to talk to her.

A sudden crash from outside had him jumping up to look out of the window.

Kerry knew the sound. It was the distinctive dull crunch of metal on metal.

'Shit.'

Grabbing his keys, he ran out of the flat, down the outside steps and round into the side road.

He could see a black Audi A3 embedded in the side of a silver estate. He recognised the cars immediately. The Audi belonged to Diana Marshall and the silver estate was Jim Hurley's.

The door of the A3 swung open and out stumbled Diana Marshall. Kerry increased his stride.

'Mrs Marshall!' he called. Diana staggered towards him. As he reached her, he put out his arms to stop her from falling over. It was then that the waft of alcohol hit him. Jesus, she wasn't concussed at all, she was steaming drunk.

'Where's that bloody Hurley girl?' Diana slurred her words as she spoke, pushing Kerry away from her. 'I need to speak to her.'

'Mrs Marshall, I don't think now is a good time,' said Kerry.

'Ah! There she is!' Diana pushed Kerry to one side and swayed with the effort, trying to maintain an upright position.

Kerry looked back towards the shops. Erin was standing on the path watching events unfold. She must have heard the crash too. He glanced up at the other flats. He could see a couple of faces at the windows, like theatre-goers in the balcony seats.

Great.

'Erin, go inside,' he called, jogging to catch up with Diana.

Erin folded her arms and stood her ground. No words needed, her body language spoke volumes.

Diana was making her way across the grass, her heels sinking into the soft turf, making her progress even more unsteady. She reminded Kerry of Storm as a toddler, just finding his feet but not being in complete control.

'Erin Hurley! This is all your fault.' Diana was shouting as she staggered. 'You have brought nothing but misery to my family. Why did you have to come back? Go back to England. You're not wanted here.'

Erin raised her chin, her arms dropped to her sides, but she didn't budge.

Kerry swore to himself again. He wondered just how much Diana knew. Maybe Roisin had confided in her mother. Somehow he doubted it, however. Now wasn't the time to mull this over. He needed to get Diana away from Erin.

'Mrs Marshall, stop this. Not here. Everyone is watching,' he said, trying to appeal to her vanity. 'You're embarrassing yourself.'

Diana leaned back, trying to focus her eyes on him. 'Whilst I appreciate your concerns, Kerry,' she said. 'This has nothing to do with you whatsoever.'

'Please, this is going to achieve nothing tonight. Let me take you home,' he said. He looked over his shoulder. 'Erin, why don't you go inside? You're making it worse.'

'Me, making it worse?' Erin gave an exaggerated huff. 'I'm not the one causing the scene.'

'You're not helping!' *Honestly, women!* 'Just go inside. Please.'

'While she stands there and rubbishes me for everyone to hear? I don't think so.'

'I'm taking her home.' He turned his attention back to Diana. 'Come on, Mrs Marshall, I'll drive you.'

Somehow he managed to get Diana moving in the direction of the car. He hoped the Audi was driveable. It looked like the front bumper of Diana's car had gone down the off-side of Jim's, gouging a furrow from the rear wing to the driver's door.

Somewhat unceremoniously, he bundled Diana into the rear of the car. He turned round to see Erin jogging across the grass towards him.

She looked at the side of her dad's car.

'Looks like she's taken a giant can opener to it,' she said.

'Don't be worrying about that now,' said Kerry. 'Can't you go inside, out of the way?'

Diana must have spotted Erin, for she started shouting again. Kerry pushed the door shut as she tried to get out.

'I'll follow you in Dad's car,' said Erin. 'You'll need a lift back. As long as this heap still works.'

Kerry didn't argue. It would save him having to call Joe out for a lift. 'Okay, but stay parked up down the road a bit, where she won't see you.'

'Don't worry, I'll be discreet.' Erin went round and got in the car. It started up and she drove out of the parking bay onto Beach Road.

Diana had calmed down and when Kerry looked in the back of the car, she was slumped to one side. 'Right, I'll be taking you home now, Mrs Marshall,' he said as he got in the driver's seat. 'You stay right where you are.'

Diana made an incoherent noise, which Kerry took as a yes.

When he reached the Marshall's house, he was glad to see Erin had parked a few houses down. He swung the A3 into the driveway, coming to a halt outside the front door.

There were no lights on in the house, but Pat Marshall's car was in the drive. Kerry rang the bell and banged on the door, before resorting to shouting through the letter-box.

Finally, a light went on in the hallway.

'Mr Marshall, it's Kerry Wright. I've got Mrs Marshall here with me!'

He could hear the lock and bolt being slid open and a bleary-eyed Pat appeared in the doorway.

'Kerry, sorry, I was upstairs. Must have dozed off.' He looked at his watch. 'Is that the time? Nine-thirty? Don't know what happened there.'

Kerry suspected that Pat, like his wife, had been on the booze. Shame it hadn't had the same effect on Mrs Marshall and sent her off to sleep long before she got it into her head to confront Erin.

'Mrs Marshall was in the village. She's in a bit of a state,' said Kerry, as he went back round to the car, followed by Pat. 'She was very upset with Erin Hurley. I'm afraid she crashed into Jim Hurley's car.'

Pat groaned. 'Any damage?'

'You could say that.' Kerry nodded at the smashed bumper of the A3. 'There's a big gouge down the side of Jim's car.'

'Send me the bill,' said Pat, with a sigh. He leaned into the car and hauled his wife out. 'Come on, Diana. Let's get you inside.' He turned to Kerry at the doorway. 'Thank you. And sorry.'

Kerry held up his hand. 'No need to apologise, Mr Marshall.' He went to walk away, but paused. 'Mr Marshall. Just to say, we're all hoping that Roisin comes back soon.'

'Thank you, Kerry. I appreciate that. Goodnight.' He closed the door.

Kerry let out a sigh. It was a sorry state of affairs all round.

Kerry crunched his way back down the gravel drive and out into the road. Erin was leaning against the side of the car, her hands in the front pockets of her jeans.

'All okay?' she asked as he neared.

'Yeah, Pat's taken her in. I think the pair of them have hit the bottle tonight. He'd been asleep. Had no idea she had even gone out.'

Erin rolled her eyes. 'That woman has a serious drink problem.'

'Is it any wonder?'

Erin got in the car and slammed the door. 'It's not my fault.'

'I know that. I wasn't saying it was,' said Kerry, as he got in the car. 'You're very defensive and there's no need to be. Not with me, at least.'

Her face softened and she gave him a small smile.

'I know. Sorry, old habits and all that.' She started the engine and pulled away down the road back towards the village. 'She does hate me, though. Her and Roisin.'

'No one hates you,' said Kerry.

'Not even you?'

'Not even me.' Far from hating her, Kerry acknowledged that his feelings for Erin were growing each day. He had thought long and hard about what she had done, about what his mother had done and he kept coming back to what Joe had said about not judging a teenager's actions through the eyes of an adult.

'What I did when I had the baby doesn't mean I didn't love her,' said Erin. It was as if she had read his mind. She continued without waiting for him to speak. 'I love my child, more than anything and giving her up was the hardest thing I have ever

244

done in my life. Nothing has ever come close to being that diffi-cult. Nothing. It doesn't make me a bad person or a bad mother. I sacrificed motherhood for my child.'

He could hear the pain in her voice. It tugged at his heart. She was still staring straight ahead, her eyes not leaving the road, but as they neared the village and passed under the streetlights, he could see her biting on her lip.

'I'm really trying to understand,' he said. 'Honest, I am. It's just… well, having been shunned by my own mother, it doesn't come easy.'

She nodded and a tear dropped down her cheek. She wiped it away with her fingertips.

'You know, after a time, bearing a grudge becomes second nature. It's easier to cut someone off and not speak to them than it is to face them and to face whatever the issue is. If you talk about things and resolve them, it means that you have to readjust everything that has kept you going for all that time, every word you've ever spoken against that person, you have to take back. You have to swallow your pride and take a very scary step into the unknown.'

As Erin turned the car onto Beach Road and drove towards the café, they saw two police cars parked in the bays.

Kerry sat up a bit straighter. 'Looks like someone called the Guards about Diana.'

'What are you going to say?'

'Nothing, she was upset so I drove her home. I won't be mentioning the alcohol. The poor woman has enough on her plate. You won't say anything either, will you?'

Erin pulled into the parking bay. 'No. What's the point?'

'Good.'

As they got out of the car, so did two guards from each of the vehicles. It was then that Kerry recognised Sean Keane.

'Hi, Sean,' said Erin. 'Everything all right?'

'There's been a development on Roisin going missing,' he said.

'We've looked at her phone records. It seems the night she disappeared she exchanged text messages with both you and Kerry at separate times.'

Kerry exchanged a look with Erin. He didn't like the tone in Sean's voice and two squad cars was overkill for just a catch-up.

'Do you want to get to the point, Sean?' he said.

'We need to interview both of you. Separately,' said Sean.

'What?' It was Erin. 'You don't think we've anything to do with Roisin's disappearance, do you?'

'Let's go down to the station,' said Sean. 'We'll chat then.'

'I'm guessing it's more than a chat,' said Kerry. He could feel the old hostility towards the local law enforcement resurrect itself. He spoke to Erin. 'You don't have to go with them. They have to formally arrest you to make you go down to the station.' Then he turned to Sean and the three officers, who were now flanking him. 'If it's just a chat, let's have it now.'

'Kerry, don't,' said Erin. 'We've nothing to hide, let's go along with them.' She came round the car and stood beside him, her hand resting on his arm. 'Please, don't make a fuss.'

She was right, of course. Kerry took her hand in his and raised it to his lips. 'Okay.'

Sean stepped forward. 'Erin, you go in the car with my two colleagues. Kerry, you come with me.'

Kerry felt Erin's grip tighten on his hand. 'Just tell the truth,' she said. 'You've done nothing wrong.'

'And neither have you,' said Kerry, before letting her hand fall and making his way to the police car.

Chapter 31

The interview room at the station was no different to any other interview room Kerry had sat in before. In his younger days they were familiar places. Regularly hauled in for many a misdemeanour, only to have his knuckles rapped and then to be released again. Kerry had always known it was his stepfather behind the harsh treatment he received for petty things such as drinking in the park with his friends, or just not being in the right place at the right time. His friends got a ticking off on the spot; Kerry got taken down to the station for a talk.

Despite the seriousness of today's interview, Kerry was as relaxed as he had ever been. Erin, on the other hand, he suspected was faring less well.

Eventually, Sean Keane and another officer came into the interview room.

'Am I likely to need a solicitor?' said Kerry.

'You're here of your own free will. You're not under arrest. We simply want a chat,' said Sean. He sat down opposite Kerry, resting his hands on the table between them. 'Do you want a coffee? Tea?'

'No. I'm good. Can we get on with this? It's late and kind of messing up my plans for the evening.'

'Can you confirm exactly when you last saw Roisin Marshall?'

'I don't know exactly. Sunday, maybe?'

'Okay, when did you last have any contact with her?' said Sean.

'If I'm being linked to her disappearance, I'd like to know on what grounds.'

'We've got a copy of Roisin's mobile-phone records. It shows all her calls and text messages, both in and out.'

Kerry shrugged. 'And...?' He looked right back at Sean and hoped his poker face wouldn't let him down.

'And...it shows a number registered to you,' said Sean, matching his stare. 'You and Roisin exchanged text messages on the night of her disappearance. What was that about?'

Kerry thought about refusing to answer. Sean couldn't demand to see his phone now, not without a warrant or a court order. By the time that was organised, Kerry would be able to wipe the text messages from it. However, if the Guards ever found Roisin's phone, then they would soon be able to see what was said. He decided to bide his time for now.

'I can't remember exactly.'

Sean leaned in. 'I suggest your memory improves or you could be here a long time.'

The other police officer opened a file he had in his hand. He looked at a few notes and then at Kerry.

'Seems you have a bit of a past. Known to the Gardai.' He ran his finger down the sheet of paper. 'Drunk and disorderly. Affray. Drugs.'

'That doesn't make me a murderer,' said Kerry, sitting up a bit straighter in his seat.

'Who said anything about murder?' said the officer.

Kerry bit down the urge to respond. He could see he was only going to dig himself in deeper. Instead, he folded his arms and leant back in the seat. 'Charge me if you think I'm involved. If not, I'd like to go home now.'

*

The interview room is sterile and hostile. I've never been in one before and can't help feeling intimidated by the oppressive surroundings. The walls, painted a neutral light grey, reflect the small stream of light coming in through the one high window. I'm sitting on a plastic chair, which reminds me of the chairs at the hospital. In front of me on the laminated table is a plastic disposable cup full of water.

'I'm Garda O'Neill,' says the first Guard sitting opposite me. 'This is my colleague Garda Murphy.'

The female Guard acknowledges me with a slight nod of her head, but doesn't speak.

'Now, I understand you're Sergeant Keane's sister-in-law,' says O'Neill. 'He speaks very highly of you and assures me you will co-operate fully with us.'

'I'll do my best,' I say, holding my hands in my lap. I wipe my palms with the tips of my fingers and concentrate on breathing normally.

'I want to run through a few details, first,' says O'Neill. He refers to a sheet Murphy passes to him. 'You used to live in Rossway until ten years ago, when you moved to England to live with your sister. Is that right?'

'That's right,' I say. 'I've come back because my father is seriously ill in hospital.'

'So I understand,' says O'Neill. 'I hope he makes a good recovery.'

'Thank you.'

It's surreal: having a civilised conversation with a stranger, all very polite, and yet at the heart of it I know this interview relates to Roisin and her disappearance.

'You went to the local school and were friends with Roisin Marshall,' says O'Neill. 'When did you last have contact with Miss Marshall?'

I take a sip of water. My hand shakes as I lift the flimsy cup towards my mouth, something neither O'Neill nor Murphy will miss, I'm sure.

'It was…' I begin.

O'Neill interrupts before I can finish. 'I should say at this stage, we have a copy of Roisin Marshall's mobile phone. It lists all her calls, incoming and outgoing, together with sent and received text messages.'

I understand what he's saying.

'I sent Roisin a text the night before last,' I say. I replace the cup on the table. My hand shakes even more.

'That will be the night she went missing?'

'Yes. I arranged to meet her, but she never showed up.'

'What were you meeting her for?'

The female Guard stops making notes and is looking at me, anticipation shining behind her eyes. O'Neill leans forward. Both are clearly eager to hear what I have to say.

I say a silent prayer. I hope to God I'm doing the right thing.

'We had a few things we needed to talk about.'

'Such as?'

'Personal stuff.' I know it's an insufficient answer, one I won't get away with. If anything, I'm arousing suspicion.

'We understand from some locals that you and Roisin had an argument in the street last week,' says Murphy. 'What was that about?'

My mouth is parched. I desperately want some more water but know my hand will shake violently if I attempt to reach for the cup. I wet my lips and swallow hard. 'It was an argument from way back when I used to live here. I went out with her brother Niall. He died in a car accident and Roisin, for some reason, holds me responsible. It was about all that.'

'So what were you meeting her for?' asks O'Neill.

'To try and sort things out once and for all.'

'And where did you meet her?'

'I didn't meet her. I arranged to, but she never turned up,' I say. 'I was supposed to meet her at The Spit. I waited for ages but she wasn't there and it was raining heavily so I went home.'

'And what time was this?' O'Neill's tone sounds harder. I'm sure he doesn't believe me.

'I got there at nine o'clock and waited for ten, fifteen minutes.'

'Can anyone confirm this?' O'Neill asks as Murphy scribbles the information down on her notepad.

I shake my head. 'No.'

'You know, Miss Hurley, this is looking very much like you were the last person to have contact with Miss Marshall that night,' says O'Neill. 'Is there anything you would like to tell us? Anything that you may have forgotten or omitted?'

'No. I've told you everything.'

'I'm going to need you to make a formal statement,' says O'Neill. 'After that, I'd ask that you don't leave the area for now. Not until we've made further inquiries.'

This time, I nod. I think of Mum, of Fiona and of the child I had.

I have no choice.

When I step out of the station, I'm relieved to see Kerry across the road. He's sitting casually on his bike, smoking a cigarette. I walk over to him. On seeing me, he drops his cigarette and grinds it out with his boot.

'They let you out, then?' he says.

'I could say the same for you,' I reply with a smile.

He wraps his arms around me and kisses me. It feels good. So reassuring and comforting after several hours' sitting in the hostile environment of the station.

'Come on, I'll take you home,' says Kerry, pulling away and reaching for the spare crash helmet.

'What time did you get out?' I ask, as I allow Kerry to fasten the strap under my chin.

'About an hour ago. Joe came and got me. I came straight back with the bike. I guessed you'd be out soon.'

'I'm assuming they asked you about phoning or texting Roisin,'

I say. The thought that he had been in touch with Roisin that night sits uncomfortably with me.

'Yeah. I texted her that night,' he says

'You texted her? What for?'

'To meet for a drink. I thought I might be able to persuade her to let things go. You know, draw a line under the past and move on.'

'And did you?'

'No. She never showed up. Look, let's not talk about it here.' He nods towards the Gardai station.

I look over my shoulder. Sean is standing in the doorway to the station observing us. A small chill runs through me. I climb on the back of Kerry's bike, wrapping my hands around his waist.

Kerry starts the Triumph and within seconds we are roaring down the road. I tighten my grip around his body. It feels good to be in physical contact with him. I don't want to let go and wish we could just keep riding and not stop.

Sex with Kerry is a strange mix of tenderness combined with urgency. Time is ticking against us and we make the most of every second we have together. And yet, the care and love surfaces time and time again.

This time we have actually made it to his bed. I nestle down in his arms, pulling the duvet up around my shoulder.

'It feels like a cocoon,' I say. 'Warm and safe. If only we could stay like this forever.'

'Sure, that would be nice,' says Kerry. He pulls me closer. 'Stay the night, won't you? There's no need to go.'

'What's the point of us both sleeping alone, especially when we're only across the road from each other,' I say. 'It's not like I've got far to go to work tomorrow.'

'How is your dad?'

'He's starting to come out of his coma. It's like he's waking from a really heavy deep sleep. It will take time.'

252

'That's good. I'm glad about that.'

'Me too,' I say. 'I want to talk to him as soon as I can. I have things to say to him that I should have said a long time ago. Bridges to build.'

'You're a very courageous woman,' says Kerry. 'I wish I had half your guts.'

I prop myself up on my elbow and drop a kiss onto him.

'I'm no braver than anyone else,' I say. 'Certainly no braver than you.' I trace my finger around his face, following the line of his jaw, biding time as I weigh up my next words. 'You're just as brave. Everything that you've been through. There's no reason why you can't build some bridges of your own.'

His eyes widen and the muscles in his face tense. 'It's easy for you to say.'

Is that a small chink in the wall he's built around him? He hasn't outright dismissed the idea.

'Why don't you let me help you?' I say, making sure there is no challenge in my voice. 'Of all the people in your life, I'm probably the only one who truly understands what you've been through. How you're feeling. How it feels to be adrift. Let me help you, please?'

Kerry rolls over and, sitting on the edge of the bed, he plants his feet on the floor, resting his arms on his knees. I shuffle over and put my hand on his back, kissing his bare shoulder. Kerry covers my hand with his.

'I don't know,' he says at last. 'You're stronger than me.'

'Strength doesn't come into it. And even if it did, you can lean on me.'

'It's too painful.'

'Don't let that pain eat you up,' I say. 'It's painful because you're scared of it. You're scared of being hurt again. I totally get all that, I really do.' I move closer and wrap both arms around his shoulders, resting my chin on him. 'It's like, if you stop being angry, you have to confront it. Deal with feelings and emotions you couldn't deal with at the time, but you're older now. Wiser and, yes, stronger. You can't be running away all your life.'

I continue to hold him, willing him to understand and to take the risk.

'Okay,' he says at last.

'Okay, what?'

'Okay, help me.' His voice is so quiet I can only just hear him. 'Help me make things right.'

'Thank you,' I say. If I can help him understand his mum and what she did, then maybe he can understand what I've done.

Kerry moves from the bed and kneels down. He pulls the box out containing the letters. 'There's a date on the back of each one,' he says.

'That's good, we'll start with the first one, then,' I say. 'But first, shall we put some clothes on?'

Five minutes later, we're sitting in the living room. The letters are laid out on the coffee table in front of us in date order. Kerry picks up the first one and slides his thumb under the flap to open the envelope.

A single sheet of A4 paper is folded in four. Kerry opens it and lays it out flat on the table.

Dear Kerry

I know you probably don't want to hear from me after what happened earlier this year but I hope and pray that you will read this letter.

I have thought about you every day since the argument and every day I've wished I could turn back time. God, I would do things differently. I never meant for things to get this bad. There's been too much hurt and loss in this family already.

Please call me. I'd love to talk to you properly.

I love you.

Mum xx

P.S. Ronan made the school hurling team.

I look at Kerry to gauge his response, but his face is impassive.

'Have you not even seen your brother?' I ask.

'I used to go and watch him in his hurling matches. If mum or her husband wasn't there, I'd go and speak to him,' says Kerry. 'Now he's older, he calls me or texts me. Sometimes we meet up.'

'That's good, at least you still keep in contact with him – that would be a shame otherwise,' I say. 'Let's try the next one.' I pick up the envelope, which is dated about ten months after the first one.

We read it together. It says much the same thing. How she wishes Kerry would get in touch and that Ronan is missing him.

Gradually, we make our way through the letters. They are all along the same lines. She wants to meet to talk through things. To make things better. She misses him and she always finishes by telling him she loves him.

We get to the final two.

'I think this is pointless,' says Kerry. 'I don't want to read any more.'

'Come on, let's read these two. We might as well now we've read all the others.' I don't wait for him to answer and open the next one. It has a date of nearly a year ago. It sounds more reflective, somehow sadder, and his mother tells Kerry how she still misses him.

'It's just the same as the others,' says Kerry. 'In not one of them has she apologised for what she said to me. It's all about her and her sorrow.'

I take the last letter and look at the date. 'This is only a few weeks old.'

'I know. Honestly, Erin, let's not bother.'

I tear open the letter before Kerry can stop me. It's the longest letter yet and goes on to a second page. I tug at his arm to stop him from getting up and begin to read it out loud.

Dear Kerry

I still don't know if you are reading these letters or not. I spoke to Max. He says he definitely gives them to you. I really hope that you are reading them.

You may have heard that Tom and I aren't together any more. He left me just before Christmas. I saw it coming, if I'm honest. And as I'm being honest, I'll tell you why. It was because of you. I've never been able to forgive myself for what happened that night. For things that were said. And I've never been able to forgive Tom either. I should not have let what happened happen. I can only imagine how you must feel and I'm tortured every time I think about it.

I never in a million years wanted things to end up like this. I can't tell you how much it hurts me to think I no longer have a relationship with my own son. Your dad would be furious if he knew. I came to Rossway last week. I came to see you. I sat in the little café next door to the workshop for a long time trying to pluck up courage to come and see you. But in the end I wasn't brave enough. I didn't want to have to face you rejecting me. How hypocritical is that? After me telling you I never wanted to see you again, I'm too scared to see you in case you say the same thing. And not without reason. I know I was wrong then, but I was scared of being alone and I had Ronan to think of. A life for my five-year-old child or a life for my seventeen -year-old who was probably going to fly the nest soon anyway. I couldn't deny another one of my sons the chance to grow up with his father. You'd already had that taken away, I couldn't take it away from Ronan.

I know this doesn't make what happened right and I know what I said was wrong, so very wrong. As soon as I said it, I regretted it. If I was able to change one thing in my life, I wouldn't choose the obvious – your dad not to have died – I would choose to take back those words. To take away the pain I caused you and the damage I've done. I know I can't and I can only tell you how sorry I am and hope that one day you will forgive me.

Please know, Kerry, that you are my son and always will be. You may not think of me as your mother any more and that is something I will have to live with. I may have got it wrong. Really wrong, but I have never stopped loving you.

I love you. Always have, always will.

Mum xx

This time Kerry picks up the letter and reads it himself. I watch him closely, but don't say anything. He shuts his eyes tight, holding his thumb and finger against the closed lids. He takes a big gulp of air and when he opens his eyes, he is crying. I hold him in my arms, not saying a word.

Eventually, he pulls away, palming his eyes and face to wipe away the tears.

'God, would you look at me?' he says.

'It's okay. You've had nine years of pent-up emotion and feelings. It needed to come out sooner or later.'

Kerry looks at the letter, which has been crumpled. He flattens it out on the table.

'She's actually sorry,' he says. 'She says so here.'

'That's a good start,' I say gently.

'You know, I always thought she didn't want me because Tom didn't like me. I thought that's why she chose him over me, but it wasn't that at all. She chose Ronan. She wanted him to be happy. She wanted him to grow up with his dad. She knew how bad it had been for me since my dad died.'

'She did what she thought was best for her child at the time,' I say. I'm aware of the similarity to my decision-making. 'She never stopped loving you, though.'

Kerry nods. 'She was sacrificing her relationship with me for what was best for Ronan. Who can blame her? Like she says, I was seventeen and probably wouldn't have stayed around for much longer anyway. Ronan was so young. She had no choice but to put him first. I still wish she hadn't said what she did. That's the thing that has stuck with me all this time.'

'It was a mistake. She says that herself. It's the one thing she wishes she could go back and change. We are all wiser after the event, aren't we?'

'I need time to take this all in,' says Kerry. He leans back on the sofa and looks up to the ceiling.

I lean back too and slip my arm around him. 'How do you feel about seeing her? Talking to her?'

'I don't know. Maybe. I need time to get used to the idea,' says Kerry. 'That's some bridge that needs building.'

'The bigger the bridge, the bigger the reward,' I say, thinking of my dad.

PART 3

'Forgiveness says you are given another chance to make a new beginning.'

Desmond Tutu

Chapter 32

The next morning Mum is surprised to see me at the hospital so early, but I explain that Kerry is standing in for me so I can be here.

'He has the day off,' I say. 'Means I could get here sooner.'

She looks at me, as if seeing me in a different way to what she has before.

'I want to be here,' I say. 'There are things I need to put right.'

Mum swallows hard and I can see her eyes shine with the first hint of tears. 'You must do whatever you need to do,' she says, placing her hand on my cheek. 'That's what we do as women, mothers and daughters.'

Her words are spoken with such sincerity and intensity. I'm sure she's trying to tell me something indirectly. I wonder again how much she knows. What secrets she is keeping.

'Mum?' I begin. I want to ask her about the key to the safe and what happened the night Dad fell. But the moment is lost as Dad gives a groan and his legs rustle against the starched bed sheets.

We both turn to look at him. Mum is saying his name and takes his hand in hers, a gesture she has done every time I've been here.

'Jim? Hello, Jim. It's me, Marie. Can you hear me?'

I position myself on the other side of the bed. His eyes are heavy. I can see he's fighting to keep them open. He frowns as he tries to focus on Mum. His lips are dry and cracked. He moves his mouth as if he's chewing a piece of food.

'Do you want a drink, Dad?' I ask. I pour some water into what is essentially a beaker for grown-ups. It has a lid and an extended spout so the patient can drink from it without having to sit up fully. Dad's probably wondering what the hell I am doing there. He looks at the cup and I offer it to him, placing the spout in his mouth and ever so slightly tipping it. He swallows the water and, like a baby, sucks on the spout for more.

I exchange a look with my mum. Is she wondering the same as me about any long-term damage he has suffered? After the third sip of water he turns his head away. I take this as a good sign. He clearly knows when he's thirsty, that water quenches his thirst and when he's had enough.

He tries to speak but his voice is rough and hoarse. The noise is no more than a rasp.

'Don't try talking,' says Mum. 'You're in hospital. Do you remember what happened?'

There's a tremor in Mum's voice. She sounds nervous. Dad makes a small nodding gesture accompanied by a grunt. I take this as confirmation that he does indeed know.

Dad raises his hand from the bed. The effort of this is clear, but as his hand shakes from the exertion, he stretches out a bony finger and points at Mum. He frowns and tries to speak, but his voice is husky and the effort too much. With an impatient rasp of air from his lungs, he drops his arm back down onto the bed.

Mum rearranges the bed sheets, which don't need rearranging at all. She seems flustered. 'You need to rest, Jim,' she's saying. 'Take your time now, won't you. Everything is fine and there's nothing for you to worry about.'

I watch my father intently for any sign of a reaction.

'Dad,' I say. 'Dad, it's me, Erin.'

His eyes transfer their gaze to me. I carry on. 'I came over from England because you haven't been well. We've all been worried about you.' I offer a smile, hoping I will get some sort of acknowledgement. He doesn't respond, but he continues to look at me. In the past, his gaze, or death stare, as I used to call it, would put the fear of God into me. I would always know when I had said something wrong or done something wrong, he'd fixed me with those dark-green eyes of his. I used to think the death stare was worse than the telling off sometimes. I'm getting the death stare now and I wonder what I've done. Maybe he doesn't appreciate me coming to see him. I want to say more to him, but Mum is there and I can't bring myself to say what I want to in front of her.

Dad's eyes begin to close and he doesn't fight the sleep that threatens. He's drifting off and within a minute his breathing becomes deeper and falls into the rhythmic pattern of sleep we have grown accustomed to in this ward.

I must have dozed off too at some point. I'm woken by a pain in the back of my neck, where my head has dropped forward. I stretch my arms and roll my head around to loosen the tightness in my neck muscles.

'Do you fancy a cup of tea, Mum?' I ask, looking on at Dad. I can't work out if he's asleep or awake. His eyes are only half open and his limbs are still. I know Mum has been speaking to him. Her words floated into my subconscious as I had drifted in and out of sleep. She's been chatting about Fiona and the children.

'Yes, please,' says Mum, in answer to my question. 'I'll come out for it in a moment.'

I head off to the kitchen and begin to make two cups of tea. I may have left behind as much Irishness in me as possible when I went to England, but tea-drinking is one thing that stayed with me. A cup of tea is the answer to everything, according to Mum.

We have lived through every celebration, every achievement, every problem and every crisis with a cup of tea. It's a natural default setting.

I leave the cups in the family room and go to fetch Mum. Dad looks to be asleep or resting, it's hard to know which, but the nurse assures us that it is perfectly normal.

'Will you be doing some test to assess the long-term prognosis?' I ask.

'The doctor will discuss all that with you,' says the nurse. 'He'll be doing his rounds later this morning. It's best to speak to him then.'

'Thank you,' I say, although I feel the nurse had sidestepped answering my question. I guide Mum through to the family room. 'There, sit yourself down, Mum, and have a proper break. I'll go and sit with Dad.'

'No, wait for me. Don't be sitting in there by yourself,' she says, standing back up.

'It's fine, Mum, you stay there.' Once again I guide Mum back into the chair. 'I would like to sit with Dad, just for a while…on my own.'

I hope I don't have to elaborate. There are things I want to say to Dad in private. I don't know when I'll get another chance.

'Don't go upsetting him, now,' says Mum.

'I won't.'

I leave before she has time to protest or insist on coming with me.

The door to the ward swishes against the floor as I walk in. The heart monitor beeps its regular rhythm. It's a lonely sound now Dad is breathing on his own, there is no *whoosh* in and *whoosh* out of the machine breathing for him. His breath rattles gently at the back of his throat like a Venetian blind fluttering on a clement breeze against an open window.

I sit down and slip my hand into his, placing my other hand over the top.

'Hello, Dad,' I say softly. 'It's me, Erin.' I stroke his hand, hoping for a response, some sort of acknowledgement that he's heard me. I look over my shoulder. The nurse is at her desk, doing something on the computer in front of her. I'm not quite sure if she really has work to do, but she's definitely making a point of being occupied.

I turn back to Dad.

'I hope you can hear me, Dad,' I begin. 'I'm not very good at this and not sure I'll be able to do it again, so you'd better be listening.' I swallow an unexpected lump that has found its way into my throat. This is going to be harder than I imagined. 'I know we haven't always seen eye to eye about everything. Okay, that's not quite right. When I was a teenager and living at home, we clashed a lot. And that animosity somehow found its way into our relationship, it got in all the little corners and grooves. It embedded itself and became the norm for us.'

I look for a response. I'll take anything – the flicker of an eyelid, a twitch of his hand, but there's nothing.

'After the accident, when I went to England, I was very angry with everyone. You, Mum, Diana Marshall. Even Niall himself. He wasn't supposed to go and die on me. And the adults in my life weren't supposed to cause me even more pain by insisting I have a termination. I couldn't cope with everything that happened. It hurt. It hurt so badly.'

Oh God, it had been so painful. The feeling of utter hopelessness comes rushing right back as if I'm living that moment all over again. It's as clear, as sharp and as fierce as it had been then. I double up, my face resting on our hands. A wave of tears comes and races down my cheeks, spreading across my hands, following the channels between my fingers, seeping through the gaps, reaching my father's skin.

I allow myself a moment to deal with the acute pain. It's the worst torture I can imagine. It feels as if my heart is being cut from me while it still beats.

After a minute or two, the pain dissipates enough so I can concentrate on what I need to say. I'm aware Mum could walk back in any time now.

'Dad, I'm sorry,' I say. 'Really sorry. I didn't understand. I didn't want to understand. I couldn't deal with it. As time went on, I began to have small inklings of what it was all about. How you thought you were doing the right thing by me. But I couldn't admit that. It would mean having to deal with the pain and loss all over again.

'If I was angry with you, it was easier. I could deal with anger. I could channel all my feelings into that anger. The more I felt, the more I began to think I understood your reasons, the more mature I became and the more life experiences I had to deal with began to make me realise that the world isn't black and white. It's full of many, many shades and tones.'

The words are tumbling out. I keep going, fearing if I stop now, I'll never say them.

'But I wouldn't let myself apply that to you. It was easier to hold you up as the villain. I could direct everything I was feeling at you. It meant I didn't have to deal with that pain.'

I pluck a tissue from the box on the bedside table and dab at my eyes and nose. I rise and put my lips to his ear.

'I'm sorry, Dad,' I say. 'So very sorry. Please forgive me.' I kiss his cheek.

At first I think the dampness on his face is that of my own tears, but as I pull away I realise the tears are coming from Dad. A tear forms in the corner of his eye from under the closed lid and, as it pools, it overflows the small well between his eye and bridge of his nose. The tear follows the path of the one before, sliding down his face. And then his eyes flick open.

'Dad?'

His mouth opens and closes. There is the tiniest of breaths and the quietest of sounds. I move my face closer. He's trying to speak, I'm sure of it.

'Erin.' It's a rasp on a small breath, barely distinguishable, but I know he's said my name. He knows it's me.

'Yes, Dad. I can hear you,' I say, my voice barely more audible than his.

'Forgive me,' he says.

I move my head to look at him and let the words sink in. After a moment I speak. 'There's nothing to forgive. Not now. Once upon a time, I might have wanted that from you, but not now. Not any more.'

His fingers move against mine. I bury my face against his and, once again, our tears merge as a tidal wave of emotion hits me. I allow myself to succumb to the feeling. I'm done fighting this battle. It's been a pointless war with no winners, only losers.

Eventually, the crying subsides. I draw back. Dad is still awake, but the rims of his eyes are red. I can see myself reflected back in those green eyes. All those feelings I thought were just my own, all that pain and hurt, it's there, plain to see in him, but I have never chosen to look for it. I've been too ready to cast him as a terrible father. My stubbornness and need to blame has prohibited me from looking at him through my adult eyes. He's forever been seen through the eyes of an angry, naive teenager, who thought the world was against her.

How had I got that so wrong? How had the rest of my life matured and yet that one part I've allowed to stay in the past? It jars with me in every way. It's as if I've been in the dark and never made any attempt to seek the light. The dark is comforting. The light means I have to look at things I don't necessarily want to see, the fear of the unknown has held me back. I don't want to have that fear again.

'I love you, Dad.'

He gives the slightest nod of the head. It's all he can manage. 'Love. You,' he says. Dad is getting weak, the effort to communicate taking its toll. He taps my hand with his finger and I lean in closer. 'I know,' he utters.

Those two words are loaded with so much, I don't know how to respond.

'He knows about the baby.' Mum's voice comes from behind me. I spin around, I hadn't heard her come in. Mum rests her hand on my shoulder. 'And so do I.'

Once again, I struggle to find any words. So much is happening, I'm finding it difficult to process it all. They know?

'How?' I finally manage to ask. I'm glad I'm sitting down already. My legs feel weak and are shaking. I look at Dad, his eyes are in that half-open state again.

Mum walks round to the other side of the bed. She adjusts the cushion on the plastic chair before settling herself down.

'I've always known you had the baby,' she says. 'I've always known that baby was Sophie.'

Chapter 33

Mum's matter-of-fact revelation poleaxes my thoughts. My whole mind goes blank. All thought pathways are numbed and blocked. The implications are far too great to compute at once.

'I had my suspicions for a long time,' says Mum. 'Probably when Fiona was supposedly pregnant. All that trouble she had conceiving in the first place and then she becomes pregnant at the same time as you. And then her only coming home in the early stages of the pregnancy. After that she said she was too ill to come and when I suggested I come over to visit, she made all sorts of excuses.'

I feel guilt and shame wash over me. I set out to deceive my mother and all this time she had known.

'We thought we had planned it so carefully,' I say at last, my voice is as small as I feel. I can't meet Mum's gaze. 'We had no idea you knew.'

'Sure, I'm not as green as the country I was born in.'

'Why didn't you say anything before?'

'Now, what would be the point of that? It would only cause problems. The way I saw it, Fiona had the child she wanted, you didn't have to go through with a termination and I still had my grandchild.'

Dad still appears to be caught between the conscious and unconscious world. 'And Dad?' I say, finding the courage to look at Mum.

Mum doesn't answer straight away. She shifts in her seat and smoothes her skirt.

'He only found out recently.'

I can sense Mum's not telling me everything. The niggling unease that has been prodding me over the last few days, one I've tried to waylay, punches me in the stomach. I draw a sharp breath.

'When exactly did he find out? And how?'

'All I've ever wanted is for my daughters to be happy. It's a natural inbuilt part of being a mother. Being a parent. I would do anything...*anything*, to ensure you and Fiona were happy,' says Mum.

'I know, Mum. I get that,' I say softly, as I try to hide the unease which has morphed into fear and is battering my stomach.

'I never told your dad. There didn't seem any need. If he knew, he would be furious that you had lied to him. You know, he too only ever wanted what was best for his girls. He truly believed a termination was the right thing to do at the time,' says Mum. 'He spent many a waking night fretting over you and what would happen. And then, it seemed my prayers were answered, but in the cruellest way possible. It was as if your baby's life was a trade-off for Niall's. God had seen it fit to answer my prayers and yet punish our family at the same time. I did not want to cause any more pain. I let your father believe that you had lost the baby and that Fiona had become pregnant. You had had too much grief in your short life already, you didn't need your father and the likes of the Marshalls on your back. It was the best way I knew to protect you.'

I listen intently. I can identify with everything Mum is saying. Haven't I only ever wanted what was best for my own child? I can justify every action on that one principle, that one belief – the best for my child, whatever the cost.

'Thank you,' I say. 'Thank you for that and for everything since.' I reach out across the bed. Mum mirrors the gesture.

'A couple of weeks ago, Roisin Marshall confronted me at the back of the café,' says Mum. 'She said she had proof that you had been pregnant.'

'The photograph,' I say. 'The one of me and Niall.'

'And the words on the back, *one plus one equals three*,' says Mum.

'I gave it to Niall shortly before the accident. We were so happy. We were also very naive. We thought we could get a place, have the baby, and go to work and college at the same time. We really believed we would show everyone, prove them wrong. Christ, looking back, we were living in some sort of dream world.'

'So you appreciate now how your father and I felt. And Diana Marshall.'

'I can now, but I couldn't then.'

'You can't put an old head on young shoulders, sure you can't,' says Mum.

'When exactly did Roisin come to you with this photograph?' I ask, as dates and times whirl through my mind.

'Do I really need to answer that?'

'The night of Dad's accident,' I say. She's right. I didn't really need to ask that. I think I had almost worked this out before. Now it's all coming together. 'What happened that night?'

'Roisin and myself, we got into an argument,' says Mum. She slips her hand from mine and sits back in her chair. 'We were arguing at the top of the outside stairs. Your father heard us and got between us. Roisin was shouting things like, "Erin was pregnant. What happened to it? She kept it all a secret." I was telling her to shut up. Your father was yelling at me to be quiet. Demanding Roisin explain herself. There was a moment when we all stopped fighting and he looked at me. I didn't say a word but then I didn't have to. He could tell.'

Mum is looking beyond me, recalling the events as if she's right back there in the moment. Part of me doesn't want to know

271

what happened next. I can guess. I wish to God I'm wrong, but something tells me I'm not. I have no choice. I have to ask. 'What happened after that?'

'There was a scuffle. Your dad lost his balance. I can remember seeing his heel hanging precariously over the edge of the top step. For one tiny moment he was suspended at the perfect point of balance, where one crucial movement would dictate success or failure, taking him to either safety or danger.' She pauses for a moment. The faraway look remains as she speaks again. 'I thought I was going to save him, to grab his hands and to stop him from toppling backwards down the steps,' says Mum. 'I genuinely thought that.'

'What did you do?' My voice catches in my throat.

'Somewhere between me reaching out for him and actually taking his hand, somewhere in that split second, I thought of all the repercussions your father knowing would have,' says Mum. 'He wouldn't have let us live the lie. He would have been on the Marshalls' side. I couldn't let that happen. So, instead of pulling him, I…pushed.'

'Oh, Mum.' The nightmare is becoming a reality.

'I couldn't let Diana Marshall have claim over your child, not after she was so against it,' Mum continues. 'She didn't deserve it.' Her voice is firm and hard. 'I didn't want anyone to know Roisin was there. I said we were to make it look like an accident or a mugging. That's why I kept the key. I think Roisin was frightened at the time. She ran off before the ambulance arrived. I thought Kerry might have seen her hiding behind the bins until it was safe to go, but he never said anything.'

I give myself a minute to take on board what Mum has told me. Roisin confronted Mum. They had a scuffle. Dad fell. They were happy to let people think it might be a mugging gone wrong. All this because of a photograph. How I wish now I'd never given it to Niall all those years ago. A stupid mistake that is catching up with me now.

I think about the picture. Is it really that crucial? 'You know what, Mum, Roisin only had a photograph,' I say. 'That didn't prove anything. It would only be assumption.'

'You're right, Erin. On its own it doesn't prove anything, but at the time I wasn't thinking straight. I grabbed it from her, that's what the scuffling was about. Anyway, I kept it for a while, but later I destroyed it. I didn't want anyone else seeing it, not least Roisin.'

'That's what you were burning in the sink,' I say, thinking back to how I had taken the milk up to Mum and she was standing at the kitchen sink. She'd got all flustered when she saw me.

'I thought that would be an end to it, but I was wrong,' says Mum. 'It was after, when she came to see me at the hospital. She got me so cross, I'm sorry, Erin, it's my fault. I let slip you had the baby. After that there was no stopping her. Photograph or no photograph.'

'But it's okay, Mum,' I say, trying to reassure her. 'I've talked this through with Fiona. Roisin may know I had the baby, but she thinks I put it up for adoption. There's nothing she can do about that. Nothing at all. After all this time, I can cope with people knowing this. I thought I couldn't, but I can. I know that now. She can't do anything to hurt us.'

Mum is shaking her head. There's such a look of sadness on her face. It unnerves me. A groan from Dad interrupts the conversation. 'You all right, Dad?' I stand and lean close to him. His eyes flicker open, but it seems to be an effort to keep them from fluttering shut.

'Family…needs mother,' he says finally.

'It's okay, Jim,' says Marie. 'Rest now. Don't worry. I have it all sorted.'

Dad grunts something inaudible.

I shiver. Again, Mum is sending chills through me. 'Mum, what's sorted?'

She hesitates before speaking.

'I wanted to protect my family. That's all I've ever wanted.'

'Something else has happened, hasn't it, Mum? What is it you're not telling me? It's something to do with Roisin, isn't it?'

Chapter 34

All the way home, Mum's words echo around my head. Something is bothering me about the conversation with Mum. I can't quite put my finger on it. I feel like I've missed something in this complicated puzzle of lies.

I have to admit Mum has surprised me. I've never thought of her as a particularly strong woman. I know she loves us fiercely and has always done her best by us, but it's Dad who has always made decisions and commanded the family. It's a traditional marriage and, in the past, I thought Dad too overbearing and Mum too soft to stand up to him. Now, I realise I'm wrong. Mum is stronger and more resilient than I ever imagined.

I think of how Mum would go about things in a quiet, assured way, how she would often speak to Dad to ensure things went the way she wanted them to go. Mum is indeed a strong woman. What she has just told me confirms that.

Like me, Mum is prepared to go to any lengths to protect her family. I think of Mum and Dad. Of Fiona and the children. I know what I have to do. This mess is all my own doing. Ultimately, I have to take responsibility for the way things have turned out, then and now. The desire to protect my family burns even deeper. I have the least to lose.

By the time I pull up outside the café, I've worked it out. I know what I have to do.

Kerry greets me as I come into the café. The lunchtime rush is over and the place is empty.

'Hey,' he says. 'How's everything?'

'Not too bad,' I say. 'Dad has been more awake this morning.'

'That's good.'

'He's not really speaking properly, although he's aware of us and is trying to communicate. The doctors are going to run some tests this afternoon to try to determine how badly he's been affected.'

'You look really tired,' says Kerry. He draws me towards him. 'Why don't you go up to the flat and get some sleep. I can stay here. I've nothing else to do.'

I let myself rest a moment in his arms. It feels good to be held, to have someone take the strain, if only for a while. I put my arms around him and hold him tightly.

'I tell you what,' I say, my face still buried in his shirt. 'Why don't we close up this afternoon and go and do something to remind us we're alive?'

Kerry tips up my chin. 'You okay?'

I smile and plant a kiss on his lips. 'Yes. I'm just weary from everything. Let's get out of here for a couple of hours.'

'If you're sure.'

'Absolutely.'

The Triumph rumbles through the lanes out of the village; Kerry steers the bike out to the countryside. I snuggle in closer to his body and look over his shoulder as the hedgerows and fields rush past us. The thoughts and feelings of today's revelations seep away from me, blown out by the wind as the bike takes us further and further away from the village. As the road begins to wind its way up to the top of the hill, the old croft comes into sight. Kerry parks the bike at the bottom of the track.

'Once a place for late-night drinking and chat about how we were going to conquer the world, now a place to sit quietly and think about nothing,' he says. Hand in hand, we begin our ascent.

The sun is bright in the sky and I squint as I look up the track towards the croft. I find myself touching the Triskelion pendant around my neck as I remember how Niall and I had sat up there, talking about our dreams for the future. He was going to be a top lawyer and I was going to have my own beauty salon. Yes, we were going to conquer the world. And then real life stepped in.

'You okay?' asks Kerry.

'Yes, fine,' I say. I pull my hand free and break into a run. 'Race you to the top!' I don't want to dwell on the past. It will sour the afternoon. I want a break from thinking about difficult stuff. This afternoon is for teenage kicks and pie-in-the-sky dreams, not the harsh realities of adulthood and responsibilities.

I make it to the top without stopping. I put my hands on my hips, catching my breath and wait for Kerry to trudge up.

'I let you win,' he says with a wink.

The view from the top of the hill is as fabulous as when I was here before with Kerry.

'Can you still get inside this place?' I ask, turning around to look at the stone building sitting atop the hill.

'I don't know. Let's have a look. They boarded it up a few years ago. Probably to stop the kids, like us, having all-night parties up here.'

We walk round to the south side. The stone doorway has, indeed, been boarded up, but three of the lower slats are missing. A splintered shard of wood hangs from one side.

'Looks like the kids still come up here,' I say. 'They're not going to let a piece of wood stop them.'

Kerry crouches down and peers into the blackness. There are plenty of holes in the roof to allow beams of light to shine through.

'It looks like someone has been camping here,' says Kerry. His voice echoes around the empty walls.

'Really?' I bend down beside Kerry and look inside. I can make out the remnants of a fire in the hearth and a bundle of what looks like bedding laid out in front of it. 'Why would they leave their stuff?'

'Perhaps they're coming back. Or perhaps they don't want it any more. Didn't you ever leave your tent and sleeping bag at a festival rather than trying to fold it up and lug it home?'

I look at Kerry and raise my eyebrows. 'What do you think?'

Kerry laughs and stands up, pulling me to my feet. 'I take that back. It was a stupid question.' He grins. 'It's not quite your thing, roughing it, is it?'

'It's not that,' I say. I know Kerry's only teasing, although there is a certain amount of truth in what he says. 'It's just...' I can't think of a reasonable argument. 'I've never been to a festival,' I finish lamely.

'We'll have to rectify that, won't we?'

'We will?'

'Sure, next month there's a small local festival. Well, you can't even really call it a festival. A local farmer puts up a beer tent, throws together a stage and invites the local bands to play. *Rock Around the Farm*, it's on every year. You can come and camp with me. If you think you can cope.'

'Is that a challenge?'

'If you want it to be.'

'Then I accept.' I plant a kiss on his lips. I ignore the voice that tells me it is never going to happen. For this moment I don't want to think about what I have to do. I smile at Kerry. 'Now let's do something that makes us feel alive.'

'Right here, on the hill?' says Kerry, kissing my neck. 'Okay, if you say so.'

I return the kiss, tugging at his leather jacket and pulling it from his shoulders. I pull open the denim jacket underneath and slide my hands underneath his t-shirt.

Kerry returns the gesture, pulling my body to his. He spins

me round and lays me down on the grass, then rolls me over so I'm on top of him.

Something makes me look up towards the croft. Out of the corner of my eye, a movement catches my attention.

Kerry lifts his head and kisses me.

'Stop,' I say. I move my head away from him, my eyes scan the grass between us and the building. I look from left to right.

'What is it?' says Kerry. He cranes his neck to look behind him.

'I thought I saw something.'

'There's nothing there. You're imagining things. Now, where were we?'

'No. Wait.' I scope the terrain again. Something doesn't feel right. The moment is lost. I give Kerry a quick kiss before climbing off him. 'Let's go back to yours.'

Kerry sighs and closes his eyes for a second before opening them again. 'I thought you wanted to feel alive.'

'Yeah, I just did,' I say, getting to my feet. 'I'll make it up to you,' I add with a coy smile as I start walking off.

'I'll hold you to that!' Kerry jumps to his feet and jogs to catch up, but carries on running past.

'Race you?' he calls over his shoulder.

I laugh. Kerry is so easy to get along with. I watch him get further and further away. It would be so easy to fall in love with him. To spend my days in his company and my nights in his bed. He's good fun and he accepts me for who I am, not who he wants me to be. My smile falters and I dismiss the romantic notion. I have no right to think of a future with Kerry. I have nothing to offer him. I haven't even told him the whole truth about the baby. About Sophie.

'Come on, slow coach!' Kerry calls, beckoning me to get a move on.

I know I have to live in the moment. I can't think back and I can't look forward; it's too painful. No, this moment is good, it makes me happy. I have to enjoy it while I can. Live for today, as tomorrow I'm going to give up everything.

Chapter 35

Kerry and Joe were standing in front of Seahorse Café. The lights were off, the sign in the door said CLOSED and there was not a soul to be seen.

'Strange,' said Joe, peering through the window. 'I've never known it to be closed. Do you think she's overslept?'

Kerry stepped back on the pavement and looked up at the flat windows above.

'She didn't oversleep,' he said, looking for any sign of life.

'You know that for a fact?' said Joe and then the penny must have dropped. 'Oh, I get it.' He grinned at his cousin.

'She got up about an hour ago, said she was opening up and she'd see me later,' said Kerry. He took out his phone and called up Erin's number.

'So, things with you two, they all great again?' said Joe.

'Great might be pushing it,' said Kerry, as he listened to the phone connect and ring through. 'Let's settle for "good" at the moment.'

Erin's phone went to voicemail. Kerry tried a couple more times but without success. 'I'll go round the back, see if I can get an answer at the flat.'

Kerry jogged round to the back of the shops and ascended the metal steps, two at a time. With each stride the feeling of unease grew. He didn't know what it was, but something didn't feel right. Especially after all that business with them both being questioned about Roisin's disappearance.

Reaching the door to the flat, Kerry banged hard on the glass. The net curtain at the window obscured his vision as he tried to look into the kitchen. There was no answer.

Where the hell was she?

'Have you tried ringing Fiona?' said Joe as Kerry came back round to the front of the café. 'Maybe something's happened at the hospital with her father.'

'That's what I was wondering,' said Kerry. 'I don't think I have Fiona's number.'

'Take a ride up there. I'll hold the fort. Although, if it's Jim, then Fiona might not be there either.'

Kerry checked his watch. 'I'll give it a while longer. I'll go up a bit later if Erin doesn't turn up.'

The niggling feeling that things weren't right didn't leave Kerry at all. He was finding it hard to concentrate on his work. Twice now he had fumbled the screwdriver when trying to take an exhaust pipe off.

'Shit,' he muttered as the screwdriver slipped and scored a gash across the newly polished pipe. Extra work now to repair the damage he'd caused. Just what he needed.

Kerry checked his phone again, even though he had done so several minutes ago. No missed calls or text messages.

'I'll go over to Fiona's now,' he said, standing up.

Joe gave a nod of acknowledgement. Kerry jumped on his Triumph and roared off up the road.

As he pulled up outside Fiona's detached house on the new estate, he was surprised to see two Guards cars parked up outside. He recognised one of the number plates as Sean's vehicle.

For a moment, Kerry contemplated leaving but his need to

find Erin overwhelmed his natural instinct to steer well clear of the Guards.

He switched off the engine and placed his crash helmet on the handlebar. Before he reached the front door, it was opened by a Guard. Kerry recognised him as the one who had taken Erin off for questioning.

'Can I help you?' said O'Neill.

'What's going on? Is everything all right?' said Kerry. 'Is Erin Hurley here?'

'It's not a good time right now,' began O'Neill.

'It's okay. Let him in.' Sean appeared in the doorway.

Straight away Kerry could see that Sean's face looked drawn; he had a haunted look about him. His shoulders drooped and his mouth was set in a downward turn.

O'Neill stepped to one side to allow Kerry in. 'What's up, Sean?' said Kerry. 'What's happened?'

He followed Sean into the living room. Fiona was sitting on the sofa and looked up as Kerry came in. Her eyes were red and swollen from crying.

Sean took a breath before he spoke. 'It's Sophie. She's gone missing.'

'Oh, Jesus,' said Kerry. 'When?'

'She went missing this morning. She was playing out in the garden. Fiona was inside seeing to Molly,' said Sean. 'Sophie's played out there on her own before. The garden's safe. There's no way she could get out, but she's simply vanished.'

'I only took my eyes off her for a few minutes. Molly had fallen over, so I was cleaning her knee up,' said Fiona. 'I came back out…and…and…she was gone.'

'Stop it, Fiona,' said Sean, sitting down next to his wife and putting his arm over her shoulder. 'It's okay. It's not your fault.'

'The Guards are out looking for her now,' said Sean. 'We're to sit tight in case she turns up or they find her. They want us to be here for her.'

'God, I'm so sorry,' said Kerry. It was a totally inadequate thing to say, he knew. He could barely believe it. 'Where's Molly now?'

'She's with a friend of Fiona's,' said Sean. 'Her daughter and Molly go to nursery together, so she's looking after her.'

'That's not all,' said Fiona. 'You'd better tell him about Erin.'

'That's what I came over for,' said Kerry. 'Where is she? She didn't open up the café this morning.'

Sean looked at Kerry for a moment. Again, something about his look told Kerry he wasn't going to like what he was about to hear.

'She's down at the station,' said Sean.

'Helping look for Sophie?' said Kerry, although in his heart he knew that wasn't the reason. Sean shifted position, searching for the right words. 'Come on, Sean, tell me.'

'Erin handed herself in at the station this morning. She's confessed to pushing Roisin into the water the other night down at The Spit,' said Sean. 'They are probably going to be charging her with murder.'

'Ah, Jesus! That is bullshit,' said Kerry. He flung his arm in the air and paced over to the window. 'Erin, arrested? Charged with Roisin's murder? We don't even know if Roisin is dead yet. No one's found a body.'

'Erin came to the station first thing this morning and made a confession,' said Sean. 'I don't know the details. I've been taken off the case. Anyway, what with Sophie going missing, I can't be there.'

'How can you have a murder without a body?' said Kerry.

'It can happen,' said Sean. 'Especially, if someone is admitting to it.'

'Erin is no more responsible for Roisin going missing than…' he searched for an example, 'than…Bex or Joe. Sure, you've got that wrong.'

'I don't believe it either,' said Fiona.

'Will you please sit down, Kerry, and stop with your pacing,' said Sean

'I thought she said she went to meet Roisin, but Roisin never showed up,' said Kerry. He paced the room some more.

'She's changed her story,' said Sean. 'Said her conscience wouldn't let her lie. Apparently, Roisin did show up. They had a row and Erin pushed Roisin into the water. For God's sake, Kerry, sit down, will you? I can't cope with your pacing.'

'Like I said, bullshit,' said Kerry as he slumped down onto the sofa. *What a fucking mess.* He ran the chain of events through his mind. What had possessed her to confess to murdering Roisin? As he mulled over the last few weeks, he began to find some clarity of thought.

'She's protecting someone,' said Kerry, sitting up and resting his forearms on his knees. 'You do know that, don't you?' Sean wouldn't meet his gaze, but instead looked down at his shoes. 'She's trying to protect the child.'

Fiona reached over to Sean, squeezing his arm. 'He knows,' she said. 'Kerry knows about the baby. Erin told him.'

Sean's body tensed and Kerry could hear him taking a deep, controlled breath. 'We were fools to think this would work,' Sean said eventually. 'I should never have let you and your sister go through with such a hair-brained idea.'

'It's a bit late for that now,' said Kerry, unable to stop himself. 'What's done is done.'

'Roisin had somehow found out,' said Fiona to her husband. 'She was threatening to tell everyone. She told Erin she had proof.'

'What? And you never thought to tell me?' Sean's mild manner broke. Kerry wasn't sure he had ever seen Sean cross. Usually his giant stature and soft country voice was enough to calm a situation. He didn't need to resort to shouting and force to get folk to see his way. Today was different. 'Why, in God's name, did you not tell me this before?'

'I've not long found out myself,' said Fiona. 'I didn't want to worry you. We seemed to have it under control.'

'We? We had it under control?' said Sean. 'Who is we?' He turned to Kerry. 'Are you involved in all this?'

Kerry held up his hands. 'Nothing to do with me,' he said. 'Erin never said anything to me.'

'What crazy plan did you and your sister come up with this time?' demanded Sean.

'We were going to call her bluff,' said Fiona. 'I don't believe she had any real evidence or proof. It was all hearsay and her imagination.'

'She must have got the idea from somewhere.' Sean was clearly keeping his temper well in check. He let out another sigh. 'Is that all you had planned?' he said. 'Tell me the truth, Fiona, because the shit is really going to hit the fan otherwise.'

'Yes. We were going to see what Roisin would do next,' said Fiona. 'Once we knew if she really had any proof, we were going to decide then.'

'So, it's quite plausible that Erin did meet Roisin and something did happen that night? Intentionally or not. Maybe, just maybe, Erin did push Roisin into the water.'

'No, that's impossible,' said Fiona. 'She wouldn't have. I just know it.'

'But you said yourself, she left the hospital early. Alone,' said Sean. 'She had the opportunity and the motive.'

Kerry ran his hands down his face. This wasn't looking good for Erin at all.

He trawled back over the other night. There must be some way to prove she wasn't telling the truth.

'She's protecting someone, I know it,' said Kerry. He looked up at Fiona. Her face had gone a deathly white. Kerry exchanged a look with Sean. Slowly, the pieces were falling into place for Kerry. 'Who would she lie for?' he said looking at the Keanes.

'Erin would put herself on the line for her family. So either you, Fiona, or...your mother.'

A silence hung between them as the implication of Kerry's words settled. Fiona shook her head. 'I can't cope with all this. It's all too much. Why is this happening to us?' She began to sob heavily now.

No one seemed to know what to say to that. Kerry tried to keep his head clear as he thought about everything that had happened. 'It's possible to prove Erin didn't do it,' said Kerry, getting to his feet. 'She was out with Ed that night. And I'll get him to back it up.'

'Kerry, please. Don't.' It was Fiona. 'If you do that, then they'll arrest Mum. That's the last thing Erin would want.'

'Fiona, what do you mean?' said Sean. His voice was soft but fearful.

'I don't know exactly what's happened. Neither Mum nor Erin would tell me, but they were talking in whispers at the hospital. I had gone out to the toilet. As I got nearer to the ward, I could see through the glass that Mum and Erin were not exactly having an argument, but they were talking and I could see the tension between them.'

'And you don't know what they were saying?' coaxed Kerry, tamping down his impatience.

'No. They stopped talking as soon as I came in. Erin was really glaring at Mum and Mum was totally ignoring her. I asked if everything was all right. Erin said nothing, but continued glaring and Mum was, like, "Sure, everything's grand." I was going to ask Erin later but she went off.'

'Did you not ask your mother on the way home?' said Kerry.

'I tried, but she brushed it off. She said Erin was just being Erin and getting stressed about the whole situation.'

'And that's it?'

Fiona rubbed her thumb over her wedding ring. 'Mum said that I wasn't to worry about anything. That she had everything under control. She was there to take the burden from us.'

'The burden?' said Kerry.

'Ah, sure, she's always saying things like that,' said Sean. 'Sometimes, I think she's speaking in code.'

'That's just it,' said Fiona. 'I actually think she was trying to tell me something.'

'Like what?' said Sean.

'It was as if she knew what was going on with Roisin, as if she knew Erin kept the baby.'

'Ah, go away,' said Sean, waving his hand dismissively. 'There's no way your mother could know and if she had, she would have said something about it. No, you're overreacting.'

Kerry let the possibility play out in his mind. 'Sean, what timeline do you have for Roisin's disappearance? When was she last seen?'

'Kerry, I can't tell you that, it's part of an ongoing investigation.'

'An investigation that you're no longer part of...' Kerry let the thought dangle there before adding, 'This could help save Erin.'

Sean sighed. 'Fine, we have an eyewitness account that states they saw Roisin heading to The Spit at around eight-thirty.'

'You got a taxi back with your mum that night, right? What time did the taxi drop your mum off at the flat?' asked Kerry.

'Erm…about quarter past eight, I suppose,' said Fiona.

'And you saw her go in? Actually into the flat?'

'Well, no. The taxi stopped in the main road, between your bike shop and the back of the café.'

Kerry pushed on. 'You went straight home after that?'

'I got the taxi to drop me off at the shop. There were a few bits I had forgotten to get. I bumped into a friend. It was nice to have someone to talk to. It's all been a bit overwhelming with Dad,' said Fiona. 'I got in just after nine-thirty. I know that for a fact as Erin phoned me on my mobile and Sean's already had me check.'

287

'Wait a minute, Kerry,' said Sean, sitting up. 'I not sure I like where you're going with this.'

'I'm trying to establish who had the opportunity to meet Roisin,' said Kerry. 'So, Fiona, you dropped your mum off but you don't know for certain she went straight home.'

'What about yourself?' said Sean. 'You've admitted to going to The Spit to meet Roisin. You had the opportunity too. How do we know you're not lying?'

Kerry shrugged. 'You don't. But I do.' The Guard looked away. Kerry continued. 'So, Marie had the opportunity, Erin had the opportunity, Fiona had the opportunity and, technically, so did I.'

There was an uneasy silence in the room as Kerry waited for Sean and Fiona to take in what he had said.

'The fact remains, though,' said Sean. 'Erin is admitting to it.'

'But Ed might be able to give her an alibi,' said Kerry. 'If Roisin was seen at The Spit at about eight-thirty, Erin was probably still with Ed then.'

'That leaves me, Mum and you still in the frame,' said Fiona. 'I swear to God, I never laid a finger on that girl. I won't pretend I haven't fantasised about her coming to a sticky end but I've never done anything.'

'I'm sure the taxi, the shop and your friend can all vouch for you being there at those times. You're in the clear,' said Kerry. 'Which leaves myself and your mum. Who has the most to lose? Or should I say, who has the most to gain from Roisin disappearing?'

Fiona rose to her feet, clasping her hands behind her neck, she walked over to the window.

'I don't know what to say,' she said. 'Whatever way, it's not looking good for one of them.'

Sean went and stood beside his wife, placing an arm around her shoulder. 'You can't stop the truth from coming out,' he said. 'If Ed can give Erin an alibi, then we can't ignore it. Whatever the consequences.'

Fiona turned and buried her face in her husband's shirt. 'I don't give a damn about anything. If the truth comes out, I really don't care. All I care about is getting Sophie back safe and well.'

'That's all anyone cares about,' said Sean. 'We just want her back safe. We all do.'

'Does Erin know that Sophie's missing?' said Kerry.

Sean shook his head. 'Not yet. They're going to tell her as soon as they've finished interviewing her about Roisin.'

'I need to get hold of Ed,' said Kerry. 'Have you got his phone number?'

'No, but you can get him on the health spa's number from their website,' said Fiona. She wiped her face with a tissue Sean had plucked from the box on the side and set about searching for Hamilton Health and Beauty Spa on her laptop. After a few minutes she found the number and Kerry immediately made the call.

'Ed Hamilton, please,' said Kerry.

'I'm afraid he's in a meeting at the moment. Can I get him to call you?'

'No. I'll hold.'

'But, I'm not sure how long he will be.'

'I'll still hold,' said Kerry. He wasn't going to be deterred that easily. 'You could try slipping a note under his nose with my name on it. Tell him it concerns a mutual friend and it's urgent. It may be that he finishes his meeting quicker.'

He gave the receptionist his name and waited patiently, listening to the piped music that played down the phone line. Some classical piece. He had no idea what it was and didn't care. Speaking to Ed was paramount.

Kerry only had to wait a couple of minutes before the receptionist came back on the line.

'Mr Hamilton will speak to you. I'll put you through,' she said.

Kerry heard the sound of the line clicking and then Ed's voice. 'Kerry. Now you're the last person I expected to hear from.

What's up? My secretary said it was urgent and I'm guessing the mutual friend is Erin.'

'Hello, Ed,' said Kerry. 'I'll get straight to the point. Erin's in a bit of bother with the Guards, you know, the Gardai, the local police.'

'Really? That doesn't sound like Erin at all.'

'Long story, but the fact of the matter is, she needs you to confirm to the Guards that you were with her the other night, here in Ireland.'

'Why does she need me to say that? What's she got herself into?' There was a certain compassion lacking in Ed's voice.

'A local girl has gone missing and the Guards think Erin had something to do with it. Erin couldn't have because she was with you.' Kerry kept a check on his growing impatience. 'Now, will you get in touch with the Guards and say so?'

'Why are you ringing me and not Erin? Where exactly is she?'

'Jesus, you ask a lot of questions,' said Kerry with a sigh. 'She's at the local station being questioned. They haven't charged her with anything yet and you could make her life a whole lot easier by making a statement saying she was with you.'

'I don't owe Erin anything,' said Ed, his voice terse. 'In fact, *she* owes *me*. Did she ever tell you how I looked after her? Gave her a job. Educated her. Gave her access to so many things: people and contacts she would never have had the chance to meet in normal circumstances. No, I don't suppose she did. Trouble with Erin, she doesn't know when she's onto a good thing. You can take the girl out of Ireland and all that...'

Christ, Kerry wanted to give the pompous Englishman a slap. He was glad the Irish Sea separated them both at the moment.

'This isn't really a great time to be pointing the finger. Erin needs your help. Seriously needs your help. Can you do this one last thing for her?'

'What happens if I refuse to help?'

'Erin is charged for murder. Something she didn't do.'

'That sounds very dramatic.' There was a scoffing tone to Ed's voice.

'As I said, it's serious.' Kerry shook his head at Sean and Fiona who were perched side by side on the sofa. Sean gave a quizzical look and mumbled something to Fiona. He then got up and went over to the desk and scribbled something on a piece of paper, before giving it to Kerry.

Ed was droning on about how busy he was and didn't know when he would find the time. 'I run my own business,' he continued. 'It's not like I can jump on a plane at the drop of a hat…'

'No one's asking you to hop on a plane. Just phone them,' said Kerry. He gave a quick glance at the paper. 'You could be charged with withholding evidence. Perverting the course of justice – if you refuse to help.'

'I'll speak to my lawyer before I decide on anything,' said Ed. 'He'll be in touch soon.' With that he hung up.

'Any luck?' said Sean.

'He'll do it,' said Kerry. 'He's just being an arsehole about it, that's all.'

Chapter 36

A night in the cells at the Guards' station isn't as bad as I imagined it would be. I stretch my arms and roll my head from side to side, sitting up straight to relieve the ache in my lower back. The pillow is wafer-thin, to match the slither of mattress, but then I assume they didn't try to make you feel comfortable. I wonder how long I'll get for murder. Maybe if I get a good solicitor I can get the sentence reduced to manslaughter.

Being here in the cell doesn't seem like real life and I'm having a hard time making the connection. I feel removed from what is happening. My emotions are numb. Is this what it's like when someone is in denial? Is this the mind's way of protecting itself? I know at some point it's going to feel real, but while my mind can shield me with this lack of conscious connection, I won't fight it.

The cell is cold and I pull the grey woollen blanket around me, ignoring the scratchy fibres and the musty smell, which has transferred from the fabric onto strands of my hair and wraps itself around me like a new skin.

I hear the sound of keys in the lock and the cell door opens.

'Breakfast,' says a female Guard. She passes me the metal tray and then retreats without saying another word, locking the door behind her.

I look at the two slices of toast and mug of what I assume is tea. It's hard to tell without tasting and I have no intention of doing that. I put the tray to one side.

I wonder what Kerry's doing? By now, he's probably discovered the café isn't open. I hadn't said anything to him. He would only try to talk me out of it. And as for telling Fiona, absolutely not. It would put her in an untenable position. No, Fiona would find out soon enough. Someone from the station would be on the phone to Sean, without a doubt. It's better this way.

I lie back down on the mattress, confident I have all bases covered.

I allow myself to zone out. I'm not asleep, yet I'm not fully conscious, refusing to sit and feel sorry for myself for fear I may lose my nerve.

I've lost all sense of time but the same female officer who had brought me something to eat earlier comes back to the cell.

'You have a visitor.'

'I do?'

'Your solicitor.' The officer waves me up from the bed. 'Come on.'

'But I haven't asked for a solicitor,' I say. 'I don't want legal representation.'

The officer gives me a sideways look. 'My advice to you, whether you think you want it or not, is to take it for now. Someone is obviously looking out for you.'

I think about refusing to go, but then decide if I want to be charged with manslaughter rather than murder, it will be wise to take the opportunity to speak to a solicitor. I guess that it was probably Fiona, or even Kerry, who has organised this.

'Okay. I'll see them,' I say, shrugging off the blanket.

The solicitor is an older man, with greying hair and glasses. I feel I've seen him somewhere before. He rises from his seat as I come into the small interview room.

'Miss Hurley,' he says holding out his hand. 'John Devlin of Devlin, Connor and Sullivan's Solicitors.'

We shake hands. 'Hello,' I say, taking the seat John Devlin holds out. I go to speak but Devlin puts his finger to his lips. He nods towards the Guard, who leaves the room.

'Best to speak in private,' he says. 'Now, I know you're not expecting me, but I've been asked to come down and offer legal representation to you.'

'I do appreciate this,' said Erin, 'but I'm not sure I can afford a solicitor. Who asked you to come?'

'Max Wright of Wright Motorcycles.'

I raise my eyebrows in surprise. 'Max?'

'Yes, I believe you know his son, Jody, and nephew, Kerry.'

'That's right, but I'm afraid I don't understand. Why has Max got involved?'

'I expect Kerry asked him,' says Devlin, pulling out a dark-green file from a rather battered-looking tan-leather briefcase.

'But I still can't afford a solicitor,' I say. 'It's not that I don't want representation, but I have no idea how I'm going to pay for you. And I know neither Max nor Kerry are in a position to be splashing out on expensive legal fees.'

'You really don't need to worry about that now,' says Devlin. He looks over the rim of his glasses at me. 'Max and I go back a long way. Don't let my suit and tie fool you into thinking I haven't ridden with the best of them in my day. No, I'm doing this as a family favour and, to be honest, from what I can see, we'll have you out of here by the end of the day.'

I quell the urge to laugh out loud. It's a ridiculous notion.

'I don't mean to be rude, but they have told you what I've done, haven't they?'

'Yes, I've been reading the notes here and your apparent confession,' says Devlin. 'You know giving false information and wasting the time of the Guards is an offence.'

I sit back in my chair. 'I haven't been giving false information.'

'Most people in your position would be delighted with the thought of getting off a murder charge,' says Devlin, taking off his glasses and resting his arm on the table. 'Anyone would think you want to spend the next twenty-five years behind bars.'

I shrug, aware I'm acting like a petulant teenager who is being admonished by their teacher. 'I'm simply telling the truth,' I say, looking down at my fingers, which are drumming silently against each other.

'Let's look at the evidence, shall we?' said Devlin.

I don't manage to contain the small intake of breath. Evidence? How could there be any evidence against my confession? I watch Devlin as he replaces his glasses and sorts through some papers in the file.

'Right, here we are,' he says pulling out a sheet of paper. 'Now, you say you went to meet Roisin Marshall at approximately eight-thirty on the night of the twenty-second this month.'

'That's right,' I confirm.

'But in your previous statement, you said you went to meet her at…' he scans through the notes in front of him, 'nine o'clock?'

'I lied last time,' I say, as if it's obvious why.

Devlin nods and continues, 'And what happened when you met Miss Marshall?'

'We argued. We had a bit of a fight. A physical fight and she fell into the estuary.'

Devlin holds up his hand. 'Wait a minute. This argument. What was it about?'

'Does it matter?'

'Humour me, please. And, yes, it does matter.'

I consider whether to comply or not. Devlin certainly seems persistent and it will probably have to come out in court anyway.

'Okay. Roisin and I were friends way back when I lived here as a child and a teenager. When I say friends, it was the sort of friendship borne out of there being no real alternative. Rossway was a much smaller village ten, twenty years ago – you didn't get much choice in friends.'

'Yes, I know what you mean. Please, carry on.'

'Our friendship was okay until we got to our mid-teens and boys came on the scene. There was a bit of competition, if you like. More on Roisin's part than mine. She was the popular one, she had lots of friends, very pretty, all the latest fashions. You know the type.' Devlin nods his understanding, so I carry on.

'I came from a less-well-off family, I had ginger hair, as you can see.' I flick one of my curls. 'And it's curly. I didn't have the latest clothes, I had to work in the café, so my life was a lot less glamorous and I became an easy target. It was easy for Roisin to look good against the backdrop of a friend like me.'

'It's a sad fact, but I've seen this a lot and it continues into adulthood,' says Devlin.

'Exactly. And that's what happened. I came back because my father has had an accident and Roisin and I picked up where we left off.'

'I get the feeling there's more to it than a bit of teenage jealousy.'

He's a perceptive man, but then it probably comes with the territory. 'Yes, there's more to it. I dated her brother, Niall Marshall. We were involved in a car accident and he died.' I drop my gaze. 'I was pregnant but I miscarried. Niall and I were running away. A naive teenage notion, which ended so tragically. Roisin has never forgiven me. She blames me for the accident.'

'I'm sorry to hear that. It must have been very difficult for everyone,' says Devlin. He allows a few moments' silence before continuing. 'And this is what you and Roisin Marshall argued about the other night?'

'Pretty much. It all came out. Ten years of anger,' I say. I hate lying, but it's partly the truth. 'It wasn't the first time we had had a confrontation,' I say. 'We argued in the street once. Kerry Wright had to step in. Ask him, he'll tell you how Roisin and I had this feud going on.'

'It's funny you should mention Kerry Wright,' says Devlin. 'I've already spoken to him and he's prepared to give a statement in your defence.'

I sit upright, trying to disguise the surprise. 'He is?'

'Yes, he is. And so is Ed Hamilton.'

'Ed? What? I don't understand.' *What the hell is Ed doing getting involved in all of this?*

'It seems that Kerry saw you on the night of the twenty-second at around seven p.m., getting into a car with Mr Edward Hamilton and driving out of the village towards Cork.'

'That's right, but I saw Roisin later. Ed dropped me off and I went to meet her, alone,' I say. I can feel the beginning of panic fluttering inside my stomach.

'See, that's not really possible,' says Devlin. 'According to Mr Hamilton, you both ate at The Courtyard Restaurant in the city and he brought you home at about nine p.m.'

'He must have got the times wrong.'

'I tell you, Miss Hurley, it's not often I have to argue with my own client to prove them innocent,' says Devlin, throwing me a disapproving look. 'We are in the process of obtaining a copy of the Visa payment Mr Hamilton made to the restaurant, which will confirm the time you left. We have also requested CCTV footage to back this up. There's no way you could have been back in Rossway by eight-thirty. Not only that, but Mr Hamilton has given a preliminary statement over the telephone and, if necessary, the Guards will be paying him a visit to collect an official statement to that effect.'

This isn't supposed to happen. I thought I had it all planned out. I curse Kerry for getting involved. This is his fault.

'Why are you so certain I couldn't have done it when I got back at nine p.m.?' I say.

'Because we have a witness who was walking their dog that

evening along the estuary, and saw Miss Marshall drive down to The Spit at eight-thirty. The witness saw Miss Marshall meet with another person.'

'That doesn't prove anything,' I say. My throat is dry and I fiddle with my necklace for something to do to disguise my shaking hands.

'That other person has been identified,' says Devlin slowly. 'They were seen getting out of a taxi and heading down there some fifteen minutes earlier. They stood out in our witness's memory as it was raining and this person didn't have a coat on.'

I feel lightheaded and sway forwards. I grip the edge of the table to stop myself and concentrate on Devlin's face. There is sorrow in his eyes.

'Motive. What motive would this other person have?' I say.

'Motive?' says Devlin. 'Being a mother, loving your child, wanting to protect them. Isn't that motive enough?'

'Who was it they saw?'

'I'm sorry, Erin,' says Devlin, using my Christian name for the first time. 'It was your mother, Marie Hurley.'

My whole body heaves. 'Where is my mother now?'

'I don't know,' says Devlin.

'Don't know or won't tell me?' I ask. 'Is she here? In the station? Have they arrested her?' I jump up and run to the door. 'Mum! Mum! Are you here? It's me, Erin!' I try to open the door, but it's locked. I pummel it with my fists, frantically shouting out my mother's name.

Devlin pulls me away from the door. In a matter of seconds the door swings open and in rush two officers.

'Where's my mother?' I scream. 'What have you done with her? Mum! Mum, where are you?'

'Miss Hurley, please be quiet,' Devlin is trying to calm me. The Guards are restraining me, holding me back from rushing out of the room.

'STOP THIS!' shouts one of the Guards. 'Pack this in and I'll tell you.'

I stop struggling. I hold my hands up in surrender and back away. 'Where is she?'

The female officer speaks. 'She's here in the station but she's being questioned. You can't see her or speak to her, not until we've finished making our inquiries.'

'It's okay. We know she's Sean Keane's mother-in-law, we're looking after her,' says the other Guard. 'She's all right. I promise ye.'

'Come and sit down,' says Devlin, guiding me back to the chair. 'That's it. Calm yourself down now. There's nothing you can do to help your mother right now. But I can.'

I look up at the solicitor. 'You can?'

'Yes, I'll represent her, if she'll let me.' He nods to the Guards to leave. Once the door is closed he speaks again. 'I figure Max Wright would be just as willing to help your mother as he was to help you.' He rubs his eyes. 'Although, God knows I must want my head examining taking on another Hurley woman if you're anything to go by.'

Despite the situation, I can't help smiling. 'I always thought I took after my dad, but now I think I'm more like my mum than I imagined.' Devlin smiles back as he rises from the chair. I stand to shake his hand. 'Thank you, Mr Devlin. What happens now?'

'You're free to go.' He pauses and his face looks troubled. 'There is just one thing I need to tell you,' he says. 'It's about your niece, Sophie Keane.'

Chapter 37

The call came mid-morning. It was Sean.

'Erin's been released,' he said. 'And Marie is helping the Guards with their inquiries.'

Kerry let out a silent sigh of relief. She was out. They weren't going to charge her. His next emotion was one of sadness. 'I'm sorry about Marie,' he said.

'Erin's here at the house with us,' said Sean.

'How is she? Does she know about Sophie?'

'She's a complete mess over it all,' said Sean.

'No news on Sophie yet?' said Kerry.

'No. They're extending their search. They've done house-to-house,' said Sean, his voice on the verge of breaking. 'They're getting divers in.'

'Shit,' said Kerry. 'That doesn't mean you're to give up hope.'

'It's okay, Kerry, I know what it means,' said Sean.

Kerry silently acknowledged this sad truth. 'I thought I might go and see Erin.'

Sean gave a laugh. 'You're a brave man,' he said. 'Or a fool. I would give Erin some space right now. You're the last person she wants to see.'

'I thought she'd be mad at me.'

'That's an understatement. You don't want to know what she thinks of you right now. She's blaming you for Marie being brought in. You know, getting Ed involved to give her an alibi. An alibi she didn't want. And now her mother's being questioned.'

Kerry wasn't surprised at all, but he had had no choice. He couldn't let Erin be charged for murder, not when he knew she was innocent, no matter what her reasons were. It was the worst luck that it put Marie in the frame.

'What do you think Marie's chances of getting off are?' said Kerry.

Sean blew out a breath. 'Ah, sure, I don't know,' he said. 'It's not looking good. She's confessing to it all, as far as I know. I've someone at the station who is keeping me up to date with things. Marie is saying she met Roisin, that there was a scuffle and that Roisin ended up in the water. Pretty much what Erin said happened.'

'And what's her motive?'

'Defending her daughter. Going with the story that Roisin was still bullying her daughter. You know, anyone would think Marie and Erin got together and hatched this story between them,' said Sean.

'It's pretty close to the truth,' said Kerry. 'They are just leaving out one crucial detail – the baby.'

'I know and I can't condemn them for that,' said Sean, his voice breaking. He took a moment before continuing. 'I love that child like she is my own. I love her as much as I love Molly. I don't differentiate between the two, I can't, it just doesn't happen. She calls me daddy and I'm her father. I was there when they brought her home, I was up in the nights feeding her when Fiona was tired. I've done nappy changes, bedtime stories, taught her to swim, to ride a bike. We've been camping in the back garden. Played football. Gone to parents' evening, school plays. Looked after her when she was ill. I've done the lot.'

It took a moment for the words to register with Kerry. 'Sean, what are saying? Are you talking about Sophie? You brought up Sophie as if she were yours?' And then it dawned on him. 'Sophie is the child Erin had.'

'Jesus, Kerry, don't tell me you didn't know?' said Sean. 'For feck's sake.'

'I knew Erin had a baby and she gave it up, but she never told me it was Sophie.' Kerry's mind raced back over all the conversations he'd had with Erin and with the Keanes. No one had directly said Sophie was Erin's baby, but now, how could he have not realised?

Somewhere amongst the shock of this, he felt a surge of understanding. He finally got what Erin was all about. She was all about protecting her family.

Sean spoke again. 'I would give up my life for that child. I really would,' he said. 'But...but in my heart of hearts, I know it's wrong what we've done. Not only that, but I look at how much Marie loves Sophie, how much pleasure she has from being her grandmother and then I look at Diana Marshall and I see how crushed she is from losing her son.' There was another pause. 'I know it's wrong to keep her grandchild from her. Morally, it's wrong. I didn't think of her at the time. I knew how angry and frightened Erin was. I only wanted to fix things for Fiona and her sister. To make things right, that's what I do. I make things right. I look after them. I always have. I wanted to take the burden from their shoulders. And that's what I did. That's why I went along with it.'

'It's okay, Sean. You don't have to justify yourself to me,' said Kerry, although he thought Sean was probably justifying it to himself as much as anything. The man had carried this secret around with him for ten years. He'd had plenty of time for recriminations. 'Do you think there's any merit in telling the truth now?'

'What use would that be?' said Sean. 'Besides, I can't see any of them going along with it. Erin might have been ready to admit

302

to having a baby, but whether she will admit to the world that the baby is Sophie, I don't know. And then there's Fiona and Marie. Individually the Hurley women are strong, together they're a force to be reckoned with,' said Sean. 'They are like one unit. They will do anything to protect Sophie, including go down for murder.'

Kerry found it hard to concentrate on anything else that afternoon. He really wanted to go and speak to Erin. He wanted to apologise for the situation her mother was now in, but at the same time, part of him wasn't sorry. He was relieved Erin wasn't going to be charged, but he knew how painful it would be for her now that her mother was in custody. Erin wouldn't thank him for his action or his visit. No, he'd give her a bit of space. Maybe tomorrow he'd speak to her.

He made his way to Apple Tree Cottage. Bex had invited him over for dinner. In her perceptive, yet subtle, way, she was looking out for him. Not letting him sit up in his flat stewing on what had happened.

'Hiya,' he said with false cheer as he entered the cottage through the kitchen door. The smell of chilli greeted him, homemade to Bex's recipe, rich from the spices she used to make the meal from scratch. Bex was standing in front of the Aga, Breeze swaddled in a multi-coloured sling, sleeping comfortably against the back of her mother. 'Ah, there's the two favourite ladies in my life.' Kerry went over and kissed both Bex and Breeze on the head.

'See now, not so long ago, I might have fallen for that line,' said Bex with a smile. 'But I know for a fact, a certain someone has taken poll position in your affections.'

'Unrequited, though,' said Kerry. He bent down and picked up Storm, who had crawled into the kitchen, pushing a toy car along. 'Hey there, little man.' He gave the boy a hug. 'What have you there? A car. Now that's a very cool car. It's an Alfa Romeo Spider.'

'Not a spider,' said Storm, wriggling for Kerry to put him down. Kerry obliged.

'Come on, out of the kitchen' said Bex. 'I'll be falling over you.'

Storm dropped to his knees and making *beep beep* noises, he pushed the car out of the room.

'He's a good lad,' said Kerry, watching the boy go.

'He is, when he wants to be,' said Bex. 'A bit like his father.' She smiled as Joe walked through the door.

Kerry greeted his cousin and accepted the bottle of beer Joe retrieved from the fridge.

'How are things in the Hurley household?' said Joe.

'Not good,' said Kerry. He took a swig from the bottle. The cool liquid slid smoothly down his throat.

'I was in the village today,' said Bex. 'Roisin's car has been found abandoned at The Spit. It was parked up in the corner, tucked away out of sight.'

'That doesn't sound good,' said Kerry.

'There was also talk of the café being closed and Marie being arrested.'

'I don't know if she's been officially arrested,' said Kerry, surprised at his immediate reaction to defend Marie. 'She's just helping them with their inquiries.' He cringed at the expression.

'Save the bullshit talk for someone else,' said Joe. 'We all know what that means.'

'There's a lot of speculation about what happened,' said Bex. She moved away from the oven and began to untie the baby wrap. Joe put his beer down and took Breeze from the sling.

'She's fast asleep,' he said.

'Her timing is great,' said Bex. She pulled a face. 'Sleep now means she'll be up half the night. At three o'clock she'll think it's wide-awake playtime.'

Kerry could hear the warmth in Bex's voice. She didn't really mind. He looked at his cousin, who was still gazing at his daughter's peaceful face. The love these two adults had for their child simply poured out of them. He thought of what Sean had said about his love for Sophie and he thought of his own feelings for his cousin's children. He could see how the love for a child would drive a person to do practically anything to protect them. Erin and Marie Hurley included.

'That's not all,' said Kerry at last. 'You obviously haven't heard about Sophie Keane.'

'No, what's that?'

'She's gone missing.'

'Gone missing? Oh, dear Lord,' said Bex. 'When?'

'This morning. I was over at Sean Keane's house. Apparently, she disappeared from the garden when Fiona was inside.'

'This is getting totally ridiculous,' said Bex.

Kerry looked over at his cousin, who so far hadn't said a word. Joe's face was one of shock.

'I can't begin to imagine how Fiona must be feeling,' said Bex. 'It's every mother's worst nightmare. And father's. Joe. Joe, did you hear what Kerry just said?'

Joe shook his head as if clearing his mind. 'Sorry, yes. Sophie Keane. That's awful, so it is.'

'You all right, there?' said Kerry. His cousin looked like he was going to be sick.

'I'm fine. A bit shocked, that's all,' said Joe. 'It's all gone a bit mad here since, well, since Erin's been back.'

Kerry shot him a warning look. 'There's a reason for that and it's not just down to Erin. Trouble is, the other half of the story is conveniently missing.'

'Roisin will turn up,' said Joe. 'It's not a new thing. She's gone missing before.'

'That's true,' said Bex. Breeze gave a little cry and nuzzled at her mother's breast. Bex adjusted her t-shirt to feed her daughter. 'I'd forgotten about that.

'She has?' said Kerry.

'Yes, right after the accident,' said Bex.

'Another beer, cuz?' said Joe opening the fridge.

Kerry shook his head. 'What made Roisin go off?'

'She couldn't handle what had happened. That was the official line, anyway,' said Bex.

'And the unofficial?'

'She felt guilty. Ultimately, she blamed herself for what happened. She spoke to Joe at the time.'

'That's right, I remember you telling me,' said Kerry. 'You didn't say she disappeared, though.'

'I forgot, to be honest,' said Joe. 'It was a long time ago. Those first few days, the first week, really, after Niall's death, it's all a bit of a blur. We were all shocked. Someone our age had died. I think that's when we realised we weren't invincible.' Joe sat down in the chair next to Bex.

'Why did she blame herself?' said Kerry. He looked across at Joe. His cousin averted his gaze, studying the bottle in front of him, picking at the label with his thumbnail. Kerry got the distinct feeling there was something else. Something Joe was holding back. He nudged Joe's foot with his own. 'What is it?'

Joe didn't look up, but his silence told Kerry his instinct was right.

'Joe?' said Bex, a wary tone in her voice. 'Joe. What's the matter?'

Chapter 38

Kerry got as far as the entrance to Fiona and Sean's road before he turned his bike around and rode off. He wanted desperately to speak to Erin, to tell her what he had found out from Joe. If she knew the whole truth about that night, it might go some way to easing her conscience. He also wanted her to understand why he had got Ed involved.

What Kerry really wanted was her forgiveness, but he wasn't sure he would ever get that now. Not if his suspicions about Roisin were true. Then she would really hate him as the series of consequences that would play out would mean there was no shying away from the lie the Hurley women had created and lived by for the past ten years.

Fuck it. He had to speak to Erin first. It wasn't his call to make whether the truth about Sophie came out or not.

He turned his bike around for the second time and, opening the throttle, headed back to Fiona's house.

The door opened before he had made it halfway up the path. It was Sean.

'All right, there, Kerry,' the Gardai sergeant greeted him.

'Sean.' Kerry gave a nod of acknowledgment. 'Any news on Sophie?'

Sean shook his head. Kerry could tell before he even answered that there was no change. 'Nothing yet. There's going to be a press conference tomorrow,' he said. 'Look, Kerry, Erin doesn't want to see you right now. She's pretty cut up by everything. We all are.'

'It's important.'

'Like I said, she doesn't want to see you.'

Kerry eyed up the big man in front of him. He didn't fancy taking on Sean physically. The man was a giant, well over Kerry's own six feet and built like the proverbial brick house. No wonder he didn't get any grief from the drunks in the city.

'I'll wait.'

'Come on, Kerry. I don't want any trouble. Not here on my own front door step.'

Kerry tried a different approach. 'What's the latest with Marie?'

'They're still questioning her,' said Sean. His shoulders relaxed a little and he hooked his thumbs into the belt loops of his jeans. 'Erin's sent her lawyer down there.'

'Devlin?'

'That's right.' Sean took a few steps towards him. 'Erin needs a bit of space right now. She and Fiona are getting ready to go to the hospital to see Jim. I'm sure she'll speak to you in her own time.'

'Yeah, you're right,' said Kerry. He lowered his head and made to turn like he was walking back to his bike. Sean may have the height and weight advantage, but it came at a cost. Kerry was banking on himself being more nimble.

In an instant he turned on his heel, took a side hop over the flower bed and ran around Sean's left side, sprinting up the path and into the house. He ignored Sean's shouts of protest and slammed the door behind him.

'Erin!' he yelled.

'Jesus, Kerry, what in God's name are you doing?' Fiona appeared in the hallway from the kitchen, flanked by a Guard. 'It's okay, I'll deal with this,' she said to the man.

308

'I need to talk to Erin,' said Kerry. Sean was mad, hammering on the closed door. Kerry saw Fiona look towards the door. He moved to the middle of the hallway, blocking her way.

'Please, don't do anything stupid now,' she said.

'Come on, Fiona, what do you take me for?'

'An interfering bastard.'

It was Erin's voice. She stood at the top of the staircase.

'I had no choice,' said Kerry.

Sean was still shouting and thumping on the front door.

'Oh for God's sake, let him in,' said Erin to her sister. 'You,' she pointed at Kerry, 'you get yourself up here out the way. I'll speak to you only because I don't want a Sean-shaped hole in the wall when he finally loses it.'

Kerry took the stairs two at a time and followed Erin into the bedroom. As he closed the door he could hear Sean blustering his way in, complaining to his wife. Fiona was pacifying him, ushering him away from the foot of the stairs.

'You're out of order, Kerry Wright!' Sean's voice travelled up the stairway.

'Sorry!' called back Kerry, although he didn't mean it in the slightest.

'Never mind all that,' said Erin. She walked over to the window and turned to face the room. 'You have five minutes.'

Kerry took a step towards her, but she folded her arms and glared at him. No words needed. He could read the body language loud and clear.

'May I?' he indicated to the stool at the dressing table.

'If you want, but don't get yourself too comfortable, you're not staying long.' She looked at her wristwatch. 'Four and a half minutes.'

Kerry ignored her and took a moment to find the right way to start off. He had rehearsed this several times on his way over, but now his mind was playing catch-up.

'Okay,' he said, conscious that he needed to get to the point.

'Now, your mother is at this very moment confessing to a murder...'

'Manslaughter,' corrected Erin.

Kerry raised his hands slightly. 'Sorry, manslaughter, and as she has no alibi whatsoever and she did, in fact, go and meet Roisin, I'm no lawyer, but I'm pretty sure she's going to find herself in jail for a long time.'

'I don't need an information broadcast on the Irish judicial system,' said Erin.

'No, I'm sure you don't. But what about a reality check? Your mum is no spring chicken. She's heading for sixty, that's nearly retirement age. How old is she going to be once she gets out? If she gets out? She's going to be in her mid-seventies at least. And what's it going to do to her in there? Think of the people she'll be locked up with!'

'I appreciate all that,' said Erin, 'but it's my mum's choice.'

'See, that's where you're wrong,' said Kerry. 'Your mum had no choice. You put her in this position. You forced her to take this course of action.'

He could see the colour slip from Erin's cheeks. She unfolded her arms and rested a hand on the windowsill.

'You have no right to say that to me,' she said.

'Why? Because it's painful? Because it's the truth?'

'You're a cruel bastard,' said Erin. She looked at her watch.

Kerry checked his. 'By my reckoning, I still have three minutes.' Erin went to stride past him towards the door, but Kerry was too quick. He jumped to his feet and pushed the palm of his hand against the white-panelled door.

Erin stood facing him. Fury firing up at the back of her eyes. 'I hate you.'

'No you don't. You just hate what I'm saying.'

'It amounts to the same thing.' She moved away and sat down on the bed. 'It doesn't matter what I say anyway. I can't make my mum retract her statement. And now Sophie's gone missing, it's all getting too much. I don't know how or where it will end.'

Kerry went and sat down beside her. The dip of the mattress causing her to lean in towards him, their shoulders resting against one another.

'Come here,' said Kerry, pulling her towards him. It cut him to pieces to see her so upset and desperate. 'There's something I want to say.'

'No. Wait. I need to tell you something first. Something I should have told you before,' she said, looking down at her hands. She fiddled with the pendant round her neck before looking up at Kerry. 'I haven't been totally honest with you about the baby.'

'It's okay,' said Kerry, wanting to save her the pain of confessing. 'I know about Sophie.'

'You do? How? God, you must really hate me now.'

'Sean let slip. He didn't mean to. He thought I knew it all.' He lifted her face and cupped her chin in his hands. 'And I don't hate you. Not at all. I couldn't possibly.' He stroked her face with his thumbs. 'I understand. I truly do.'

'I wanted to tell you, I really did,' said Erin, she took his hands from her face and held them to her heart. 'But I couldn't. It wasn't only my secret to tell. All this time I wanted to tell you that I hadn't really given her up. Not totally, just to my sister.'

'You don't have to explain,' said Kerry.

'I do, though. You've hated me for what you think I did…'

'It's not you I hated, it's what I thought you did. Deep down I've never quite been able to reconcile your actions with the person I thought I knew. Something didn't sit right. It bothered me. That's why I never totally gave up on you.' He looked directly into her eyes as he spoke.

'I figured this way, I could still be part of Sophie's family, I could watch her grow and still have contact with her. She doesn't know I'm her mother, we've kept that from her, so far,' said Erin, her voice heavy with emotion. 'I knew Fiona and Sean would love her. And it meant she could grow up and know her grand-

311

parents and me, even if it broke my heart not being a mother to her.'

'And now I understand why you were so determined to keep it a secret,' said Kerry. 'I get it.'

'Anyway, what does it all matter? The truth is going to come out now, I'm sure of it. Roisin knows about Sophie being my child. She told Mum that she was going to expose the truth.'

'How did she find out?'

'Roisin looked at the blood groups on our medical records,' said Erin. 'They're all there. Fiona from when she was pregnant with Molly. Sean from his Guards' medical. Sophie from when they tested for glandular fever.'

'And…' said Kerry, not sure of the significance of this.

'Fiona and Sean's blood groups mean they can't have a child with a blood group B. Sophie is B.'

'Okay, but why can't they have adopted her? What makes Roisin think Sophie is yours?'

'Sophie is rhesus negative. She can only be that if both her parents carry it.'

'And you and Niall both do, or did,' said Kerry.

'Yep. That, along with a photograph Roisin found that I had given to Niall, one of us together and I'd put what I thought was a clever message on the back. *One plus one equals three.* It doesn't take a genius to work it all out.'

Kerry took a moment to get everything straight in his mind. 'And I suppose, what with Sophie being the right sort of age too. Roisin must have thought she'd hit the jackpot when she put all this information together.'

'In her eyes she did,' said Erin. 'And whether she turns up now or not, it's all going to have to come out in the open, especially if they're charging Mum with her…her…disappearance.'

'Did your Mum not say anything to you about the night Roisin disappeared?' he asked.

'She said she'd met her. She'd tried to convince Roisin not to say anything, but Roisin was set on doing so,' said Erin. 'Mum said we weren't going to admit anything and if Roisin had time and money to waste dragging it through the courts, then that was up to her. I think Mum was trying to call her bluff.'

'I'm not convinced anything happened to Roisin the other night,' said Kerry. 'I think your mum left Roisin there safe and well.'

'So where is she now?'

'Hiding.'

'What? I don't understand. Why would she be hiding?'

'All Roisin has wanted from the start was for the truth to come out. She had a hunch that you had the baby. She couldn't seem to force you or your mum to admit to Sophie being yours and Niall's,' said Kerry, taking Erin's hand. 'So she's decided to force it out into the open. Knowing that your mum was the last person to see her, and once the Guards really started digging around it would only be a matter of time before the truth came out about Sophie. That way, it was out of everyone's hands and in the hands of the law.'

'Do you really think she'd do that? Put her own mother through all this, despite what's happened in the past?'

'I think she would,' said Kerry.

'The truth about Sophie will come out.'

'And is that so bad?' said Kerry. 'Isn't it best that Sophie knows who her real parents are? She won't lose anything. She'll gain another family, the Marshalls – not to replace the Hurleys or the Keanes, but to sit alongside. She will be the most loved little girl in the whole of County Cork.'

'You make it sound so simple,' said Erin. 'You need to take off your rose-tinted spectacles.'

'I've no doubt it will be a bumpy road,' said Kerry. 'No doubt at all, but isn't it time you all stopped running and hiding from this? You can't outrun it.'

Erin held her face in her hands. 'I don't know if I'm strong enough.'

'Oh, you're strong enough. I've witnessed that first hand. You are all strong enough,' said Kerry. 'What you've actually got to do is find forgiveness.'

'Forgive Diana Marshall, you mean?'

'And Roisin. Your father. Yourself. And Niall. It is no one person's fault. It was a series of events, decisions and judgements that were made at the time with the best possible intent. Love. How can you not forgive love? Think about it, Erin,' said Kerry. 'It's the only way forwards, for all of you.'

'I've already made peace with Dad,' she said.

'You have? That's great. And that must show you that you can do it.'

'It's all irrelevant now,' said Erin. 'What does it all matter without Sophie?'

'I have a theory about Sophie,' said Kerry. 'And it involves Roisin.'

Chapter 39

'Erin! You okay?' Sean's voice called from the foot of the stairs.

'We'd better go down,' said Erin.

'We need to talk to you,' said Sean as Erin and Kerry reached the bottom of the stairs. He glanced over at Kerry.

Erin held Kerry's hand. 'Whatever it is, I want Kerry to stay. I've no secrets from him. None at all.'

Sean nodded. He looked at Kerry. 'Not impressed with that stunt you pulled back there.'

'Sorry about that,' said Kerry. 'It was a kind of spur-of-the-moment thing.' He held out his hand to Sean. 'No hard feelings?'

Sean accepted the proverbial olive branch with good grace.

'What did you want to talk to me about?' said Erin.

'Come into the living room,' said Sean. 'I've sent O'Neill outside. This needs to stay between us.'

Entering the living room, Fiona came over to her sister and grasped her hand. Kerry watched the sisters as they looked intently at each other and exchanged silent words. Fiona blinked hard but could not stop the tears from falling. Erin, a mirror reflection of emotion.

'Nothing lasts forever,' said Fiona. Her voice so quiet, Kerry could only just hear her.

'I know,' said Erin.

'It will be okay, I promise. I'll…' Fiona looked over at Sean, stretching out her other hand to her husband. He moved towards her. Fiona continued. 'We'll make sure of that. All three of us. We'll get through this, together.'

Kerry stood awkwardly in the living room as the three of them held onto each other. He thought he saw Sean wipe tears from his own eyes. Kerry turned away, not wanting to be a voyeur to their deeply private moment.

He walked over and looked out of the window. He wanted to be out there looking for Roisin. He had an idea where she might be and chided himself for not thinking of it earlier. Erin's hand on his shoulder brought him from his thoughts. He turned round to her.

'Okay?' he said.

'Yes. It's fine. We all knew the truth might come out sooner or later. We just never expected it to happen quite like this. We thought we would be in control of the situation, rather than the situation controlling us.' She rested her head on his shoulder and Kerry dropped a kiss on her head, holding her close to him. After a while, she pulled away. 'Sean and Fiona are going to tell the family liaison officer the truth about Sophie. They've been pushing to make some connection already. We can't keep it a secret any longer.' She looked away out of the window. 'Roisin wins, after all.'

Fiona looked round. 'You don't think Roisin has got anything to do with Sophie going missing, do you?'

'It's possible,' said Erin going over to her sister. 'Who knows? She's desperate enough.'

'Oh God, I hope she doesn't do anything stupid,' said Fiona.

'I don't think she will,' said Erin. 'She wanted to truth to come out. What would she gain from not bringing Sophie back? The more I think about it, the more I'm sure this is just a stunt to force our hand.'

Sean took his wife in his arms and guided her to the chair. 'We'll call the station and get someone onto this right away.'

'I need to get off,' said Kerry.

Erin followed him out to the hall. She picked up her jacket. 'I'm coming with you.'

'I don't think that's a good idea. Your sister needs you.'

'Sophie needs me too and if she's with Roisin, I want to be there when you find them.'

Kerry could see the determined look on Erin's face. He wasn't particularly surprised and had, in fact, brought a spare crash helmet with him in anticipation of this decision. 'Okay, let's go.'

Kerry started the Triumph and waited for Erin to swing her leg over the seat and get comfortable. He loved the feel of her arms around him and liked the fact that she wasn't confident enough yet to hold onto the back of the seat. 'Ready?' he shouted above the rumble of the 750cc engine. She gave him a squeeze and nodded.

The roads were quiet and Kerry steered the bike steadily through the village and out onto the coast road. They headed north and after fifteen minutes the landmark he was heading for came into sight. Kerry pulled up at the bottom of the hill underneath a line of trees.

'The croft?' said Erin, climbing off the bike.

'You know when we were here the other day and we saw the old sleeping bag?'

'You think that's Roisin?'

'I'm almost certain. You thought we were being watched, remember?'

'Oh God, yes.'

'It adds up. It's a safe dry place for her to hide out. No one comes up here any more and if they do, she's got a clear view of them and time to hide.'

'She'll see us come up, though.'

'Not if we go round the other side. That's why I've parked up here out of the way. We can't be seen from the road and she can't see this part of the road from there,' said Kerry. 'We can use the hedgerow as cover to get round.'

Kerry led the way, keeping close to the hedge, and within five minutes they were on the north side of the hill. The trees and bushes were denser and the path overgrown in places. No other roads or footpaths approached the derelict house from the north side. The track they had just followed was essentially a loop around the foot of the hill.

'So what now?' said Erin, as she looked up at the old stone building.

'As quietly as we can, we go up the hill. Keep as low as you can.'

'And when we get to the top?'

'Take her by surprise. Hope she's in the croft. If not, we'll go inside and wait for her.'

'You're making it sound very simple.'

'It is,' said Kerry. 'In theory.'

The scramble up the side of the hill was tougher than Kerry anticipated, but the long grass gave them something to grab onto and the rough terrain, pot-holed with rabbit burrows, gave them extra leverage. As they got nearer the top, the incline was steeper. Kerry looked over his shoulder to check Erin was okay. She was right behind him, a little out of breath, but she was managing fine.

When they got to the top, Kerry peered over the brow, scanning the area in front of him. The wind had picked up and a dark rain cloud was heading inland from the stormy-looking sea. Erin scrambled up next to him.

'I can't see anyone,' said Kerry in a whisper. 'Come on.'

As light-footed as he could with his heavy boots on, he scurried over to the derelict building. The buckle on his leather jacket jangled and he held it in his hand to stop the noise. Erin, much lighter on her feet, was soundless as she darted over with him. From his inside pocket, Kerry took out a torch he'd had the foresight to bring.

It felt slightly ridiculous creeping around the wall of the building, like some SAS assault team. As they got to the entrance, Kerry switched on the light. He gave Erin a questioning look and mouthed 'ready' to her. She nodded. He swung around into the entrance of the croft.

'Roisin?' he said. 'Are you there? It's me, Kerry. And Erin.'

The beam of the torch illuminated the interior of the building. The black rain cloud was moving in on them, limiting the natural light. 'Roisin. Are you there?' he said again.

Stepping inside, Kerry noted that the sleeping bag was still there, although this time it was folded up on top of an old milk crate. He walked over and behind the crate was a sports holdall. Erin looked over his shoulder as he unzipped the bag and, without taking anything out, examined the contents.

'Looks like female clothing, judging by the pink t-shirt and that pair of socks,' said Erin. 'And look here.' She picked up a pair of trainers that were next to the bag. 'These are definitely women's trainers.'

'Okay, I think it's safe to say that it probably is Roisin here,' said Kerry.

'What about Sophie?' said Erin. 'Let's have a look around.'

They went into the second room. The ceiling had totally collapsed here and looking up, Erin could see the roof had caved in too, above them was the black stormy sky. 'It's really ramshackle now,' she said. 'A bit different to when we used to come here.'

'Let's see if we can get upstairs,' said Kerry. He shone the light into the corner, where a flight of wooden stairs disappeared round behind the central fire breast. 'Mind your step, some of these treads have rotted right through.'

The wood creaked and groaned as they made their way carefully up to the first floor. They reached the landing at the top.

To the left was the room, or rather hole, that they had peered up through from the downstairs. To the right was a closed door. This side of the building had remained more intact.

Erin grabbed Kerry's arm. 'What's that? Did you hear that noise?'

Kerry listened but couldn't hear anything. 'From in here?' he indicated to the closed door. Erin nodded. Kerry placed his hand on the latch. 'Ready?'

'Be careful,' said Erin.

Kerry lifted the latch and pushed opened the door. It creaked as it swung back on its hinges. Kerry shone the light into the room. The floorboards were patchy, several of them missing and the window had been boarded up, making the room very dark. As the torch light swept the room, in the corner beside the fireplace was a bundle of blankets.

'Wait,' said Erin grabbing his arm. 'Go back. The blankets.'

Kerry moved the torch beam back to the bundle and then picked his way across the broken boards towards the corner. Erin followed him. A small whimper came from the blankets.

'Sophie? Quick Kerry, it's Sophie.' Erin dropped to her knees and pulled at the fabric. A little face appeared in the spotlight. 'Sophie. Oh, Sophie. It's me. Erin. Aunty Erin. It's okay, darling, you're safe now.' Within seconds the little ten-year-old was in Erin's arms. Both were crying as Erin held her tightly. 'It's okay. It's okay,' she repeated.

'I want Mammy,' said Sophie through her tears. 'I want to go home.'

Kerry knelt down. 'We're going to take you home. Everything is going to be fine. Don't be crying now. There's a good girl.' He stroked her head.

'Roisin said she would take me home. She promised, but she keeps saying I have to stay a bit longer,' said Sophie. 'She scared me.'

'Everything will be fine. I promise,' said Erin. 'What happened,

Sophie? Why did you go with Roisin?' Sophie dropped her gaze. 'It's okay. You're not in trouble.'

'I was in the garden. She came to the side gate and said Mammy wanted her to go to the shop and did I want to go with her. She said she'd get me some sweets and we wouldn't be very long.'

Erin looked up at Kerry. 'As simple as that.' She looked back down at Sophie. 'I suppose you thought it was okay because you know Roisin.'

'She's a friend of Mammy's. She goes into Nanny's café. I was just wanting some sweets, that's all. I didn't know this was going to happen. I promise.' Sophie began to cry again.

'Sophie, sweetheart,' said Kerry. 'How did you get here? It's a long way to walk?'

'She had a car. A blue one,' said Sophie.

Kerry let out a small groan.

'What is it?' said Erin.

'Doesn't matter right now. I may be wrong,' said Kerry.

'I want to go home,' said Sophie.

'That's what we're here for,' said Erin. 'Don't cry. It's okay.'

'Do you know where Roisin is now?' said Kerry.

'She said she was going to get something to eat.'

'She won't have gone far,' said Kerry. 'She can't afford to be seen just yet.' He gave Sophie's head another stroke. 'Listen now, we're going to go downstairs and sit very quietly while we wait for Roisin to get back.'

'I want to go home,' said Sophie. 'Please, Erin, take me home.'

'We will,' said Erin. 'We need to wait for Roisin first. She's in a lot of trouble for bringing you here. I promise as soon as she's back we can go. I'll even text Mummy now to let her know we're coming home soon.' Erin took her phone from her pocket and fired off a quick text to Fiona.

'Roisin won't have gone far. We'll sit and wait for her in the back room, out of the way,' said Kerry.

'You'd better switch off that light,' said Erin as they reached the bottom of the stairs. 'She'll see that before she even comes in. We don't want to give her any warning we're here.'

'Good idea. Let's sit over here, it's really dark this side. I'll be able to see her coming from this window.'

The stone floor wasn't the most comfortable of spots and the wind was whipping around them, the draught racing in from the doorway and from the gaps in the crumbling brickwork. Erin put a protective arm around her niece.

As the wind picked up some more, it carried a light mist of rain with it. The sky above them darkened again and within a few minutes, drops of rain were falling. Fortunately, Erin and Sophie were protected by what was left of the roof, while Kerry was standing by the window, keeping a look out for Roisin.

It was then he saw her. Her head appeared first over the top of the hill, bent down, shielding the rain from her face and, as she neared, Kerry could tell it was definitely Roisin. However, she wasn't alone.

'What the hell?' said Kerry.

Erin stood up and came to peer over his shoulder.

Chapter 40

I can't quite believe what I'm seeing. I take a quick look at Kerry's face and all I can see is anger. I don't blame him. For me, the surprise isn't that much of a surprise. They say a leopard never changes its spots. It's certainly true in this case. Jody Wright may have had me fooled for a while, but not any longer.

I beckon Sophie to me and whisper to her to stay very still and very quiet. 'Don't worry,' I say in her ear. 'Me and Kerry will look after you. You're safe with us.'

I can see through the doorway into the main room as Roisin and Joe come into the house. She pushes a wet strand of hair from her face.

'You've got to stop this now. If you don't, I will,' Joe is saying. 'You can't let Marie Hurley go to prison. And as for taking Sophie Keane, for feck's sake, Roisin, that's kidnapping and I'm now a party to it.'

'Man up, for God's sake,' says Roisin. 'To tell the truth, I'm past caring. Maybe I really will disappear and then the Hurleys will get what's coming to them.'

This time it's me who is held back. Kerry grips my hand. They haven't noticed us here, pushed back in the shadows. They are too busy arguing. Jody puts a carrier bag down on the floor beside the campfire.

'You can do what you like, but I'm taking that child back to her mother,' he says.

'And you'll be charged as an accessory,' says Roisin.

'Like you, I really don't care. What I care about is doing the right thing.'

'You didn't worry about that the night of the accident,' says Roisin.

'I was a kid then. I'm not now. I'm a father myself. This is all wrong. You hear me? All wrong.'

At this point Kerry moves out of the shadows.

'Funny,' he says, 'I was just thinking the same thing.' He steps into the main room and I follow, keeping Sophie close to me.

Roisin gives a small scream of alarm. Jody swears.

'Jesus! What the feck are you doing there?' he cries.

'Again. I was just thinking the same thing,' says Kerry. He moves into the centre of the room. His jaw is set tight and I can see him clenching and unclenching his fists.

'Oh and look who's with you! It's Mammy Erin,' says Roisin. Her ability to regain her composure amazes me. 'Might have known your sidekick would be with you, Kerry.'

'Now we're all over the shock of seeing each other,' says Kerry, his voice like steel. 'Perhaps you can explain what's going on.'

'Oh, please, Kerry,' says Roisin. 'Don't be so hick and naive.'

'Leave it out,' says Joe. He's keeping a wary eye on Kerry. I think he must recognise the anger that's bubbling away just under the surface. I'm not sure how long Kerry will be able to contain the rage.

'Shut up, Joe,' says Roisin. 'You're such a wimp. Frightened of upsetting your cousin now. First it was your wife, then it was her,' she waves a hand in my direction, 'and now it's Kerry. Grow some balls, man.'

'I didn't want to get involved in this,' says Joe, turning to Kerry.

'I've just this minute been trying to talk her out of it. I was saying this has gone too far and has to stop.'

'Shut the fuck up, Joe,' snaps Kerry. Joe looks at me. If he thinks he's getting some sort of support or empathy, then he can think again. Roisin sits down on an upturned milk crate in front of the hearth with a total look of nonchalance. God, I want to slap that unconcerned, superior look right off her face.

'What exactly did you expect to gain from all this?' I ask. 'Taking Sophie. Have you any idea what Fiona is going through right now? Not to mention that my mother is currently under arrest for your murder. And have you not stopped to think about your own mother?'

Roisin stands up, her face contorts. 'Don't you dare lecture me about what my mother may or may not feel. You have absolutely no idea.' She pauses, the muscles in her face relax and she sits down again. A contemptuous looks descends upon her. 'Not nice is it? *Thinking* you've lost someone you love. *Knowing* you've lost someone is even worse. I thought you Hurley girls needed a taste of your own medicine; to know what fear really tastes like, to feel that pain of losing a child. Not nice, is it?'

'Is that what this little stunt is all about? Was that it? Or is there something else in that warped mind of yours?' Sophie's arms slip around my waist. She gives a little whimper.

'Now we're getting down to the nitty gritty,' says Roisin. 'What I want is the truth about Sophie. Nothing more, nothing less. I want you to confess to what you and your sister did. I want Sophie to be part of my family, her family. The Marshalls are as much her family as the Hurleys and, you, Erin, have denied her that. You and your family have kept her a secret from us for all this time.' She comes to stand in front of me.

'Stop, Roisin,' I say. I draw Sophie behind me, aware that she is listening to every word Roisin is saying. 'Not here.'

'You should have thought about that before,' says Roisin. 'You had absolutely no right to do what you did. No right whatsoever.

She is my brother's child. My brother who died because of you.'

'So, what now?' I ask, wanting to prevent Sophie hearing any more of Roisin's ranting.

'You and I go to the solicitors and make this all official. I want it in writing that you will let us, that's my family, have regular contact with Sophie. That my mum can see her, the child can stay with her, she can take her out, treat her exactly like she should as a grandmother.'

I nod, ignoring the pain that's racing to my heart. I don't want to share Sophie with Diana Marshall. She didn't want her in the first place. What if she doesn't want her now? 'Does your mum know?' I ask.

'Not yet. But that's none of your business anyway. What do you care about my mam? You never bothered about her feelings when you went off to England.'

'She didn't deserve to know, then,' I say. 'She didn't want me to have the baby in the first place. What I told you before, that she wanted me to have an abortion, was true.' The words blurt out before I have time to check myself.

'You're a liar,' says Roisin.

'Why would I lie about that? Why would I continue to lie, when you're about to tell your mum?' I stand my ground; we are inches apart. For the first time I see an uncertainty in her eyes.

'My mam would never agree to an abortion,' she says.

'Your mother did not want to ruin Niall's chances at university,' I reply. 'If she hadn't been so set on Niall having a glittering career, one that she could be proud of, one that she could show off about, then we wouldn't have had to run away.' Sophie moves further behind me, but I barely register this. All I can focus on is Roisin.

'If you had gone along with what she wanted then you wouldn't have had to run away!' Roisin is shouting, but her voice is full of raw emotion. 'If you hadn't run away then you wouldn't have had the accident.' She pushes me in the shoulder. I stumble back. For a moment I think I'm going to stumble over Sophie, but she

326

moves quickly to the side, sinking into the corner. Once again I am back to focusing on Roisin. It all happens in a few seconds. I regain my balance and I return the shove. Roisin grabs my arm and for a moment we engage in some sort of strange rocking-from-side-to-side motion, like two Sumo wrestlers getting ready to start throwing each other about.

'Not again,' groans Kerry and then he's forcing his way between us. Joe grabs at Roisin.

'That's not fair, Roisin. You can't blame Erin for the accident. You know that. I know that,' says Joe.

'Calm down the pair of you,' says Kerry.

'Tell her to keep her hands to herself.' I'm fuming. All the anger from ten years ago comes rushing back to join forces with the anger I'm feeling now. Kerry is still holding onto me. I shrug his hands from my arms, but he pulls me closer. He kisses my head and mutters soothing words, like he might if Storm or Breeze needed calming. It has the desired effect after a minute or so. 'I'm okay,' I say. 'Honest, I have it under control.' I go over to Sophie and reassure her with words and another hug. I feel ashamed that I let things get out of hand in front of her. She has had enough to deal with.

Roisin wipes tears from her eyes. I wonder if she really does believe me now. It must be hard to accept that your own mother could do something like that. But something tells me there's more to those tears. There is still something I don't know, something she is hiding. I look at Joe. He looks away, but it's too late, I've seen it. I've seen it in his eyes. Guilt.

His words of just a moment ago, coming rushing back to me.

'Joe,' I say, my voice one of total calm and composure. 'What did you mean just now, when you said I wasn't to blame for the accident?'

'Nothing,' says Joe.

'You said Roisin knew I wasn't to blame and that you knew it too.'

'Tell her, Joe. Tell Erin what you told me earlier,' says Kerry. 'I don't want to have to knock it out of you, much as I'd like to give you a feckin' good thumping right now.'

Kerry's threat isn't wasted, although I'm not so sure it's just a threat. I'm pretty certain Kerry means every word.

'Don't!' cries Roisin. 'Don't say anything.'

Joe hesitates. He looks at each and every one of us.

'Erin needs to know. She has a right to,' he says at last. Roisin goes to protest some more, but Joe continues to speak. 'Just as your mother has a right to know about Sophie, Erin has a right to know about the accident.'

My legs suddenly feel weak and my throat closes, making breathing difficult. I take a gulp of air. Kerry holds onto my elbow. 'You okay?'

I nod. 'I'm fine.' All I want now is to hear what Joe has to say.

Chapter 41

I look at Joe. 'What do I need to know?'

Joe looks uncomfortable. I get the feeling I'm not going to like everything I hear.

'Remember, Erin,' he says. 'We were all just teenagers then. We did things, made decisions as seventeen-, eighteen-year-olds, not as the adults we are today.'

'I get that,' I say, impatient for him to begin.

'Oh, for God's sake, Joe, get on with it,' says Roisin. For once, I'm in complete agreement with her. Roisin doesn't wait for him. 'I'll tell you my bit,' she says, seemingly accepting it's going to happen whether she likes it or not.

'We're all ears,' says Kerry. He takes my hand in his and I appreciate the gesture of solidarity.

'The night of the accident, Niall came to tell me he was leaving. That you and him were running away. He didn't say anything about you being pregnant. He just said that Mam didn't approve, that he couldn't tell me everything that night, but once he was settled he would be in contact and he'd tell me then.

'Anyway, naturally, I didn't want him to go. I didn't want him to go with you. I begged him not to, but he wouldn't listen. He said he loved you and wanted to be with you.'

For a moment I'm transported back to that night and the rush of emotion takes me by surprise. We did love each other, so very much. We really did. But now, as I look back, I know that it was teenage love and I'm realistic enough to know that it probably wouldn't have lasted. Not with the odds so stacked against us. We were innocent and totally oblivious to how hard the adult world would be.

'We did really love each other,' I say quietly. I want Roisin to know that.

She ignores me and carries on. 'I hated the fact that you were causing so much upset in our family. I didn't know why Mam disliked you so much, but all I knew was that it was causing problems. If you were gone, out of the picture, then I thought our family would be happy and whole again.'

She pauses and looks down at her hands.

'Go on,' says Kerry.

'I was desperate for Niall to stay,' she says. 'I was prepared to say anything to make him change his mind. I knew he had some weed on him, he often did, but I had seen him put the little box he kept it in in his rucksack. I persuaded him to sit outside with me and have a joint, you know, one for the road sort of thing. I got a couple of beers out of the fridge and we went down to the end of the garden.'

'I always suspected he was a little bit high or tipsy,' I say. 'He had that glazed sort of look when he picked me up and his driving was all over the place.'

There's a small silence.

'Tell her the rest,' urges Joe.

'I'm getting to that,' says Roisin. 'I...I told Niall something about you.'

For the first time, Roisin actually looks guilty, even a bit remorseful.

'What did you tell him?' I ask, wracking my brains as to what it could possibly have been. I didn't have any secrets then, not from Niall. He knew everything about me. To be fair, at sixteen, there wasn't a lot to know.

'I said that you and Joe had slept together.'

'What?' I can't quite believe what I've just heard. 'You said what?'

'I was sixteen, remember,' snaps Roisin. 'It's the sort of thing you say when you're that age. I was desperate for Niall to ditch you. I thought if he believed that you and Joe had slept together, then he wouldn't want anything more to do with you.'

'This is where you all tell me that's bollocks,' says Kerry. He's talking to all of us, but his eyes are fixed on his cousin.

'Ah, Jesus, Kerry. Of course, it's bollocks,' says Joe straight away. 'Sure, I can't even believe you're asking that.'

'Well, it is the night for surprises,' says Kerry. 'I just wanted to get that bit clear.'

'What did Niall say?' I ask. 'Did he believe you?'

'Sort of.'

'Yes or no?' I need to know whether Niall doubted me. Was his last thought of me one where he believed I had cheated on him? An overwhelming feeling of sadness seeps through me and settles in my bones. 'Did he believe you?'

'He said he was going to have it out with Joe. See what Joe had to say about it,' says Roisin.

'So, he did believe you.' The sadness consumes me. Niall doubted me. It hurts. Badly.

'He texted me,' says Joe. 'Told me to meet him up here, at the croft. Said it was important.'

'So that's why we were heading up this way,' I say. It starts to make sense. I sink to the ground. 'He said we had to go this way. The coast road would be quieter. I had no idea of the real reason. His driving was all over the place. We argued. He was driving too fast. I pleaded with him to stop.'

Kerry kneels down beside me. One hand rests on my back, the other tucks a strand of hair behind my ear.

'I saw the crash,' says Joe eventually. His voice is quiet and I'm not sure if I've heard him right. A howl of wind rushes up from under the semi-boarded doorway and swirls around the room. I look up at Joe. He repeats his words. 'I saw the crash.'

'Was it you?' I ask. 'Was it you who pulled us from the car?'

Joe nods. 'You. Yes.'

Joe knows my secret.

'I didn't have any choice,' I say. 'I genuinely thought he was going to kill us both. Oh, dear God, the irony of that. How many times have I wished it was so?'

'Erin, what are you talking about?' It's Kerry. He doesn't know. Joe must never have told him. 'Don't be saying things like that. He was drunk and high; he had no right to be driving.'

'I know. He had absolutely no right. And he wasn't,' I say, looking up, first at Kerry, then Joe and finally Roisin. 'I was driving.' There's a stunned silence as both Kerry and Roisin take in the new information. Joe, of course, has always known this.

'*You* were driving?' Roisin strides over to me and pulls me up by the lapels of my jacket. 'You were driving? You crashed the car? You killed my brother?' She slaps me hard across the face. It stings and I can feel the heat from it immediately.

Once again, Joe is restraining Roisin.

'I was only driving because he was too stoned and drunk to be driving himself,' I say. 'I didn't give him the joint. I didn't give him the beer. If you're apportioning blame, then you, Roisin, have to take some of that yourself.'

'We all have to take some of the blame,' says Joe.

'You did nothing wrong,' says Kerry. 'Or is there more?'

'There's more,' says Joe.

'Of course there's more,' says Roisin. 'What I want to know is why the Guards' report never mentioned Erin driving.'

Kerry curses, pulls his tobacco pouch from his pocket and rolls two cigarettes. He throws one in Joe's direction. They take a moment while they light their cigs. If I smoked, I'd be having one too – I know what's coming next.

Joe blows out a lungful of smoke.

'I saw the crash. I was with Bex. We were up here on the hill. We could see the road clearly. There wasn't so much hedgerow or trees then. We raced down straight away. Niall had been thrown out.' He looked at Roisin. 'I'm sorry, Roisin, but he had already gone. He must have died instantly.'

Roisin lets out a cry. It's one of pure pain. I turn away as I throw up. The events of that night way too strong in my mind, but this version I have never heard before.

'What about Erin?' says Kerry, after I wipe my face.

Joe addresses me. 'You were in the driver's seat. Slumped over the wheel,' says Joe. 'You had your seat belt on.'

'Niall wouldn't wear his,' I say quietly, remembering how he had refused to put it on.

'We pulled you clear,' says Joe. 'There was petrol everywhere. We were worried the car would catch fire. You were in a bad way. You were bleeding. Everywhere.'

I remember the blood. It was the only thing I could focus on when I came round. I don't remember Joe being there at all. I remember waking up on the cold, damp grass, surrounded by people. The car was ablaze from the ruptured fuel tank, where it had tumbled and rolled down the hillside. 'Did you know?' I ask Joe.

'You began to come round and mumbled something about a baby. Then you passed out again. It was afterwards, when Bex and I were talking about it. She guessed.'

'You never said.'

'What was the point? To be honest, we assumed you lost the baby in the accident. We thought it was best not to say anything.'

'You never suspected anything afterwards?' I say.

Joe shakes his head. 'No. There was no reason. We were all too shocked about Niall's death. Then you moved away. It wouldn't have served any purpose to say anything.'

'Why didn't you wait around for the Guards at the time?' I ask. 'I don't remember them interviewing you.'

'We never said we were there.' He looks at Roisin. 'We were all young and what we did then, we thought was the right thing at the time. Roisin didn't want to get into trouble for making Niall have a smoke and a drink and I didn't want to get into trouble for supplying him with the weed or for leaving the scene of an accident. It wouldn't have made any difference to the outcome. Niall would still be dead. You'd still be away in England. And Roisin and her family would still be grieving. No, there seemed little point.'

'I can't believe you never told me,' said Kerry. 'Especially with all that's been going on.'

'Again, there seemed little point,' says Joe.

'So, why are you helping Roisin now?'

I can tell Kerry is more than a little pissed off with his cousin.

'You might as well tell him,' says Roisin. 'You've told him everything else.'

'Joe?' I say.

'Please tell me it's not what I think it is,' says Kerry, clasping his hands behind his head. 'Jesus, Joe.'

Roisin laughs. 'Oh, God, he thinks we're having an affair,' she says, once she's controlled her laughter.

'What is it, then?' says Kerry.

'We, Roisin and I, we...' Joe can't quite find the words.

'God, you're pathetic at times, Joe Wright,' says Roisin. She turns to face me and Kerry and I swear she's enjoying this moment in the spotlight. 'Joe and I had a one-night stand. Years ago.'

'She was going to tell Bex,' says Joe. 'She was going to make out it was more than just a one-nighter.'

'She's going to find out now, isn't she,' says Roisin. I can't help but feel Roisin is rather pleased about this.

334

'We were both drunk,' says Joe. 'I know that's no excuse. Bex and I had had a row. A big row. We even called the wedding off. Bex went away for a couple of weeks on holiday with her sister. Roisin and I…' His voice trails off.

'That's a shitty excuse,' says Kerry. 'And why the hell didn't you ever tell Bex?'

Joe rubs his hands up and down his face. 'I've no feckin' idea.'

'So, you've known all along that Roisin was alive and well,' I say.

'She contacted me. She needed some food. I've been trying to talk her out of this the whole time,' explains Joe. 'I tried to tell you. I kept saying she'd turn up.'

It's true, he did say that, but we all assumed it was Joe being his usual laid-back self.

'And Sophie?' I ask. 'Did you know that's what she had planned?'

'I swear on my kids' lives, I never knew anything about Sophie. Not until Kerry came to me today,' says Joe. He looks mortified and I believe him. 'I came up here as soon as I could. I was going to bring Sophie back with me, even if Roisin didn't agree.'

'But you lent her your old car,' says Kerry.

'I didn't know what she was going to do,' says Joe. 'She asked me yesterday if she could borrow it. I left it parked up with the keys on the front wheel. I had no idea she was going to take Sophie. To be honest, I thought she was going to go off for a few days. Find somewhere else to hide out.'

'You're an idiot, you know that don't you?' said Kerry. I can see the contempt in his eyes for his cousin.

'I'm sorry. I really am,' says Joe.

Roisin lets out a scoffing sort of noise. 'Pathetic, Joe Wright, absolutely pathetic.'

'Didn't you stop to think what this was doing to your own mother?' says Kerry, turning to Roisin.

'The end justifies the means,' says Roisin. 'This way, my mother gets the grandchild she has been denied all this time. She gets a part of her son that has been lost forever.'

'And you get atonement,' I say.

'We all get that,' says Roisin.

Chapter 42

The shower was warm and welcoming. Roisin had it on full blast and needle-sharp water pummelled her skin. She took the exfoliating scrunchy and scrubbed at her skin. Roisin was tired. She had been home for two hours, having spent the best part of the day at the Gardai station, explaining away her disappearance and reasons for taking Sophie.

It had been a total surprise to both her and the Guards when Sean and Fiona Keane had insisted they didn't want to press charges. Sean had convinced the Guards to let her off with a lecture about how much upset and trouble she had caused. How her mother had been beside herself with worry, how the Keanes and the Hurleys had been distraught, not to mention the time and manpower wasted by the Guards. She did actually feel guilty about her mam, but it had to be done. The Hurleys, well, she wasn't too worried about them. As she had said to Erin, the end justified the means. She had what she wanted. What her mam needed. What her family needed. The pain of today would heal and the pain of the past ten years would ease.

Roisin stood under the shower for another five minutes, rehearsing for the one-hundredth time what she was going to say to her mam. She had been waiting for this moment for a long time. She wanted to get it right.

Diana was waiting in the living room with Pat. This in itself was unusual. Roisin suspected that Pat had banned his wife from the drawing room. Too close to the sherry. He knew there was a big announcement coming, but Roisin had little doubt either of them knew what it was.

'Ah, there you are,' said her father. He stood up and kissed Roisin's cheek. Taking her hand, he guided his daughter over to the sofa, next to her mother.

'You look better,' said Diana.

'And smell better too,' said her father. He laughed at his own joke.

'There's something important I need to tell you,' said Roisin, cutting to the chase. She had never been any good at small talk and she knew they were itching to find out what she had to say. Roisin smiled at her mother. For the first time since finding out about the baby, Roisin doubted herself. She so wanted this to be the answer to her mother's problems, but what if it wasn't? What if Diana didn't want to know the child? Then Roisin would have to go back to the Hurleys with her tail between her legs. She didn't care that she had caused them upset, but she cared about her mam.

'What is it?' said Diana.

'It's about Niall and Erin Hurley.' Diana caught her breath, but said nothing, so Roisin continued, 'I found out recently that Erin was pregnant when Niall died.'

'Oh, that's nonsense,' said Diana. 'What a preposterous idea.'

'It's the truth, Mam. I know. Erin told me.'

'And you believe the lies of someone like her. Don't be ridiculous, Roisin.'

'Mam! Stop.' Roisin laid her hand on her mam's. 'You don't have to pretend. I know the truth.'

Diana pulled her hand away and began disputing this, telling Roisin it was the most ridiculous thing she'd heard in all her days. Roisin looked at her father. He hadn't said a word so far. He closed his eyes for a moment. When he opened them he looked straight at Roisin.

'Diana, please. Stop,' he said. 'Roisin is right. We know that, don't we?'

Diana went to protest, but her voice was silenced as Pat held his finger to his lips. He gave a slight shake of the head.

Diana looked down, her eyes not able to meet those of her daughter's. 'Yes, it's true,' she said eventually, her voice was only just audible.

'You, Dad, Jim and Marie Hurley all wanted her to have an abortion,' said Roisin.

Diana tutted. 'Termination. The word is termination. Abortion sounds so, so…crude.'

'So that's true too,' said Roisin. Her heart dropped a little. Her own mother, a GP, sworn to save life, wanted to terminate life.

'They were young. Niall was about to go off to university. He was going to be a lawyer. Move to America. He had dreams. We had it all planned out. A baby wasn't in the plan,' said Diana, her voice growing stronger with every word. 'It was for the best. We all agreed on that. We wanted our children to have the best start, the best chance in life. Having a baby wouldn't have done that. There was plenty of time for children. They were only children themselves.' She stared at the fireplace for a moment. 'God, I could do with a drink.'

Pat went into the drawing room, reappearing with a small glass of sherry, which Diana downed in one go.

'The thing is,' said Roisin, once Diana had placed the empty glass on the coffee table. 'After the accident, everyone assumed Erin had lost the baby.'

'Yes. She did,' said Diana. 'Her mother told me so.'

'Mam, she didn't have a miscarriage. She was okay in the end.

She went to England straight after the funeral. She had the baby over there.'

'What do you mean?' Diana sounded a mix of anger and surprise.

'She went through with the pregnancy,' said Roisin, knowing there was no way back now, despite the incredulous look on her mother's face and the knowledge that this would poleaxe her. 'She had the baby. She had Niall's baby. Your grandchild.'

'No. That's not possible,' said Diana, flapping Roisin away with her hand, like she would an irritating fly. 'Marie Hurley made a point of coming to me after the funeral and telling me that Erin had had a heavy bleed and there was no need for a termination.'

'That, I suppose, was the truth,' said Roisin. 'Marie Hurley left out a few details, though.'

'Jesus Christ,' muttered Pat. He left the room and came back this time with the sherry bottle and two more glasses. He poured one for them all.

Diana took another drink. 'What happened to the baby?' she said. Her voice was quiet. 'What happened to my son's child?'

'They named her Sophie,' said Roisin, trying to break the news gently. 'Sophie Keane.'

Her father looked blank. It didn't mean anything to him. Her mother, however, made the connection. 'Sophie Keane?' she repeated.

'That's right. Fiona and Sean's oldest girl,' said Roisin. 'They have brought her up as their own.'

Diana stared at her daughter for a minute before speaking. 'I have a grandchild living in this village and I didn't know?' She rose and walked across to the French doors, which overlooked the gardens. She gazed out of the window and hugged her arms around her waist, pulling her cardigan around her. 'Niall has a daughter. Part of Niall lives on.' Her hand went to her mouth to stifle a sob and then she collapsed onto the parquet flooring.

As Roisin and her father rushed over and picked her up, Diana was crying but smiling at the same time. Supporting her, one under each arm, they took her over to the sofa and put her feet up.

'Just rest there, Mam.'

Diana reached out for her husband and grasped his hands within her own.

'Pat, we have a grandchild. Niall hasn't gone completely,' she said through her sobs. Roisin realised these were sobs of joy. 'He's still with us. We have a grandchild.' Diana repeated these two sentences several times.

'Go and get your mother's pills,' said Pat.

'I don't want to be sedated. Those tablets are to stop me feeling pain. This isn't pain. This is pure joy. I want to feel every moment of it,' said Diana through her tears.

Roisin found herself crying too. Even her father couldn't stop the tears from falling. For the first time since Niall had died Roisin could see the happy, joyous mother she had once known. Perhaps her father could see it too. There was a glimmer of her mother, the one who laughed and sang and played games with her. Her mam was coming back to them. No matter what anyone said, Roisin knew she had done the right thing.

The silence lies heavy across Fiona's kitchen table. My mum sits beside me with Fiona and Sean opposite. After the initial relief that mum has been released by the Guards, the harsh reality of what we must face is now upon us.

'How's your father?' Mum ventures at last.

'I went to see him today,' says Fiona. 'He was awake for much longer than the last time and the sleeps in between were much shorter.'

'And his speech?'

'It's getting better. A little slurred and slow, but the doctor says it's all good signs. They are going to get him out of bed tomorrow and see how his gross motor skills are.'

341

'There's something you need to know,' says Mum. 'About your dad's fall.'

Fiona reaches across the table. 'It's okay, Mum. We know.'

'I told them,' I say. 'I thought they should know. No more secrets.'

'I'll have to tell the Guards,' says Mum.

'You can't do that,' I say. The thought of my mum being questioned again and possibly charged for attempted murder for real, fills me with horror. Fiona protests too.

'Now, you three listen to me,' says Sean. 'This conversation need never be had again. What happened at the top of the steps was an accident. You can't be prosecuted for your thoughts, only your actions. You didn't push Jim. He fell. End of.' He looks purposefully at each of us in turn. We nod in agreement. 'Good. Now, I suggest we move on and sort out what we're going to tell Sophie. How do we play this? What I mean is, not only what do we tell Sophie, but what happens to her now?'

I speak before anyone else has a chance to.

'She heard a lot of it up at the croft. I don't know how much she took in. She was in a lot of shock.'

'We have to speak to her, though, all together,' says Fiona.

'I agree,' I say. 'I don't want Sophie to ever think that what I did wasn't because I didn't love her. She must know I wasn't rejecting her. In fact, it was the complete opposite. It was the only way I could keep her.'

Mum takes Molly out into the garden and occupies her with a tea party for her toys. I can see how much Mum loves Molly. I know how much she loves Sophie. In trying to protect me, she has protected them too; her love as a mother has no boundaries, extending through the generations.

I can hear Fiona talking to Sophie and taking her into the living room. I take a deep breath and pray to God that we get this right as I follow them in.

'Sophie, there's something very important that we need to talk

342

to you about,' says Fiona. Her voice is steady, yet I know inside she's trembling with fear. It's a new notion, Fiona being frightened. All my life she has been confident and strong, knowing what to do and how to fix things. To have her uncertain has a ripple effect and I can feel the butterflies in my stomach. The last thing I want is to confuse Sophie. I want her to be one-hundred percent safe with the knowledge that above everything else, she is loved. Fiona continues to speak. 'After what happened with Roisin, there's something we need to talk to you about.'

Sophie nods. 'Okay,' she says. She fiddles with the iPad in her hand, opening and closing the magnetic catch.

'You know how much Mummy and Daddy love you, don't you?' says Fiona. She waits for her to look up. She smiles. Fiona returns the smile. 'And you know how much your family love you too. Nanny loves you. Gramps loves you. Erin loves you. All very much.' Her voice wobbles a touch, but Sophie doesn't seem to notice. 'We love you because we are family and family all look after each other.'

'And some families don't have mammies or daddies, or grand-parents,' says Sean. 'Families are all made up differently.'

'I know. Eamon Donnelly has no father,' says Sophie. 'Eamon Donnelly's mother says his father is a no-good-drunken...'

'Okay, we don't need to know that,' says Sean, hiding the smile on his face. 'But, yes, some families are different.'

'And that's like your family,' says Fiona. 'Your family is different.' Sophie looks back down. She flicks the catch on the iPad a little bit faster. 'Roisin said my family wasn't real.'

'Oh, darling, your family is real,' says Fiona. 'It's very real but... but there are things you don't yet know about your family.'

Fiona falls into a silence and looks at Sean. Neither knows what to say next. It's hard for them. It's hard for all of us. We are about to twist everything Sophie thought she knew about herself. We are going to twist it out of shape and then try to bend it back again, only it won't ever be quite the same. There will be dents, scratches, marks and scars that will always be testament to how we distorted the truth.

'When I was younger,' I say. 'I had a baby.'

'That's what Roisin said,' says Sophie.

'Yes, she's right. I was very young and I was on my own. The baby was a little girl and we all loved her very much, so I asked my family to help look after my baby.' I let the idea settle. Sophie's stops fiddling with the iPad now and is looking at me as if she's going over the words I've just spoken and sorting them into some sort of order. 'I asked your mummy and daddy to help me look after the baby. And because we are all family and we all love each other, which includes the baby, they were delighted to be able to help. That way the baby could grow up with her family and be loved by everyone.'

There's an uncertain look on Sophie's face. Sean puts an arm around her shoulder. Fiona looks at me and I nod.

'Do you think you know who that baby might be?' asks Fiona. She twiddles her wedding ring round and round on her finger.

Sophie looks uncertain. I sense she knows the answer, but is too scared to say it.

'That baby,' I say, my voice catches in my throat and I try again. 'That baby was you, Sophie.' Sophie looks at each one of us. She doesn't know if this is good or bad news. She doesn't know how to respond, how she's supposed to respond. 'Do you understand what we're saying?' I probe gently.

'You're my mammy?' she says.

'That's right.'

Sophie considers this information. The words weigh heavy in the room. 'What about Molly? Are you her mammy too?'

'No,' I say. 'I'm not Molly's mummy, but I love her as if I was. The same way I love you. The same way Mummy and Daddy love her and the same way they love you.'

'What about my daddy?' says Sophie looking up at Sean.

'Sean is your daddy, in the same way as Fiona is your mummy,'

I say. 'But the daddy who I loved when I became pregnant with you, he was killed in a car accident. That's how I came to be on my own when you were born. And that's one of the reasons why I couldn't look after you alone. I needed the help of my family – your family.'

'Do I have to go and live with you now?' says Sophie. Her voice is brave, but I can see in her eyes she's frightened. My heart breaks and mends itself all in one moment.

Living with me is not what she wants. My heart breaks.

Living with her mummy, daddy and her sister is what she does want. My heart mends.

I don't want to take her away from everything she has known. I don't want to cause my sister and her husband pain beyond words. I don't want to break the family. All I've ever wanted is to keep the family together and by not keeping Sophie I have managed to do that. We, as a family, have done that. What right am I to ruin the bond we have created?

'No, darling,' I say. 'You don't have to come and live with me if you don't want to. You can stay right here with Mummy, Daddy and Molly. You can come and stay with me if you want, the same way Molly can. And if ever in the future you want to do things differently,' I cast a glance at Fiona to make sure I have her blessing. She gives a small smile that tells me I'm doing okay. I turn back to Sophie. 'If you change your mind, we can sit down again, all of us and talk about it. Just like we're doing now.'

The relief floods her face and she buries her head against Sean's arm. Fiona wipes tears away. She passes me a tissue for my own and I'm sure Sean is blinking furiously to stop his from falling.

It takes a few minutes, but we all manage to compose ourselves.

'There is one other thing,' says Fiona.

I know what it is. It's the thorny issue of the Marshall family. We wanted to tell Sophie another day, when she had had time to digest and understand her new family history. But Roisin is intent

345

on telling her mother straight away. We have no choice but to push on now.

Sean sits Sophie up and gives her a reassuring smile. 'Listen to what your mother has to say.'

'Your daddy, the young man that Erin had you with, he lived here in Rossway,' says Fiona. 'He had a mammy and a daddy and a sister.'

Sophie nods. I don't think she realises the implications.

'The thing is, Sophie,' I say. 'You know that Nanny is your mummy's mum, the same way she is my mum. And you know your Nanny Keane is your daddy's mum.' Sophie nods. 'Because you had another daddy, and he had a family, that makes them your family too.'

'I have a new family?' says Sophie.

'That's right. Another nanny and granddad and another aunty.' We all watch while she takes in this new information.

'Is that Roisin's family?'

'That's right. Roisin is your aunty and her mammy and daddy are your nanny and granddad,' says Sean.

'I have a big family now,' she says at last. 'I'm not sure if I like Roisin.'

'Well, now, the thing is,' says Sean, 'Roisin has been very sad for a long time. Sometimes when you're that sad, you do things that aren't very nice. It's a bit like being unwell. Your mind doesn't let you behave as you should.'

'Roisin is unwell?'

'She was, but she's going to be okay,' I say. 'You may have to give her another chance.' The words spike at my heart. I feel like a traitor saying such things, but I know for Sophie to move on and accept her new history, she cannot have any negative feelings about the Marshalls. We all have to move past this point for Sophie's sake if nothing else.

She picks up the iPad. 'Can I finish my game now?'

For a second we are all a bit stunned. That's it? That's how a ten-year-old takes the news she has a new family. I'm not sure it's sunk in yet, but I feel whatever she has taken on board is enough for the time being.

'Can we all have one big group hug?' I say. Sophie pulls a face, but Sean laughs and pulls his daughter towards him.

'Ah, sure, you're not too big for a hug.' He stretches out his other arm and embraces Fiona. 'And you,' he says looking at me. 'You're not too big for a cuddle either.'

I dive in for the best group hug of my life.

Chapter 43

After a quiet afternoon at Fiona's and a family tea together, I drive Mum up to the hospital.

'I think I'll stay the night with your father,' says Mum, as we pull up outside.

'You sure?'

'Yes, I want to tell him what's happened. I don't want any surprises for him. If it sets him back at all, at least he'll be in the right place and I'll be here.' Mum unfastens her seat belt.

'Mum,' I say. 'You don't have to feel guilty about what happened, you know. We all understand.'

'And the same applies to you. We are very lucky to come out of this all intact, apart from your father, but nothing that won't mend, by the looks of things. It could have been a lot worse.'

'I know it's been forced on us, but I'm glad it's out in the open now,' I say. 'Fiona and I had some romantic notion that we could keep the secret forever, but I think both of us knew deep down that we couldn't. We were just putting off the inevitable.'

'I know. I tried my hardest to protect you all,' says Mum, looking over and placing her hand on the side of my face. 'I really did. I would have done whatever was needed.'

I rest my hand on hers. 'Me too,' I whisper.

348

I leave Mum at the hospital an hour or so later. Dad was quite tired this afternoon, but we did have something resembling a conversation. He hasn't got the concentration at the moment to hold a long discussion, but he asked me if I was okay. I got the feeling it was a more in-depth question. I told him everything was fine and couldn't be better. I think he knew what I meant. Mum is going to tell him this evening. An abridged version of events. Myself, I have one final loose end to tie up.

As I park the car in the bay in front of the café, I look up at the flat above the bike shop. There's no light on. I go round the back and up the steps to try the door anyway. I knock loudly a couple of times, but there's no answer. I'm not sure I want to go in the pub, not right now. I may be ready to face Kerry again, but I'm not ready to face any of the villagers or questions they might throw my way.

I take out my phone and call Kerry's mobile.

As it rings in my ear, I hear the sound of a phone ringing down in the street. I lean over the railings and there, under the streetlight, is Kerry. He's looking up at me as he takes his phone from his pocket and answers.

'Hey,' he says.

'Hey, back atcha.'

'I was wondering if you'd call by,' he says, still standing under the amber glow of the light.

'Is there any reason why I wouldn't?'

'Have you forgiven me?'

'Forgiven you?' I say. 'There's nothing to forgive.'

'Goodbye, then? You've come to say goodbye.'

'I wasn't planning to.'

'So, what are you here for?' I can hear a smile in his voice and the corners of his mouth tip up as proof.

'I've come to say thank you.' I'm smiling as I speak.

'Is that right?' He begins to walk to the bottom of the steps.

'I always pay my debts,' I say. 'In full.'

'I have some of my own to repay,' he says, as he strides up the steps and comes to a stop right in front of me. We both still have our phones to our ears. 'And how long will that take?' he says. 'Full repayment, that is.'

I close the gap between us. Our faces almost touching, our mouths separated by only our breath.

'How long?' I say. 'A long time. A very long time.' I drop the phone from my ear. 'What about yours?'

'A lifetime?' says Kerry, his whisper matching mine.

'Sounds good to me.'

In one swift movement, he pulls me into his arms, his kiss is gentle, and then as I respond it becomes more urgent. Reaching round, Kerry somehow unlocks the door before we practically bundle our way into the flat, down the hall and into the bedroom.

EPILOGUE

'Yours is the light by which my spirit's born: You are my sun, my moon and all my stars'

E. E. Cummings

'It's only me, Mum,' I call, opening the front door to the two-bedroom bungalow my parents now live in. I go into the sitting room, where Mum is helping Dad on with his coat. 'Great, you're ready,' I say, kissing both my parents in turn. 'How are you today, Dad?'

'Not too bad,' he replies.

'We're going to try it without the wheelchair today,' says Mum. 'Just the sticks.'

'No chair yesterday,' says Dad. His speech seems to improve each time I see him. It's been six months since the accident and although he can't speak quite so quickly, the words are definitely more distinguishable. His walking has come on quite well, but it's a slow process. His physio assures him it's only a matter of time, patience and practice. Poor Dad, having to learn to walk again at his age. Still, we are grateful for small mercies, it could have been a whole lot worse.

'We went to the café yesterday,' says Mum passing Dad his sticks. He begins his laboured walk to the front door. 'We thought we'd see how the new owners are getting on.'

'They seem to be doing very well,' I say. 'It's very modern in there now.'

'Yes, it's very nice,' says Mum. 'Now, what about Kerry? How did it go yesterday?'

'Good,' I say. 'He and his mum are getting on really well now. It's taken some time to get there, but I think it's going to be okay. It makes it easier that she's not with her husband any more.'

'It's a shame about the divorce,' says Mum. 'But it's a fact, nothing will break a mother's love.'

I smile at her. She is, of course, right. We make our way out the door.

'What's this?' says Dad, nodding towards the Land Rover that's parked outside. Kerry jumps out to open the passenger door and Storm waves madly from the child seat he is strapped into at the very back of the vehicle. Breeze is in her car seat on the other side. Skip is at the window too. Front paws on the glass, he gives a little yap as if to say 'hurry up'.

'I finally persuaded Kerry to buy a new Land Rover,' I say. 'The other one was fit for the scrap yard.'

'Sure, it's very grand,' says Mum.

'Good job I'm back at work full time and have plenty of paint jobs coming in. Your daughter has expensive tastes,' says Kerry. He winks at me as he helps Dad into the front seat and then myself and Mum into the middle row of seats.

'Hello, Storm,' says Mum. 'And hello darling little Breeze. My, what a bonny baby you are. And how are you Storm? Are you being good for Kerry and Erin?'

'He most certainly is,' I say.

'Mummy and Daddy have gone on honeymoon,' says Storm.

'I know,' says Mum. She smiles at me. I think she's as relieved as everyone that Joe and Bex have got over the hurdle of his one-night stand with Roisin. 'You have a very special mummy, there,' says Mum.

'You can say that again,' says Kerry. 'Their daddy is a very lucky man.'

He starts the engine and we head off to Fiona's house.

'Now, have I got the presents?' says Mum. 'Did I pick them up?' She looks around her feet.

'I've got them,' I say. 'I put them in the back.'

'I can't believe Sophie is eleven,' says Mum.

Storm starts singing happy birthday and we all join in. After the fourth rendition, we arrive at Fiona's house.

Sophie rushes out to meet us excitedly. Molly and Storm are equally as excited and somehow, amongst all the fuss, we manage to get out of the Land Rover and into the house.

Fiona has done a great job of decorating the room with balloons and banners and the buffet of finger food is laid out on a pink tablecloth in the conservatory.

I get Mum and Dad settled in the living room. Kerry and Sean have cracked open a beer each. Sean comes through with a glass of wine for me and Fiona. Before I take the glass, I hand Sophie her present. It's a small box wrapped in pink paper with a white ribbon.

Sophie tears off the paper eagerly. The small blue trinket box sits in the palm of her hand. She opens the lid and, with great care, takes out the necklace. Her face lights up. 'It's like yours,' she says.

I shake my head. 'No, Sophie, it is mine. Was mine. It's yours now. It belongs to you.'

She lets the Triskelion pendant swing on the end of the chain, looking at it for a moment before looking up at me. 'Was it the one Niall gave to you?'

'That's right. I spoke to your mummy and daddy and we all agree it's time for you to have it now.'

Sophie smiles and then hugs me. I hold her tightly and then to distract myself because I don't want to cry on her birthday, I say, 'Shall we put it on you?'

'Yes, please!' Sophie lifts her hair and turns around while I fix the necklace.

'Happy birthday, my darling Sophie,' I say softly as she skips off to answer the doorbell.

'It's Nanny Diana!' shouts Sophie as she opens the door. 'And Granddad Pat and Aunty Roisin.'

I look at Fiona.

'You ready for this?' It's the first time both families have got together.

'As I'll ever be,' says Fiona.

After another whirlwind of hellos and greetings, the Marshalls sit in the living room with Mum and Dad.

Sean brings in the champagne and pours everyone a glass before gathering us all together to make a toast.

'To families,' he says. 'In all their forms.'

'To love, in all its forms,' adds Kerry.

I look at Diana and we exchange a small smile. It's another gesture of our truce and gradual acceptance of the past we share.

'To mothers and daughters…in all their forms,' she says.

I look around at the happy faces of both families. Never did I think it would turn out this way. For a brief moment I cast my mind back to eleven years ago. I think of Niall, as I always do every year on this day and I tell him I'm sorry he's not here and I send my love to him, my love as a teenager and my love for giving me the most precious gift I've ever had. This year I take more comfort in knowing that although nothing will ever make up for his passing, his family now have more than just a memory of him.

Looking around at the scene before me, I ask myself if coming home was the right decision, but before I can answer, Roisin comes to stand next to me. We have a less strained relationship these days. We're definitely at peace with each other.

'Has it all been worth it?' she says.

'Yes, it has,' I say. And then I silently answer my own question. Coming home was most definitely the right decision.

THE END

Acknowledgements

A huge thank you to the HarperImpulse team and all those associated who have worked on this book - I really appreciate it. Wrong as it may be to single out individuals, I must thank Charlotte Ledger for all her support and hard work in getting The Girl Who Lied out there - you're a star!

Thanks also to Margaret James and the London School of Journalism where this story first took root, and although it has gone through many transformations since then, the essence has remained.

Much love and gratitude to my husband, Ged, and my children who never stop believing in me - love you all very much.

And, finally, a heartfelt thank you to all my readers who make writing a pleasure.